'Ian McDonald writes science fiction like no one else; not just today, but ever before. After reading his latest novel, I think he might be best compared to a futuristic Charles Dickens. Diverse plot strands come together, past and future reflecting each other in an amazing book that easily matches McDonald's award winning *Brasyl* in ambition, scope and achievement'

The Times

'Another epic, complex and intelligent offering from McDonald'

Total SciFi

'A brilliant, jewelled machine of a novel'   *Independent*

'A lush, complex and hugely entertaining novel'   *Guardian*

'This is as good as contemporary literary SF gets'   *SFX*

'Subtle, intelligent and beautifully-crafted'   *The Spectator*

'A novel that is his [Ian McDonald's] best yet by a whole new order of imaginative and sensuous magnitude'

Richard Morgan

The Dervish House

IAN McDONALD

First published in Great Britain in 2010 by
Gollancz
An imprint of the Orion Publishing Group
Orion House, 5 Upper St Martin's Lane,
London WC2H 9EA
An Hachette UK Company

This edition published in Great Britain in 2011
by Gollancz

1 3 5 7 9 10 8 6 4 2

A CIP catalogue record for this book
is available from the British Library

ISBN 978 0 575 08862 7

Printed and bound in the UK
by CPI Mackays, Chatham, Kent

The Orion Publishing Group's policy is to use papers
that are natural, renewable and recyclable products and
made from wood grown in sustainable forests. The logging
and manufacturing processes are expected to conform to
the environmental regulations of the country of origin.

www.orionbooks.co.uk

To Enid

Turkish Spelling and Pronunciation

In 1928 the new Republic adopted a modified Roman alphabet of twenty-nine letters.

Consonants are similar to English, except that:

c is pronounced j as in joy

ç is ch as in chair

ğ is an almost silent aspirate that lengthens the preceding vowel

j is pronounced as in the French je

ş is sh as in ship

h and y are pronounced as consonants, as in hit and yellow

Vowels:

a as in father

e as in pen

i as in pin (the capital also carries the dot, which I have not reproduced here for typographical reasons)

ı has no direct sound in English, the closest being an unrounded vowel sound similar to er

o as in pot

ö as in the German, or the French eu

u as in room

ü as in the German, or the English few

Monday

1

The white bird climbs above the city of Istanbul: a stork, riding the rising air in a spiral of black-tipped wings. A flare of the feathers; it wheels on the exhalations of twenty million people, one among ten thousand that have followed the invisible terrain of thermals from Africa to Europe, gliding one to the next, rising up from Lake Victoria and the Rift Valley, following the silver line of the Nile, across the Sinai and the Lebanon to the great quadrilateral of Asia Minor. There the migration splits. Some head north to the shores of the Black Sea, some east to Lake Van and the foothills of Ararat but the greatest part flies west, across Anatolia to the glitter of the Bosphorus and beyond, to the breeding grounds of the Balkans and Central Europe. In the autumn the stork will return to the wintering grounds in Africa, a round trip of twenty thousand kilometres. There has been a city on this strait for twenty-seven centuries but the storks have been crossing twice a year for time only held by the memory of God.

High above Üsküdar storks peel off from the top of the thermal, wing-tips spread wide, feeling the air. In twos and threes they glide down towards the quays and mosques of Sultanahmet and Beyoğlu. There is a mathematics to the wheeling flock, a complex beauty spun out of simple impulses and algorithms. As the stork spills out from the top of the gyre, its sense for heat tells it there is something different this migration, an added strength to the uplift of warm air. Beneath its wings the city stifles under an unseasonable heatwave.

It is after the hour of prayer but not yet the hour of money. Istanbul, Queen of Cities, wakes with a shout. There is a brassy top note to the early traffic, the shrill of gas engines. Midnotes from taxis and dolmuşes, the trams on their lines and tunnels, the trains in their deeper diggings through the fault zones beneath the Bosphorus. From the strait comes the bass thrum of heavy shipping: bulk carriers piled high with containers edge past Russian liquid gas carriers like floating mosques, pressure domes fully charged from the terminals at Odessa and Supsa. The throb of marine engines is the heartbeat of Istanbul. Between them scurry the opportunistic ferries. Sirens and horns, call and response; motors reversing and burbling as they warp in to Eminönü's quays. Gulls' cries; always gulls. Dirty, conniving gulls. No one builds platforms on their chimneys for gulls to nest. Gulls are never blessings. The clatter of roller shutters, the bang of van doors. Morning radio, pop and talk. Much talk, of football. Champions' League quarter-final. Galatasaray/London Arsenal. The pundits are in full flow from a hundred thousand balconies and rooftop terraces. Pop, football and heat. This is the tenth day of the heatwave. Thirty-three degrees in April, at seven in the morning. Unthinkable. The climate pundits speculate on whether it could be another Big Heat of Twenty-Two when eight thousand people died in Istanbul alone. That was insane heat. Now some witty phone-in caller is fusing the two punditries together and speculating that if it flattens those pale English footballers, can that be such a bad thing?

Over all, through all, the chorus of air-conditioners. A box in a window, a vent on a wall, an array of fans on a rooftop, one by one they spin up, stirring the heat into ever-greater gyres of warm air. The city exhales a subtle breath of spirals within spirals, updrafts and microthermals.

The stork's pin-feathers feel out the rising airscape. The city's waste heat may save it those few wing beats it needs to carry it to the next thermal or away from the stooping eagle. Its life is an unconscious algebra, balancing equations between energy opportunity and energy expenditure. Black feather-tips flutter as it slides down across the rooftops.

The explosion goes almost unnoticed in the greater roar of the waking city. A flat crack. Then silence. The first voices are the pigeons and gulls, bursting upwards in clattering wings and shrieks. Then come the voices of the machines: car alarms, security alarms, personal alarms, the hip-hop of call tones. Last come the human shrieks and cries.

The tram has come a halt in the centre of Necatibey Cadessi, a few metres away from the halt. The bomb detonated at the rear; the blue roof is bellied up, the windows and doors blown out. A little smoke leaks from the back end of the second car. The passengers have made their own escapes on to the street and now mill around uncertain what they are to do. Some sit on the ground, knees pulled up, deep in shock. Pedestrians have to come to help. Some offer coats or jackets; some are making cell calls, hands trying to describe the scene; more stand around feeling the need to offer help but uncertain what to do. Most stand back, watching and feeling guilty for watching. A few without guilt shoot video on their cepteps. The news channels pay money for citizen journalism.

The tram driver goes from group to group asking is everyone there, is anyone missing, are they all right? And they are all right. She doesn't know what to do either. No one knows. Now come the sirens. Here are people who will know what to do. Lights flash beyond the press of bodies, the crowd parts. It's hard to tell victims from helpers; the blood is smeared everywhere. Necatibey Cadessi is a street of global banks and insurance combines but the ripples from the blast have spread out along the lines of the light rail system. Station by station, street by street, tram by stalled tram, Beyoğlu seizes up. Everyone knows about the bombing now.

From the eye of a white stork riding in from the Bosphorus the paralysis can be seen spreading out from the heart of the outrage. Its eye has no comprehension of these things; the sirens are just another unremarkable note in the clamour of a waking city. City and stork occupy overlapping but discrete universes. Its descent carries it over the bombed-out tram surrounded by flashing blue lights and into the heel of the next thermal. Then the rising heat plumes of Istanbul spiral the stork up in a wheel of white bodies and black wings, up above the eastern suburbs, up and onwards into Thrace.

Necdet sees the woman's head explode. He was only trying to avoid more direct, challenging eye contact with the young woman with the good cheekbones and the red-highlighted hair who had caught him looking in her direction three times. He's not staring at her. He's not a creep. Necdet lets his eyes unfocus and wander mildly across the passengers, wedged so politely together. This is a new tram at a new time: twenty minutes earlier but the connections get him into work less than an hour late, thus not upsetting Mustafa, who hates having to act the boss. So: his tram-mates. The boy and girl in their old-fashioned high-button blue school uniforms and white collars that Necdet thought they didn't make kids wear any more. They carried OhJeeWah Gumi backpacks and played insatiably with their ceptep phones. The gum-chewing man staring out the window, his mastication amplified by his superb moustache. Beside him the smart man of business and fashion scanning the sports news on his ceptep. That purple velvet suit must be that new nano-fabric that is cool in summer, warm in winter and changes from silk to velvet at a touch. The woman with the curl of silver hair straying over her brow from under her headscarf and the look of distant rue on her face. She frees her right hand from the crowd, lifts it to touch the jewel at her throat. And detonates her head.

The sound of an exploding skull is a deep bass boom that sucks every other sound into itself so that for a moment after the blast there is only a very pure silence. Then the silence shatters into screaming. The tram jerks to a halt; the momentum almost throws Necdet from his feet. To go down in this panic is to die. Necdet can't reach a handrail and steadies himself against the bodies of roaring passengers. The crowd surges against the still-locked doors. Their bodies hold the headless woman upright. The man in the fine velvet suit shrieks in an insane, high-pitched voice. One side of his purple jacket is dark glossy red. Necdet feels wet on his face but he can't raise a hand to test it or wipe it away. The doors sigh open. The press is so tight Necdet fears his ribs will splinter. Then he spills out on to the street with no sense of direction or purpose, of anything except a need not to be on the tram.

The tram driver moves from group to group asking is anyone missing, is anyone hurt? There is nothing really she can do but she is a representative of IETT so she must do something and she hands out moist wipes from a pull-tube in her large green handbag. Necdet admires that her tram has been suicide-attacked but she's remembered to bring her bag with her.

The wet wipe smells of lemon. To Necdet the folded cone of white is the purest, most holy thing he has ever seen.

'Please move away from the tram,' the driver is saying as he marvels at the little square of cool citrus white. 'There may be another explosion.' She wears an expensive Hermes headscarf. It links Necdet to that other scarf he saw around the woman's head. In the final moment he had seen the wistful regret on her face resolve as if she had received a revelation into some long-rooted family woe. She smiled. Then she touched the jewel at her throat.

Passengers crouch around the schoolchildren, trying to ease their crying with word of comfort, offered hugs. *Can't you see the blood on your faces is scaring them all the more?* Necdet thinks. He remembers the warm, wet spray into his own face. He looks at the wet wipe balled up in his hand. It isn't red. It wasn't blood.

Everyone looks up at the beat of a helicopter. It slides in over the rooftops, defying talk and phone calls. Now sirens lift above the morning traffic noise. It will be the police before the ambulances. Necdet doesn't want to be near police. They will aks him questions he doesn't want to answer. He has ID; everyone has ID. The police would scan it. They would read the carbon debit Necdet used to buy his ticket that morning and a cash withdrawal the night before and another carbon debit that previous evening at eighteen thirty. They might ask about the cash. It's grey but not yet illegal.

And is this your current address?

No, I'm staying at the old Adem Dede dervish house in Eskiköy. With my brother.

Who is your brother? Here they might find they had more questions.

Ismet had replaced the padlock with the new one he had bought. Bright brass, a golden medal on a chain. The tekke's shuttered wooden balconies overhung the steps; this was a private, shadowed entrance, behind the industrial steel bins of the Fethi Bey teashop, miasmic and greasy with the ventings from the kitchen extractor fans. The door was of old Ottoman wood, grey and cracked from centuries of summer heat and winter damp, elaborately worked with tulip and rose motifs. A door into mysteries. It opened on to gloom and the acidic reek of pigeon. Necdet stepped gingerly into the enfolding dark. Light fell in slats through the closed and barred window shutters.

'We shouldn't be doing this,' Necdet whispered. It was an architecture that commanded whispers. 'People live here.'

'Some old Greek and a married couple at the front. And an office girl on her own. And that shop for blasphemies in the old semahane. We'll sort that eventually. This end's been left to rot for fifty years, just falling apart.' Ismet stood proudly in the centre of the floor. It was his already. 'That's the crime here. God wants this to be what it was before. This is where we'll bring the brothers. Look at this.'

Ismet flung open a matching door across the dusty room. Colour flooded in and more than colour: a growing verdure of clipped box; the perfume of sun-warmed wood; the burble of water and the sudden song of birds. Ismet might have opened a door on to Paradise.

The garden was six paces across but it contained a universe. A shady cloister walled with floral Iznik tiles ran around the courtyard affording shade or shelter in every season. The fountain was a single piece of sun-warmed marble, releasing water over a lily-lip into a basin. A jewel-bright lizard started from repose in the sun and dashed along the scalloped rim to vanish into the shade beneath. Herbaceous plants grew tall and cool in small box-bordered beds.

The soil was dark and rich as chocolate. A green place. House martins dipped and bobbed along the eaves of the wooden gallery directly above the cloister. Their shrills filled the air. A copy of yesterday's *Cumhuriyet* lay sun-yellowing on a marble bench.

'It's all still here,' Ismet said. 'The redevelopers never got around to the back. The old cells are being used for storage – we'll clear them out.'

'Someone looks after this,' Necdet said. He could imagine himself here. He would come in the evening, when the light would fall over that roof on to that bench in a single pane of sun. He could sit and smoke blow. It would a good place for a smoke.

'We'll be all right here,' Ismet said, looking around at the over-hanging balconies, the little rectangle of blue sky. 'I'll look after you.'

Necdet can't let the security police know he has moved into the dervish house which his brother intends to make the home of the secret Islamic order to which he belongs. The police think secret Islamic orders blow up trams. And if they look at his old address, they'll see what he did, back there in Başibüyük, and why Ismet Hasgüler took his brother of the flesh under his care. No, he just wants to go to work quietly and soberly. No, no police thank you.

The air above the still-smoking tram thickens in buzzing, insect motion. Swarmbots. The gnat-sized devices can lock together into different forms for different purposes; above Necatibey Cadessi they coalesce like raindrops into scene-of-crime drones. The sparrow-sized robots flit on humming fans among the milling pigeons, sam-pling the air for chemical tracers, reading movement logs from vehicles and personal cepteps, imaging the crime scene, seeking out survivors and photographing their blood-smeared, smoke-stained faces.

Necdet drifts to the periphery of the mill of survivors, haphazard enough to elude the darting drones. Two women in green paramed coveralls crouch with the tram driver. She's shaking and crying now. She says something about the head. She saw it wedged up under the roof behind the grab-bars, looking down at her. Necdet has heard that about suicide bombers. The head just goes up into the air. They find them in trees, electric poles, wedged under eaves, caught up in shop signs.

Necdet subtly merges with the circle of onlookers, presses gently through them towards the open street. 'Excuse me, excuse me.' But there is this one guy, this big guy in an outsize white T-shirt right in front of him, with his hand up to the ceptep curled over his eye; a gesture that these days means: *I am videoing you.* Necdet tries to cover his face with his hand but the big man moves backwards, videoing and videoing and videoing. Maybe he is thinking, *this is a couple of hundred euro on the news;* maybe, *I can post this online.* Maybe he just thinks his friends will be impressed. But he is in Necdet's way and Necdet can hear the thrum of swarmbot engines behind him like soul-sucking mosquitoes.

'Out of my way!' He pushes at the big man with his two hands, knocks him backwards, and again. The big man's mouth is open but when Necdet hears the voice say his name, it is a woman's voice speaking directly behind him.

He turns. The head hovers at his eye level. It's her. The woman who left her head in the roof of the tram. The same scarf, the same wisp of grey hair coiling from beneath it, the same sad, apologetic smile. A cone of light beams from her severed neck, golden light. She opens her mouth to speak again.

Necdet's shoulder charge sends the big man reeling. 'Hey!' he shouts. The surveillance drones rise up, fizzing at the edges as they prepare to dissolve and reform into a new configuration. Then they firm back into their surveillance modes and swoop around the flashing blue lights which have only now made it through the city-wide traffic jam rippling out from the destruction of Tram 157.

In the hushed world of Can Durukan the explosion is a small, soft clap. His world is the five streets along which he is driven to the special school, the seven streets and one highway to the mall, the square in front of the Adem Dede tekke, the corridors and balconies, the rooms and rooftops and hidden courtyards of the dervish house in which he lives. Within this world, lived at the level of a whisper, he knows all the noises intimately. This is new, other.

Can looks up from the flat screen in his lap. He turns his head from side to side. Can has developed an almost supernatural skill at judging the distance and location of the nano-sounds that are allowed to enter his world. He is as acute and weird as a bat. Two, three blocks to the south. Probably Necatibey Cadessi. The living room has a sliver of a view down on to Necatibey Cadessi, and if he squeezes right into the corner of the rooftop terrace that leans out over Vermilion-Maker Lane, a silver shard of the Bosphorus.

His mother is busy in the kitchen with the yoghurt and sunflower-seed breakfast she believes will help Can's heart.

No running! she signs. Şekure Durukan has many faces she can put on to augment the hands. This is furious-tired-of-telling-you-concerned face.

'It's a bomb!' Can shouts. Can refuses to sign. There is nothing wrong with his hearing. It's his heart. And there is nothing wrong with his mum's hearing either. Can often forgets that.

Can has found that his greatest power in the first-floor apartment is to turn his back. Half a world can be ignored. His mother will not dare shout. A single shout can kill.

Long QT Syndrome. A dry, form-filler's name. It should be called Cardio-shock; Sheer Heart Attack; like a title you would give to the kind of freak-show TV documentary featuring a nine-year-old boy with a bizarre and potentially fatal heart condition. Patterns of chaos flow across Can's heart. Potassium and sodium ions clash in wavefronts and graphs of fractal beauty like black tulips. A shock can disrupt those synchronized electrical pulses. A single loud sudden noise is enough to stop his heart. The shriek of a car alarm, the clang of a shutter dropping, the sudden blare of a muezzin or a popped party balloon could kill Can Durukan. So Şekure and Osman have devised a tight, muffling world for him.

Odysseus, ancient sailor of these narrow seas, plugged the ears of his crew with wax to resist the killing song of the Sirens. Jason, a subtler seafarer, drowned them out with the lyre-work of Orpheus. Can's earplugs are inspired by both those heroes. They are smart polymer woven with nanocircuitry. They exactly fit the contours of his ears. They don't drown out reality. They take it, invert it, phase shift it and feed it back so that it almost precisely cancels itself. Almost. Total precision would be deafness. A whisper of the world steals into Can's ears.

Once a month his mother removes the clever coiled little plugs to clean out the ear wax. It's a fraught half hour, carried out in a specially converted closet at the centre of the apartment into which Can and his mother fit like seeds into a pomegranate. It is padded to recording studio standards but Can's mother still starts and widens her eyes at every muted thud or rattle that transmits itself through the old timbers of the tekke. This is the time she speaks to him, in the softest whisper. For half an hour a month Can hears his mother's voice as she tends to his ear canal with medicated cotton buds.

The day the sounds went away is the earliest memory Can trusts. He was four years old. The white hospital was square and modern with much glass and seemed to flash in the sun. It was a very good hospital, his father said. Expensive, his mother said, and said still, when she reminded Can of the health insurance that kept them in this dilapidated old tekke in a faded part of town. Can had known it must be expensive because it stood by the water. Beyond the window of the ear clinic was a great ship loaded high with containers, closer and bigger than any moving thing he had seen before. He sat on the disposable sanitized sheet and swung his legs and watched more and more ship come into view until it filled the window. They were looking at his ears.

'How does that feel?' his father said. Can turned his head one way, then the other, sensing out the new presences in his ears.

'There will be some discomfort for a few days,' the ear doctor said. On came the great ship, huge as an island. 'You will need to clean them once a month. The electronics are very robust. You've no need to worry about breaking them. Shall we try it? Can ...' And his hearing had flown away, every sound in the world driven to the furthest edge of the universe. The doctor, his father, became like tiny birds. His own name turned into a whisper. The ship sailed past silently. Can thinks of it as the ship that took all the sound in the world away. When he goes up on to the terrace to peer down steep Vermilion-Maker Lane at that tiny vee of Bosphorus, he still hopes that he will see the ship that brings it back again, a different sound in each container.

His mother made aşure that night. A special pudding for a special time. Aşure was a big treat in her family; they were from the east. Can had heard the story of Noah's pudding, how it was made up from the seven things left uneaten when the ark came to rest on Ararat, many times from his mother and his grandmother when she was still alive, but that night Mum and Dad told it with their hands. High on sugar and twitching at the discomfort in his ears, Can had not been able to sleep. Airbursts flashed on to the Barney Bugs wallpaper. He had flung open the shutters. The sky was exploding. Fireworks blossomed above Istanbul, dropping silver rain. Arcs of yellow and blue stabbed up into the night. Bronze fire cascaded silver from starbursts of gold so high Can craned hard to see them. All in a hush of muffled thuds and whispered whooshes, detonations muted as a bread-crust breaking. The near silence made the lights in the sky brighter and stranger than anything Can had ever seen. The world might be ending up there, the seven heavens cracking apart and raining fire on to the earth. Mortars lobbed their payloads higher and higher. Can heard them as pops on the edge of his perceptions, like pea-pods releasing their seeds. Now luminous armies battled above the solar water heaters and satellite dishes of Istanbul: battalions of blazing janissaries armed with flash and artillery against swift, sparkling sipahis who galloped from one side of the sky to the other in a whisper. Above, a little lower than the stars themselves, the angels of the seven heavens warred with the angels of the seven hells and for one searing moment the sky blazed as if the light of every star since the birth of the universe had arrived at once over Istanbul. Can felt its silver warmth on his upturned face.

As the light faded so the city returned the gift. From the Bosphorus first, the soft flute of a ship's siren, building in a chorus of tankers, ferries, hydrofoils and water taxis. The streets replied with tram hooters, delicate as prayers, then the brassier, flatter blare of car and truck horns. Can leaned forward, trying to hear. He thought he could make out dance music spilling from the Adem Dede teahouse. He could feel its beat, a pulse against his own. Beneath it all, human voices, cheering and whooping, laughing and singing, shouting nothing at all except for the joy of making pure noise; all bleeding into an aggregate of *crowd*. To Can it was a hiss of static. The people packed the streets, the little square with its two teahouses and one minimarket. Many carried little flags, more had bottles. Can could not believe so many people lived in tight, enclosed Adem Dede Square. Cars sounded their horns in exuberance and flew flags from their windows; the white-on-red crescent and star of Turkey, and a blue flag bearing a circle of golden stars. Those same flags were in the hands of the people in Adem Dede Square: crescents and stars. Can watched a young bare-chested man dance-swing along the balcony of the konak on the corner of Vermilion-Maker and Stolen Chicken Lanes. His country's crescent and star was painted white on his red face. The crescent made him look as if he were smiling. He turned to wave down to the crowd. They waved up. He pretended he was going to jump down. Can held his breath. It was the same height as his viewpoint. The crowd now seemed to be cheering the man on. Suddenly he let go. Can always remembers him falling through the streetlight, his skin shiny with sweat, his face eternally grinning in the face of gravity. He vanished into the crowd. Can never learned what happened to him.

He only knew his mother was beside him by the touch on his arm.

'What's happening?' Can asked. His own voice seemed small as a lizard's. His mother knelt beside him, pressed her lips close to his ear. When she spoke he felt its tickle as much as heard the words.

'Can, love, we're Europeans now.'

Can runs through the hushed corridors of the dervish house. He knows all the best vantages on to the world beyond. Can runs up to the terrace. It smells of hot wooden patio furniture and desiccating geraniums. Can lifts himself up on his tiptoes to peer over the wobbly wooden shuttering. His parents will condemn him to a world of whispers but they never think that he might just fall off the terrace. He sees smoke rising up between the circling storks. There is not very much of it. Necatibey Cadessi, as he thought. Then his fingers grip white on the age-silvered balcony rail. The air above Adem Dede Square fills with grainy motion, as if from a dust dervish or a plague of locusts. The flock of insect-sized swarmbots barrels through the middle air, flowing around streetlights and electricity cables, channelled into a stream of furious motion by the close-pressing apartment blocks. Can beats his fists on the rail in excitement. Every nine-year-old-boy loves bots. Right in front of his eyes they turn in mid-air and pour down steep Vermilion-Maker Lane like water over rocks. In the open sky above the rooftops, the dancing-hall of storks, the wind would overwhelm their nano-fan engines and disperse them like dust. Can finds flocks within flocking, flows within flows, strange currents, fractal forms, self-organizing entities. Mr Ferentinou has taught him to see the blood beneath the world's skin: the simple rules of the very small that build into the seeming complexity of the great.

'Monkey Monkey Monkey!' Can Durukan shouts as the tail end of the swarm vanishes around the twists and staggers of Vermilion-Maker Lane. 'After them!'

A stir in the still-shadowed corners of the dining room, a scurrying in the intricate woodwork of the terrace screen. From nooks and crevices the machines come clambering, scampering, rolling. Tumbling balls fuse into scuttling crabs; many-limbed climbing things link and twist into arms. Piece by piece the disparate units self-assemble until the last section locks and a plastic monkey leaps up on to the rail, clinging with hands and feet and prehensile tail, and turns its sensor-dotted head on its master.

Can pulls the smartsilk computer out of his pocket, unfolds it and opens the haptic field. He flexes a finger. The robot monkey twitches alert. Can points and it is off in a thrilling spring up on to the power line and a hand-and-foot gallop over the street to a coiled jump to the balcony opposite where the Georgian woman insists on hanging her underwear out to dry. Up up and up again. Can sees it perched on the parapet, a shadow against the sky.

Can's toy BitBots cannot compare to the police machines that flocked past him but Mr Ferentinou has pushed them far beyond the manufacturer's specifications. Can clicks the Monkey icon. Bird, Snake, Rat and Monkey are the four manifestations of his BitBots. Between their four elements, they create the city that is barred to Can. He sees through their eyes. Can giggles in excitement as he falls in behind Monkey's many sensors and careers across rooftops, weaves through mazes of aerial and cable, leaps the thrilling gaps between close-shouldering konaks. By map and the point-of-view camera link Can steers his eyes down through the roofs of crumbling old Eskiköy. Only a boy could do it. He is part superhero, part extreme-sports free-runner, part city-racer, part ninja. It is the greatest computer game. Parapet to parapet to pole to hands feet and tail scramble down the plastic sign of the Allianz Insurance. Can Durukan arrives at the scene of the blast, clinging upside down to the bottom of a giant letter I.

It disappoints. It is not a very big explosion. There are ambulances and fire trucks and police cars with flashing lights and news crews arriving by the minute but the tram hardly looks damaged at all. Can scans the crowd. Faces cameras faces cameras. A face he recognizes among the onlookers; that rat-faced guy who has moved into the empty quarter of the old house; the one with the brother who is some kind of street judge. At first Can resented their squatting. The deserted rooms filled with dust and pigeon shit were his undiscovered country. He had thought of sending Monkey – the only one of his agents with hands – to move things around, pretend to be the ghosts of old unquiet dervishes– but Rat-Face might lay a trap for mischievous Monkey and capture him before he could split into his separate units and slip away. Observation was the game.

Rat-Face is trying to slip away. He almost starts a fight with a big man in a white shirt. What is he doing now? He looks as if he's seen a ghost. Now he's barging his way through the crowd. If the Scene-of-Crime bots see him they'll needle him with their stings. That would be exciting. Can still wishes ill on Rat-Face and his kadı brother, defilers of his sacred space. No, he's made it out.

Monkey uncurls his tail from the stanchion and prepares to swing back up into the rooftops. Nothing decent to post online. Then Can notices a glint of movement in the Commerzbank sign on the building to the left. There's something in there. Monkey swivels his sensor-studded head and zooms in. Click click click. Movement, a glitter of plastic. Then the disparate motions come together. Can holds his breath. He looks close up into the face of another many-eyed monkey bot. And as he stares the head turns, the smart-plastic camera eyes bulge and focus and stare back.

The confectioner Lefteres used to say that all the Greeks in Eskiköy could fit into one teashop. Now they fit around one table.

'Here he comes now.'

Georgios Ferentinou waddles across Adem Dede Square. *Square* is too grand for what is little more than a widening of the street that runs past the Mevlevi tekke. An old public fountain stands in a niche in a wall, dry longer than any Eskiköyu's memory. Room enough for two çayhanes, Aydin's kiosk on the corner of Stolen Chicken Lane with its spectacular display of Russian porn clothes-pegged to the bottom of the canopy, Arslan's NanoMart, the Improving Bookstore that specializes in colourful publications for elementary schoolchildren, and That Woman's Art Shop. Aydin the pornographer takes his morning tea in the Fethi Bey çayhane, on the insalubrious staircase on the derelict side of the dervish house. Adem Dede Square is small enough for two teashops but big enough for rivalries.

'Hot,' Georgios Ferentinou wheezes. He fans himself with a laminated menu. The order is immutable as the stones of Aghia Sofia but Bülent the çayhane owner always lays out the menus. That cheap bastard Aykut across the square never takes that trouble. 'Again.' He sweats freely. Georgios Ferentinou is a fat bulb of a man, balanced on tiny, dancer's feet so that he seems permanently on the teeter-totter. None of his çayhane compatriots have ever seen him in anything lesser than the high-waisted trousers and the white linen jacket he wears today. A hat perhaps, in the highest of summers, like the terrible Twenty Two and when the sun gets low and shines through the slot of sky along Vermilion-Maker Lane, a pair of tiny, round dark glasses that turn his eyes into two black raisins. On those increasingly rare days when snow falls in Adem Dede Square and the tea-drinkers are driven inside behind breath-steamed windows, a red woollen scarf and a great black coat like some old Crimean trader from the last days of the empire.

'Hot as hell,' Constantin agrees. 'Already.'

'We've saved you a leg.' Lefteres pushes a plate across the small café table. Upon it a marzipan lamb lies slaughtered, its body broken. Delicate red frosting crosses adorn its grainy, yellow flanks. For over one hundred and fifty years since they arrived from Salonika into the capital of the empire, the family Lefteres made marzipan Paschal lambs for the Christians of Constantinople. Lambs for Easter, crystallized fruit made lustrous with edible gold and silver foils, the gifts of the Magi, for Christmas. Muslims were not ignored by the Lefteres: sesame candies and brittle sugary confection dishes for Sweet Bayram at the end of Ramazan. Boxes of special lokum and pistachio brittles for wedding calls and sweetening conversations. Family Lefteres sold the shop before the end of the century but the last of the line still makes his sweet lambs and jewelled fruit, his Bayram delights for Adem Dede Square. And he is still known as Lefteres the Confectioner.

Bülent sets down Georgios Ferentinou's invariable glass of apple tea.

'Here's the Father now,' he says. The last of the four old Greeks of Aden Dede Square sets himself down heavily in his ordained seat beside Georgios Ferentinou.

'God save all here.' Father Ioannis stretches his legs painfully out under the table. 'God damn my knees.' Without a word Bülent sets down his linden tea in its delicate tulip glass. Father Ioannis takes a sip. 'Ah. Great. Bastards have been at it again.'

'What are they doing this time?' Bülent asks.

'Someone slopped a bucket of piss into the porch. Half of it ran under the door into the sanctuary. I've been up since four trying to scrub it all off. Bastards. What I can't figure is, they must have been storing it up for days. All those teenagers standing around pissing in a bucket and giggling to themselves.'

'This is assuming,' says the most quiet of the Adem Dede çayhane divan, 'that it was actually human urine. It could have been some large animal.'

'In the middle of this city?' says Father Ioannis. 'Anyway, God and his Mother preserve me, I know what human piss smells like.'

Constantin the Alexandrian shrugs and examines the cigarette burning close to his yellow fingertips.

'It's going to take a lot of incense to get rid of the stink before Easter and who's going to pay for that?' Father Ioannis grumbles. 'I can't even get the Patriarchate to fix that tile on the roof.'

Georgios Ferentinou thinks this Easter he might visit the shrine of Aghia Panteleimon. He has no belief; faith is beneath his dignity but he enjoys the designed madness of religion. The minuscule church is tucked away down an alley off an alley off an alley. Older than any name in Eskiköy, Aghia Panteleimon let the district grow up around it like a fruit around a seed. It houses the sword that bent rather than behead its eponymous martyr (until he so decided) and a fine collection of icons of its patron saint, some in the alternate, Russian, style, with his hands nailed to his head. The woman who owns the art gallery in the former dancing hall has made Father Ioannis a fine offer for his macabre icons. They are not his to sell. If he does go this Easter, Georgios Ferentinou knows he may well be the only attendee. Perhaps a couple of old widows, come from Christ knows where in their raven black. Even before the ethnic cleansing of 1955 the tide of faith had ebbed from Eskiköy. Yet lately he has sensed it stealing back in little seepings and runnels, feeling its way over the cobbles and around the lintel stones. It's a more strident faith than either that of Aghia Panteleimon or the Mevlevi Order. It has an easterly aspect. It's rawer, younger, more impatient, more confident.

'It's the heat I say, the heat,' says Lefteres the Confectioner. 'Makes them fighting mad.'

'And the football,' Bülent adds. 'There'll be some English fan stabbed before the end of the week. Heat and football.'

The Greeks of the Adem Dede teahouse nod and murmur their agreement.

'So have you finished that lampoon then?' Father Ioannis asks.

Lefteres unfolds a sheet of A4 and slides it to the centre of the table. It is blank white.

'I have decided not to do this one.'

Lefteres, master of sugar and succulence, paschal lambs and gilded fruit, is the resident Lampoonist of Eskiköy. A pestering boyfriend, an unrecovered debt, unwelcome big beats or somebody fly-tipping in your dumpster: go to Lefteres at the Adem Dede çayhane. Pay him what he asks. It will not be cheap. Quality is never cheap. But the very next morning Eskiköy will wake to find a single sheet of A4, always handwritten, thumb-tacked to the offending door, gaffer-taped to a window, gunged to the windscreen of a parked car. In the best Turkish verse and scansion and the highest of style, every vice is listed and shamed, every personal attribute ridiculed. Every intimate detail is excoriated. Lefteres' research is immaculate. It works without fail. The crowd at the door is an ancient and powerful sanction. Word of a new lampoon travels fast. People come from far beyond Eskiköy to read and marvel. There are international websites dedicated to the lampoons of Lefteres the Confectioner of Eskiköy.

'Have you told Sibel Hanım?' Georgios Ferentinou says.

'I have indeed,' Lefteres says. 'She wasn't happy. But I told her that part of my commission is that I must be absolutely satisfied myself that there is just cause as well as clear social need. That's always been the case. Always. The woman is not a prostitute. Simple as that. Georgian she may be but that doesn't make her a prostitute.'

Since the Caucasus and central Asia found that the front door to Europe now opened on to theirs, Georgians, Armenians, Azeris, Ukrainians, workers from as far as Kazakhstan and Turkmenistan, Syrians, Lebanese, Iranians, Kurds in their tens of thousand have flooded across Anatolia, the buckle strapped across the girth of great Eurasia, Istanbul the pin. And that is how Georgios knows Lefteres' reasons for not accepting the lampoon. Istanbul was a city of peoples before and knows it shall be again, a true cosmopolis. The time of the Turk is ending. Georgians, Greeks: sojourners alike.

'Here, do you know who I saw yesterday on Güneşli Sok?' Constantin asks. 'Ariana Sinanidis.'

'How long is it since she went to Greece?' asks Lefteres.

'Forty-seven years,' says Georgios Ferentinou. 'What's she doing back here?'

'Either a will or a property dispute. What else does anyone come back for?' Constantin says.

'I haven't heard of any deaths,' Father Ioannis says. In as small and intimate a community as the Greeks of Istanbul, every death is a small holocaust. Then the bomb goes off. The sound of the explosion echoes flatly, flappingly from the house fronts. It is a little blast, barely distinguishable from the growl of morning traffic, but the four men at the table look up.

'How far was that?'

'Under a kilometre, I'd say.'

'Well under a kilo. It might well have been just the detonator.'

'Whereabouts would you say?'

'I would guess down towards Tophane Meydanı.'

'No guesses. This is an exact science.'

Constantin taps up news feeds on the smartpaper lying among the tea glasses and coffee cups.

'Necatibey Cadessi. Tram bomb,' Constantin says.

Behind the counter, Bülent clenches a fist.

'Yes!'

'Bastard!' says Lefteres. 'What's he made now?'

Georgios Ferentinou pulls out his ceptep. His thumb moves unswervingly over the icons.

'The Terror Market is up twenty points.'

'Lord Jesus Son of God have mercy on us,' says Father Ioannis. His fingers tie a knot on his prayer rope.

'Breakfast is on the house then,' says Bülent.

Georgios Ferentinou never saw economics as the Dismal Science. To him it is applied psychology, the most human of sciences. There are profound human truths in the romance between want and aversion; delicate beauties in the meshing intricacies of complex financial instruments as precise and jewelled as any Isfahan miniature. The blind wisdom of the mass still amazes him as it did when he first discovered it in a jar of plushy toys. The jar had sat on the desk of Göksel Hanım, his morning-school teacher. She had brought it back from a visit to her sister in Fort Lauderdale. Seduced by the Mouse, she had gone on a plushy spree across Disneyworld. Goofies and Mickies, Plutos and Stitches and little Simbas were packed together like pickles, eyes gazing out at eight-year-old Georgios Ferentinou. Çiftçi, Göksel Hanım had insisted on calling him. A Turkish transliteration of his name. Çiftçi had found the compressed figures strangely attractive. It would be quite good, he thought, to be squeezed into a jar full of other soft bodies.

'Guess how many there are,' Göksel Hanım said to her class, 'and you will win them.'

Çiftçi was lazy. He was told that every day by Göksel Hanım. Lazy and dull. He wanted the bodies in the jar so he did what any lazy and dull boy would. He asked his classmates. Their answers ranged for fifteen to fifty. Dull, lazy and reluctant to commit to decisions, Çiftçi added the answers and divided them by the number of pupils in the class, rounding up for luck.

'Thirty-seven,' he said confidently to Göksel Hanım. Thirty-seven there were, exactly. Göksel Hanım gave him the jar grudgingly. He stared at it for months, on his bedside table, enjoying their captivity. Then one day his mother had taken them away to clean them. She returned them all to their confinement but damp had got in and within two weeks they were green and bad-smelling and were thrown out. It was his first exposure to the power of aggregation. The mass decides.

There is a market for anything. Debts. Carbon pollution. The value of future orange harvests in Brazil and gas output in the Ukraine. Telecommunications bandwidth. Weather insurance. Buy low, sell high. Self-interest is the engine; aggregation, like the class of '71, the gear-train. Georgios Ferentinou has merely extended the free market principle to terrorism.

The market is played this way. A network of a thousand traders is strung across Istanbul. They range from economics students to schoolchildren and their mothers to real traders on the Stamboul Carbon Bourse. All night AI sift the news networks – those deep channels that Georgios Ferentinou took with him when he left academia, and less exalted sources like chatrooms, forums and social and political networking sites. By dawn they have drawn up a long list of potential future news. Georgios Ferentinou's first task of the day, even before he takes his breakfast tea at the Adem Dede teahouse, is to draw up that day's list of tradable contracts in his pyjamas and slippers. By the time he shuffles across the square to his table, the offers are out across the city like soft-gliding storks and the bids are coming in. I'll buy twenty contracts at a settlement price of one hundred on Galatasaray beating the Arsenal two one on Thursday. How much do you want to pay for them? That depends on how likely you think it is that Galatasaray will beat Arsenal two one.

This is the easiest future contract, a straight sporting bet. There is a clear termination point at which the contract is fulfilled – the sound of the referee's final whistle in the Galatasaray Stadium – and a simple pay-out. All you have to do is decide how much you will buy that pay-out for, and for others to decide how much they will pay to buy that contract off you. All trading is betting.

How much would you pay for a contract with a settlement of one hundred on a bet that the price of gas will rise by fifteen per cent by close of trade next Monday? Thirty? Fifty, for a hundred pay-out? What if you see the price rising on the Carbon Bourse? Seventy, eighty? Turn those prices into percentages and you have a probability; you have a prediction of future news.

Thirty, fifty, one hundred, what are these? Kudos: the artificial currency of Georgios Ferentinou's Terror Market. A light, odourless virtual money, but not without value. Kudos are not points in a game. They can be exchanged for other virtual-world or social networking or online-game currencies, some of which can be converted up into real world, pocketable cash. They can be traded. That is another one of Georgios Ferentinou's behavioural economics experiments. Kudos is worth something. Georgios Ferentinou understands there is no market without real gain, and the possibility of real loss. The money makes it work.

Here's another contract. Settlement price one hundred kudos. There will be a suicide strike on Istanbul public transport on a major arterial during the current heatwave. Do you buy it?

Georgios Ferentinou checks the closing price. Eighty-three kudos. High, given the plethora of speculative factors: the time since the bombing at the bus station; Ankara's announcement of a clamp-down on political organizations opposed to the national secular agenda; the possibility that the heatwave might break in glorious lightning among the minarets of Istanbul. Then he tracks the price since the contract was offered. It has risen as steadily as the therm-ometer. This is the miracle of the Terror Market. Buying and selling, petty greed, are more powerful prophets than the experts and artificial intelligence models of the National MIT Security Service. Complex behaviour from simple processes.

The woman who runs the religious art shop in the bottom of the dervish house crosses the square. She squats down to unlock the security shutter. Her heels come a little off the ground as she balances on the balls of her feet. She wears good boots and patterned tights, a smart skirt not too short, a well-cut jacket. Hot for this weather but stylish. Georgios Ferentinou watches her run up the shutter with a rolling clatter. Such unconscious ease costs gym fees. Her ceptep rings, the calltone a spray of silvery sitar music. Georgios Ferentinou looks away with a small grimace of regret. He was admired once too. A disturbance in the air draws his eyes up, a shiver like heat haze, a plague of tiny mites, the visual equivalent of the glittering glissando of the art-shop woman's calltone.

The swarm of gnat-sized machines swirls in the choked air of Adem Dede. Even the boy bringing the sesame-dusted simits from Aydin's kiosk looks up. Then the cloud of nanorobots pours down Vermilion-Maker Lane like water over a weir, following the stepped terrain beneath them, flowing around the schoolchildren, the women, old Sibel Hanım labouring up and down the steps. Follow the flock. Avoid near neighbours but try to maintain an equal distance from them. Cohesion, alignment, separation. Three rudimentary rules; the well of complex liquid beauty.

In the corner of his vision Georgios Ferentinou glimpses the little monkey-bot go helter-skelter across the electricity line and jump to the offending Georgian woman's balcony. *A strange world that boy inhabits*, he thinks. A world of whispers, of distant tintinnabulations on the edge of hearing, like angel voices. But is it any stranger than four old Greeks, flotsam adrift for decades in the crash and suck of history, gathering over tea and doughnuts to divine the future?

And Ariana is back. Almost half a century and she is in Eskiköy. No deal, no play of trades and future outcomes could have predicted that. Ariana is back and nothing is safe now.

*

The yalı leans over the salt water, balcony upon balcony. Adnan opens the roof terrace's wooden shutters. The heat of the morning beats in mingled with coils of cool from the Bosphorus. The current is dark. Adnan has always felt the Bosphorus to be dark, dark as blood, dark as the birth-canal. It feels deep to him, deep and drowning. He knows where this fear comes from; from his father's boat and the endless sunlit afternoons of a childhood lived on water. This is why his seal of success has always been a place by the edge of the water. It is the lure of the fear, the reminder that everything you have won may be lost in an unconsidered moment. The early sun turns the side of a Russian gas carrier into a wall of light. It is a monster. Adnan Sarioğlu smiles to himself. Gas is power.

'One million two hundred you say?'

The real estate agent waits by the door. He isn't even properly awake, but he's shaved and suited. You have to get up early to sell to the gas lords. A dealer knows a dealer.

'It's a very sought-after location and, as you can see, you can move straight in. You have your own boat dock and waterside terrace for entertaining.'

Adnan Sarioğlu shoots some video.

'We've had a lot of interest in this property,' the realtor presses. 'These old yalıs do go fast.'

'Of course they do,' says Adnan Sarioğlu. It is not a real yalı, those were all bought up long ago, or are collapsing under the weight of their decaying timbers in forgotten coves along the Bosphorus, or have burned decades since. It is a fake, but a good fake. Turkey is the land of the masterful fake. But it is far far from that hateful little eighth-floor apartment huddling between the roar of the expressway and the blare of the mosque.

He pans the ceptep across the terrace. Already he is filling the space with skinny Scandinavian furniture. This could be an office. It would just be leather sofas and old Ottoman coffee tables, lifestyle magazines and a killing sound system. He would come in in the morning and summon his avatars to spin around him hauling in spot prices from Baku to Berlin. The big dealers, the Paşas, all work this way; from the boat club, from the gym, from the restaurant. Perfectly weightless. Yes, this is a house to start his dynasty. He can't afford it. The realtor's background checks will have disclosed that. But they will have shown that he is the kind of man who could have money, very very much money and that's the reason the agent has got up in the pre-dawn and showered and shaved and scented and put on his good suit.

He pans the ceptep across the reach of the waterway. He blinks the zoom in on to the pastel houses along the European shore. Bigger cars, faster boats, deeper docks, further from their neighbours' shadows. Money and class have always clung to the edge of Europe. He double-takes, pans back. Between the shiny slick twenty-first century yalıs with their low-sloping photosynthetic roofs is a pile of timbers, grey and lone as a widow, roof caved in, front wall slumping towards the water, window frames eyeless and half closed. A ghost of a house, abandoned and neglected among its young, tall, brilliant neighbours. A true yalı. It may have stood, decaying year upon year, from the Ottoman centuries. He blinks closer on to its empty windows, its sagging lintels and eaves. He cannot begin to imagine how much it would cost to return it to habitability, let alone make it a place to raise a family, but he knows where he will go next. He begins here, he ends on the shadow of the bridge, on the toes of Europe.

On the edge of his vision he glimpses smoke. The plume goes up straight as a flagpole into the clear blue air. In an instant he has zoomed in on it. A map overlay gives him a location: Beyoğlu. Now a news mite bursts into the steady procession of gas spot prices across his retina: *TRAM BOMBING ON NECATIBEY CADESSI. PIX TO FOLLOW.*

Ayşe rides that tram.

Her ceptep rings three times, four times, five times, six.

'Hi there.'

'You took your time.'

'That shutter's sticking worse than ever. It's going to need replacing.'

'So you totally missed the bomb, then?'

'Oh that was down on Necatibey Cadessi. A swarm of police bots just went past.'

Adnan wonders if Ayşe's otherwordliness is her natural aristocratic nonchalance or some emanation from the art and artefacts that surround her. That shop, for all the hedge fund managers and carbon Paşas looking for a little investment in religious art; it's not a proper business. It's a lady's pursuit. She'll give it up when they move in here, when the babies start to come.

'It was your tram.'

'Do you not remember I said I was going in early? There's a potential supplier calling before work.'

'Well, you watch yourself. These things never happen in ones.'

'I'll keep an eye out for suicide bombers. How's the yalı?'

'I'll send you the video. I may be late back. I'm trying to get a meeting with Ferid Bey tonight.' The name-drop is as much for the realtor as for his wife. There is a beat of radio silence that is the equivalent of an exasperated sigh.

'I'll see you when I see you then.'

At some dark hour he will slip back through the curve of taillights arching over the bridge to the eighth-floor apartment. She may be watching television, or half-watching it while she puts on laundry, or if his meetings have hauled on and on, be in bed. Then he will slip in without turning on the lights, a quick mumble as she surfaces through sleep like a dolphin, in behind her to press the rough warmth of his dick against the bed-heat of her smooth ass and the return press, then down with her, lured down into sleep so fast there is not even time for the twitch of the terror of drowning. All around, the sweet incense of fabric conditioner. It's no way to live. But he has seen the end of it. A few more days of effort and it's over.

Adnan Sarioğlu snaps off his ceptep.

'One million two hundred thousand you say?' he asks.

'We've had a number of offers,' the realtor says.

'I'll give you one million one.'

'Offers are generally in excess of the asking price.'

'I'm sure they are. But this isn't an offer, this is a price. In cash.'

The realtor flusters. Adnan drives home his advantage.

'One point one million euro in cash to your office by noon Friday.'

'We, ah, don't usually deal in cash.'

'You don't deal in cash? Cash is king, is what cash is. Do anything with cash, you can. Friday, lunchtime. You have the contract on the desk and I'll sign it and shake your hand and you take my fucking cash.'

Three minutes later Adnan Sarioğlu's car leans into the on-ramp to the bridge, accelerating into the stream of Europe-bound vehicles. Autodrive makes microadjustments to the car's speed; the other vehicles read Adnan's signals and correspondingly adjust their distances and velocities to accommodate him. All across the Bosphorus Bridge, through every arterial of vast Istanbul, every second the ceaseless pump of traffic shifts and adjusts, a flock of vehicles.

Drive-time radio news at the top of the hour. The tram bomb is already downgraded. No one dead besides the suicide bomber. A woman. Unusual. No promise of Paradise's rewards for her; just eternity married to the same old twat. Something in the family. It always is. Men die for abstractions, women for their families. No, the big story is the weather. Hot hot hot again. High of thirty-eight and humidity eighty per cent and no end in sight. Adnan nods in satisfaction as the Far-East gas spot-price ticker crawls across the bottom of the windshield. His forty-eight hour delivery options on Caspian Gas will hit their strike this morning. Nice little earner. He'll need the premiums for a few small necessary purchases on Turquoise. Cash is always king. Adnan slips the nozzle of the inhaler up his nostril. The rush of inhaled nano breaks across his forebrain and the numbers become sharp, the focus clear. He hovers high above the golden fabric of deals and derivatives, spots and strikes. Only the concentration-enhancing nano makes it possible for Adnan to pick a pattern from the weave of transactions. The old traders use more and more to keep pace with the young Turks. He's seen the shake in their hands and the blur in their eyes as he rides down the express elevator with them to the underground car park after the back office has settled out. Nano, Caspian gas, CO_2 and traders: all the many ways of carbon.

Music: the special calltone of his Paşa, his white knight. Adnan clicks him up on the windshield.

'Adnan Bey.'

'Ferid Bey.'

He is a fat-faced man with skin smooth from the barber's razor, almost doll-like in its sheer buffed finish. Adnan recalls from his research that Ferid is very vain, very groomed.

'I'm interested in this. Of course I'll need much more detail but I think we can do business. I'll be at the Hacı Kadın baths from seven thirty.' He laughs hugely though there is no comedy in his words.

'I'll see you there.'

The call ends. The Audi stitches itself in and out of the traffic and Adnan Sarioğlu beats his hands on the dashboard and whoops with delight. A new call chimes in; a poppier tune, the theme from an animated TV series that Adnan and his three fellow Ultralords of the Universe grew up with.

'Hail Draksor.'

'Hail Terrak.'

Adnan and Oğuz graduated from the MBA and entered Özer together. Adnan floated into lofty hydrocarbons and the realm of abstract money, Oğuz was pumped into Distribution, the all-too-solid domain of pipelines and compression stations, tanker terminals and holding centres. It's lowly, unglamorous; very far from lunch at Olcay and champagne at Su come bonus time. Too easily overlooked. That was why, when the idea of Turquoise struck in its full, lightning intensity as he rode the elevator up the glass face of the Özer tower, Oğuz was the first call of his old college friends.

'Volkan's got a fitness test at twelve.'

'He'll never make it,' Adnan says. 'Fat bastard's so out of condition he can't even touch his toes.'

Oğuz's face grins in the smartglass of the windscreen. The four Ultralords of the Universe are also ultra-Galatasaray fans. On their bonuses they could easily afford a corporate box at Aslantepe but they like to be in the stands, with the fans, with their kebabs and their small flasks of sipping rakı. Cimbom Cimbom Cimbom! Fighting stuff that rakı. The Ultralords understand going to games. It is not about sport. There is no such thing as sport. It is about seeing the other team lose. One million goals would not be enough to crush the opposition. When he is up there with the rest of the boys, Adnan wants to see the opposition all die on stakes. The Romans had it right. It's fighting stuff. Give us blood.

'So where are you?' Oğuz asks.

Adnan flicks on his transponder. A map of mid-Istanbul overlays Oğuz's grinning face on his windshield. Oğuz is on the Fatih Sultan Bridge to the north. The distances are comparable; the driveware calculates traffic densities. A little jockey-programme generates odds. Oğuz's grin widens. He likes those odds.

'I'll go five hundred euro.'

'Eight hundred.' Adnan likes those odds too. 'And the tip.' There is etiquette to the Ultralords of the Universe's street races. The tip is that the loser pays the winner's traffic fines.

'Element of Air assist me!' Adnan shouts. 'In three. Two. One.' He grabs the steering handset and flicks off the autodrive. Warnings blare through the car. Adnan ignores them and floors the pedal. The gas engine barely raises a note but the car leaps forward into the traffic. The self-guiding cars fluster and part like panicked chickens as Adnan piles through. There is a time to peel out from the flock. Adnan Sarioğlu laughs as he spears through the traffic. The Audi leans like a motorbike as he crosses lanes. Cars peel away like the bow-wave of a Russian gas-tanker. The game is on. Adnan feels the roar build inside him, the roar that never goes away, that is in the kick of the nanotuned gas engine of his street-sweet German car, that wells in him when Ayşe moves against him on those nights he slips home in the dark, when she murmurs so and opens to let him press inside her; but most, most in the shriek of gas hurtling down the Blue Line, under the Bosphorus, out into the world of money, that is the deal, every deal, every closing. The roar that never, never stops. In seven minutes he will take Oğuz for three hundred euro and a dozen traffic-cam fines. Tonight he will meet the manager of one of Istanbul's fattest hedge funds. On Friday he will slap down a briefcase full of notes in front of that piss-eyed realtor in his hideous shiny little Lidl suit and set the name of Sarioğlu down by the waters of the Bosphorus. It is the game, the only game and the always game.

The angel is blind and shackled by an iron band around his right foot. His eyes are blank stone orbs. He is naked and wreathed in flame, male, marvellously muscular and lithe, yet sexless. He flies by the power of his own will, arms outstretched, intent but ignorant, blind to his own blindness, straining against the single shackle. The blind angel's left arm claws for the child. He craves it with sense other than sight.

The second angel cradles the child away from that grasp. He too is male, defined yet kept chaste by the leg of the child. He stands on a ribbon of cloud low on an indefinite sea. He looks to the blind angel with an expression of incomprehension. The child, a sturdy lad improbably muscled, faces away. His arm is held up in a plea for help. His hair is very curly. The succouring angel looks like a prig. All the passion, all the energy, is in the blind, burning angel.

'William Blake, Good and Evil Angels,' Ayşe Erkoç says, leaning close over the print. 'I love William Blake. I love his vision, I love the prophetic fire that burns through his art and his poetry, I love the completeness of his cosmology. I've studied William Blake, I've read William Blake, I've seen William Blake, in folio, and in London. On very rare, very special occasions, I've sold William Blake. Original William Blake. This is not William Blake. This is garbage.

The paper's all wrong, the line is like a five-year-old's, I can smell the bleach from here and there's a spelling error in the text. This is an offence to my professionalism.'

Topaloğlu's cheeks quiver in embarrassment. Ayşe thinks of them as two slabs of condemned liver. Offal propped apart by a wide, rural moustache.

'I mean no insult, Mrs Erkoç.'

'There's a world – no, a universe – of difference between unclear provenance and a Grand Bazaar fake,' Ayşe continues. 'If I can see it, my buyers can see it. They know at least as much as I do. These are collectors, aficionados, investors, people who purely love religious art, who love nothing else. They may not care where or how I get a piece. They care very much that it's genuine. The moment they hear I'm selling fakes, they go to Antalya Fine Arts or the Salyan Gallery.'

Topaloğlu's humiliation deepens. *He is cheap little pedlar with the soul of a carpet seller*, Ayşe thinks. Abdurrahman recommended him to Ayşe as a man who could get Isfahan miniatures. She will have to have a word with Abdurrahman Bey.

'I may have to reconsider our business relationship.'

He's pale now. Hafize, the gallery assistant, eavesdropper and interferer in concerns not hers, dips in and haughtily sweeps away his tea glass on her tray. She's wearing the headscarf again. Ayşe will have to have a word with her. She's become bolder in her flaunting of it since the tarikat, the Islamic study group, began meetings in the old kitchen quarters. Ayşe's seen how the young men look at her as she locks the gallery shutter of an evening. They want her and her idolatrous images out. Let them try. The Erkoçs have good connections and deep purses.

'What else have you got?' Ayşe asks.

Topaloğlu sets out miniatures like fortune-telling cards. He has donkey teeth, yellow plates of enamel. They make Ayşe feel ill. She bends over the miniatures laid out on the table in the private viewing room and clicks down the magnifier lens in her ceptep eyepiece.

'These are genuine,' Topaloğlu says.

But very poor, Ayşe thinks, scanning the brushwork, the framing, the fine detail of the backgrounds. In the Isfahan and Topkapı schools, miniatures were the work of many hands. Each artist had his specialization and spent all his life perfecting it. There were masters of roses, of cloudscapes, of rocks, there were maestros who never painted anything but tile work. These are obvious apprentice pieces. The contrast between the exquisitely drawn figures and the crude backgrounds is glaring. The fine eye, the minuscule detail has not yet emerged. The great miniaturists, anonymous all of them but for their style, could paint a trellis, a window screen, a tiled wall, with a single hair. These are production line works for volumes of Sufi poetry, the kind which minor paşas and beys bought by the shelf to impress their inferiors.

'Rubbish, rubbish, rubbish. Is that it? What's in the shoe box?'

Topaloğlu has been keeping it by his side, half hidden under the flap of his jacket. A Nike box, a style from five years back, Ayşe notes. At least he is wearing proper gentlemen's shoes for this meeting, decently polished. Shoes speak loud, in Ayşe's experience.

'Just a few what you might call trinkets.'

'Show me.' Ayşe does not wait for Topaloğlu to open the box; she snatches off the lid. Inside there is indeed a rattle of junk; Armenian crosses, Orthodox censers, a couple of verdigrised Koran covers. Grand Bazaar tourist tat. Amidst the tarnished brass, glints of silver. Miniature Korans. Ayşe greedily lays them out in a row along the table. The recessed ceiling bulbs strike brilliants from the thumb-sized silver cases.

'These I'm interested in.'

'They're twenty euro pilgrim curios,' Topaloğlu says.

'To you, Mr Topaloğlu. To me, and to the people who collect them, they're stories.' She taps the cover of a twentieth-century electroplate silver case, the crystal magnifier an eye, a good-luck boncuk charm. 'A boy goes off to military service. Despite her best efforts his mother can't get him into a soft option like the jandarmeri or the tourist police, so gives him a Holy Koran. Keep the word of

God close and God will keep you folded into his breast.' An early nineteenth-century gold shell case, exquisitely filigreed. 'A merchant from Konya, after years building up his material goods, finally frees himself from his worldly obligations to undertake the Hac. His concubine gives him a keep-sake. Remember, the world will be waiting.'

'How can you tell it's a Konya piece?'

'It's in the Mevlevi style, but it's not a souvenir from the Rumi pilgrimage — those usually are cheap mass-produced tourist junk. This is altogether a much more fine work. There's money and devotion here. Once you learn to see, you begin to hear the stories.' Ayşe rests her finger on tiny silver Koran no larger than a thumb, delicate as a prayer. 'This is eighteenth-century Persian. But there's only half a Koran. A Holy Koran, divided?' She opens the case and sets the little Persian scripture in the palm of her hand. 'What's the story there? A promise made, a couple divided, a family at war with itself, a pledge, a contract? You want to know. That's the market. The Korans, as you say, are trinkets. Stories; people will always buy those.' Ayşe sets the tiny hemi-Koran back into its case. 'I'll take these three. The rest is rubbish. Fifty euro each.'

'I was thinking three hundred would be more appropriate.'

'Did I hear you say that they were only twenty euro pilgrim curios? Two hundred.'

'Cash.'

'Cash.'

Topaloğlu shakes on two hundred.

'Hafize will arrange payment. You can bring me more of these. Then we'll see about the miniatures.'

Topaloğlu almost bares his rural teeth in a smile.

'Good to do business, Mrs Erkoç.'

Footsteps on the stairs and along the wooden gallery; Hafize's heels. Modest headscarf and fashion heels. A tap at the door. The look on her face is part puzzlement, part suspicion.

'Madam, a customer.'

'I'll see him. Could you deal with Mr Topaloğlu? We've settled at two hundred euro for these three.'

'Cash,' Topaloğlu says. Hafize will screw another twenty per cent off the price; her 'administration fee'. For a young woman with aspirations to respectability, she's as tough a bargainer as any street seller spreading his knock-off football shirts on the quay at Eminönü.

From the encircling balcony, Ayşe looks down into the old semahane, the dance-floor where in another age dervishes spun themselves into the ecstasy of God. A man bends over a case of Torahs. The great brass chandelier hides him, but Ayşe catches a ripple of gloss, like oil sheen in an Eskiköy puddle, across his back. Nanoweave fabric. Expensive suit.

As Ayşe descends the stairs Adnan warbles a video clip on to her ceptep. She glimpses wide Bosphorus, a white boat at a jetty, dipping gulls, a slow pan along the strait to the bridge. A gas tanker passes. So Adnan to let the camera linger on the gas tanker. His palace, his dream, when he closes Turquoise. Still the wrong side of the Bosphorus, Anatolian boy. She needs to get back to Europe.

'I am Ayşe Erkoç.'

The customer takes her proffered hand. Electronic business cards crackle from palm to palm.

'Haydar Akgün. I was just looking at your Jewish manuscripts. There is some very fine micrography here.' Moiré patterns, blacker on black, mesh across the fabric of his suit. Silver at his cuffs. Ayşe admires silver. There is restraint in silver.

'It's actually double micrography. If you look closely you'll see there is calligraphy within the calligraphy.'

Akgün bends closer to the page. He blinks up his ceptep. Lasers dance across his eye, drawing a magnified image on the retina. The folio is from a Pentateuch, the panel of lettering set within a decorative frame of twining flower stems, trellises and fantastical heraldic beasts, dragon-headed, serpent tailed. The decoration teases the eye, the look beyond the surface dazzle shows the outlines to be made up of minuscule writing. It is only under magnification that the second level of micrography appears: those letters are in turn made up of chains of smaller writing. Akgün's eyes widen.

'This is quite extraordinary. I've only seen this in two places before. One was a dealer in Paris, the other was in a codex in the British Library. Sephardic I presume? Spanish, Portuguese?'

'You're correct on Portuguese. The family fled from Porto to Constantinople in the fifteenth century. The micrographic border is a genealogy of King David from the Book of Ruth.'

'Exceptional,' Akgün says, poring over the weave of calligraphy.

'Thank you,' Ayşe says. It is one of her most adored pieces. It took a lot of discreet envelopes of euro to get it away from the police art crime department. The moment her police contact showed the Pentateuch to her, she had to possess it. For others it might be the prestige they could garner, the thrill of control, the money they could make. With Ayşe it was the beauty, that cursive of beauty spiralling through Aramaic and Syriac texts to the demotic Greek of the Oxyrhynchus, the painstakingly squared-off Hebrew of the Talmudic scholars of Lisbon and Milan, the divine calligraphy of the Koranic scribes of Baghdad and Fes and learned Granada. It flowed into the organic lines of gospel illumination from monasteries from St Catherine's to Cluny, in the eternal light of Greek and Armenian icons, through the hair-fine, eye-blinding detail of the Persian miniaturist to the burning line of Blake's fires of Imagination. Why deal in beauty, but for beauty?

'You wonder how far down it can go, writing within writing within writing within writing,' Akgün says. 'Nanography, perhaps? Do you think it could be like nanotechnology, the smaller it gets, the more powerful it becomes? Are there levels so fine we can't read them but which have the most profound, subliminal influences?'

Ayşe glances up to the balcony where Hafize is guiding Topaloğlu to the back stairs down into the old tekke cemetery. She subtly unfolds three fingers. Thirty per cent discount. Good girl. Gallery Erkoç needs every cent it can find.

'Pardon?'

'A nanography that slips into the brain and compels us to believe in God?'

'If anyone could it would be the Sephardim,' Ayşe says.

'A subtle people,' Akgün says. He unbends from the codex. 'They say you can get hard-to-find items.'

'One should always take the praise of one's rivals with a pinch of salt but I do have a certain ... facility. Is there a particular piece you're looking for? I have private viewing facilities upstairs.'

'I think it's unlikely you'd have it in stock. It is a very rare, very precious item and if it can be found anywhere it will be in Istanbul but if you can source it for me I will pay you one million euro.'

Ayşe has often wondered how she would feel if a life-transfiguring sum of money walked into her gallery. Adnan talks of the fist-solid thrill of the leveraged millions of his gas trades solidifying into profit. *Don't let it seduce you*, he says. That way is death. Now a thousand euro suit offers her a million euro on a Monday morning, how could she not be seduced?

'That's a lot of money Mr Akgün.'

'It is, and I wouldn't expect you to embark on such a project without a development fee.'

He takes a white envelope from inside his jacket and gives it to Ayşe. It's fat with cash. She holds the envelope in her hand and orders her fingers not to feel out the thickness and number of the notes.

'You still haven't told me what you'd like me to find.'

Hafize has returned from exiting Mr Topaloğlu. Her customary haste to make tea – tea for every customer; tea, tea – is frozen by those words, *one million euro*.

'It's quite simple,' Akgün says. 'I want to buy a Mellified Man.'

Leyla on the Number 19, wedged hard against the stanchion in her good going-to-interview suit and business heels. Her chin is almost on the breastbone of a tall foreign youth who smells of milk, behind her is a fat middle-aged man whose hand keeps falling under social gravity to her ass. If he does that one more time she'll knee him in the nuts. What is keeping the tram? Five minutes ago it jolted to a stop dead in the middle of the Necatibey Cadessi. Doesn't IETT know she has an interview to get to? And it's hot, getting hotter. And she's sweating in her one and only going-to-interview suit.

The driver announces an incident on the line ahead. That usually means a suicide. In Istanbul the preferred self-exit-strategy is the dark lure of the Bosphorus but a simple kneel and prostration of the head to the guillotine of the wheels will do it quick and smart. Down in Demre, where the sun glints bright from the endless polytunnel roofs, it was always the hose pipe through the car window.

'There's been a bomb!' shrieks a woman in a better business suit than Leyla's. There is a ceptep over her eye. She is reading the morning headlines. 'A bomb on a tram.'

The effect on the Number 19 is total. The sudden surge of commuters lifts little Leyla Gültaşli from her feet and swings her so hard into wandering-hand-man that he grunts. People push at the doors but they remain sealed. Now everyone is thrown again as the tram lurches into motion. It's going backwards. Wheels grind and flange on the track.

'Hey hey, I've got an interview!' Leyla shouts.

The tram jolts to a stop. The doors open. The crowd pushes her out on to the same halt at which she boarded. She has thirty-five minutes to get to this interview. Her shoes are trampled and her suit is rumpled and her hair is ruffled and she is lathered in sweat but her face is right so she puts her head down and pushes out through the turnstile into the traffic.

Leyla had organized the interview preparations like a wedding. With the hot night greying into day outside her balcony she was striding around in her underwear, unfolding the ironing board, flicking water over her one good suit and blouse as she applied the hot metal. She has got into terrible habits since Zehra announced she was moving back to Antalya. While the suit relaxed on the hanger, losing the just-ironed smell of fabric conditioner, she showered. The water was as mean and fitful as ever. Leyla wove and shimmied under the ribbon of tepid water. Seventy seconds, including shampoo. No more. The landlord last week had slipped a leaflet under every door explaining that the municipal water charges were going up again. Unquenchable Istanbul. The hair straighteners were already plugged in and coming up to temperature. Leyla Gültaşli got jiggly with the hair-dryer and went over her pitch.

Gençler Toys. Toys for boys. Six- to eleven-year-olds. Lead lines: BattleCats TM; Gü-Yen-Ji, their ceptep-handshake trading card game, was EU Toy of the Year two years ago. Their success is built on BitBots. The creepy kid upstairs has them. Leyla's sure he watches her with them. But they have a vacancy in their marketing department and Leyla is Marketing Girl so she'll talk BitBots and Battle-Cats TM as good as any of them.

The suit, then the slap. One hour twenty to get to Gençler. Plenty of time. Bag; a good brand not so high-marque as to be obviously a fake. Which it is. A girl of business needs one convincing accessory in her wardrobe. And the shoes and out.

Twenty-two minutes now and she curses herself for not thinking to wear trainers. Put the good shoes in the bag and change in the ladies' room when you're making the final adjustments to your face. She can run – just – in these shoes. But the crowd is growing thicker on Necatibey Cadessi and now she hits the police line and before her is the tram with its windows blown out and its roof bowed up and people standing around among the crisis vehicles with their red and blue flashing lights. The road is sealed. Leyla gives a cry of frustration.

'Let me through, let me through!'

A policeman shouts, 'Hey, where do you think you're going?' but Leyla plunges on. 'Hey!' To her left is a narrow sok, more stairs than is sensible in this heat and these shoes. Fifteen minutes. Leyla Gültaşli takes a deep breath, slings her bag over her shoulder and begins to climb.

Once there were four girls from the south. They were all born within fifty kilometres of each other within the smell of the sea but they didn't discover that until the dervish house. The condition of Leyla moving from the plasticland of Demre to Istanbul was that she place herself under the care of Great-Aunt Sezen. Leyla had never met Great-Aunt Sezen or any of the distant Istanbul side of the family. Their third-floor apartment in the sound-footprint of Atatürk Airport had a Turkish flag draped over the balcony and a Honda engine under the kitchen table and was full of noisy, clattering relations and generations over whom Great-Aunt Sezen, a matriarch of seventy-something, ruled by hint and dint and tilt of head. The country girl from the Med found herself plunged into an involuntary soap-opera of husbands and wives and children, of boyfriends and girlfriends and partners and rivals and feuds and makings-up, of screaming fights and tearful, sex-raucous reconciliations. In the midst of this storm of emotions Leyla Gültaşli tried to work, seated at the kitchen table, her knees oily from the manifold of the Honda engine while her extended family raged around her. They thought her dull. They called her Little Tomato, after her hometown's most famous export. That and Santa, its other global brand. Her studies suffered. She began to fail course elements.

She went to Sub-Aunt Kevser, Grand Vizier of the Gültaşlis, who called Leyla's mother in Demre. The two women talked for an hour. It was decided. Leyla could share an apartment with suitable girls, provided she report to Sub-Aunt Kevser every Friday. No boys of course. There was a respectable girl from Antalya at the Business College who had a place, very central, very good value, in Beyoğlu. So Leyla entered the dervish house and discovered that it was central because it was tatty, sorrowful Eskiköy and good value because the apartment had not been renovated since the declaration of the Republic a century ago. Among three Marketing and Business students, Leyla had even less peace than she ever knew in Honda kitchen. They still called her Little Tomato. She liked it from the girls. Sub-Aunt Kevser called faithfully every Friday. Leyla answered as conscientiously. After two years she graduated with honours. Her parents came up on the bus for her graduation. The Istanbul branch moved family members around rooms like tiles in some plastic game to find space for the Demre tomato-growers in Runway View Apartments. Her mother clung to her father throughout the event at the campus. They gave her gold and had their eyes closed in every single photograph.

So: these four girls from the south who shared a small smelly apartment in Adem Dede tekke. They all graduated from Marmara Business College on the same day. Then one went to Frankfurt to work in an investment bank. One moved out to a Big Box start-up on a bare hill outside Ankara. Five weeks ago Zehra announced she was moving back to Antalya to marry a hitherto-unsuspected boyfriend and Leyla was left friendless cashless and jobless in the crumbling old dervish house, the only one not to have secured some shape of future. Istanbul was over-commodified with bright young girls with diplomas in marketing. Day by day, bill by bill, the money was running down but one thing was sure. She was never moving back to that apartment full of screaming lives and jet engines.

Leyla's counting the steps: thirty-one, thirty-two, thirty-three. The lie of the streets is familiar: there's the end of Vermilion-Maker Lane. She's within a couple of hundred metres of home. She could slip back for comfortable shoes. Twelve minutes. If she can get up on to Inönü Cadessi there are buses and dolmuşes and even, though they would consume the last of her cash, taxis, but it all has to connect sweet and this is Istanbul. Her fingers shake from exertion. There is a humming in her ears. God she is so unfit. Too many nights in front of the television because it is voices and lives in the apartment. Then Leyla realizes it's not the thrum of her own body. This is something outside her. She is fogged in a cloud of mosquitoes. She waves her hand at the swarm – shoo, evil things. The bulge of black sways away from her hand and thickens into a hovering dragon-fly. Her breath catches in fear. Even Leyla Gütaşli has heard of these things. Up and down Vermilion-Maker Lane morning people stand in place while the dragonfly bots ascertain identities. The machine hovers on its ducted-fan wings. Hurry up hurry up hurry up. She's got an interview in ten minutes, minutes *ten*. Leyla could crush the thing in her hand and be on her way but it scares her. Soldiers you can flash eyes at, flirt a little to make their day and they'll nod you on. Soldiers are men. These things carry poison darts, she's heard, evil little nanotechnology stings. Defy them at your peril. But it's slow slow slow and she's late late late. She blinks at a wink of laser light: the security drone is reading her iris. The dragonfly bot lifts on its wings then blows into a puff of mites. On your way now. Up and down the stairs, along Vermilion-Maker Lane, the dragonflies evaporate into smart smoke. She's passed but she is horribly hideously fatally late.

All the traffic that has been diverted from the bomb blast has been pushed on to Inönü Cadessi. Leyla wails at the immobile mass of vehicles, nose to tail, door to door. Horns blare constantly. She squeezes between the stationary cars. A little bubble citicar comes to a sudden stop and Leyla shimmies in front of it. The driver beats his hand on the horn but she sashays away with a cheeky wave of the hand. There's a bus there's a bus there's a bus. She dances a deadly bullfighter's dance through the pressing traffic, closer, ever closer to the bus. The line of passengers is getting shorter. The doors are closing. Damn these stupid shoes, what possessed her to put them on? Men never look at shoes. The bus is pulling away from the stop but she can make it she can make it. Leyla beats on the door. Two schoolboys leer at her. She runs alongside the crawling bus, banging on the side. 'Stop stop stop stop!' Then a gap opens in front of it and it surges away from her in an aromatic waft of biodiesel. Leyla stands and curses, the traffic steering around her; good, long, southern tomato-grower curses.

Dolmuş dolmuş dolmuş. There's a cluster of them, slope-backed minibuses huddling together like pious women but they're too far down the street, too distant from the stop and even if she could hail one it would have to travel at the speed of light to get there on time.

Faster. Not even the Prophet on Burak could get to Gençler Toys in time for the interview. Leyla wails, throws up her arms in despair in the middle of gridlocked Inönü Cadessi. Her ceptep alert chimes to reinforce her failure. Out of time. Over. No point even calling. Istanbul is too too full of Leyla Gültaşlis.

'I could do that job!' she shouts to the street. 'I could do that job easy!'

She's sick to her stomach, sick in her suddenly-stupid and vain suit and shoes, her cheap knock-off bag. She needs that job, she needs that money, she needs not to go back to Runway View Apartments but most of all she needs never again to see the sun glinting from the endless kilometres of plastic roof over the fields and gardens of Demre and breathe in the cloying, narcotic perfume of tomatoes. Leyla is very close to crying in the middle of traffic-clogged Inönü Cadessi. This won't do. She can't be seen like this. Go home. Tomorrow you can pick yourself up and smarten yourself and get out there again and show them you're good. Today, rage and cry and kick things around where no one can see you. Why why why did this have to be the day that a suicide bomber decided to blow himself up to God? It's so selfish, like any suicide.

She is halfway down the steps to Adem Dede Square when her ceptep calls. Sub-Aunt Kevser. The last person she needs to talk to. Her thumb hovers over the reject icon. She can't. You are always available. The mantra was drummed into her at business school.

'You took your time.' As ever when she talks with Leyla, she looks like a school-teacher.

'I was just doing something.'

'Doing?' There's always been the assumption that Leyla's aspirations are dispensable. The women drop everything for the family, it was the way down in Demre, it's the way up in Istanbul.

'It's all right, nothing much.'

'Good good good. Remind me, what was that course you did?'

You know full well what I do, Leyla thinks. *I can't see her, but Great-Aunt Sezen is behind you directing this from her chair.*

'Marketing.'

'Would that include raising finance and finding backers?'

'It does.'

'Hmm.'

Just tell me, you bad old crow.

Sub-Aunt Kevser continues, 'Did you ever meet Yaşar Ceylan?'

'Who's he?'

'He'd be your second cousin. Smart boy. University educated.' *Rub it in, sterile spinster. Yes, I only went to a business college.* 'He's set up this new business start-up thing over in Fenerbahçe with some boy he did his doctorate with. I've no idea what it is; some new technology thing. Anyway, they're very smart, very clever but useless at anything practical. Yaşar wants to expand but doesn't know how to get to the people with the money. He needs someone to get him to the money men.'

You see, you knew all the time.

'When does he need someone?'

'Right away. But you said you were doing something, so I don't know ...'

'Has he got any money?' Ever the drawback to working with family.

'He'll pay you. So you'll do it?'

'I'll do it. Give me his number.' Sub-Aunt Kevser's face is replaced by a ceptep number. Leyla stores it quickly. God God thank you God. Sometimes family is your friend. She almost skips down the last few steps into Adem Dede Square. From desolation to ludicrous exultation in seven steps. Fenerbahçe. Business start-up. New tech. Fresh university graduates. It all means only one thing. The big one, the one that promises to build the future and change the world, the one where you can really make your name.

Nanotechnology.

2

The alien robot is an ungainly spider thing concealed among the graphics of the Commerzbank. Can observes it from his hiding place in the shadows of Allianz Insurance. An ugly boxy yellow industrial unit; a Xu-Hsi, or maybe a customized General Robotics. Licence number covered up with gaffer tape. An inspection machine would carry warning chevrons and flashers. Can Durukan knows his robots like other kids know cars or footballers or Chinese comics. An industrial bot wouldn't pay a wink of interest even if the world were ending down there. What else could it be? On his adventures high above Eskiköy Can has encountered photodrones: machines set wandering on month-long journeys across the city by art students to capture the random and spontaneous. Those pause, shoot, stalk on. He has also met unofficial press bots upon the rooftops: stealthy, secretive surveillers used by investigative journalists and photographers looking for the news behind the press releases. Ghost machines that can flash-burn their memories to slag if detected by the state and its agents. Everything deniable. If this is a press drone, the photographer's timing is brilliant. Too brilliant. And then there are the black drones: the ones they like to mutter about on the conspiracy sites. Invisible to official police bots, surveilling the surveillers. If this clunky chunk of yellow plastic is a legendary black drone, it's in some very deep cover altogether. And then hide the licence number? This is none of these. This is proper mystery. Can's monkey creeps closer, hand by careful hand, prehensile tail coiling and uncoiling, trying to see better without being seen. The mystery bot is scanning the bomb victims inside the police cordon. Its sensory arrays, clusters of fly-eyes lenses, rotate and refocus from survivor to survivor. Click whir click whir. That woman with blood speckled all over her face like freckles. Those shivering children in blue with schoolbags so big they could fold themselves inside. That dazed-looking businessman clutching his briefcase. That man, wandering away from the main group, between the ambulances, not wanting to be seen. Can watches Rat-Face, the guy from the tekke garden, move slowly, mingle subtly, merge with the crowd beyond the Do Not Cross lines. So intently does Can watch, so tightly does he hold his breath in excitement, that he almost misses the ninja robot detach itself from its roost and slowly, subtly, with no sudden movements to catch the attention of the police bots, work its way up the stanchions to the roof of the Commerzbank building. He sees a flash of anonymized yellow vanish over the parapet. Hissing in frustration, Can wills Monkey up on to the roof of the Allianz building. There: the mystery surveiller is working along the building tops, following Necatibey Cadessi. Slowly, stealthily, Can follows. His eyes are wide, his tongue rolled in concentration, his heart loud with excitement. This is mystery. This is adventure. This is what every boy and his robot want.

'Aie!' Can stifles the involuntary cry of excitement. Too loud too loud; it's far too easy to be too loud when the world is reduced to a whisper. But it's a huge huge discovery. Mystery bot is following Necdet, stoner-boy. Up in the balcony Can almost gibbers at the excitement. This isn't just curiosity, or even a mystery any more. This is a case. He is Can: Boy Detective now. The case is afoot!

Carefully carefully, with one half of his eyes on the stalker, the other half on the crazed, reeling guy down in the street, Can creeps across the rooftops of Beyoğlu. Release a hand here, take a grip there. It is following him. Necdet, stoner-boy. Of all people to follow. Like the lizard stalking the hunting mantis feels the shadow of the hawk; it's only Can's over-compensating secondary senses, that instinctive knowing before knowing that makes his hand stab out and make Monkey roll forward, out of the pincer jaws that would have fried his BitBot circuitry with EMP.

As he was the follower, he too was followed. He reconfigures his eyes as he gallops away from the attacker. Another anonymous hack-drone. He has stumbled into the surveillance range of another watcher and triggered an alert. It's big and it's fast and it's strong. It can take Can's BitBots to pieces. It's behind him and Can's power management panel is telling him he is down to two-thirds battery power. He has to bring Monkey back, but it will lead the pursuer straight to him.

Run robot run. Monkey leap, monkey scuttle. Behind him, half a roof away, comes the destroyer. Can gasps in mental exertion and flexes his hand to send his monkey up a wall in two bounds, over a parapet and across a sheltered green-painted garden where morning washing hangs limply in the heat-weary air. The hunter follows. It's bigger, faster and even closer. Can flicks a glance at the battery meter. Half charge now, and at this rate of exertion Monkey eats power. And *leap*. Even as Monkey is in mid-air Can reconfigures him into a ball. The BitBot hits and rolls, bounding from the air-conditioning fans and photosynth panels to crash hard against the further parapet. The hunter bounds after him, crossing the roof in a few strides but the BitBot has morphed back into Monkey mode and is hand-over-handing it down the fire escape for the leap to the roof of the adjoining building. Can has stolen a few dozen metres.

Can doesn't hear the door open. Can doesn't hear anything. The chase across the rooftops is silent. He only looks up from the robot-versus-robot action when light from the open door dazzles him. A shadow, a sun-blurred spindly alien-thing. His mum. She signs. Can frowns. He always sits facing the door so that he will know when someone comes in but also because the visitor can't see what he is doing on his computer. Can isn't allowed excitement. She would cry. Unable to shout or shake or strike, she's forced into self-martyrdom. See how you've made me feel?

She signs again. *Have you got a clean shirt for school this afternoon?*

Can knows better than to nod. That would make her feel hurt because he was being rude and disrespectful. She might even ask what was so important he couldn't talk to his mother. His hands can't afford the time away from the screen but he signs: *There's one in the wardrobe.*

Good, she says. The silhouette moves in the bright light as if to go, then turns back. *What are you doing anyway?*

Can's heart flutters.

'Just playing with Monkey.' It's no lie.

Well, just you don't go annoying anyone with him, all right? Then she vanishes into the light and the door closes. Can lets out a hiss of concentration and bends over his roll-up screen. Speed power navigation security. A cat flees as Monkey and its hunter gallop across the rooftop and swing up a water-tank gantry on to the next roof. Distance five metres, power at twelve per cent. Can wonders who is behind those insect eyes; what face lit by what screen.

Whoever you are, Can Durukan Boy Detective will amaze and bamboozle you! Can clenches his fist to summon the reserves from the batteries, then flings his hand open to send Monkey leaping high over the concrete coaming. The hunter-bot leaps after him. *Got you! You thought there was a roof but there is nothing but twenty metres of empty air.* Can brings his hands together in a silent clap. Falling Monkey explodes into its component BitBots. Nanorobots rain down on to Vermilion-Maker Lane. Can crosses his thumbs and waggles his fingers. The cloud of mite-machines ripples, darkens into smoke and coalesces into a pair of gossamer wings. A bird; Can's Bird. Power is critical, but Bird beats its wings, swoops over the heads of the men squatting on their teashop stools, so low they duck. Three beats four, and he pulls up out of Vermilion-Maker Lane. In his rear-view camera he sees the hunting bot smashed like a porcelain crab on the cobbles. Shards and splinters and scraps of yellow shell. He turns over Adem Dede square, a great white stork sliding home.

Can's hands shake. There's a tightness in the back of his throat and nose of wanting to cry and he needs a pee. His heart thuds tight in his chest, his breath flutters in his throat, his face burns with excitement now that he realizes he was in danger. While he was running it was a game, the best game he has ever played. Now he can think about what would have happened if the men behind the robot had followed him, had come to his door and knocked on it. Now he can be afraid. But he is proud; more proud of escaping the hunter than of anything he has ever done. He wants to tell people. But the kids in the special school are too stupid to understand or have something very wrong with them. His parents: Can knows he would never crawl out from under his mother's self-flagellation and his father's silence.

Mr Ferentinou. He will listen. He will know. What he doesn't know he can guess and his guesses are always right. He was famous for that, so he tells Can. Can Durukan goes to the edge of the balcony, peers into the brilliant morning breaking over Eskiköy and lifts a hand to catch Bird coming home.

You are a fine gentleman of Iskenderun, old Alexandretta, some time in the middle decades of Eighteenth Christian Century, a subject of Sultan Osman III. His empire has ebbed far from its zenith at the gates of Vienna. It is the magic blue hour of the house of Ösmanli. All seems radiant and still and suspended as if it might carry on in this shell-like turquoise forever. But the night draws inexorably in. Imperial Constantinople may console itself in grand buildings of mosques and baths and imperial tombs but Alexandretta is far from the Sublime Porte and feels the winds from the east and the north more closely. It has always been a cosmopolis of many races and confessions where the trade routes from Central Asia meet the sea-lanes from Italy and the far Atlantic. In those caravanserais and hans you made your wealth. In your prime you were a travelled man, west to Marseilles and Cadiz, east to Lahore and Samarkand; to the north, Moscow and, as befits a religious man once in his life, south to Mecca as a hacı. Now you are old; you have retired to your shaded house where the cool sea breeze brings news from the corners of the empire and the greater world beyond. The great age of peace and prosperity is ending. Your wife is dead these five years; your sons manage your interests and your daughters are adequately married. Life's obligations are fulfilled. It is time to leave. One morning you order your staff, *bring me a bowl of pine honey.* You eat it all up with a silver spoon in a quiet room of your house that has no clocks. Again, for your midday meal: *bring me a bowl of pine honey.* In the evening; a bowl of pine honey. Only honey.

By the third day of nothing but honey the servants have gossiped it abroad. By Friday prayers it is all across the city. Your many friends come to call, a river of them for you are a household name in Alexandretta, but not before your sons and daughters. The women weep, the men ask, *What possessed you to choose this bizarre act? You say, a tumour the size of a pomegranate. I can feel it inside me, it is months since I could enjoy a piss without pain. It would be the death of me and I can't defeat that but I can arrange a different appointment with Azrael.* By now the servants have soaked the curtains in vinegar to keep the flies from you.

Doctors are called, European trained. They come from the room that now smells of sweet honey-sweat to tell the waiting sons and sons-in-law that there is nothing they can do, you are set upon this process and it will take its course. Not even the imam can sway you from what you have decided to become. It is unusual but it has a long and noble history. In the second week of your transformation you express a taste for exotic and rare honeys: the blends and the regionals, from the potent aphid-sucked honey-dew of the fir forests of the Vosges and southern Germany to the delicately floral Thousand Flower honey of Bordeaux. In the third week of your transfiguration you explore honeys of theft and peril; wild acacia honey of the savage hives of Africa where the foragers have grown immune to stings that would kill lesser men; honey from the Sundarbans of Bengal where tigers stalk the hive-hunters in the mangrove forests; the carob honeys from the bazaars of Fes, stolen in the high Atlas from legendary hives the size of houses. In your moments of lucidity between swimming in golden sugar-hallucinations you realize that you are now the empire's greatest connoisseur of honey and that this precious knowledge could easily pass from the world. You hire an amanuensis, a tarikat-trained boy of a good family and excellent calligraphy to write down your ravings on the honeys that your servants now drip by the spoonful on to your tongue. In the fourth week you explore the high paths of sweetness; the single flower honeys. Such is your skill now that you can taste a single drop and say that this is a myrrh honey from Arabia, that is a thyme honey from Cyprus, that is orange blossom honey from Bulgaria and that, unmistakably, is cedar honey from the Levant. Beyond the borders of the empire you discover sleep-scented lavender honey from Spain and the cactus honey of Mexico. For two days you savour and describe the bitter, mentholic darkness of the Sardinian Corbozello honey made from the flowers of the wild arbutus. Over three days you are gripped in hallucinations of the rhododendron honey of the Himalayas. Towards the end there are days when you are lost entirely in the golden light that glows behind your permanently-drawn blinds and you utter honey-prophecies and oozing sugar-visions but when you ask your secretary to read your ravings back there is not one word written on his page. By now your pores exude not sweat but a gold-tinged ichor. Your urine is as sweet as a confection, your excrement a soft amber unguent. Honey permeates every vessel of your body; honey swaddles your organs and drips in oozing globules through the spaces of your brain.

The transition from waking world to dream, from dream to coma and from coma to death is sweet, subtle and as slow as the fall of a tear of honey from a spoon. The doctor confirms with his little mirror that all breath has left your body. Your secretary stands shaking with hidden tears, clutching his treatise on honey as the blinds are thrown open. Your daughters are already keening, your sons have one last task to perform. The imam makes the consignment as the servants wash the corpse that smells of thyme and lavender, pine and myrrh and orange-flower. Now your sons must work fast. The great stone coffin, an ancient pagan Roman thing, has already been filled with honey. Your body is slowly submerged in it; great bubbles rising slowly through the amber liquid as you sink. The lid is slid into position and as it is sealed with lead the remaining spaces are filled with yet more honey poured through a hole bored through the mouth of the pagan goddess until a single drop of gold forms on her lips. Then that too is sealed with molten lead. Men and many horses – all the men of goodwill who knew you in life – carry you through the streets of Alexandretta to the warehouse where you have caused the grave to be dug. The marker is set in the place of the paving slab. It reads, Hacı Ferhat, 1191–1268 – and a second date: Berat Kandili 1450.

Every trade has its fabled beasts, its Rocs and Cyclops and Djinni that can whisk you from the dome of Baghdad to Samarkand in a thought. Lawyers have monster murderers and celebrity defendants who have defamed Turkishness or merely pulled off a breathtaking scam. Traders have their stellar players who read the market in one moment of piercing insight and made unimaginable fortunes. The media is rife with the vices of actors and the eccentricities of editors, producers and directors. Musicians' whims and contract riders are legendary. The neglected, dusty corner of antiquarians and manuscript dealers is no different. There are its grails, its lost codices, forbidden grimoires and Hands of Glory and, stalking the honeyed path between them, the Mellified Man.

They are creatures of antiquarians' legends, Mellified Men. Once in a lifetime one may turn up in the vast bazaars of Damascus or Cairo, walking out of a remote and alien history. They command fearful prices, insane money, for they are the embodiment of powerful magics. Even the djinn respect a Mellified Man. At the due date on the tombstone the casket is unsealed. When the lid is removed what remains is a human confection. Honey suffuses every channel and organ, honey fuses with flesh, honey permeates every cell. Sugar is a powerful preservative and antibacterial. The unfamiliar sun turns the thing in the coffin to gold. Now the Mellified Man's true work begins.

The body is broken up into pieces the size of a cube of baklava. These are applied to cure all manners of ill and wounds. The flesh of a Mellified Man, soft as semolina halva, has the power to cure diseases, heal wounds, mend broken bones. Smeared on the eyelids it melts away cataracts; it can restore hearing to deaf ears. Spread on the genitals, it renews potency. Taken internally is the most efficacious method. A tiny dose melted on the tongue will dissolve cancers, clear phlegm from clogged lungs, refresh the great organs, stoke up cooling digestive fires, eradicate any stone or gall or ulcer. Even the hair from the mummy's head, thick and syrupy as a strand of kedayıf pastry, is a famous cure for baldness.

'You don't work for any length of time in this business without someone boasting that they've seen a Mellified Man,' Ayşe says. She is very aware of her own breathing. 'And I am aware that they're more than just legends but in my experience they were strictly medieval.' A void has opened in the sanity of things and she teeters on the brink. The Persian miniatures of Belkis and the Prophet that line the walls swirl without ever changing position. This is an echo of the age of miracles in this third decade of the twenty-first century. But if there is one place where a Mellified Man could walk out of magical time, where the fantastical and the mundane routinely come into contact, where the djinn touch toe to earth, it is surely Istanbul.

'Oh no no no,' says Akgün. In the private viewing room Ayşe can closely study her guest. The nanoweave fabric of his suit has closed in the air-conditioned cool and his clothing shimmers like Damascus steel. The watch is high-marque, the manicure exquisite from the tips of his nails to his cufflinks. The shave is business-close but there is something about the man does not smell right. His cologne is *Arslan*. Even an ultra Cimbom fan like Adnan would never wear an aroma branded for a Galatasaray striker. 'People put too much faith in Li Shizhen's account. There is good evidence that a Mellified Man was sold in Tashkent to traditional Chinese medical practitioners as recently as 1912.'

'Yes, but that's a long way from an eighteenth-century Mellified Man from Alexandretta.'

'You are absolutely right to be sceptical. That's why I've brought provenances.'

Inside the impact-carbon briefcase is another, in supple honey-coloured leather. It would not surprise Ayşe if it were human skin. It carries a small tulip-shaped tattoo. Her scanners tell her the mark is a blossom of tracker molecules. Within the case is a waxed paper wallet, within that the folio itself, leather bound with an ornate rosette in gold leaf set on a medallion on the cover.

'May I?'

Akgün slides the book across the table. It lies beside the envelope of cash. Ayşe wills down the lights as she studies the binding. The stitching seems authentic, strong linen thread; the header tapes of their time. Dust falls from the right places and the leather smells of old skin and is creased where a book should be, like a face lined with experience. It crackles as Ayşe opens it. Inside is in the swift, clear Sumbuli script of a lad who has transcribed the Holy Koran from memory, setting down the thoughts of God as they form in his memory like water welling from a spring.

Heather honey, from the uplands of the barbarous realm of Scotland, which comprises the northernmost part of the island of Britain. Heather is a small ground-covering plant, with springy woody boughs and small, thyme-like leaves which commonly grows on the sides of the hills and mountains that characterize that country. Trees are almost entirely unknown in upland Scotland due to the proximity of the pole and the general inclemency of the weather, which is of a wet, gloomy and sunless nature and of a boggy disposition.

'So?'

'On a cursory inspection it looks authentic, but we are the world capital of fakery. To be sure I'd need to carry out a molecular analysis,' Ayşe says. The small room is filled with the cedary perfume of an old book opened to the light. Smell is the djinni of memory, all times are one to it. As she pores over the book, her eye-write scanning the calligraphy, Ayşe is simultaneously in her grandfather's bookstore in Sirkeci that rambled through a series of seemingly arbitrarily connected rooms (were they in different cities, different ages, different universes?), the books becoming older and more compressed the deeper and darker you went, like a geology of words. As a nine-year-old she would close her eyes and wander surely through the warren, guided by the sharp, spicy ketones and esters of modern pulps and A-format paperbacks through the teetering towers of remaindered hardbacks and the glossy, oily tang of coffee-table books to the musks and spices of the antiquarian volumes on their sagging shelves, many of which were written in letters she could not understand and which read the wrong way. Understanding did not matter; Ayşe could wander, entranced, for hours along the lines of Arabic cursive. Often it was enough to stand, eyes firmly shut, under the little coloured mosque lamps with their low-voltage bulbs and breathe in the perfume of history, the pheromones of the dead. 'It would involve destroying a small sample.'

Akgün's shock is genuine. *Here is a man who knows and loves books, Ayşe thinks. And cannot countenance any violence to them. He would return borrowed paperbacks on time, their spines uncracked, the covers of their corners un-foxed. But he doesn't know that with modern nano–assay chips the clipping is a few fibres of paper, a few molecules of ink.* That he doesn't know that is another circling suspicion. After the adrenaline always comes clarity and judgement. A Mellified Man, the blood burns, the brain blazes at even the possibility of it being true. But like djinn in a house, her doubts will not be driven out: of all the shops of all the dealers and all the antiquarians in all of Istanbul, why this shop, this dealer? The world is simple but it is never neat. This man in the right suit and the wrong aftershave is too neat. Ayşe Erkoc closes the book and slides the envelope of five-hundred-euro notes across the table.

'You tempt me but I can't take this commission.'

'May I ask why?'

'You said I can obtain hard-to-get items – that's because I've built up a network of dealers and antiquarians and experts. I've built it up by word of mouth. I guard it very jealously. This is a very small business. Everyone knows everyone else and rumour moves like wildfire. You live or you die by reputation. When word got around

that Ünal Bey was passing Kazakhstani fakes off as Timurid miniatures he was shunned. Two weeks later he drove his car through
the crash barrier of the Bosphorus Bridge in shame. Maybe you
heard about it on the news? I know my suppliers and my agents and
I know my clients – many of them are very wealthy and influential
men, but everything is done by personal recommendation. Now,
I have no doubts that your provenances are genuine and that this
Alexandretta mummy has washed up in Istanbul and I'd be lying if
I said I wasn't very very tempted. But there's an etiquette in this
business. I am very sorry, Mr Akgün.'

He chews his lower lip, flicks his head.

'You have my card.' He straightens the cuffs of his shirt. 'I hope
you'll reconsider.'

'Trust me, nothing would give me more pleasure than to track
down a mellified man,' says Ayşe. She extends a hand. Akgün's grasp
is firm and dry. No spark of data between them. She waits on the
balcony as Akgün descends the stairs. Hafize's eyes are wide and
hands spread in astonishment as the street door closes behind him.
She has been watching, as she always watches, the deal on the
security cameras. Her hands say, *You turned down a million euro?*

Yes, Ayşe will tell her when Akgün is gone. *You didn't smell his
aftershave.*

His was love in a time of military rule. It was the late summer when
Georgios Ferentinou looked up from the beautiful abstract weave of
statistical regressions and complexity algorithms and saw the tumbling curling hair and magnificent sullen cheekbones of Ariana
Sinanidis across Meryem Nasi's pool. A fresh and zealous undergraduate, he had been engaged in a season-long combative cor-
respondence with a New York-based Lebanese economist. Georgios'
enemy argued that random events beyond the predictions of theory
shaped the world. People and lives bobbed in a storm of probability.
Georgios argued back that complexity theory folded the spikes and
pits of randomness back into the everyday, the humdrum. All storms

whimper out in the end. That summer they argued across the Atlantic by flimsy blue airmail while in Istanbul demonstrators marched and protestors rallied and political parties formed and drew up manifestos and made alliances and schismed into new parties and bombs went off in Istiklal Cadessi litter bins. In Ankara generals and admirals and jandarmeri commanders met in each other's houses. In the university library Georgios Ferentinou – thin and lithe and luminous-eyed as a deer – worked on, as oblivious to the deteriorating political climate as to the season.

Then the invitation came to Meryem's party. Meryem Nasi was as close as modern Istanbul came to aristocracy, of an intellectual Jewish family that claimed to have lived by the Bosphorus since the Diaspora. Of no special gift herself, she was hopelessly attracted to talented people. She collected them. She enjoyed bringing disparate, even antagonistic talents together to see if they would achieve a critical mass, if they would fuse or fission or generate some other burst of creative energy.

'If there is one thing will kill Turkey,' she would say, 'it is a famine of ideas.'

No one in her coterie dared mention that if anything was killing Turkey it was a surfeit of ideas, too many political visions and ideologies. But the head of the school of economics did mention a particularly bright and aggressive undergraduate who was fighting a ridiculous but valorous battle against an American academic of ten times his experience and a hundred times his reputation. Three days later the invitation arrived on Georgios Ferentinou's desk. Not even his unworldliness could ignore a summons from Meryem Nasi. So he found himself stiff as a wire in a hired suit and cheap shoes clutching a glass on her Yeniköy terrace, grimacing nervously at anyone who moved through his personal space.

'Darling, there's someone I want you to meet.' Meryem was a short, big-haired gravel-voiced fifty-something in shoulderpads and wasp-waist jacket but she seized Georgios Ferentinou by the arm like a wrestler and hauled him to the group of men by the pool steps.

'This is Sabri Iliç from *Hürriyet*, Aziz Albayrak from the State Planning Organization and Arif Hikmet from the faculty you already know. This is Georgios Ferentinou; he's the bad boy's been baiting Nabi Nassim at Columbia.'

In the warmth of an early September evening their talk turned to the oil crisis of the previous winter when old women froze in their apartments in Istanbul. Stammering at first in such prodigious company, Georgios suggested that a more secure energy future could be fuelled by natural gas. It was less subject to the political price fluctuations of OPEC, the TransCaspian area had so much of it they burned it off in tail flares and it would hook Turkey back into its traditional hinterland of the Caucasus. Arif Hikmet, with a wink to his student, said that the Americans would not look well on their prime security partner in the Middle East tying itself to its ideological enemy for energy policy. Sabri Iliç, *Hürriyet*'s new business editor, commented that it was the Americans who had driven the oil prices up in the first place. Aziz Albayrak from Ankara maintained that Turkey must always look west, not north, to the EEC, not the USSR. Georgios was nineteen years old in a funeral suit and bad shoes; people whose opinions shaped the nation nodded when he spoke. He felt weightless, filled with light ready to burst from every pore, giddy with intellectual excitement yet at the same time assured and controlled. He could trust his mouth not to open and scuttle him. Now they were energetically debating the ongoing effects of the lira's devaluation and convertibility; how it opened the Central Bank to international markets and investors but also made it vulnerable to currency speculators. What did Georgios Bey think? Georgios Bey had been glancing away from the debate for a moment but in that moment a woman in equally rapt conversation across the pool also looked away. Their eyes met. That look wiped away all thought. Georgios Ferentinou was struck by the lightning of his oldest gods. Her gaze moved on, the moment was gone. She returned to her conversation but he was lost. With the skill of an academic son used to studying between television, blaring radio, shouts and calls and raucous animated conversations, he screened out his own party and tuned, like a radio telescope eavesdropping on a distant and radiant star, to hers. She was talking politics with a group of entranced men, sitting around on the marble poolside benches like the *demos* of ancient Athens. She was theorizing on the Deep State; that enduring Turkish paranoia that the nation really was a conspiracy run by a cabal of generals, judges, industrialists and gangsters. The Taksim Square massacre of three years before, the Kahramanmaraş slaughter of Alevis a few months after, the oil crisis and the enduring economic instability, even the ubiquity of the Grey Wolves nationalist youth movement handing out their patriotic leaflets and defiling Greek Churches: all were links in an accelerating chain of events running through the fingers of the Derin Devlet. *To what end?* the men asked. *Coup*, she said, leaning forward, her fingers pursed. It was then that Georgios Ferentinou adored her. The classic profile, the strength of her jaw and fine cheekbones. The way she shook her head when the men disagreed with her, how her bobbed, curling hair swayed. The way she would not argue but set her lips and stared, as if their stupidity was a stubborn offence against nature. Her animation in argument balanced against her marvellous stillness when listening, considering, drawing up a new answer. How she paused, feeling the regard of another, then turned to Georgios and smiled.

In the late summer of 1980 Georgios Ferentinou fell in love with Ariana Sinanidis by Meryem Nasi's swimming pool. Three days later, on September 12th, Chief of General Staff Kenan Evren over-threw the government and banned all political activity.

Now Ariana is back in this tangle of streets, on this square beneath him. He tries to imagine how time might engrain itself in her face, deepening lines, accentuating her sharp features, adding shadows. She would not have coarsened, grown gross like him. She would always move like a muse. Why has she come back? He's old, it's been forty-seven years. Dare he seek her out?

All minorities possess a sense for being watched. Georgios turns slowly in the creaking chair. The snake clings to the wall, fixing

Georgios in its jewel-bright eyes. Georgios Ferentinou nods to the watching robot and lumbers down the stairs to his library. He is so stiff today. The machine slides ahead of him along the wall. That same old Fener-Greek instinct introduced Georgios to neighbour Can Durukan. Poring over his smart paper screen one winter afternoon with the Karayel, the Black Wind, seeking out the gaps in the window frame, a prickle on the back of his neck had made him look up. There, a tiny watcher tucked into the carved wooden fitting for the chandelier. He stood up on his chair to peer at it and the thing dropped to the floor and made a break for the door. But Georgios was in the heart of his demesne. In a thought he whipped his jacket from the back of his chair and flung it over the scuttling thing. He snatched it up, only to drop the jacket, startled. It squirmed and boiled as if infested. A swarm of tiny spider robots scattered in every direction. Georgios shook his head with wonder. As the last spider headed for the gap at the bottom of the library door he grabbed a glass and brought it down over the device. 'I've got you!'

An hour later came the knock on his apartment door.

'Come on in,' he said. 'I think I have something of yours.' The boy frowned, leaned forward. Of course. The heart condition. Like every other occupant of the dervish house Georgios received a note under the door every New Year reminding him to avoid rows, heavy footwear, power tools, excessive thumping or dropping heavy pans and keep the volume on his music and television down. It was twenty years since Georgios Ferentinou kept anything heavier than a kettle for tea in his cramped kitchen and, unusually for a mathematician, he had no ear for music. *It's down in the library*, he wrote in propelling pencil on the wall by the door. The boy goggled at such nonchalant vandalism.

'This is a library?' Can said in his too-loud, flat voice. He stared around at the simple whitewashed dervish cell with its single brass lamp and small, shuttered window. 'The woman downstairs has hundreds and hundreds of books.'

But those are not books for reading, Georgios wrote on the smart-paper sheet on the old Ottoman desk. *A library full of books that are never read is not a library.* He lets the words erase themselves, letter by letter. *This library has only one book, but it is every book in the world.*

He set the BitBot under the upturned tea-glass in which he had imprisoned it on the desk. He wrote, *This is clever technology.* He gestured for Can to lift the glass. The little robot ran up the boy's forefinger, under the sleeve of his T-shirt to curl in the hair at his temple. *It could be so much more than just a toy.*

'What do you mean?'

We could reprogramme it. Make it do really interesting things.

Can blinked twice at him.

'I have to go now. My mum will wonder where I am. She wouldn't like it if she knew I'd been to see you. She thinks you're a paedo. I know you're not but I'm still going.'

Come back, Georgios thought at the closing door. Can did return the next day, Monkey riding on his shoulder. The slow, careful education began.

In a different season of another year Can waits in the Library of All Books. He beckons. Snake scurries across the ceiling and drops. In mid-air it breaks into its component mites, then the cloud of microrobots reconfigure into Bird. It flies up to perch on his shoulder. Can carefully carefully removes the plugs from his ears. Georgios always holds his breath as Can extracts the delicate technology. He seems not himself today. He fidgets, his face is flushed. Georgios makes tea. Two glasses, two saucers, two spoons. Man to man across the tiny white table.

'Mr Ferentinou, I went to look at the bomb. You know, down on Necatibey Cadessi.' Georgios stirs the lazy sugar crystals in the bottom of his glass. Can's small world is full of big stories. Can continues in his slightly-too-loud voice, 'I hid up on the front of the Allianz building, and there was another robot on the building next door, hiding like me. I thought it was watching the bomb, but it wasn't. It was watching the people, the ones caught on the tram. It looked at all of them, and then it followed one. Mr Ferentinou, it was following Mr Hasguler from downstairs.'

'Ismet?' Georgios fears Shaykh Ismet. He is the antithesis of his life.

'No, the other one.'

'Necdet. I didn't know that Necdet had been caught in the bombing, but why would anyone be interested in him?'

'Well, it was following him; and it wasn't the only one. There was another robot: I didn't see it, but it saw me. It came right up behind me and it would have had me if Monkey hadn't jumped just in time. It chased me, Mr Ferentinou.'

'Chased?'

'Over the roofs. It was scary but really brilliant. It was big and fast. But it wasn't as clever. I did this trick I've been practising where I jump and morph into Bird in mid-air. It thought there was another roof there. It fell and smashed. Just out beside Kenan's.'

Georgios Ferentinou's spoon slips from his fingers and takes a quadrant off the fragile, tulip-shaped tea-glass. The tea floods the table. He will clean it up later.

'It knows where you live?'

'No, like I said, I tricked it and killed it.'

'Just outside Kenan's you say? I wouldn't mind taking a look at that.'

Can is on his air-soled feet, Snake riding his shoulder like a wave. Georgios points him back down into his seat.

'You stay there. Whoever sent it could have come looking for it. I don't think it would be good should these people know that you live here.'

'Do you think it's a conspiracy?'

'Mr Durukan, if God is dead then everything is conspiracy.'

Can presses his forehead against the window of the tiny tearoom. Mr Ferentinou waddles painfully down the steps, greets Bülent and Aydin the simit seller and pokes around behind the Coke machine outside Kenan's. *Right, to your right*, Can mouths at him, mutely waving him toward the street door. *There there, right there!* Georgios Ferentinou prods and pokes, hunkers down, face red like it could explode. He opens his hands in a gesture of incomprehension. *Nothing*.

'There was a robot, there really was, it really chased me and I did kill it,' Can says on Mr Ferentinou's return.

'Oh I believe you,' Georgios says. 'They've already taken it away. They will have video footage of your robots. And, if, for some reason they are interested in Mr Hasgüler, they will come back to this dervish house.'

'But then if they're watching that Necdet guy, then I could watch them.'

'Mr Durukan, I think you and your robots should keep a low profile.'

'But I know places in this building that no one else does. I know all the secret places. No one will ever find me.' *I watch you*, Can thinks. *I watch that Leyla girl, the one who watches too much television too and she never knows. I watch everyone.*

'I forbid it. I would be very angry if I thought you were doing that.'

'But it's a conspiracy, only it's on my own doorstep. It's cool. A real conspiracy!'

'Mr Durukan, take it from my own personal experience, real conspiracies are not cool. Real conspiracies are dangerous and bewildering and exhausting and so, so frightening. In real conspiracies, you are all on your own. Whatever this is, it's no matter for a nine-year-old boy. Leave it.'

Georgios Ferentinou gets a sponge and mops up the tea, careful of the shards of glass.

Necdet sees the first djinni perched on the hot-air hand-drier as he exits the toilet cubicle. The djinni is like a grossly obese baby, slit-eyed and puff-faced. And it's on fire. Necdet can feel the heat from the toilet door. It seethes and roars like burning fat.

'I'd, uh, kind of like to dry my hands? It's hygienic?'

The djinni cocks its bloated head to one side and holds out its pudgy hands. Necdet lifts his own hands towards them. The heat is incredible. His hands are dry in an instant.

'I'm going now.'

The question strikes him in the corridor: why didn't the hand-drier melt? Necdet ducks back into the toilet. Nothing of course. Djinn are never there when you look for them. Then the shakes hit. Necdet leans over the sink, stomach heaving. He presses his head against the cool porcelain. It is solid, it is dependable, it is cool certainty. He daren't look up. It could be there again, perched on the hand-drier with its horrid horrid baby face. Or there could be something worse. Or the head of the woman who blew herself up on the tram. Necdet puts his mouth under the tap and gulps down clear cold water, lets it run down his face, into his eyes. Wash away what they have seen today. When he looks up the toilet is still empty.

In the lobby Mustafa practises his pitch shots. Mustafa is never without a plan. None have ever earned him a cent, let alone broken him out of this pressed-aluminium barn of a Business Rescue Centre but his theory is that if he generates enough ideas one of them will stick. His latest is to exploit the fact that he is trapped in a Business Rescue Centre by turning it into an Urban Golf Facility.

'It's a new urban sport,' Mustafa says. 'Turn a building into a golf course. Corridors become fairways, offices are greens. But what makes it much much cooler than just golf is that you have to get your ball around corners and up flights of stairs. All the office furniture and partitions and workstations: those are like hazards and bunkers and all that stuff. You're never quite sure where your ball is going to go. Sort of like handball or squash – or three-d crazy golf? Maybe we should include safety helmets and goggles, what do you think? I'm going to write up a prospectus, I'm sure I can raise some venture capital. It's another great Turkish idea.'

Mustafa hits a five-iron down the corridor from his tee-off position on the empty reception desk. A sweetly angled shot, the ball strikes the wall just before the turn and ricochets around the corner. Mustafa swings his club over his shoulder. He has a lot of time to practise.

You could walk over and around the Levent Business Rescue Centre and never know it was there. Hundreds do every day. It is forty thousand square metres of office space built into the underpinnings of the Emirates Tower. Cavernous halls, office spaces, corridors and meetings rooms, storage and kitchen and toilet facilities, even a recreation room and a gym, buried away, never seeing the light of day. Should earthquake, fire or flood ever strike down those shining towers, a corporation could seamlessly move its business down to the Rescue Centre. It's big enough to handle the entire Istanbul Stock Exchange. In the year and half Necdet has been here, the red telephone has rung once and that was a wrong number. Mustafa has been here since day one. Necdet is Mustafa's only partner to stick it more than six months. Mustafa likes the dusty, neon-lit solitude of the rows of empty workstations, the meeting rooms with their chairs all set at perfectly regular intervals around the oval tables. It's room for creative thought. A thousand flowers have bloomed among these server farms.

'On for even par,' says Mustafa with a golfer's follow-through airpunch. 'What's with you? You look like you saw a ghost.'

'Not a ghost. I did see a djinni in the toilet.'

'Well, that is a traditional haunt of djinn.' Unfazed, Mustafa swings his club over his shoulder and jumps off the reception desk. He has time – buckets of time – to become a minor expert on everything. 'According to those mystics and Sufis who make a study of such things, you're supposed to ask permission every time you piss.'

'It was on the hand-drier, and it was a baby. A burning baby.'

'Ah. That's different then. Carry these for me, would you?' Mustafa hands Necdet a pitching wedge, putter and a clatter of irons. He is only three years older than Necdet – they've talked about their ages, they've talked about everything down in the bunker – but he conducts himself like a worldly-wise cosmopolite. 'I incline to the theory that djinn are spare thoughts left over from creation, memories of the Big Bang, so to speak. That would fit with them being creatures of fire. There's a new theory among the imams who have a little quantum physics that the djinn are ourselves in a universe at an angle to ours. But I think in this case they are most likely to be some lingering trauma from being in the epicentre of a tram bomb. You don't just walk away from these things you know. I'm sure they have counselling available. If it were me, I'd have given you the day off, but it's not in my gift, alas.' The Levent Business Rescue Centre is managed by Gum-Chewing Suzan. When she phones in twice a week to make sure Necdet and Mustafa haven't killed each other with the fire axes she sounds as if she is chewing a wad of gum the size of a car. Neither Necdet nor Mustafa have ever met her. 'Either that or all that skunk you smoke is finally catching up with you. Pitching wedge, please.'

And that would also explain the floating luminous head of the suicide bomber, Necdet thinks as he picks the wedge out of the clutch of clubs in his grasp. *I didn't tell you about her because I thought that too. But I felt the heat of the djinni of the hand-drier on my face. I dried my hands on it. Traumas don't dry hands.*

Mustafa addresses the ball. He has a good lie in the centre of the corridor, well-positioned for a chip up the staircase at the end on to the return. Mustafa wiggles his ass. A flicker in the corner of Necdet's vision makes him glance over his shoulder. Behind the glass wall is the main back-office; twenty-seven thousand square metres of dusty desks, tucked-in chairs and outdated workstations. Every monitor, as far as Necdet can see into the regress of screens, crackles with static and the ghost of a face from another universe.

The Roman Emperor Vespasian said that money has no smell. The emperor lied. Money is every breath Adnan Sarioğlu takes on the trading floor. The smell of money is the ionic charge of Özer Gas and Commodities; sweat and musk, electricity and the hydrocarbon scent of power-warmed plastics, time and tension. To beach-boy-turned-commodities-trader Adnan, money is the smell of a wetsuit worn by a woman.

The commodity pit is a cylinder at the heart of Özer's glass tower, eight floors ringed around a central shaft and capped with a stained-glass dome that throws shards of colour across the traders ranged around the Money Tree. That is Adnan's name for the IT core that runs from floor to ceiling, tier upon tier of suspended servers and network links, each level keyed to a specific commodity. Gas is a lowly so its traders are on the second tier, one above crude and dirty oil, and Adnan is only rarely surprised by a shard of blue or gold falling through the jungle of routers and servers and power conduits on to his face. Carbon is the highest, right up there under the dome. Carbon is exalted, carbon is pure.

Adnan Sarioğlu reaches up and slides trading screens around the branches of the Money Tree. He brings in new panes of prices, expands some, pushes others away into the recesses of the central tree. To the virtual eye of the Özer trader, the information core at the centre is dense with leaves of information, almost impenetrable in their total coverage of the global markets. Commodity trading floors, once roaring pits of open-outcry bids and buys, have all become silent as dervish monasteries now that trading information is beamed directly on to the eyeball and AI assistants murmur in the inner ear. Adnan knew the old pit of the ITB exchange only as a red-jacket junior but the roar of the traders screaming into each other's faces shook his blood vessels, echoed in the ventricles of his heart. When the bell rang, when trading closed and he stepped out to the back office the hush hit him like a breaking wave. Now he only gets that breaker of sound on the terraces of Aslanteppe Stadium.

In the new bourse the clamour is visual. Adnan moves through a storm of information, screens and panels swooping around him like starlings on a winter afternoon. The traders are peacock bright, far from the formal colour coding of dealers, traders and back office team. Many have customized their jackets with panels of nanoweave or had them cut from whole animated fabric. Flickering flames at cuffs, hem and lapels are the thing. Others sport Heavy Metal devils, roaring dinosaurs, spinning euro signs, nudes or football team logos. Onur Bey's bandwidth trading team has adopted the Lâle Devri tulip motif. Adnan thinks that decadent and effeminate. He wears the front-and-back quartered red and silver of Özer. Simple, direct, unaffected; what a man should have on his back. His single affectation is his tag; it reads *DRK*. Draksor: once an Ultralord of the Universe, always an Ultralord of the Universe.

Adnan reaches up and flicks open a screen from the cloak of display panels wrapped around him. Ten minutes to the closing bell at the Baku Commodity Exchange, the big central Asian gas market. In that rush to close, price differences open between Baku and Istanbul. In those few seconds while the market reacts, dealers like Adnan Sarioğlu can make money. It's all about arbitrage. Özer's man in Baku is Fat Ali. Adnan met him on an Özer away-day trail-biking in Cappadocia. Adnan wasn't a very good trail-biker. Neither was Fat Ali. They both preferred cars. They left the corporate boys to their leathers and dust and spent the afternoon drinking wine on the hotel's rooftop terrace and speculating if buying the winery might be a sound investment. They drank a lot of wine. As well as car and wine enthusiasts they were both Cimbom fans. They work well together. But Fat Ali isn't an Ultralord.

Adnan's eyes flick from screen to screen to screen. Every two seconds Adnan checks the prices on Baku June delivery. The nano blowing in gales through his head makes this level of concentration sustainable.

'Four forty-six and trading small,' Adnan says. 'Someone out there long? Come on Ali, one of your camel-fuckers has to be going long.'

The angel of arbitrage is the angel of the gaps. The AI agents can react to a market more quickly than any human but when they attempt to push that market any real intelligence can see them coming like a train. Some of the dealers rely heavily on their agents. Adnan trusts his own wit and his ability to see patterns those value-adding few seconds before they appear on the screens. *Come to me, angel of the gaps.*

'Four forty-seven and pretty thin stuff,' Fat Ali says in Baku. But at some point as the clock ticks down to the bell there will be some local trader buying in Baku who does not have a seat in Istanbul's central ITB and so cannot trade there. The price will move in Baku

and for the few seconds before the market shifts in Istanbul, Adnan
Sarioğlu and Fat Ali can make money.

'What's Branobel doing?'

'Sitting long.'

The Baku screen swoops to a halt in front of Adnan. 'We're at
four forty-five.' And there is the gap. Now all he needs is a way to
exploit it. Adnan whirls screens around him. 'Someone wants to sell
fat. Come on you bastard, I can feel you.'

'Flush him out and we'll shoot him down.'

Adnan moves his hands, a dance, a code. A new offer of four
hundred and forty-five dollars flows out from him across the many
screens of the Money Tree like a wind rippling leaves. Instantly the
AIs swarm. *This'll rattle you out*, Adnan thinks. There will be a seller
out there with a limit on the daily downward movement of his contracts. Adnan's scare-price is designed to look as if the market is headed
down further yet. Faced with the possibility of unlimited loss, that
trader will be forced to sell. And there. One star, burning bright in
laser light on the back of Adnan's retina. The stop-loss seller. Adnan
buys two hundred. In the same instant Fat Ali sells those same two
hundred across the price gap in Baku. Buy Istanbul at four forty-five,
sell Baku at four forty seven. Forty thousand euro profit for two
seconds' work. Another two seconds later the market adjusts and
closes the differential. The angel of the gaps moves on. At no time
does anyone sniff the gas that Adnan has arbitraged. That would be
a grievous error. This is the secret of Özer Gas and Commodities:
never carry any gas, never inventory any commodities, never get left
holding. Promises and options of future prices are the currency.

Adnan's AIs book the sale and throw it to Kemal in the back
office. Forty thousand euro. A waft of woman-warmed sun-scalded
neoprene waves across his money. It was a sweet deal and few play
it better than Adnan Sarioğlu and Fat Ali but it's not where the real
money lies. Commodities money will always be quickie money,
money you have to cajole into coming to you, wit and speed money.
For you to make it means someone has to lose it. It's a closed system.

There are no draws in Özer. But Turquoise, that's real money. That's money enough to get out of the wheedling and the carpet-selling. Turquoise is magic money that comes out of nowhere. Five minutes to close in Baku, an hour to the bell in Istanbul. Adnan Sarioğlu opens his hands, pulls the twenty-four-hour spot price screen in before his face. There's something in there; a shadow of a pattern, a watermark in a banknote. *Now how can I make money here?*

Leyla at the Nano Bazaar. This wall of pressed construction carbon business units is the caravanserai of the business of the infinitesimally small. Banners and windsocks share the roofline of Big Box industrial units with the Turkish crescent moon and the European Union stars. The street wall is decorated with a huge mural depicting the orders of magnitude of the universe, from the cosmological on the left to the quantum on the extreme right, worked in the floral abstractions of Iznik ceramics. The centre, where the gate like the entrance to a han has been cut, represents the human scale. As Leyla reads the wall of Nano Bazaar a dozen trucks and buses and dolmuşes draw up or depart, mopeds and yellow taxis and little three-wheel citicars steer around her. Leyla's heart leaps.

This is always always always what she wished a bazaar to be. Demre, proudly claiming to be the birthplace of Santa Claus, was direly lacking in workshops of wonder. Small corner stores, an understocked chain supermarket on the permanent edge of bankruptcy and a huge cash and carry that serviced the farms and the hotels squeezed between the plastic sky and the shingle shore. Russians flew there by the charter load to sun themselves and get wrecked on drink. Drip irrigation equipment and imported vodka, a typical Demre combination. But Istanbul; Istanbul was the magic. Away from home, free from the humid claustrophobia of the greenhouses, hectare after hectare after hectare; a speck of dust in the biggest city in Europe, anonymous yet freed by that anonymity to be foolish, to be frivolous and fabulous, to live fantasies. The Grand Bazaar! This was a name of wonder. This was hectare upon hectare of Cathay silk and Tashkent carpets, bolts of damask and muslin, brass and silver and gold and rare spices that would send the air heady. It was merchants and traders and caravan masters; the cornucopia where the Silk Road finally set down its cargoes. The Grand Bazaar of Istanbul was shit and sharks. Over-priced stuff for tourists, shoddy and glittery. Buy buy buy. The Egyptian Market was no different. In that season she went to every old bazaar in Sultanahmet and Beyoğlu. The magic wasn't there.

This, this is the magic. This is dangerous, like the true magic always is. This is the new terminus of the Silk Road; central Asia's engineers and nanoware programmers the merchants and caravan masters of the Third Industrial Revolution. Leyla steps boldly through the gate.

The air of Nano Bazaar air is heady; every breath a new emotion. She reels from blissed-up euphoria into nervy paranoia into awed dread in as many steps. Dust swirls in front of her, glittering in the pinhole sunbeams shining through the patchy plastic awning. The dust coalesces into a ghostly image of her face. It frowns, moves its lips to speak and is gone in a burst of glitter. Tiny ratbots scuttle around her heels. Windows flicker with oil-sheen television pictures, rolled-down shutters drip big brand logos; all the lovely labels she will enjoy when she gets proper marketing-job money. Bubbles waft across her face, she recoils as they burst, then gives a little 'oh!' of delight as each delicate detonation plays a fragment of Gülsen's last-summer hit *Şinaney*. The birds that look down from the gutters of the industrial units aren't birds. Atatürk's face on a passing T-shirt suddenly turns its eyes on her and scowls. Leyla wants to clap her hands in wonder.

'Unit 229?' she asks a bearded man with curly hair. He's bent over the engine of a little three-wheeler delivery truck. *Bekşir Borscht and Blini*, it says on the side. She's heard Russian food is very fashionable with these tech guys. Vodka freezing in the reactor cooling cells. The lad frowns at her and mutters something in Russian. She knows it well from too many drunken tourists. A guttural, peasant tongue to her, next to the music of Turkish, but here it's exciting, salty, exotic.

Two dozen languages from as many nations ring around this former military airbase on the cheap edge of Fenerbahçe.

'Unit 229?'

The guy has just bought coffees from a franchise wagon; one in each hand, those Western-style coffees that are just flavoured milk and come in cardboard buckets with wooden stirrers. He's tall and sallow and lanky with an older face than his clothes, a slightly over-defined jaw and thoughtful puppy eyes that keep darting away from her gaze.

'That's over in Smaller.'

'Where?'

'We're arranged in order of technology scale,' he says. 'Milli, micro, nano. Small, Smaller, Smallest. Small is beautiful. Size matters. I'm going that way.'

Leyla offers a hand. Her business card is primed. The man lifts high his buckets of coffee in apology.

'I'm Leyla Gültaşli, I'm a freelance marketing consultant, I've an appointment with Yaşar Ceylan from Ceylan-Besarani.'

'So what do you want with Yaşar?'

'He wants me to build a business development plan to upscale the company. Access finance, White Knights, venture capitalists, that sort of thing.'

'Venture capitalists.' He sucks in breath. 'You see, I find money talk kind of scary.'

'It's not when you know what to do with it.'

Despite Sub-Aunt Kevser's explanation Leyla still isn't clear how she's related to Yaşar but he was nice and polite when she called him, interested with none of the geeky self-fascination.

'Fenerbahçe, yeah, got that.' It was a trek; five different modes of transport. With good connections it was an hour and half. Give it three. Once again she showered in costly water, ironed out the frustration rumples in her going-to-interview suit, set out with plenty time.

'Nanotechnology.'

'Sort of yes.'

Nanotechnology, even sort-of nanotechnology; what does she know about nanotechnology? What does anyone really know about nanotechnology, except that it is the hot new revolution that promises to change the world as radically as information technology a generation before. Leyla has no preparation other than a well ironed suit and her own insuperable belief in her own ability. This is as far as she could possibly be from Demre.

'Unit 229.' The man gestures with his coffee cups. He follows Leyla through the low door into an anonymous single bay front office. 'Yaşar, this is Leyla Gültaşli. She's our freelance marketing consultant.'

'Oh, ah, yes; pleased to meet you.' Leyla fights down the blush of her mistake as she shakes the hand of the young man getting to his feet from the cramped seat pressed up by the desk against the wall. Yaşar Ceylan's hair is too long and his belly is too big and he has facial hair but his eyes are bright and he holds her look and his grip is sincere. Information crackles, palm to palm, business card to business card.

'I see you've already met Aso, my business partner.'

'Business partner, yes, of course, I should have guessed, Aunt Kevser didn't tell me, partner, of course.' She's gabbling, gabbling; gabbling girl from the sticks.

'And Zeliha.' The fourth person in the tiny office is a woman in her late twenties almost lost behind the piles of invoices and printouts that cover her tiny desk. She frowns at Leyla, looks baffled and buries her face in one of the coffee buckets. Two desks, three chairs, a filing cabinet with a printer on the top, a row of too too fashionable ugly Urban Toy figures on the window ledge behind Yaşar. The four of them fit into the tiny office like segments of an orange.

'So what is it you actually do here?'

Yaşar and Aso look at each other.

'Programmable nucleic bio-informatics.'

'Okay,' says Leyla Gültaşli. 'Maybe this is the point where I should tell you that I haven't a clue what that means.'

'And you're not really a marketing consultant either,' says Yaşar. 'Sorry. Aunt Kevser. She told me.'

Zeliha sniggers into her coffee.

'But we still need you,' Aso adds quickly. 'We know as little about marketing as you do about programmable nucleic bio-informatics.'

'Except that if I'm to pitch it, I need some comprehension of what it is.'

Yaşar and Aso look at each other again. They're like comedy presenters on children's television.

'You see, we're small,' Yaşar says.

'But not smallest,' Aso concludes.

'We're not micro-robotics and smart sand.'

'Neither are we true nano, let alone femto.'

'We're kind of in between.'

'Cellular.'

'Technology that becomes like biology.'

'Biology that becomes technological.'

'Bio informatics.'

'Stop,' says Leyla Gültaşli. 'Maybe I'm not a marketing executive – yet – but I do know that if you talk to a venture capitalist like that, they'll throw you straight out.'

'Okay okay.' Yaşar holds his hands up. 'Let's go back to basics. The scales. Small tech: micro-robotics, swarm computing, that kind of scale.'

'Like BitBots,' Leyla says brightly. 'Or police bots.'

'Okay,' Yaşar says. 'And at the other end of the scale, there's smallest – if you don't count quantum dots – which is nanotechnology, which only starts at the scale of a tenth of a wavelength of light.'

'It's what I snort when I need to remember stuff or have to concentrate or want to play at being someone else for a while,' Leyla says. 'It's what makes pictures on T-shirts move and lets you have smartpaper and scrubs extra cholesterol out of your arteries or alcohol out of your liver. It's why my ceptep and car, if I had a car, recharge in five seconds flat.'

'Well, there is a bit more to it than that,' Yaşar says.

'There's a scale in between, which is Smaller, and that's the scale we work at. We're working with the cells of the human body,' says Aso.

'What, like little submarines in the bloodstream?' Leyla asks.

They both look at her. Zeliha sniggers again.

'I think you'll find that is science fiction,' Aso says.

'You see, at the cellular level, the viscosity of blood is so enormous . . .'

'Stop. Enough of the double act. Tell me, this isn't to do with those replicator things?'

Yaşar and Aso look aghast, as if she has accused them of paedophilia. Even Zeliha is ruffled.

'We do bio-informatics,' Yaşar says.

'Studies into replicators are subject to strict government licence and oversight,' Aso says. 'Replicator experiments can only be carried out at government approved research facilities and they're all in Ankara.'

So someone in this bazaar of wonders is experimenting with replicators, Leyla thinks. Would that be Small, Smaller or Smallest? Replicators were danger. Replicators were the new nuclear. Replicators got you shot, no questions, no appeal. Replicators were the end of the world creeping up, one relentless atom after another. An enduring childhood terror: unable to sleep, Leyla had gone down the stairs. Quietly quietly, no one hearing. Mummy and Daddy were there on their respective sofas and chairs, big brother Aziz and sister Hasibe sprawling across the floor. News time; their faces were blue with the world pouring from the flat screen that occupied an entire wall. At that scale the horror can't be avoided. The world was coming to the worst possible end. Later Leyla learned that there was a name for this apocalypse; the Grey Goo scenario. She saw a slow tide of grey devour a town like Demre. Houses, streets, the mosque, the shopping centre, the bus station, the buses, the cars in the street, all were gradually over-run by this creeping corruption, silver as the botrytis mould that stalked the greenhouses and reduced tomatoes and aubergines to undulating velvety grey.

There were no people in this death-Demre. But the film did show a cat, a black cat with white feet and tail, cornered by the inevitable grey, swamped, reduced to a cat-shaped patch of silver carpet that heaved and kicked for a few moments and then melted. She started screaming.

'It's all right darling, it's all right darling, it's only the television, it's just made up, just a silly old thing.' Her mother scooped her up as her father flicked away to some psychic show. But Leyla had seen the logo in the corner of the screen and knew what it meant. This was the news, this was true. Where had this come from, where was it going? She was seven, maybe halfway to eight, but the image of her world, her parents, everything and everyone she loved but especially Bubu the cat who hunted polytunnel vermin, being turned to grey mould still gave her screaming nightmares. Years later, when she retold the story at a family gathering, she had finally learned that it was an opinion piece in response to Ankara announcing special economic status for new nanotechnology developments to boost Turkey's research status as an EU candidate state. It was a clever computer animation of runaway replicator nanotech devouring the world. The prophet of nanotechnological doom was a tight, elegant man with a very well trimmed grey moustache and the narrowest eyes she had ever seen. She's seen Hasan Eken many times since – he's still the expert-of-choice on the dangers of the race to nanotech: Dr Goo, the columnists call him but that night he was the angel of death. He terrified her more purely than anyone before or since. Replicators are death.

She's accused her potential new clients of being geek boys and criminal replicator-runners. This isn't how it works in the client management hand-outs.

'Okay, bio-informatics is the science of how the DNA – that's the material in the nucleus of every single cell of your body that programmes how the proteins that build living material are put together,' Yaşar says.

'I know what DNA is.'

'Well, bio-informatics looks at DNA not so much from the

point of view of inheritance and cell-building, but as information processing; programming almost. Each strand of DNA is a complex piece of biological software that the ribosomes process to print out proteins. DNA can be used to make chemical computers, and I'm sure even you've heard of biochips – there are half a dozen labs here working on biochip projects – the media are always on about them, direct interface between technology and the human brain, the self as the final frontier, opening up the skull, ceptep calls right into someone else's brain, sending pictures straight into someone's visual cortex, all you have to do is think a thought at someone and it will go through the ceptep net straight into their brains.'

'Now that sounds like science fiction to me,' says Leyla. She's only said this because she's noticed that Aso, when he tries hard to explain, has a nice, introverted frown, as if he must convince himself before he tries to persuade anyone else.

'Do you know what non-coding DNA is?' Yaşar asks.

Leyla tries to think of a smart answer but shakes her head.

'Well, the human genome has massive redundancy – that means that two per cent of the DNA does all the work of instructing the ribosomes that build the proteins that make up the cells of your body. Ninety-eight per cent of your DNA just sits there doing nothing. Taking up space in the gene.'

'To bio-informaticists, that's memory space going begging,' says Aso. 'Wasted processing power. Until the Besarani-Ceylan Transcriber.'

'Ceylan-Besarani Transcriber,' Yaşar says quickly.

Aso holds up a finger. He has started so he will finish.

'The Besarani-Ceylan transcriber is a molecular engine that takes information from bloodstream programmed nano and transcribes it on to junk DNA.'

Leyla knows she is supposed to look impressed here.

'This transcriber writes information on to the spare capacity of this non-coding DNA,' she says.

They're still waiting.

'Okay.'

'Think a minute about the implications,' Aso says.

'You're storing information inside cells.' They're expecting more. 'You're turning living cells into . . . tiny computers?'

They're looking happier now.

'And how many cells are there in the human body?' Yaşar asks.

'As many as there are stars in the sky!' declares Zeliha unexpectedly.

'Ten trillion cells,' Aso says. 'And inside each cell are thirty-two thousand one hundred and eighty-five genes, three billion bases, eighty-five per cent of which are non-coding.' There's an odd look, fundamentalist look in his eyes now.

'So multiply the numbers,' Yaşar cajoles. Leyla has never been very good at carrying zeroes in her head.

'A thousand billion,' she says uncertainly. 'Zillion.'

Yaşar shakes his head. 'No no no. One thousand three hundred and fifty zettabytes of information, storable inside every human being. That's *zetta*bytes. These are numbers they haven't made up names for yet. And what can write can also read. And what is a computer other than something that reads an instruction in one place and writes the answer in another?'

'All human music ever written fits into your appendix,' Aso says. 'Every book in every library is a few millimetres of your small intestine. Every detail of your life can be recorded – and replayed. That's maybe the size of your stomach. You can live other people's lives. Talents and abilities and new skills can be downloaded and stored permanently. Not like now where it wears off as the nano is purged from the system. The Besarani-Ceylan transcriber writes it into the cells of your body. You want to play the piano? It's yours. You want to memorize a play, or you want to learn every test case in the law library? Foreign languages, home plumbing, programming code, physics, chemistry, you've got them. Now, what you do with them once you've got them, what you make of them, that's up to you. We don't guarantee expertise, only that it's there, coded into your DNA.'

'Come and see,' says Yaşar. Everyone shuffles round to let Yaşar out from behind his desk and round to a door in the back wall.

The warehouse behind the door is as dark and cool and spacious as the front office is bright and hot and crammed. It smells of fresh cinder-block, still drying cement, paint and electronics. Aso clicks on batteries of lights. In the centre of the unit stands a single bladeserver tower, swathed in pipes that run to a massive cooling unit on the ceiling. Other than that the unit is the domain of cobwebs and birds' nests glued under the eaves and dust sparkling in the light that slants through the narrow, high windows. She draws an arc with the point of her good shoes in the dust on the concrete floor.

'What am I looking at exactly?' Leyla Gültaşli shouts. The roar of fans and cooling pumps and dust extractors from the black monolith defeats conversation.

'A real-time modelling farm running X-cis, Atomage and Cell-render 7,' Aso announces proudly.

'Licensed copies,' Yaşar adds.

'You're looking at forty thousand euro of high-end commercial molecular modelling ware,' Aso shouts.

'And that's a reconditioned ex-EnGen render unit,' Yaşar says. 'We've made ten thousand euro worth of modifications and upgrades – it's a Refiğ Brothers custom overclock; that's almost five hundred terraflops Rpeak. You don't want to know how much electricity and water this thing eats.'

'I'm looking at a big computer.'

'You're looking at a state-of-the-art real-time molecular design and modelling suite.'

'Let me get this right, you don't actually make anything here.'

The men looked as shocked as if she has accused them of running a porn studio.

'We're designers,' Yaşar says coldly. 'Nobody who's anybody makes stuff. That's just production.'

'I think you need to see it,' Aso says. 'What's the bandwidth on your ceptep?'

Leyla meekly offers up the base unit from her bag. The boys

huddle over it, stork and starling, turning it over in their hands, taking it without a word from each other.

'It should be all right but you'll need these.' Aso gingerly fits a pair of lenseless spectacle frames on Leyla's face, adjusting their set on her nose with an optician's care. 'You really only get the full idea in 3D.'

Leyla blinks and flinches as the write-lasers drop down in front of her eyes. Her ceptep rings in her bag, then she is dropped face-forward into the world of DNA. The dusty concrete vault is filled with helical hawsers like the bridge cables reaching out before her, through the walls of the fabrication unit. They rotate along their axes, corkscrews, spiral staircases, Archimedes screws. DNA; the double-helices linked by rungs of base pairs. The atoms waltz around her, stately, relentless. It is engulfing, huge, hypnotic yet deeply relaxing. Leyla is thinking how she could market it as a spa experience when she becomes aware of movement up ahead of her. Little scurrying whirligig things, like the beetles she used to see on the water tanks back at home, gyring around on the surface tension, haul themselves atom by atom up the endless spiral staircases of the DNA helices. The simulation focuses on a cluster of DNA strands, bringing Leyla in closer, closer until the DNA climbers seem the size of buses. This is the atomic scale; a tinker-toy universe built from balls: beach balls and footballs and tennis balls and tiny bouncing ping-pong balls. Cogs made of linked spheres, cranks and levers and wheels, built from balls. Balls made from smaller balls from smaller balls. It's a crèche playroom reality, everything soft and rounded and playful. But these are not soft children's toys. They are purposeful, tireless, unstoppable crawlers, base pair by base pair heaving the thread of DNA through their interiors, snapping the bases, fusing them together behind them, but changed, spinning like blobs of spider glue running down a thread of spun silk. She watches molecular shears snap atomic bonds and reweave them into new patterns. Heave, shear, weave, heave. Atom by atom up the endless chain of DNA.

When she was a tiny thing, Leyla had gone down with a raging tonsillitis that spread into her brain and unfolded into full fever. For two nights she had bumped along the ceiling of death, sweating, hallucinating things like these atom-crawlers; unstoppably climbing endless spirals yet never advancing one single centimetre forward. This was an unending fever-march through the molecules of her body.

She takes off the eyewriter frame.

'What is it you want me to do?'

They go back out into the front office for the money talk.

'We're going to go to a production prototype,' Yaşar says.

'Proof of concept,' Aso adds. This double-act is starting to grate.

'We've budgeted at two hundred and seventy-five thousand euro at this stage. We're looking for venture capital, a White Knight of some kind, even an established industry. In return we put up fifty per cent of the company.'

'Okay,' says Leyla. 'This sounds do-able. I can certainly look at the business plan and draw up a funding strategy. I can also front up a pitch. Now, my fees . . .'

'Two things before you rush into agreeing to anything,' says Aso. He looks at Yaşar. Yaşar sucks in his bottom lip.

'We need to move fast on this. There is a rival project. We've heard they're about to move into a production model.'

'How fast?' Leyla asks.

'Two weeks, max.'

'There is another thing,' Aso says. Yaşar winces uncomfortably.

'The company's not entirely ours.'

'How much do you own?'

'Fifty per cent. We needed money up front for the modelling farm and the software.'

'Where did you get it?' Leyla asks.

'Where do you think two boys just out of post-doc with no credit history are going to get fifty thousand euro?' Yaşar says.

'Family,' says Aso. 'His family. Your family.'

'Mehmet Ali.'

'Who?' Leyla asks.

'Second cousin,' Yaşar explains. 'He's one of these relatives can always get things.'

'Is there a contract?' Leyla asks.

'It's an informal agreement,' Yaşar says. 'A family thing. There's a token: whoever owns it has half of Ceylan-Besarani.'

'Why do I get the feeling this isn't going to be as simple as just making Mehmet Ali an offer he can't refuse?'

'No one's heard from Mehmet Ali for a couple of months. He's not answering calls.'

'And the token?'

Yaşar opens his hands in helpless supplication.

'You have to get this token back. If some dodgy distant relation can saunter in, slap a piece of paper down and claim fifty per cent . . . .'

'It's not a piece of paper.' Aso fishes in his jacket pocket and offers an object in his palm to Leyla. It's a miniature Koran, the kind people buy as souvenirs after visiting saints' tombs. Quite a nice one; an old family heirloom. I heard someone say it was Persian. At some point in its history it got cut cleanly in half.

The Ultralords of the Universe eat köfte at the Kebab Prophet's kiosk across Levent Plaza from the Özer Tower. They sit in order of Elemental Mastery on their assigned stools at the tin counter and eat very good, very messy meatballs, their napkins tucked into shirt collars. They are coming down from nano-high. It works this way. First they talk a lot, incessantly, chirruping and clattering. In this stage bets are settled and forfeits like speed camera fines are paid. In the second phase everyone is very quiet, very withdrawn and introspective. Distance vision blurs so that the glass and money towers of Levent sway like reeds. Then the close vision smears so the diners at the Kebab Prophet's have to hold their hand-meals at arm's length to focus on them. Then comes the killing, killing low, which if it lasted any more than a couple of minutes would send you off a bridge or under a tram. And then you are just yourself again and the Ultralords of the Universe go back to being merely men.

Kemal bangs down late on to his red-topped bar stool between Adnan and Kadir Yinanç in Risk Management.

'Element of Fire, fight with me!' he shouts. The Kebab Prophet slaps the paper-wrapped kebab down on the mirror-bright counter.

'Element of Air, assist me!' Adnan cries.

'Element of Water, wage war with me,' says Kadir. He's always known he has the shit line.

'Element of Earth, empower me,' mutters Öguz.

Draksor, Ultror, Terrak and Hydror. Once there were, once there weren't, in a land not so far away and as close as the atrium of Özer Gas and Commodities, four fresh faces and sharp suits. They had things in common. They were men, they were part of a group of new recruits starting at Istanbul's biggest and shiniest commodities firm on the same day, and they were all mad mad Cimbom fans. The supercilious woman leading the induction had in the course of her tour given her party a glimpse of the heaven-like golden luxury of the boardroom: *and who knows, you may even make it all the way up to a seat around this table*. The cocky don't-give-a-fuck one from the south coast made the comment, *Looks more like Slavor's Temple of Doom*. Three caught the reference to the old kids' cartoon and creased up in suppressed laughter. Afterwards they sought each other out and the Ultralords of the Universe were born. None have yet made it to that golden temple. Instead, they're planning the financial coup of the decade.

Ultror, Ultralord of Fire, put the business plan together in the back office; a hundred AI devoting a fragment of their bandwidth, each a part, none comprehending the whole.

Terrak, Ultralord of Earth, will disguise it as just another Baku gas deal, barrelling down the Nabucco Line from Erzurum.

Hydror, Ultralord of Water, will conceal it in the labyrinth of Özer's audit systems, like a mystic name of God within a mosque's ornate calligraphies.

Draksor, Ultralord of Air, makes the deal. He gets the money.

And when he has the money, when the deal is down, when the price is right and only when the price is right, he gives the word to all the other Ultralords to swing Turquoise into operation.

'I'm seeing Ferid Bey again tonight,' Adnan says. 'He says he needs more information.'

'More?' says Kemal. He's always been an irritable man but this is beyond nature or nano. 'He's got the business plan.'

'He wants the market analysis.'

Kemal rolls his eyes again. *The heat*, Adnan thinks. *It draws the strength out of us and makes us brittle and edgy as street dogs but as long as it lasts, Turquoise lives*. Kemal offers a hand over the debris of köfte and bread. Adnan takes it.

'Here's your fucking market analysis.' Information sparks between them, page after page of breakdowns and charts and forecasts. It's a fine and dark art for which Adnan has neither the talent nor the patience. The deal, the handshake, the people, those are his gifts.

'Where are you meeting him?'

'At a private executive bathhouse.'

'Watch out he doesn't stick it up you,' snorts Öguz.

'That'll be the sweetest your balls have smelled all year,' says Kemal.

'And if he bites?' Kadir asks. Ferid Bey is far from the first oligarch the Ultralords of the Universe have approached. But he is the first to have fixed a second meeting, the first to ask for more detail.

'Is the Iranian still in town?'

'I can arrange that.'

'Then it's champagne in the box,' declares Adnan.

'And the ball in the back of the net,' chorus the Ultralords and the Kebab Prophet.

'Did you look at that yalı?' the Kebab Prophet asks. He is called the Prophet because he restores harmony, heals souls, subtly guides the words and thoughts of four Levent money boys blazing with autistic levels of focus and synthetic aggression. He's the ultimate come-down treatment.

'I certainly did,' Adnan says. 'And I shall make them an offer.'

'Too close to the water for me,' says Kemal. 'You get vermin. Rats the size of fucking dogs. I've seen them. Cats are scared of them. Give me one of those new-builds up in Ulus.'

'Sure Adnan wants to raise an old-fashioned Ottoman dynasty,' says Kadir.

'Well I wouldn't raise any kids there,' says Öguz. 'You get bad vapours from the Bosphorus. I know what I'm talking about here. All that marine pollution just hangs there. It's like smog. And then that double-tide thing, the water never really gets changed. Sewage can hang around for a week or even longer. And there's worse. I know this – don't argue – this cop friend of mine told me when something goes in off the bridges, the bodies can go up and down for months.'

'Well girls,' Adnan says wiping his mouth with a paper napkin. 'If we're quite finished discussing suicides, shit and the cleanliness of my testicles, let's do some work shall we?'

Kemal scrunches up his kebab paper and shies it towards the refuse sack in its hoop at the back of the stall. He misses. The Kebab Prophet picks it up and disposes of it in the black plastic bag.

The man of words and the man of numbers see a white room differently. To the writer it's a cube of horror, a blank needing to be filled with the spurt of imagination. It is that space you write about when you have looked at nothing else for days. It is writing about writing. To the mathematician it's the void, the pure white light which, falling through a prism of analysis, breaks into the numbers that are ultimate reality. The walls of the white room are the walls of the universe and beyond them lies mathematics.

Georgios Ferentinou does not fear his white, one-book library, as austere as a monk's cell. The one small window, guarded by a pierced wooden screen, allows glimpses of Adem Dede Square and its stooping apartment buildings. In the white room, the walls open on to other Istanbuls where the streets and buildings are drawn by their inhabitants' supermarket spending habits or their diseases and medical interventions or the subtle interactions of their geographical, social and religious affiliations. There are the restless Istanbuls of traffics and tracks and tunnels. There are wiry Istanbuls, nervous as a skinned man, of gas and power and data. There are Istanbuls built entirely out of football gossip. For every commodity, for every activity that can be analysed and modelled, there is a city.

To Georgios Ferentinou economics is the most human of sciences. It is the science of wants and frustrations. It is psychology subject to the abstract, amplifying forces of mathematics. An individual bet on a news story, one elementary school child's guess at the number of Disney plushics in a jar, is a product of value and experience. Aggregate them, by a simple average or financial instruments with the promise of future gain, and they become oracular. Mathematics is the power that lies behind the white walls of the one-book library. Georgios is an old agnostic who can't believe in any god who would believe in him, but increasingly he feels it is a Platonic universe. Mathematics is too unfeasibly accurate in its ability to describe physical and human reality. At the bottom of everything is number. When he dies, and Georgios thinks about that a little every day, as old men should, he will evaporate into carbon atoms. He will become white and merge with the walls of mathematics and pass through them into those other Istanbuls.

Georgios Ferentinou's thoughts meander, as an old man's should, a walk through the intricate city of memory, to Ariana. He pictures her in Eskiköy's steep streets. She hasn't aged a day. She can't have aged. Time has been suspended since he saw her walk from the ferry to the station. As the Greek community has grown smaller, it has grown tighter. He could find her easily, but Georgios wonders not if he can find Ariana, but if he dare. Why has she come back after forty-seven years?

Georgios shakes himself out of his meanderings. He looks again at the jerking footage Can sent him from his BitBot. A watching robot implies that the tram-bomber was not a lone agent. Lone killers are usually socially inept males and need the theatre of their own apotheosis. They post elaborate sermons of alienation on social networking sites before they strap on the guns and walk into the school or mall or government office. Suicide bombers, female or male, deliver diatribes of social justice and transformation and promises of Paradise. There is a structure behind this desperate, headless woman.

Turkey's many terror groups each has its own signature. The Kurds tend to the theatrical. They need to attract global attention to themselves as a nation. The anti-EU Grey Wolf nationalists see themselves in the romantic tradition of the Young Turks and favour individual assassinations and street shootings. This is a classic Islamist martyrdom on a Number 119 tram. It is the violence of a faithful family dog that turns and rends the baby, the neighbour who stabs her husband, the unexplained suicide of a work colleague. Forces unseen and unsuspected press for years, warping lives and relationships. The organization behind the Necatibey bomb – probably a cell of three or four individuals, certainly with a ridiculous name— would want to record the moment of immolation. Wahhabist sites are full of explosions and martyrdoms, with home-brew graphics and heroic music. So why risk that information chasing the boy's BitBot? Why the need to hack the signal? Why try to follow it back to this house? Strange indeed here. Strange is that grain of order in the seethe of randomness. Strange is information.

The jerky, disjointed images hurt Georgios' eyes. He looks up to the visual peace of his white walls.

The door buzzer is so loud, so sudden it stabs his heart. A man at the door. Georgios' heart hammers. They've found him, they've come for him. They know everything. They are at his door. His heart flutters, unable to land on the beat. Be logical. Killers would not ring the doorbell. They would kill quietly, strangle him like an old Ottoman prince.

The buzzer jars again. The man looks up into the camera.

'Georgios Ferentinou?' He is well spoken, educated. They usually are. Fanaticism is a middle-class vice. Decent suit, clean shirt and neatly knotted tie. 'My name is Heydar Bekdil.' Georgios sits back from the screen. The smartpaper can't see him but the man at the door frowns as if he is looking right into the room. A third buzz. 'Mr Ferentinou, it's quite important that I talk to you.' He presses a palm to the doorplate. An identification flows through his hand to the computer. MIT. The National Intelligence Organization. What interest could the intelligence services have in him? 'Mr Ferentinou?' Georgios buzzes him in.

'I'm sorry about the dust,' Georgios apologizes as he shows the visitor into his living room. The room is another converted cell; two sofas face each other rather too closely over a long narrow table. 'I've grown rather accustomed to my own rules of living. After a few months the dust doesn't seem to get any worse, I've found. You'll take some tea.'

In the adjoining kitchen Georgios Ferentinou boils the kettle and finds two unbroken glasses of the same design. He balances a cube of Lefteres' sesame halva on the edge of each saucer. The visitor has wiped a small section of the table clean with a handkerchief, a landing pad for the hovering saucer.

'If it's about the news feeds,' Georgios says. He lowers himself heavily on to the sofa. The two men's faces are close over the table, too intimate for strangers.

'It's nothing to do with the news feeds.' The man smiles to himself. 'No, that's a ... privilege. No, that will continue, you'll be glad to hear.' He is nervous, his glass rattles. 'Mr Ferentinou, I have a confession to make. I am actually a player. I'm a trader in the Terror Market.' Now Georgios realizes that the man may be in mild awe of him. 'Longsightedson?'

Georgios cannot conceal his distaste. Anonymity is part of the rules. He likes it that the man at the low table at the Fethi Bey çayhane across the square, that driver tapping his fingers on the steering wheel impatient at traffic lights, that woman he passes at the frozen food section on his weekly trip to the supermarket, may be Terror Traders incognito.

'Thank you, I'm glad the game enjoys attention at such high levels. So what does MIT need with me?'

Bekdil puts his hands together.

'You are aware of the Haceteppe Group?'

'I was a founder member.'

'Forgive me. I was not aware. You may not be aware that MIT has recently set up a second research group with a much lower profile, working in parallel with the Haceteppe Group, based in Istanbul and using unorthodox and speculative techniques. We believe that the creative tension between the two methodologies may yield fresh insights into our security situation.'

Georgios Ferentinou turns his tea saucer so the spoon lies like a compass needle trained on Bekdir's heart.

'You want me to join this group.'

'We do.'

Georgios laughs to himself, a heaving grunt of humour.

'Security must be in a pretty sorry pass if you need me to save the country. Why do you think I should have any desire to be part of this ...'

'Kadiköy Group. Curiosity, Mr Ferentinou?' Bekdir takes a small plastic phial with an inhaler nozzle from the jacket of his cheap suit and sets it on the little dusty table. 'There's a one-use number in there. Your questions will be answered there. The memory carbon is coded to your DNA so if anyone else tries all they'll get is a brief auditory hallucination of bird wings.' It does not surprise Georgios that MIT still holds his DNA. The State is always reluctant to relinquish its grip. 'I'd be quick about it, though; the nano is time coded. You'll forget it one hour exactly after you inhale it. Well, thank you for the tea, Mr Ferentinou and, whatever you choose, I will keep playing the Terror Market. It'll be a different username though.' Bekdir offers a hand. Georgios shakes it dazedly, hypnotized by the unlabelled translucent phial.

The djinn are waiting for Necdet as he comes blinking up the concrete steps from the Levent Business Rescue Centre into the sun-blast of drive-time. Djinn by the flock, djinn by the blizzard, watching from every rooftop and balcony and elevator shaft and window-washing cradle, perched on every street light and road sign and advertising hoarding, every electricity and telecom cable, jammed together on the roof of every passing bus and dolmuş, peering down from the glass cornices of the towers of Istanbul and the minarets of the ugly new mosque with its cheap silvery dome – there especially. The djinn have always been drawn to mosques. They flicker in and out of reality like cold flames, more than there are souls in great Istanbul.

'What?' he shouts at the waiting djinn. 'What is it?' A woman bustling homewards stares. Eccentric is suspicious in this time when everyone has a grudge and a means to express it. Necdet glares at her. When he looks away, the plaza is empty, a million soap-bubbles bursting silently, simultaneously.

Necdet takes the dolmuş. Bombs haunt the trams and metro. Most of Levent has made the same calculation. The Gayreteppe Road is clogged with trucks, inter-continental executive coaches, citicars and blue-and-cream dolmuşes. The little microbus starts and fits a metre at a time through the clog of traffic. Horns shout on every side, traffic policemen blow whistles. A three-quarters-empty tram sweeps past. Necdet is buried at the back of the dolmuş behind a ruck of cheap business suits, fearing djinn. He dreads the head, the woman's head, the shining head. He glances out the window. A still, blue flame, as motionless as if carved from sapphire, hovers over the hood of every vehicle on Cumhuriyet Avenue. The djinn of internal combustion. Necdet closes his eyes and does not open them again until he hears the shared taxi pull into the great roaring traffic gyre of Taksim.

Walking down the sweating alleys between the lowering, exhausted apartment blocks, windows open, air-conditioners rattling, Necdet feels the djinn as a closer heat, heat within heat, knots and whirls of electrical energy trapped between the old buildings. In Adem Dede Square, dark and filled with the whistlings of pigeon wings, they swirl, feeding on the exhalations of the trapped day-heat and the stench of rancid cooking fat from the Fethi Bey çayhane, making themselves solid. Necdet fumbles for the key to the big brass padlock. They're at his back, piled high as a thunderhead. He can smell them like cooking oil.

'Necdet.' A woman's voice, a voice he knows though it's never spoken directly to him before. It's the girl who helps at the art shop, walking down the steps between the dervish house and the teahouse. She is upside down. She is inside the earth. The steps, the square, the buildings are obdurately solid, but by some trick of djinn-sight Necdet can see into the earth and the woman walking there, her feet to his feet. She is identical to the shop-girl except that she is pregnant. She leans back, takes it easy on her back, her knees as she climbs the staircase. She stops on the step ahead of Necdet and looks up at him between her feet. She rests her hands lightly on her belly, sighs and labours on up the steps, climbing the imperceptible upward curve of her hollow world. A karin. They are minor spiritual beings – theologians differ over whether they are creatures of clay, like men, or fire, like the djinn – but they are no less capable than the djinn of envy and petty spite. Maiden aunts and dervishes and back street healers sometimes sense them; shaykhs hear and speak with them and may command them. All agree that each karin is a mirror, underneath the earth, of the life lived above ground, guardians of the happiness and peacefulness of their siblings. Necdet staggers against the tekke door, it falls open.

'Ismet! Ismet! Man, I need you. Ismet!' Necdet stumbles into the kitchen, heart hammering. Ismet sits on one side of the cheap Ikea table, the Holy Koran in his hands. Ismet Hasgüler is one to whom the book speaks. His readings from the Holy Koran are light and musical and delight the ears. They cure ills, banish baleful influences, purify houses and bless children. When a woman comes knocking on the door with a question that has no answer in this world – and they are invariably women – in Ismet's hands the book always falls open at the perfect ayah. Two women in headscarves sit across from him, close together. All look up, startled, as if guilty at having been caught divining God's will. It's her. The girl from the art shop, the sniffy one who's never tried to conceal her contempt for Necdet. The one he saw upside down under the earth a few footsteps ago.

'I saw you,' Necdet stammers. He points. The woman recoils. The other woman, older, an aunt most likely, clings to her arm. 'I saw you, outside. Just this second. Your karin, your earth sister. I saw her under the ground. She said my name. I saw you and you were pregnant.'

The young woman's mouth and eyes are wide. Then her face crumples up into tears. She wails and hugs her aunt-mother-older-sister.

'A sign, a sign!' the older woman says, hands held up in praise. 'God is good! Here, here.' She pushes euro notes at Ismet. He steps back out of his chair as if the money is poisoned.

'What?' Necdet asks. 'What is it? What's going on?'

'You are a real shaykh,' the art shop girl says and Necdet realizes that she's weeping in shivering joy. 'I heard about your brother, that he's a good judge, very straight, very fair, very fast; so Uncle Hasan said after he sorted the problem with his cousin at the sports shop. And Sibel Hanım said he was very good with the word of God too after he drove the djinni out of her daughter's bedroom mirror. But you, you're the master of djinn. Two brothers together; that's a force from God. Thank you, thank you so much, thank you!'

Necdet scoops up the soiled notes and throws them at the women. 'Here, here you are then. Are you answered?'

'Yes,' says the art-shop girl. She touches her hand to her belly, the same gesture her sister under the earth had made. 'Oh yes I am, God is very good indeed.'

Aunt-mother-sister hears the crazy in Necdet's voice, takes the art-shop girl by the hand and bustles her out of the kitchen into the street. The cash she leaves where it lies on the table among the tea glasses.

'What was that about?' Ismet demands. 'You were incredibly rude to those women. Bundling them out like that. God willing, I'm trying to build some kind of reputation here and that's never going to happen if you scare away people who need my help.'

Necdet closes his eyes. The room swarms with half-glimpsed spiritual and emotional forces, the air buzzes with dread and energy.

'Listen. I was on that tram today, you know, the one where the bomb went off. I was on the tram, I saw the woman who did it. I saw her pull the strings and her head blew off. I was on that tram.'

'Oh man, why didn't you tell me? You should be in hospital. Necdet, you need to go to the hospital.'

Necdet shakes his head, trying to shake off the dizzying buzz of another world.

'Doctors won't help me. I see djinn. Do you understand that? I see djinn.'

Needles of yellow light fall on to Adnan Sarioğlu prone on the marble octagon. Steams wisps around him. Sweat pools on his belly – more fat there than he likes – trembles a moment then rolls down his side on to the warm marble. He stretches. His skin pulls against the slab. Every bone and sinew glows as if hammered in a forge. The tellak's steel fingers left no muscle unraked, no joint uncracked.

Ferid Adataş, proprietor of one of Turkey's largest non-military investment funds, is a member of the newest and most exclusive private bathhouse in the city. The hamam is fashionable again. The old bathhouses are appointment only; new private-members' hamams open every week. It's another post-EU incongruity. Spas are sissy, indulgent, European. Hamams are authentic and Turkish.

Drained on the slab under the starry dome – that bastard tellak had tried to get him to squeal like a virgin – Adnan melts into perfect relaxation. Muscles he did not know he possessed release and purr. Every cell is electric. Adnan gazes up into the dark dome pierced with concentric rings of circular skylights. He might be alone in a private universe.

Water splashes and runs in a film across the glass floor suspended above the mosaics. The Hacı Kadın hamam is a typical post-Union fusion of architectures; Ottoman domes and niches built over some forgotten Byzantine palace, years and decades of trash blinding, gagging, burying the angel-eyed Greek faces in the mosaic floor; century upon century. That haunted face was only exposed to the light again when the builders tore down the cheap apartment blocks and discovered a wonder. But Istanbul is wonder upon wonder, sedimented wonder, metamorphic cross-bedded wonder. You can't plant a row of beans without turning up some saint or Sufi. At some point every country realizes it must eat its history. Romans ate Greeks, Byzantines ate Romans, Ottomans ate Byzantines, Turks ate Ottomans. The EU eats everything. Again, the splash and run as Ferid Bey scoops warm water in a bronze bowl from the marble basin and pours it over his head.

'Great!' he roars. 'Great.'

Ferid Bey hauls himself up from the warm glass and waddles across the floor to the steam cubicle. He is not a fat man or greasy from luxury but his chest hair is grey and he is stiff in the hips. Adnan unseals himself from the slab and follows him into the marble-walled steam room. Beneath the glass floor, subtly lit Patriarchs and Palaeologi gaze up at his balls. Ferid Bey spreads his legs wide and settles back against the marble wall. Adnan matches Ferid Bey's comfort. For the first time in months he feels properly alive.

'I've had a look through your more detailed projections,' Ferid Bey says. Water drips from the hem of the peştemal wrapped around his waist. 'The only obvious flaw is that you're asking me to become a gas smuggler.'

'We think of it as an alternative supply chain.'

'Tell that to the judge if you get caught.'

It's in the air. It's that long ball crossed into the box that the wind gets underneath and floats. Anyone could get to it. Adnan must trust his own skill.

'They're just flaring it off. The Tabriz pipeline can't handle the volume, so they burn it. Whoosh. Like setting a match to a suitcase full of euro.'

'I don't believe it's as simple as turning a stop-cock with a spanner.'

95

'Oğuz our pipeline man says it's two commands on a computer. Close that, open this. Clickety-click.'

'So tell me, how did you find out about this?' The two men lean close to each other in the tomb-narrow confines of the steam room.

'While everyone else spent their military service in the Land of Opportunity bitching and whining about how the Kurds were going to turn them into eunuchs if they caught them, I used my time a little more profitably.'

'And how did you find the East?'

'It's a shit-hole. But it's our shit-hole.'

Sweat gathers in a bead on Ferid Bey's chin, swells, drops to the glass floor, a flaw in the eye of the mosaic saint.

'I'm an investor not a scientist, but I need to be sure it's safe. I can't go irradiating Greeks, much as I'd like to.'

Adnan smiles at the joke but he thinks, *he said* I. I *can't go irradiating Greeks. He's buying into it.*

On that day everyone remembers, Adnan had been repairing wetsuits on the quay. That day was bright and the sun was high, it was early in the season and the first dive boats were going out to the drowned Lycian towns. Fresh-looking Swedish girls and short intense Danes were the best of the early arrivals. Scandinavians liked a man who looked busy in an intricate task. News burbled on the flatscreen set up under the awning at the Octopus Bar for the sport. Adnan worked on the quay not the boats and so always knew what was happening before anyone else, and what it might mean. So that day at the wetsuits his half-listening ear picked up the newsreaders' change of tone and he turned his full attention to the screen. Grave expressions, a ticker along the bottom of the picture, shaky camera work of a sky lit by flashes beneath the horizon. Adnan set down the glue gun and drifted toward the edge of the bar. *Adnan's interested.* Every head on the quayside turned. Men left their ropes, their dive gear, their boats, their vans and mopeds. The Swedes and Danes hung back, unsure of their right to participate in whatever the screens in the harbour bars were showing.

At eleven twenty Ankara time, Fandoglu Mountain in western Iran's Azarbaijan province had been struck by forty missile-borne thermobaric warheads. Satellite footage showed blossom after blossom after blossom of flame unfold from the mountain-creased earth; beautiful as tulips. Fireball after fireball after fireball. New pictures, cellphone shot, showed a perfect mushroom cloud of fire climbing into the sapphire sky; then another. Then another. Then the footage shook and ended.

'Are those nukes?' a voice asked. 'Someone's using nukes!'

'No, it's not nukes,' Adnan said staring at the screen. 'Vacuum bombs; they're supposed to be safe and clean, though it's pretty fucking academic if you get caught by one.'

'And how would you know?' an idle old man asked.

'I saw it on the Discovery Channel. They're specifically designed for use against underground bunkers.'

'What would they have out there? It's a hole in the ground.'

'It is now,' someone muttered.

'Only one thing,' Adnan said. 'Real nukes.'

'That was Qom, the UN inspected it, everyone knows that!'

'Qom was the one they wanted you to see.'

Then a voice simply said, 'The Jews.' Topal had worked for twenty years out of Northern Cyprus up and down the Levant and was considered the most cosmopolitan man in Kaş. 'The fucking Jews have finally done it!' The Octopus Bar exploded into roaring voices and waving fists.

'Shut up, I want to hear what's happening,' Adnan shouted. What he could see of the screen showed a graphic of a red plume, like a cypress tree or a feather, going up thousands of metres into the air, leaning to the east like a pillar of smoke, towards Tabriz. The look on the newsreader's face was beyond grave. This was apocalyptic. 'Shut the fuck up!' Adnan roared into a momentary lull in the uproar. There was silence. 'Thank you. Listen. Listen!'

Adnan tried to imagine the CG simulation on to real flesh and lives. A single thermobaric strike would turn the tunnels beneath

Fandoglu Mountain into hell. Shockwaves pulped human organs and shattered limbs and ribcages. The firestorm raced at near-supersonic speeds along corridors, through rooms into every level of the facility; those that survived incineration suffocated as the inferno consumed all available oxygen. What Discovery never showed was what happened when forty strikes, arriving in succession to create a continuous rolling explosion, were aimed at a pressurised water nuclear reactor. At the heart of Fandoglu Mountain, the controls were incinerated, back-ups turned to slag, fail-safes melted and jammed. Cooling systems failed, core temperature soared. Containment breached; the molten mass of the fuel core hit the cooling water. A titanic steam explosion sent a geyser of radioactive material blasting out from the tunnels and vents into the atmosphere. Carried on a westerly wind, the radiation plume was now fifteen kilometres high and a hundred long. Under Fandoglu Mountain not even a bacterium was alive.

The good-cheek-boned Swedes and the chubby Danes had slipped away.

All the Kaş men were in the bars, the restaurants, the çayhanes, watching television. In their homes the women came together around their flatscreens. The terror unfolded. The plume had touched down on the Marand gas field eighty kilometres to the east. Everything died. The field would be unusable for a generation. Tabriz was being evacuated. Prime Minister Yetkin had promised the help of the Turkish people. Adnan watched footage of an old woman hosed clean of fall-out particles. She held her hands up, turned her face up to heaven, not knowing that it was from there that the poison dropped. The Knesset confirmed in a press conference that it had attacked and destroyed Iran's nuclear facility at Fandoglu Mountain. Silence became muttering. Two words were said again and again: *fucking Jews*. Then someone threw a stool. It struck the TV and set it swinging on its stand. A cheer went up. Hands tore down the traitorous screen. Tables were smashed, chairs broken. The bottles behind the bar were shattered one by one and the hanging mosque lamps torn down and ground into the floor. The men ransacked the

Octopus Café. That was not enough. Someone set a fire. It fed greedily on the smashed wood and alcohol. When the staff tried to fight it with extinguishers the men pelted them. At midnight the roof fell in in a spray of coals and sparks. The next morning the building was still too hot to approach. Adnan could not understand it. In their anger at the Jews and their American stoolpigeons the people of Kaş had destroyed the livelihood of their own neighbours. All across Turkey, across the reach of Islam, that self-mutilation was mirrored in burnings and bombings and small pointless martyrdoms.

For a time the world teetered on a brink. But Israel had calculated shrewdly. Iran threatened to close the straits of Hormuz to oil traffic; the US fleet moved against it. With millions displaced, Tehran realized it could gain the upper hand by playing the victim. Pakistan blew and blustered and bombed embassies but backed down faced with the patient might of its superpower neighbour India. Afghanistan continued its long self-immolation, as exquisitely worked as a carpet. Syria's call for the destruction of Israel was no more than posturing, a ritual shouting of insults. Those thermobaric cruise missiles and worse were only minutes from Damascus. China protested and threatened sanctions but its own slow environmental apocalypse was more intimate and threatening. India showed refined displeasure. The European Union lectured. The South Americans mouthed moral outrage but they were downwind of no one's fallout. The US Security Council veto blocked any formal condemnation from the UN. The Russians issued stern reprimands and thin threats but were secretly pleased that the massive western Iranian gas fields had effectively been put out of production for decades, buried beneath the slow snow of radioactive dust that was all that remained of the Fandoglu Mountain nuclear facility. The world staggered, then picked up its step again. The general dance spun on.

And in Turkey, by the turquoise Mediterranean, on the day after that day everyone remembers, a seaside surf-shop boy bought in a case of cheap ninety-nine-bead rosaries and sold them all within the hour at three hundred per cent mark-up. While Kaş waited for the sky to open and the Mahdi utter the secret hundredth name of God to end the world, Adnan witnessed a different miracle, that of the market.

Fifteen years after Fandoglu Mountain western Iran is still a radiological burn zone, the border closed and its pipelines internationally embargoed. But that same surf-shop boy turned trader has found a way to channel unsaleable gas through a long disused, almost forgotten branch into the Nabucco pipeline that runs from the Caspian Sea to the Adriatic. Gas so cheap the Iranians are almost giving it away, gas that will net a fortune in the crazy heat of the Istanbul spot markets.

The deal is clever and intricate but robust. Adnan sets up the deal with the Iranians. The White Knight – Ferid Bey – puts up the liquidity. The Ultralords swap full price Caspian gas for cut-price Iranian at a pumping station out in the deep east where the old, sealed off Green Line from Iran meets the Nabucco pipeline from Baku. Everyone profits when the gas is sold on the spot market in gas-hungry Istanbul. Everyone ends in the money. But the deal is dead until Ferid Bey's chop is on the contract.

'When do you close the deal?' Ferid Bey leans back against the hot marble. His belly lolls over the cheap plaid-weave cloth.

'The day before the weather breaks.'

'You can predict the weather? Then what do you need my money for? Tell me, I'm not the first; who else turned you down before you came to me?'

To let Adnan into this hot room, this hararet, this private Turkish bath, Ferid Bey will have researched him so thoroughly he will spot a lie before it's on Adnan's lips.

'A fair few of them are here tonight.' *And you've already talked to them.*

Ferid Bey stands up, slaps his thighs, his belly, shakes drops of sweat from his thick hair.

'Right. Enough of this. Come and rinse off. I like you, Adnan Bey. I know your paperwork, I know your figures, but I don't know you. You've got balls but I don't like to do business with people I don't know. Come to dinner, tomorrow. My place on Heybeliada. There'll be a boat at Eminönü at eight. Are you married, have a significant?'

'My wife's Ayşe. She trades in religious artwork.'

'Does she now? I like that. Women should have careers. I'd like to meet her.'

'There are the others I work with.'

'You're the one I'm doing the deal with; you come and bring your wife. I'll have a few other friends over.'

'So when can I expect a contract?' Adnan says as Ferid Bey slips into his wooden hamam clogs and totters across the wet glass to the basins.

'Plenty of time. We'll talk tomorrow. Dress informal.'

Adnan Sarioğlu bows his head and lets sweat beads roll down either side of his nose, merge at the tip to swell and drip on to the glass floor. He breathes in the hot, aromatic vapour. It burns his nostrils, but it smells of money.

The air in the bedroom is hot and clinging and motionless but Ayşe in her underwear shivers and dives into the new dress. Once you leave your childhood bedroom you can never be comfortable or warm in it again. She shakes the dress down over her breasts and shoulders, adjusts the fall and hang then turns to look at herself in the mirror on the old closet. So many reflections, so many dresses and undresses in that mirror, so many admirings of herself; the flatness of her belly, the fullness of her breasts, the cut of her jaw and the firmness of her arms, the quest for the first curl of a pube or the proud swell of a tit that marked the end of childhood and the flowering of womanhood. Ayşe remembers the first set of killing lingerie she smuggled in at the age of seventeen from the bold and brash new Agent Provocateur at Cevahir Mall, the long, luxurious ritual of putting it on, item by item, hooking and buttoning and strapping up all its complicated and inefficient fastenings, getting her pose just right so that when she turned to face the mirror it would be like a model swirling on a catwalk or a smoky twentieth-century lady-spy meeting a contact in her red velvet boudoir. The static rub of thigh against thigh had amazed her, the tiny pink bows placed just so: that she could be so sexy. She could not keep her fingers away from the lace and mesh and gloss. She felt worth all the riches in Istanbul. Ayşe had lounged for hours on her bed exploring the sensations and emotions five pieces of gauzy fabric could bring out in a seventeen-year-old; catching sight of herself as a wild thing in that plain, stolid wardrobe mirror. She sat, legs wide, on the edge of the bed, smoking, studying her image. She dreaded and half-hoped that the bedroom door would open and her mother catch her. She had discovered a sensual woman in this old room with its posters of girlie popstars on the walls.

'Here I come. What do you think?' Ayşe strides down the hall that has smelled of cooking onions and trapped grease as long as she can recall and into the living room. Her mother sits in her chair in the window bay where she can survey both inner and outer worlds. 'Now, it's not designed to be worn with these boots, but will it do?'

'Do for what?'

'I told you ten minutes ago, this dinner with Ferid Adataş tomorrow.'

'Ferid who?'

Tulip Apartment was a House of Memory. Ayşe had first encountered these edifices in the pages of Renaissance writings from fifteenth-century Florence. There masters of the art of memory constructed fabulous Palladian palazzos of visualization in which every hall and room and painting and statue, every piece of furniture and ornament on that furniture was the key to a painstakingly remembered fact. Contracts, legal cases, poems and discourses, were parsed into phrases of memory and assigned to locations in the mnemonic palace. A walk from the portico through the vestibule and along the loggia could be a complex argument in logic; another walk from that same starting point, by way of a certain niche, into the withdrawing room to a balcony overlooking a formal garden of cypress trees like dark flames could be a family genealogy or a marriage contract. As the ties between Fatma Hanım's memories grew less coherent, Ayşe's mother devised her own informal art of memory, investing the lamps and ornaments and family photographs, the books and years-out-of-date magazines and little jewelled boxes she loved so much with moments and recollections. She had set them at precise angles that Dicle the cleaner was forbidden from moving, for that would completely change the memory. A shift of twenty degrees might transmute a school prize into a cousin's wedding; the brother's graduation in the silver frame on the table beside the sagging sofa could, by a single move to the other side of the table, turn into New Year fireworks for the turn of the century and be utterly lost. As even those associations disintegrated, Fatma Hanım had taken to sticking yellow Post-its inscribed with cryptic, SMS-like memos to her mementoes. She raged with the spectacular spite of the old at Dicle when the little *aides-memoires* started disappearing. What had happened was that the glue dried out and the sun-paled yellow notes, the handwriting faded almost to invisibility, fell through the dusty air to the ground like leaves. Memory by memory, Fatma Hanım was being indexed on to the Erkoç Apartment. To Ayşe it seems like the necessary entropy of Fatma Hanım's life as family archivist. While she and her sisters and brother, her cousins and aunts and the whole carnival of the extended Erkoçs ran around going to school and falling in love and getting married and having babies or careers or both and splitting up and living big and wide, her mother picked up the memories, cleaned them off and arranged them in sense and place for when they might be needed, years or lifetimes later. Now the house was too full of rememberings and Fatma Hanım too empty of them. To her that was success: it was all written, had you eyes to read it.

'Mother, what do you think?' Ayşe's sister Güneş calls. Fatma Hanım's gaze had been sliding from Ayşe to the veins on her hands folded in her lap, the annotated ornaments on the mantel, the blue flicker of the television in the corner furthest from the light. The ebb of her mother's memory had grown stronger in the past three months, sucking details and names and even faces out into forgetting. Fearful of water left running and gas hissing in the kitchen, Günes had moved in with the children. Recep and Hülya, her nine- and five-year-olds, cantered around the apartment heedless of meaningless heirlooms and carefully positioned *aides-memoires*, liberated by the sudden spaciousness of the generous old Ottoman rooms. Ibrahim, her husband, remained at the crammed little modern apartment at Bayrampaşa. Günes had been waiting years for this. She had long wanted the messy and unpredictable being-married part of her life to be over so she could fold herself back into family. She had always been a carer and a coper. Ayşe had always been a chaser and a smoker. Günes' haughty moral superiority, her mother's enduring grey disappointment that Ayşe had married beneath herself did not trouble Ayşe any more. God or DNA had ordained it. You don't argue with them.

'Yes, lovely dress dear; what did you say it was for?' Fatma Hanım asks.

'The dinner, out on the Princes Islands.'

'The Princes Islands? Who would you know out there?'

'Ferid Adataş.'

'I think you mentioned that name. Who is he? Do we know him?'

'He's an investment fund manager. A businessman, very successful.'

Fatma Hanım shook her head.

'Sorry dear.'

A diplomat, a bureaucrat or a nouveau eurocrat; even a member of that most endangered species, a prince: that was the kind of society the Erkoçs enjoyed in the Princes Islands when Fatma and the most dashing Captain in the Northern Sea Command would be whisked out to a ball in a navy launch by smartly uniformed ratings, the red star and crescent billowing behind them. Businessmen have fingers yellow with money. Businessmen have beady peery eyes from looking at the bottom line, not the dazzling horizon of the blood-dark Black Sea.

'He's a friend of Adnan's.'

Fatma Hanım's gaze slides away again. That's it said now, good and proper. Business. Not a decent society thing at all. Across the room in the chair by the window where the light is good for needlework, Güneş presses the tip of her tongue to her lips in a soft lizard-hiss of disapproval. That name is not to be spoken in front of Fatma Hanım. Any reminder of what her youngest daughter could have and refused to marry into moved the easy tears of old age.

Ayşe kisses her mother on the forehead. As she closes the door Fatma Hanım asks again,

'Where is it she's going?'

'The Princes Islands,' Güneş says patiently.

The Marmaray out from Sirkeci is solid with bodies. Ayşe strap-hangs under the Bosphorus. The carriage smells of electricity and the light is migrainous. There is fear in the train: everyone knows where there was one bomb there will be another, from the same group or from another wanting a shine of the glory. Ayşe tries not to imagine a bomb in this deep tunnel. She tries not to imagine the blast of white light, the roof cracking open, the tunnel splitting, the water blasting in like a knife under millions of tons of pressure. The train sways over the points, blue lightning illuminates the tunnel. Ayşe knows everyone else thinks the same thought. Deep tunnels, tall buildings, fast trains and high-flying aircraft, all these things are irresistible to angry males. All these things defy God.

A million euro and she never has to do this again.

Tonight the dolmuş winds interminably between the spindly apartment blocks of Ferhatpaşa. Roads, eroded, dusty verges, concrete facades and the scrubby hillside are doused in yellow light. Ayşe can no longer stand the ugliness. A million euro would take her across the Bosphorus, back to Europe again. Kids hang around the lobby of the apartment block. Doesn't the new mosque run some kind of youth club?

He's not home. He won't be for hours. After the hamam, there'll be drinks, more talk. She won't wait up for the signature purr of the Audi pulling into the parking lot. The apartment is still with trapped heat and smells of fabric conditioner. Ayşe can hear upstairs' television through the floor. Whatever channel they watch seems to consist of constant cheering. She drinks cherry juice from the carton, so cold it hurts. Ayşe lays out tomorrow's clothes on her dresser. It is bliss to unzip and slip off the boots, a ridiculous fashion in such weather, but the fashion nonetheless. She slips naked beneath the sheet but even that is too much covering. Sleep won't come. Ayşe tries her comfortable side, her less comfortable side, her back, moving to the cooler part of the bed, arranging one leg over the other so, one arm under the other so. Nothing. Her mind races. She sees Adnan at the bath-house, so serious, as he is so beautifully serious when he does business; Adnan over drinks – he loves a party but he will always be at least one drink behind his host. She imagines the dinner tomorrow; the men talking to each other about football and politics and deals, the women around the table discussing family and gossip and society. *And what do you do to pass the time, Ms Erkoç?* I'm on a quest for a mellified man. Which is more absurd in Istanbul, a legend bubbling up out of a magical past or turning down a million on the smell of man's aftershave?

She pulls on a robe to make the call. Akgün takes a moment to recognize her name.

'Ms Erkoç. Forgive me, what can I do for you?' She catches a phantom wisp of *Arslan* aftershave.

'Your mellified man.'

'Yes?'

'I'll do it.'

Tuesday

'Hot,' says Father Ioannis.

'Hotter than yesterday,' says Georgios Ferentinou.

'Hottest yet,' says Lefteres the Confectioner. 'It'll break thirty-eight.'

'Hot as hell,' says Constantin. 'Your pardon, Father.'

'Hell is hotter,' says Father Ioannis.

Bülent brings a stick with simits threaded on it.

'What are these for this time?' Lefteres asks. He stirs his tea, sugar crystals whirl and blur in the hot liquid.

'Volkan passed the fitness test, didn't he?'

Lefteres throws his hands up in despair.

'How do you do this?'

'I'm a natural-born entrepreneur, I have deep-rooted market instincts.'

'So why are you still running this place?' says Lefteres the lampoonist.

'I wouldn't be if it were real money,' says Bülent. 'Maybe I'm scared of success. It's our abiding national failing.'

Constantin tears a piece from his simit.

'Here, Ferentinou, anything on that bomb yesterday?'

'Why are you asking him?' asks Father Ioannis.

'You weren't here for this bit,' says Lefteres. 'Our good doctor here is all of a sudden a security consultant. Right in the middle of his morning tea there's a knock on the door and who should be there but some spook from MIT.'

'For a start, I'm not a security consultant,' says Georgios Ferentinou. 'What I have done is agree to work with a new government think tank. They want people with heterodox ideas. The orthodox ones don't seem to be working. And it's good *professor*.'

'He means, they don't predict tram bombs,' says Lefteres.

Bülent lifts empty glasses on to his tray.

'Call me naïve, but surely one of the first things about a security think tank is that it's, well, secure?'

'All I'm saying to you is that I'm a member of the Kadiköy Group. That's no national secret.'

'You're going to Kadiköy?' says Lefteres.

'Yes. This afternoon. Is this so very strange?'

'I'm trying to remember the last time you went further than Taksim.'

'They're sending a car,' says Georgios Ferentinou but the lampoonist has sunk a barb into him. For years now he has let his world contract until it is as close and comfortable as an old suit. The ghost Istanbuls of his white room have replaced the old wonderful names of the streets and alleys: The Street of a Thousand Earthquakes, Alley of the Chicken that Thought It Could Fly, Avenue of the Bushy Beard, the Street of Nafi of the Golden Hair.

'So what were you poking around at yesterday up the side of Kenan's shop?' Bülent asks.

'Young Mr Durukan claims he was chased by a robot.'

'You still letting that kid visit you?' asks Constantin.

'You're a fool to yourself, Georgios,' says Lefteres.

'Now I did see something yesterday,' Bülent says. 'That kid's toy bird-robot thing, and another one as well. I thought it was a flowerpot or a satellite dish come off a roof or something.'

'The boy went down to have a look at the bomb on Necatibey Cadessi,' Georgios says. 'He finds he's not the only robot watching the events. And what's more, they're following someone. He goes to investigate, but another robot – a third robot – spots him and tries to grab him but he escapes. It chases him all the way back here but he manages to trick it into a jump it hadn't foreseen, and it falls and smashes.'

'That would be what I saw then,' Bülent says.

'Go back a bit,' says Father Ioannis. 'You said they were following someone.'

Georgios raises an admonitory finger.

'Yes, and someone known to us.'

Every breath is bated.

'One of the young men from the basement,' Georgios says.

'Well, in that case I hope it's the police and that they find him and evict him,' says Father Ioannis. 'Those boys have been nothing but trouble since they moved in. It's them poured piss over my church, I'm sure of it. Get the lot of them out; this has always been a mixed area.'

'Well, I'll tell you something,' says Bülent leaning over his counter as if it is a pulpit. 'That same guy, he sees djinn.'

'He smokes his head off on marijuana all day,' drawls Constantin.

'Well, what about this then, unbelievers,' Bülent says. 'Hafize, who works with Erkoç Hanım over in the art gallery – right underneath you, Georgios. Well, the brother Ismet – the street kadı, he has a reputation for being good at opening the book, so she went to see him and get a reading because she thought she might be pregnant. Necdet takes one look at her and tells her straight to her face, you most certainly are pregnant. How does he know? Because he's seen her karin, upside down in the earth, with the big bulging belly. A karin.'

'For a natural-born entrepreneur who professes deep-rooted market instincts, you do talk such fearful shit,' declares Constantin.

Father Ioannis throws up his hand. 'A kadı, and now a miracle worker. That's the last thing we need. Lefteres ...'

'I can only intervene if someone asks me,' says the confectioner.

'The bomb must have knocked something loose,' Constantin growls.

'This young man is caught in the tram bomb and sees djinn,' says Georgios fanning himself with a menu card. A silver brow of sun has risen over the roof of Ismet İnönü Apartments. Soon it will pour its full heat into Adem Dede Square and drive the old men to shelter.

'Can Durukan was chased over the roof by a robot after he was caught spying on the bomb scene. That robot is destroyed but someone removed the evidence.'

'And that bomb, there's something not right about that,' Bülent says. 'Suicide blast; martyrdom video. That's the rule. Glorious martyrdom against Turkish prostitution in the arms of the decadent West. It's up on the internet before you can say Inshallah.'

'You know rather a lot about this,' Lefteres says.

'I've watched a few. I like rating them. I've this idea for a TV show: people send in their martyrdom videos, people vote and the winner gets a suicide bomb mission.'

'God forgive you,' says Father Ioannis. 'That's not even funny.'

'It seems odd that whoever planted the bomb put a robot there to make sure there were no videos at all.'

'They were watching for something else,' Constantin says with a rap of his cane on the cobbles. 'Something they needed to follow closely, without being seen or suspected. And they were afraid your young friend saw it too.'

'Exactly,' says Georgios Ferentinou, leaning forward and pursing his fingers, an unconscious gesture from the days when his debating circle was wider than old Greeks and a çayhane owner. 'Let's review what we know. One small bomb, no casualties beyond the bomber. There is no martyrdom video. The bombers – or someone else, it's a possibility – leaves a robot there at the scene. It may be recording something, but when someone else comes to investigate, it pursues him and tries to find out his identity. This is all very interesting.'

'Are you suggesting we play amateur detectives?' Lefteres asks. He gets creakingly up from the low stool, shakes hands quickly with his friends. 'A bunch of old Greeks and a çayhane owner?'

Father Ioannis is next to leave.

'Whatever it means, it will all come down on us,' he says. 'It always does. God and His Mother be with all here.'

'What time does the car take you to Kadiköy?' Constantin asks.

'The afternoon.'

'Plenty of time then.' Constantin pulls out the backgammon board from the rack under the table and unfolds it.

'Now you know I beat you at this every time,' Georgios says.

'I do.' Constantin lays out the counters on the points and folds up the leather dice cup. 'I just thought you might welcome a reason to spend a little more time with me.'

'Why would I want to do that? I see you every bloody day.'

'There might be something you want to ask me.'

'What would I want to ask you?'

'Like where you might find Ariana Sinanidis.'

A flicker of movement catches Georgios' attention. A little plastic monkey-thing scurries with soft gripping pads along a cable slung from the dervish house to Ismet İnönü Apartments, scuttles up the wall, over a coaming and is gone. Bülent brings fresh tea on his swinging tray.

'Just roll the damn dice,' says Georgios Ferentinou.

Can is the Boy Detective and he is on patrol up on the rooftops of Eskiköy. From his vantage parapet on Ismet İnönü Apartments, he looks down into Adem Dede Square. There is Mr Ferentinou with his old friend, the nasty one he doesn't like. There is Bülent leaning against the counter reading something off his ceptep. The Georgian woman comes out on to her verandah beneath him to take in her washing. She is smoking and her television is blaring. She doesn't see the Boy Detective. That's because he is a master of disguise, the wearer of many shapes. There is that stupid girl who works in the shop full of dead books, opening up the locks. She always looks furtive when she opens up the store. In she slips, as if she has committed a crime.

Monkey turns until the camera locator matches with the GPS log from yesterday's rooftop chase. *Size of a rat!* the Boy Detective commands. Monkey explodes into his component BitBots and reforms into creeping, careful Rat, sniffing and snooping and sampling the roof for clues. What kind of clues? The sort of thing that crime scene investigators on television clear entire rooms to keep safe, and put on masks to lift with long tweezers, and put into plastic bags. Clues. An empty cigarette packet isn't a clue. A lottery ticket torn almost in half, a pair of pants long fallen from a line, grey and gritty from years of rooftop exposure. Rat goes sniffing across the rooftops. Seagulls lift, braying in irritation at being disturbed and settle again. Rat perches on his little sprung feet on the edge of the parapet, tasting the air. There is Mr Ferentinou playing tavla with that nasty Egyptian one. There is the Boy Detective's mom going to bring the little silver car up from the garage on Vermilion-Maker Lane. The Gas Bubble, he calls it. The Boy Detective has ten minutes to get a start on this case before he has to pull on his blue uniform and stick his big pack on his back. Think Rat think. Bülent sets out saucers of milk for the cats of Adem Dede. He feeds them because Aykut across the square hates them. Think Rat think. The Boy Detective clicks up the GPS log. This is where Monkey leaped into mad mid-air; here the hunter robot fell and smashed. Look, look well, concentrate. The Boy Detective makes a new movement through the haptic field and Rat transforms into Snake; freaky, go anywhere Snake. Walls are no object to Snake's sticky-smart belly; down he goes, scanning, scanning. Can's eyes flick across five panes of information, looking for the overlooked, something small and unconsidered that the clean-up crew might have missed. But the men who controlled the hunter robot are big and old and slow. The Boy Detective is young and quick and brilliant. His brain is naturally attuned to pick visual clues out of the world that others miss. It's rewired itself this way, Mr Ferentinou says; compensating for his muffled, sound-poor world.

There. What's that? In a gutter along the side of Kenan's store. Something small and sharp-edged and orange. Snake loops across the side of Ismet Inönü Apartments. Snakes have no hands so Can reconfigures it into Monkey and snatches the orange ort out of the dried, cracked sludge. In three bounds Monkey is on the window ledge of the dervish house balcony. It drops the treasure into the Boy Detective's hand. A sliver of plastic, chipped cleanly from the hunter robot's shell. It must have flown a long way from the impact. There is printing on it. NG428. Can squeezes the piece of plastic in his fist until it cuts. God is good, God is very good.

Do like the CSI cops do. Tag it. It's the work of a moment to take a high-resolution photograph on your ceptep. Bag it. Into the plastic lunch bag on which he's written the word EVIDENCE, and that bag into your school bag. Can is doing up his blue school tie when Mom enters and signs, *All ready to go then?*

'Right and ready,' says Can the Boy Detective.

'A karin,' says Mustafa as he boils up his ritual start-every-morning coffee in the Business Rescue Centre's immense kitchen, 'is not a thing you see every day, even you.'

A topic that regularly surfaces in the Levent Business Rescue Centre is what talent its two wardens already possess might become a superpower. Mustafa's is becoming an expert overnight. He can catch an obsession in the blink of an eye. Urban Golf, that's just so old. Djinn, now they are endlessly fascinating.

Necdet, whose superpower is now all-too manifest and genuine – Djinn-Boy – is certain that Mustafa now knows more than Necdet ever will about the djinn; their ranks and orders, their foibles and weaknesses and the words of power by which a strong shaykh may master them. The Mustafa Bağli Guide to Djinn, Ifrits and the Lesser Members of the Creation of Fire.

'Upside down, inside the earth, now that's very interesting.' Mustafa pours two tiny cups of frothy, grainy coffee from the brass pot. The coffee is strong and very good – another of Mustafa's small researched expertises, when he became obsessed with the sacks of coffee the Ottomans abandoned on their retreat from the gates of Vienna, at the height of imperial ambition. 'That's kind of a North African interpretation – specifically from Cairo. Tell me, if you look down, do you see anything at my feet?'

'No, but there is something on your shoulder.'

Mustafa almost upsets his coffee.

'Describe this . . . entity.'

'It's like a hand on your shoulder, if a hand looked like a crab made of clay.'

'Clay, you say?'

'Clay, or rocks, sort of like that American superhero who's made of rocks.' Necdet decides not to mention the eyes, which are between the fingers.

'I think the comic character you're referring to is Benjamin Grimm, aka The Thing. You see, there is a different interpretation of the karin, that they are creatures of clay rather than creatures of fire and that they sit on your shoulder, like angels or demons.'

'It's drumming its fingers on your shoulder.'

Now Mustafa's coffee cup does hit the grey carpet tiles. After he has cleaned up the spill he wanders down along the aisles of dusty workstations to where Necdet now sits clicking vacantly at a gossip site.

'Is it still there?' Mustafa asks. 'The thing – the karin– on my shoulder?'

Necdet doesn't want to tell Mustafa what he really has at his shoulder so he mumbles, 'Yeah.'

Mustafa pulls a chair over from the next work cube.

'This interests me. It pains me to say this, being a rationalist and a modern European as well as a modern Turk, but we do seem to be living in a new age of mental recidivism. For every reaction there has to be an equal and opposite reaction, as much in the spiritual world as the physical, it seems. Just as we finally cast off our mantle of being the Sick Man of Europe, the eternal barbarous Turk, we find the most primitive and superstitious kind of Anatolian folk religion rearing its head in our cities. Djinn, shaykhs, street kadıs administering their own brand of the shariat. Dervishes and everything. Action, reaction. It's a cloud of unreason. Some Islamist woman blows herself up on the tram and you see a djinni on the hot-air drier, meet a karin under the doorstep and find Ben Grimm's hand on my shoulder.

'Now, I don't know how this works – it's obviously some post-traumatic hallucination – but I tell you this most sincerely, once that pregnant girl starts talking, half the neighbourhood will be round looking for prayers and readings and healings. You'll never hear the end of it. Your brother may go on about wanting an Islam for the street that's pure and fresh and modern – so far, so old school Sufi, if you ask me – but I tell you this too, there was never an imam – or a kadı, for that matter – could resist a quick euro. There's money to be made and to be honest, what you need is marketing. Good, creative marketing, with vision and a long-term plan. An investment structure. Get you out of this hole. Get you some kind of life.'

'When you say marketing, you mean you.'

'Well, yes.'

'You run a Business Rescue Centre no one's ever used.'

'Yes, but with entrepreneurial flair.'

Necdet can't deny this. The doctor-fish health spa for American psoriasis sufferers, the Roses from Turkey company, Hazelnuts for Health and Happiness: the new superfood, Your Cave in Cappadocia! and most recently the Urban Golf; all business schemes of Mustafa's. All fantasy.

Mustafa goes to take the morning call from Gum-Chewing Suzan. There's a directive to cut down on the air-conditioning. The price of gas on the micro-markets has peaked again. Mustafa reasonably argues that the rescue centre only needs air-conditioning because of the heat thrown out by the hundreds of purring workstations. Shut down the computers and the gas price system is solved at a stroke. Simple. Brilliant.

Necdet is seized by sudden, low-grade panic, the rushing, roaring of a landslide in his head; all the places and faces of his life slipping away from him, tumbling and bowling and grinding each other ever smaller until they are nothing but walls of dust billowing out on every side of him. Necdet looks again at Mustafa, arguing on the screen with Gum-Chewing Suzan and knows him. Somewhere outside this dungeon is Ismet. Necdet can see his face, hear his voice and speak his name. He knows there are others, brothers of the tarikat who come around on a Thursday afternoon to argue new, good, street law from the Koran and the Hadith but he can't see their faces or hear their names. On the tram, hadn't there been a woman whose head came off? He had seen her as a vision, floating in front of him as he tried to flee the crowd before the police asked him questions he didn't want to answer, it must have been just yesterday but the face, the place, the time, even the dull boom of the necklace of explosives detonating, are clouded, memories of memories. What had he so feared from the police? Before Ismet let him into the sun-dusty cellars beneath the dervish house, what had he done, where had he been? He can't remember. His memory is just a storm of djinn.

The panic leaps to become absolute, gibbering, paralysing; the panic of total loss and total helplessness. Then Necdet hears the music of a single flute. He turns in his swivel chair to identify the source of the notes. Djinn stream through the air, like smoke or water running away through subtle, unseen courses. Djinn constantly changing shape and size, from motes of dust to birds or scurrying things swimming in air to veils and scarves of twisting silver fire. Creatures from beyond the world, more than living. He knows he is meant to follow. Mustafa, still rapt in argument with Suzan, does not notice when Necdet slips out of his work cube and goes with the flow.

The stream of djinn slips under the utility room door. Of course. It eddies around the leaning brooms and mops, the buckets and dustpans, the squat cylinder of the floor-polishing robot which hasn't worked since Mustafa tried to turn it into a self-guided cocktail bar. Under another door to the electricity meter cupboard and fuseboards. The energies contained here excite the djinn; they boil and deliquesce, shifting from vapour to fluid in gushes and plumes of silver but Necdet carefully follows their course to an air-conditioning grille low in the wall. The spiritual fluid pours through the mesh. All the while the flute calls.

The vent is fitted with plastic pegs, cheap like everything else; they give at the first tug. Necdet pushes head and shoulders into the dark passageway beyond. There's a cold draught with a current of old stone and deep earth. The river of djinn flows past him. They feel like cat fur against his body. This is thrilling and heady and the only thing Necdet can do is go forward. Lights flicker on and he's in a man-sized service shaft, lined with ducts and cables, pipes and wiring. The service way leads steadily downward; the smells of old earth and a more ancient damp grow stronger and condensation glistens on the walls and drips from the pipes. It's cold. The djinn foam and gush around his feet like rapids. At the end of the tunnel is a door; the djinn force themselves under it like water through a mill race. The door opens to his touch. Beyond is darkness and age. Blinking in the deep dark, senses more intimate than sight tell Necdet he is in a place from another age. Stone. A drip of water. Moving air tells him there is a dome over his head. Echoes suggest pillars. He realizes it's some time since he heard the flute. The djinn pool at his feet. Photon by photon his eyes adjust to the light. He is in a pillared stone vault. The exact dimensions are beyond him, the darkness reaches beyond his seeing, there are pillars all the way. Alcoves, domes, cupolas above his head. This is a deep place, this is an old place. Now he begins to make out an object in front him, massive, low, sculpted. It reminds him of the fountain in the dervish house garden where he goes to sit and smoke. His memories are coming back. With that moment of recognition comes another: a figure sits on the coping of the fountain.

Necdet starts, then, as the djinn flow towards the sitter's feet, gathering and for the first time giving light, a tremendous peace fills him. The robes, the long beard, the green eyes of deepest penetration, the green turban wound loosely around the head. How can Necdet be afraid of him? He is the oldest one, the Green Saint, older than Allah, older than God's Christ and his mother Mary, older than Yahweh. If he now wears the green robe of a Sufi it is because Islam took the colour of life from him. His is the green of the floods of the Tigris and Euphrates, of the Anatolian spring of Hattuşa and Çatalhöyük. He is Hızır, Khidr, Al-Khidir, saint, prophet and angel.

He is water, he is life. He is the help from beyond comprehension; his the hand that pulls you back from in front of the tram, that inflates the airbag, that pulls you out of the air crash. He is the obstreperous parking lot attendant, the obstructive security official who makes you miss that doomed plane in the first place.

But yet Necdet is afraid. Hızır is the unpredictability of water, the lawlessness of a higher law. Hızır can bless, Hızır can kill, he is creation and destruction, the drought and the flood. Now he turns his green eyes on Necdet.

Recite.

Recite what? Necdet asks. But he already knows the answer to that. Any medrese-trained boy knows that. He learned that in the Friday school where he sat with Ismet, reciting until he knew it like he knew his own heartbeat. Afterwards he would go with Ismet to the big dusty pitch with the goalposts sagged in the middle. Ismet played. Ismet was a good central defender. Necdet sat on the dirt bank minding the jackets and watching the big truck trains rolling up the expressway to the bridge. Necdet was never any good at ball games. He couldn't see the point of them. He learned to recognize the alphabets on their taut-buckled sides and know that this truck came from Russia and that one from Syria and that other one from Georgia and this last one of all, well, that's easy because it's in Arabic, God's language. That was another thing he couldn't see the point of: sitting on a Friday afternoon on the floor nodding to those words in God's language. Why couldn't God just talk like everyone else? If he was God he could say it as well in Turkish as Arabic. He would blink out the windows at the sun in the dusty sky and then one day, without thinking, almost without realizing it, he found his hand was up.

'What's the point of this?'

The other boys had been shocked and angry but the imam was a patient man, quietly addicted to televised sport.

'The point is that someday this will be asked of you. It may be tomorrow, it may be at the end of the world when you stand before

God, but asked it will be, and you will have to answer. And what shall you say?'

Another memory. The djinn shift at the feet of the Green Saint, casting long shadows over the dome of the old cistern. Again, Hızır says, *Recite.*

The assault of memory reels Necdet backwards.

He hears the point-blank bang of nailguns, the rev of the chainsaw cutting roof timbers. All the uncles had turned out to help build the house. They began at sunset, by the law. Concrete blocks and mortar. Row upon row. Plastic windows from the double-glazing centre: this was no slum. Towards midnight the roof went up, the uncles holding the bucking plastic sheeting against the rising wind, while Necdet's father picked his way carefully over the chainsaw-cut joists, water-proofing the tie-bolts with his sealant gun. He took his time for there is no house without a roof but he worked with one eye on the horizon. If the roof was raised before sunrise, no one could take the house away from you. That was the law. Under highway inter-sections, at the back of industrial parks, on eroded hillsides and flash-flood valleys, whole neighbourhoods sprung up like flowers after rain. Townships – gecekondus – built on the law and hope.

The women sat in the cars and made food and tea in the gas cooker that would be proudly wheeled into the new kitchen. They talked, they laughed, they listened to the radio and kept an eye on the children. The memory is so old Necdet is not sure if it's something he has been told that has turned into a memory. He is certain he was very small. New sister Kizbes was even smaller, bouncing on her mother's lap in the back of the pick-up. Ismet, only two years older but big enough for men's work; running up with boxes of nails for the gun or new tubes of sealant or cleaning mortar from trowels. Necdet wanted that; the attention, the feeling of being useful. He saw the nailgun lying by the back of Uncle Soli's pick-up and lifted it up the night sky. *Dang!* he went, *dank-an-dang-a-dank*, the banging of big nails right into things. It was a beautiful thing, the nail gun held up against the sky glow of great Istanbul; the noise it made, the way it left things permanently, unalterably changed, two things that had been apart forever joined.

'Hey, hey stop him, get him away from that thing!' Uncle Soli had shouted too slow too late, for Necdet rolled over on to his side and with a dang! pulled the trigger and sent a ten centimetre nail clean through Aunt Nevval's foot into the dusty ground.

Houses terraced along the hillside, plastic roofs one by one replaced by red tile as the gecekondus became official suburbs. The dazzling aluminium dome of the new mosque down at the side of the expressway, built, like the attendant religious school, with Saudi money. Aunt Nevval coming slowly up from the dolmuş stop on the stick she needed ever after the nail gun, the baptism of the home, for Necdet understood even then that no house can stand without blood. Before the dervish house, this was where he lived, this hot, dusty ex-urb strung like a hundred others along the expressways into Anatolia. Istanbul was a rumour here; where the trucks came from, where the buses and dolmuşes went. Başibüyük, home and heart.

'What is this?' Necdet shouts. 'Is this true, is this real, what is this? Get out of my head green man! Get out, just get out, get out, get out!'

Hızır holds Necdet's glare, raises a finger.

Recite.

The burning girl comes plunging out the house into the street. The light polyester of her sports top is perfect fuel: the burning fabric drops blazing, smoking drips of molten plastic on to her jeans, her shoes. Her hands are held up, flapping, beating at herself. She shrieks like nothing Necdet has ever imagined coming from a human throat. She is wreathed in flames now; the screams stop, choked for oxygen. Kizbes falls to the ground but the men are there, rushing from their tea, rolling her in the dirt. Neighbour of the left Etyen has the fire-extinguisher from his pick-up, Semih the neighbour of the right calls an ambulance though Başibüyük is far from hospitals and emergency services. Now the women have Kizbes, cutting away her shirt where polyester has fused to skin. Her cries are terrible.

Her hair is half burned away. To Necdet, watching from the kitchen window, it is one of the most interesting things he has ever seen. Now Necdet's father comes pounding up the hill from the gas station where he washes buses; he stops only a minute at the huddle of women around Kizbes, then runs into the house and drags Necdet out into the light. His father and all the men from the neighbourhood kick Necdet down the hill. He breaks free from their hands and runs straight out into the highway. Trucks blare their horns, cars swerve. A bus grazes his heel. He can see the looks on the faces of the passengers. Speed and insanity get him to the other side of the high-speed steel. Some of the bolder Başibüyük boys risk the highway – the bully boys, the ones who have always despised Necdet – but by now Necdet is way up into the maze of houses and alleys on the south side of the valley.

'Why are you showing me this?'

Hızır fixes Necdet with his gaze.

'Why are you looking at me? I didn't do it!'

Djinn-light eddies around the Green Saint's feet.

'I didn't do it. It was an accident she was smoking she dropped a cigarette.'

Hızır raises an eyebrow

'She was bugging me, right? She was bugging me, just standing there and getting in the way, I couldn't get away from her. Wherever I went she was there. She wanted some stuff and I didn't have any but she wouldn't listen to me when I said I didn't have any.'

But he hadn't felt anything. Numb; he was numb. He had watched Kizbes go up in a wreath of flame with remote, intellectual dispassion. Her cries were just the sound of breaking machinery. It was seen through glass, on a screen, a news report from a distant battle front. His own father had kicked him to the ground, kick after kick after kick, fighting through the other men and boys to get a kick in. Necdet knew terrible damage was being done to his body but he felt nothing. He had borne the whole thing with a mild smile on his face. He hadn't thrown the cigarette on to Kizbes because she was bugging him, because she had made him angry. He felt no anger, he felt no impatience; he felt nothing at all. She had merely been the closest thing to hand when he wondered how well a woman might burn.

Necdet hid four nights at the house of his dealer. Ümit's parents knew him, the man who set his sister on fire. Even Ümit seemed wary of him but he knew that a man who set fire to his sister would as casually inform on him to the police if he was refused hospitality. The fifth day Ismet – good, mosque-going, committed – came with a deal of his own. He would take Necdet with him to the European side, keep him in the care of the Islamic order he was setting up with a few like-minded brothers he had met online. Get him away from the downward ramp of slacking, small time cannabis dealing, sitting on a stool by the front door staring down at the highway. Give him order, stability, quiet, a sense of right and the divine. It was that or live like a wolf up in the hills. There was no welcome for Necdet back in Başibüyük. Kizbes would live. She was in the hospital. The imam was holding a fund-raiser. The hair would never grow back the same; she could cover that with a wig but not the glossy burn scars on her face. She would probably never marry.

Hızır the Green Saint lowers his finger and looks away.

'There's something wrong in my head!' Necdet cries. He beats his temples with his fists. 'Get in there get in there get in there! Why can't I feel anything? There's nothing there, it's just wood. Nothing real.'

Hızır looks back. The smallest, holiest, most unworldly of smiles creases his mouth.

But you do feel. Anger and fear and numb and dazed, confused beyond belief half the time and the other half out of your head seeing things other people wouldn't dare imagine. The most real thing that has happened to you, Necdet Hasgüler, is this Sufi saint and his legion of djinn. Hızır, help from beyond the world, but also perilous in his gifts. He's offered you a childhood. Here it is, take it, but it's a horror. A monster child. Now you must ask yourself, can you trust it? Is it a true childhood, or just what you think you remember? Old memories or new ones? In this old stone cistern, close to the waters which are his heart and his blood, is Hızır turning him into something different, a new Necdet?

Recite, yes. Recite. Recite, in the name of God, who made you from a clot of blood.

Unclean oven, trapped cooking, the cigarette smoke absorbed into the wallpaper, unemptied vacuum-cleaner dust-bags. The air fresheners placed by the concierge on window ledges and work surfaces and cisterns add a sickly, death-ward stink. This empty, clattery apartment with the dust thick on the blinds and the floorboards gritty and the dead pigeon souring on the balcony, stinks of single man. There's a packet of instant tea granules in the sticky kitchen cabinet. Letters and catalogues swept by the openings of the front door against the wall. A peeling patch under the balcony window. A soft dark oval of hair-grease on the bedroom wallpaper, above the ghostly outline of the bed head. The mattress is stained, the toilet brown with lime scale. Grey gum is fused to the kitchen tiles.

Leyla fights a gag reflex.

'There's two months' rent owing,' the concierge says. He is small, pot-bellied, troglodytic. Leyla thought his subspecies had died out decades ago, the mean-souled, nosy house-snoop. He took a wad of petty cash to lead her and Yaşar into this eighth-floor apartment. The lifts at Kemal House stopped working long before Mehmet Ali's lease. Residents glowered as they squeezed past on the landings and staircases. Everyone had children and a television blaring in their living room. On the third floor Leyla kicked off her business heels. They were death on the worn concrete risers. 'Are you friends of his, relatives?'

'It's business,' Leyla says. 'How long has he been gone?'

'Since February,' the concierge says.

'Is it not customary to wait until someone's dead before you sell their stuff?' Leyla asks.

The kapıcı shrugs. 'Landlord's decision. He owed. The stuff just about covered the first couple of months. Are you sure you're not related to him?'

'Not our problem,' Yaşar says from the kitchen space.

'Well, someone owes it.'

'Do you mind if we have a look round?' Leyla asks.

The concierge seems not to have heard, casually lighting up a cigarette. Leyla peels twenty euro from her purse. The Istanbul kapıcı's reputation for venality is in safe hands. A hope too far that it would have been as simple as knocking on the door and Mehmet welcoming them with tea and sweets. Mehmet gone, but his possessions intact and in place would have been even better. This is detective work now and she hasn't even seen a contract from the viperish Zeliha. Family is the worst employer. Leyla kneels and peers down cracks in the floorboards and under skirting boards, stands on her tiptoes to peer along high shelves, pokes in the corners of wardrobes. An old pair of underpants once used as a duster and cellophane pull-strips from cigarette packets. The floral bouquet of air-freshener is giving her a headache. She'll have the smell in her head for days. She lifts the lid of the vile toilet cistern.

The other half of this, Yaşar had said in the Ceylan-Besarani company car, a battered Peugeot citicar stuck permanently in manual due to the autodrive having picked up a virus. He took both hands off the wheel to rummage in his pockets. Leyla grabbed it with her left hand and steered them around the back of a long-distance coach with neat lace curtains. Leyla took the beautiful silver miniature Koran, no bigger than her thumb. Yaşar retook the wheel.

'This is old.'

'Persian. It's genuine silver.'

Leyla turned it over and the sense of violation at the naked page, the Holy Koran cut in two, was a reminder that she had not travelled so far from Demre.

'How does it come to be half a Koran?'

'There's a family story in that. Everything's a family story with us.'

'Well tell me. I like family stories.'

'It goes back to the start of the twentieth century, to the First World War. My great-great-whatever grandfather Abdulkadir – they made us learn his name, like he was a father of the nation or something – got sent to Çanakkale. Çanak Bayırı, the hill where Mustafa Kemal made his name. Even in Istanbul everyone knew it was basically a death sentence. The Koran was an old family heirloom; when she heard that Abdulkadir was going to the front, his mother went to a Jewish jeweller and had him cut it very carefully in half. No Muslim would do that, so the story goes. She gave him the front half and kept the back half. The Holy Koran is one thing, indivisible, and would always seek its other half and bring him home again.'

'Did he come home? Did he survive?'

'Oh yes. Great-great Abdulkadir was a born survivor. He worked out pretty quickly that the way to keep your head on your shoulders was to stay well away from Kemal and his death-and-glory boys. He lived to be eighty-eight and dropped dead in the middle of a New Year party.'

'I think you should be proud of him. I think everyone who was at Çanakkale was a hero.'

'He was the only one to come back from his unit without a scratch on him.'

'That's some Koran.'

'That's some self-preservation skills.'

Leyla peeps into the cistern. Nothing wrapped up in six condoms and bubble wrap at the bottom of the cistern. Good. She doesn't want to have to put her hand into that water. Nothing here at all.

'Take a look at this.' Yaşar's soft call from the kitchen. He has opened a cutlery drawer. The landlord's house-clearers have even sent the knives and forks to auction but left empty plastic vials. The drawer is full of them. Yaşar opens each drawer. They are all full of plastic vials. Yaşar holds one up between thumb and forefinger.

'Nano.'

'You're sure he's not a relative?' the concierge says.

'He's not a relative,' Leyla lies.

'Good, then I can tell you what I really think. He was not a good man, this Mehmet Ali. All sorts of people here at all hours. Not the sort we want round here – this is a family apartment block. Bulgarians. Bad, the lot of them, Bulgarians. Knife you as soon as look at you. And Georgians and Russians – they are a nation of gangsters. And women. You know the type I mean. And bags, out of the backs of vans. Always buying and selling, buying and selling. And boxes and boxes of empty plastic bottles, tiny little bottles. I know what that means. I went over this place with one of those allergic vacuum cleaners. You know, for people who can't have dust. I don't want that stuff getting down between the floorboards, making its way into the wiring and the pipes and all. God help us, what if it got into the vermin?'

'Hyper-intelligent mutant rats,' Yaşar says. 'Cool.'

Nano still scares Leyla Gültaşli. No matter how safe or respectable or ubiquitous it has become, she imagines it crawling inside her, like legends of terrible old mountain men invaded and hollowed out by lice so that they were nothing inside but swarming vileness. She imagines it like ash in the veins, like she has heard people who inject drugs feel; dirty inside. At the college she had always declined it, going bare-brained to exams and assignments even if it disadvantaged her against her focused, sharp, pattern-recognizing course-mates. She weakened under the pressure of the final exams. There was always someone who knew someone who could get the good stuff, the grey stuff, the stuff that really worked. The vial had worked its way up the supply chain, perhaps from this kitchen work-top. It stood on her bedside cabinet, leaking nightmares. The morning of the first exam she had snapped the top and poured the nano, fine and fluid as water, down the toilet. Two flushes to be safe. Let the fish of the Galata Bridge be focused and sharp and recognize patterns they've never seen before. She could not bear the thought of dirt and ashes inside her.

'Do you know who bought all the fixtures?' Leyla says.

'You'd have to ask . . . .'

'. . . the landlord. Can I have his number?'

The concierge shrugs. Leyla peels out another twenty. It's sole remaining cousin is lonely, nestled in the silk lining. Another note to Zeliha: everything can be done with petty cash.

Leyla slips her shoes off again; the stairs are more treacherous going down than coming up.

'Yaşar.' He trots diligently two steps behind. Out of the office he's a pussy cat. In the office he's bullish and aggressive. Leyla's grown up in a house of brothers and knows boys and their incessant competition. Leyla wonders how Yaşar and Aso ever built a working business. It's not working. That's why she's here. Who writes loan agreements on hemi-Korans? 'Two things. One: I've set up a meeting with the European Emerging Technologies Investment Board for this afternoon. They have a fast track scheme, though I'm not sure how fast fast track is.' She had been up until three this morning, clicking through the Byzantine levels of European funds and bursaries and development loans and start-up funds and Next-Step programmes. She had begged a last-minute cancellation slot on the ceptep on the metro that morning. 'I'd like Aso to go to that. You're a brilliant designer but you look and dress like a drummer from a metal band.'

'The fuck . . .'

'It'll mean a haircut. And a suit.'

'Absolutely not.'

'Aso goes then. Two: I'd like the chip to the car. You are the worst driver I have ever seen.'

'You drive?'

'Of course I drive.'

'That's Demre driving. This is Istanbul driving.'

'Give me the chip.'

No one is driving. The Peugeot has been hauled up onto the back of a big red tow truck emblazoned with salutations and improving religious mottoes. Leyla raps the driver's door. The driver winds down the window but it's the passenger who leans over to speak to her.

'You're looking for Mehmet Ali.' The passenger is a bullet-headed, baby-faced man, piggy eyes and pursed lips. His voice is low and sweet. 'We're looking for him too.'

'Who are you? Are you the landlord? I told the kapıcı we're not related. Give me my car back.'

'No, I'm not the landlord. Does he owe him money as well? That wouldn't surprise me. It was the kapıcı messaged me. I'm a former business associate of Mehmet Ali Bey. He does owe me money. It's quite a sum.'

'That's not my business. Give me my car back.'

'Well, it is your business. I've made it your business, in that if you find out where he is you'll let me know.'

Where is Yaşar? Leyla is too too conscious that she is standing at the side of the truck with her heels in her hand and very few options. Her one advantage is that he doesn't know that she isn't looking for Mehmet Ali for money. She isn't necessarily looking for Mehmet Ali, just his half of a miniature Koran. 'Deal,' she says. The bullet-headed man's baby-face is genuinely surprised but the tow-truck driver hits a button, a winch whines and the Peugeot is lowered off the flat bed. It runs a little way off the ramps before the winch brakes it.

'I'll need some way of getting in touch with you,' Leyla says.

'I'd prefer not to do that,' the bullet-headed man says. The driver starts the engine. 'We'll keep an eye on you.'

Leyla waits until the red tow-truck has rounded the corner and is out of sight. She turns on Yaşar.

'Give me the chip. Give me the starter chip. The starter chip.' He surrenders it meekly. He is genuinely scared, whether of her or the tow-truck incident she can't say. Leyla is shaking with fear and anger now. She slips in behind the wheel. The heels go in the back. She can drive this heap of scrap barefoot. 'I'll drive, you navigate. Family conference. Right now. Having my car kidnapped by thugs is not in my terms and conditions.'

*

In Kuzguncuk, old wooden Ottoman houses step down the street beneath generous trees. They are painted bold and bright; chrome yellow, ultramarine, crimson and pink. Upper storeys overhang; old men and cats sit in the shade, world-watching. Screens of pierced and painted wood shelter top-floor balconies. Everyone who is sensible enough not to have a job to go to is up there, trying to catch any wind. Old men and cats have never been sensible.

Ayşe goes slowly up between the bright houses. The street is steep, the day is hot, the boots are tight, the cobbles treacherous to heels. The old men look over their glasses at her; someone madder than they. She is looking for a blue house; blue as a cornflower. A city witch lives there; an urbomancer, a psychogeographer. Ayşe loves this neighbourhood, its sheltered green valley pulled around it like a shawl. For a time she had entertained Kuzguncuk as a location for the gallery. The Bosphorus Bridge ran a kilometre to the north, the expressway looped over the ridge at the head of the valley, ferryboats could be glimpsed down through the leaning houses and fairy-light-strewn branches, but none spoiled the perfumed charm of Kuzguncuk. Kuzguncuk's seclusion was its limitation: she would have sat days on end waiting for the door bell to tinkle. People came to look, to wander, to waste time and chance upon small joys. No one can build a business on serendipity. Eskiköy was grey and dirty and old but it was in the heart of the antiquarian district. For wanderers and meanderers and stumblers-over of trifles, historians of the spirit of place, psychogeographers, Kuzguncuk is perfect.

The blue house is the last in the row, hard against the chain-link fence. Behind it, judas trees climb the steep valley side. Ayşe rattles the wind chimes by the front door. A face appears from a heart-shaped opening in the balcony screen; a woman of middle age and wild big curling hair, frog-featured, bright eyed.

'The door's open, come on up.' Kuzguncuk famously closed its police station from a dearth of crime.

Selma the urbomancer is dressed in floppy silk pyjamas and toe rings. Cushions and bolsters line three sides of the balcony, a proper divan. Ayşe eases her killing fashion boots off. There is not a breath of wind up on the balcony either. Tea there is, and sesame halva.

'The Jews, darling. They make the best halva.' A remnant Jewish community survives in Kuzguncuk. Also Greeks and Armenians. Churches, mosque and synagogue face each other over a crossroads. Selma Özgün's purpose is to know these things, and why. Urbomancer. City witch. Selma Özgün had been Ayşe's tutor in Ottoman divan calligraphy but discovered that a better living could be made just walking the city's streets charting mental maps, recording how history was attracted to certain locations in layer upon layer of impacted lives in a cartography of meaning; delineating a spiritual geography of many gods and theisms; compiling an encyclopaedia of how space had shaped mind and mind had shaped space through three thousand years of the Queen of Cities. Hers was a walking discipline, like the practices of the peripatetic dervishes. It proceeded at the speed of footsteps, which is the speed of history, and at that speed, on those long walks which are the science's method, connections and correspondences appear. Strange symmetries appear between separated buildings as if some urban continental drift has taken place. Streets follow ancient, atavistic needs. Tramlines track ancient watercourses, the words of gods and emperors are spoken in stone. Human geographies, maps of the heart; fish markets far from the sea, districts in which trades have become fossilized, or die out in one generation only to return decades later. Subtle demarcations; odd transitions between restaurant cuisines: Aegean on this junction, eastern down that alley; cursed sites where no business had ever succeeded though a neighbour two doors down will flourish; addresses where if you live on one side of the street you are ten times more likely to be burgled than on the other. All these things Ayşe has learned on long evening walks with Selma Özgün through the city, seemingly meandering, always rich with hidden purpose and secret intent. The lost peoples of Istanbul fascinate Selma Özgün most; the Greeks, the Jews, the Armenians and the Syrians, the Rom and the Rus, the remnants of the old empire, and how the incomers from the hinterland of the new European empire have unconsciously taken up the districts and streets and lives and voices of the displaced ghosts.

Articles and papers Selma Özgün has produced:

A list of Bosphorus wrecks.

Outbreaks of contagious suicides.

The homosexual map of Istanbul, from the days of the Janissaries to the present.

The seemingly spontaneous paths called desire lines that humans track across any newly bared piece of terrain.

Geographic clusters of needs and desires in small ads on online forums.

Evolution in populations of fish that became isolated in lost Roman tanks and cisterns; towards paleness, clamminess, eyelessness.

Today Selma Özgün paints her toenails, puffing with effort as she leans forward to apply the brush; she's a rurally built woman.

'I've been invited on to a bastarding government think-tank,' Selma Özgün says, pushing her toes into the light and the air, the better to dry the polish. 'I tried to tell them they'd made some kind of ridiculous mistake – me, for all that's holy – but no. A car is being sent, apparently. So I'd better look worth the money they're lavishing on me. So how's the gallery doing? Are you still selling those iffy Armenian gospels?'

'They're all perfectly genuine.'

'That's the problem.' Selma has never concealed that she thinks Ayşe a smuggler, a looter, a calligraphic mercenary, a Jimmy Choo tomb-raider. 'So what whim brought you over to Asia this pleasant morning?'

'I'm trying to find a Mellified Man.'

'Roc eggs, Prophet's swords, djinn lanterns; any other impossible things you'd like me to find before dinner?'

'I've taken a commission from a client. He seems to think it's entirely possible.'

Selma Özgün pulls her shameful feet out of the air and public view. Even in easy-going, accommodating multicultural Kuzguncuk, she is considered an eccentric of English proportions.

'And who is this client?'

'Professional confidentiality.'

'Professional confidentiality be damned. Tell me.'

Selma Özgün finds the idea of skin-to-skin data transfer horrifying so Ayşe writes the client's name on a card. Selma Özgün dons reading glasses on a gold chain around her neck.

'No, nothing, darling. Is he from Iskenderun?'

'Should he be?'

Selma Özgün sighs.

'It'll be the Iskenderun mummy. He pops up every ten, fifteen years or so. You're not the first; very far from it, my dear. There's an entire minor industry built up around the Mellified Man of Iskenderun. It's one of the great legends of Istanbul, up there with the Lost Jewels of Aya Sofya. People have followed entire careers and published libraries of veritable tripe and squandered all-too-real fortunes on the Mellified Man of Iskenderun without any of them getting close to a single whiff of honey.'

'And I'm just the owner of a fine-art gallery who's good at the hard-to-get stuff.'

Selma Özgün pours more tea from the brass pot perched atop the double-boiler.

'According to Ergün Şaş at the Boğazici, the Mellified Man of Iskenderun is Hacı Ferhat, a member of a prosperous Alexandretta mercantile family whose fortunes faded spectacularly through the late eighteenth and nineteenth centuries. He has evidence of a series of theological disputes and shariat judgements between the resident imam and an itinerant dervish known as the Hairy Man from Cappadocia who fancied himself as a legalist, over the religious status of the Mellified Man. The Hairy Man declared it haram, which was why the Ferhats were suffering the judgement of God. Not only had Hacı Ferhat not been buried properly, in the earth, but he had been laid in a pagan coffin and, most heinous of all, mummification was an indirect attempt to avoid the Day of Judgement. The curse could only be lifted if they freed themselves of that pagan object and returned to true submission to God.'

'Sounds to me like the Hairy Man from Cappadocia knew a valuable religious artefact when he saw one.'

'I'm sure the point wasn't lost on the Ferhats. Anyway, they gave it to the Hairy Man who recited a couple of suras at them, proclaimed them halal and buggered off with Hacı Ferhat. The principle is simple, darling, find the dervish, find the Mellified Man of Iskenderun. Hacı Ferhat's journey in the company of the dervish and how he found his way to Istanbul, that's where theories come in. Sunni and Shi'a are nothing compared to the Mellified Man-hunters. They're a pack of vicious old queens. They get scratchy when their theories are criticized. One man you can trust spends his days down fishing off the Galata Bridge, everyone knows him as Red. Him you can trust; he's as mad as a lorry but he's neutral and everyone trusts him. He is Istanbul's greatest living authority on the Mellified Man of Iskenderun. You can't miss him but ask for him in my name, otherwise he'll just talk about fishing. Me, I'm not about truth, I'm about the beautiful lies that make up this city. And speaking of those . . .'

Selma Özgün heaves herself up off the divan. She has grown larger and more luxuriously ungainly since Ayşe met her last at a gallery opening in the autumn with the Storm of the Mating Ram blowing dust across the tiled floor. The days of the great meandering peregrinations across Istanbul may be ending. Selma Özgün's future pilgrimages will be through memory cities.

Selma Özgün's ascent of the stairs is heavier than her descent. She sets a small jar of amber fluid on the tea table.

'Go on.'

Ayşe holds the jar up to the broken light. Tiny flecks and flakes float suspended in the gold. It moves thickly, mellifluously when she tilts the jar. The lid is rusty, the smell confirms her analysis.

'Is it?'

'What do you want it to be?'

'Can I taste it?'

'If I said it was five hundred years old and I paid a three thousand old New Turkish lira for it, would that change the way it tastes?'

Ayşe unhesitatingly dips a forefinger into the amber fluid and puts it into her mouth.

'How did it taste?'

'Like honey.'

'Or I might have bought it from the corner shop.' Selma Özgün takes a spoonful and stirs it into her tea. The flecks swirl: flowers fragments, bee scales, flakes and shreds of human flesh. She drains the glass in a toast. 'Live forever. Well, darling, you're obviously intent on this and there's nothing I can do about it. Part of me fears what might happen if you find it. It's a treasure, a wonder of the world. Legends should stay legends, otherwise they just become history, when the natural course of things is the other way around, from history to legend. But I think that if anyone can, you can, darling.'

A car crunches big and heavy on the dead-end street. Its engine is very quiet. Selma Özgün glances through the pierced woodwork.

'That's the man from the ministry, come to take me away. Finish your tea, linger as long as you like, just leave the door. Good hunting my dear.' She embraces Ayşe, kisses her on each cheek. Her toenails gleam as she waddles down the stairs. Ayşe sits back in the divan and watches Selma bundle into the big car. She will finish her tea, but not linger because she has just enough time and Red is in just the right place to call on him among the fishing lines before she meets Adnan on the quay.

4

'Have you come for me?' Georgios Ferentinou asks the driver of the black car at his front step. It has black windows. The driver wears black. Heat shimmers from its black curves. The driver opens the door for Georgios Ferentinou. Clutching his briefcase to his chest, Georgios gingerly pats the upholstery as if he is sitting on living skin, as if his Greek body might defile it. The car is very quiet and smooth running. Georgios looks over his shoulder to see the frontage of the dervish house disappear around the crook in Stolen Chicken Lane. He has lost connection with his small world. The driver indicates right on Inönü Cadessi.

'Could we go the other way, by the ferry?' Georgios asks.

The driver flicks the indicator left.

The last black government car Georgios was in had turned right, over the Bosphorus Bridge into Asia.

The room was the colour of a diseased lung. Tobacco smoke had permeated the thick, glossy paint. Georgios had reckoned he could have run a licked fingertip over the wall and it would have come away brown. The three men across the trestle table smoked constantly and rhythmically, an ordered sequence of stubbings out, tapping a new cigarette out of a packet, the scratch of a cheap disposable lighter, the next grinding of a dead filter into the growing pile in the Efes ash tray. It was part of the intimidation, as was the smell; cigarette smoke mingled with the oils and phenols of military paint and a persistent hack of bleach. You could imagine anything being covered up by the bleach: urine, vomit, blood and excrement. It masked everything and concealed nothing.

'I will help any way I can,' Georgios had said. The seat was placed far enough away from the table to afford no psychological protection. 'I want you to know that I am a good citizen.' The men looked up, frowning, from their typed notes. They studied the sheets, showed lines to each other.

'Your parents,' said the man in the middle. The man on the right uncapped a blue ballpoint pen and held it poised over lined paper. Georgios Ferentinou began to feel more afraid than he had ever been in his life, ball-afraid, gut-afraid, bone-afraid; the afraid you will never be free from again.

'They've left the country,' Georgios Ferentinou said. Ballpoint man began to write. He did not stop for twenty minutes. The men, their room, their constant constant cigarettes, the smell of something concealed and the ever-present fear that his future depended completely on what happened in this room forced the words from Georgios like water from a pump. He had always imagined he would be stout in the face of intimidation, the interrogatee they would never break. It gushed from him. He was entirely in their power. Georgios was too young to have experienced the 1955 riots that would drive half of Istanbul's ancient Greek population – the last children of Byzantium – from their city. But the stories of that September night were the terrifying folk tales of his childhood: arson, rape, men forcibly circumcised on the street, the beards ripped from priests' faces, a man carefully smashing pearls one by one with a hammer in a looted Istiklal Cadessi store, blind to worth and beauty alike. The threats of 1980 hid behind a paint-sprayed shop shutter, an excrement-daubed church, an Advice to Quit taped to the door of Georgios' father's dental surgery. They took the advice. Spitefully, the new government stripped them of their citizenship.

Now he sat in a cigarette-smoke-coloured room pouring out his heart as if he were in love to three Intelligence men. How many traitors had he met? Well there was Arif Hikmet from the faculty and Sabri Iliç the economics editor from *Hürriyet* and Aziz Albayrak but he was from the State Planning Organization, he couldn't possibly be a traitor, and Recep Gül the mathematician and Devlet

Sezer the novelist. The names went down on ballpoint-pen man's pad. All day Georgios babbled out answers. At seven o'clock they set down their pens and folded their hands.

'Can I go now?' Georgios Ferentinou asked.

'One last question,' said the lead interrogator. 'Do you know Ariana Sinanidis?'

A smoke-yellow room in Üsküdar, in Asia, over the Bosphorus Bridge in a black car.

An involuntary sigh leaves Georgios Ferentinou at the sight of the Sultanahmet skyline from the Galata Bridge, the panoply of domes and minarets above the Golden Horn. From Aya Sofya and the Blue Mosque to the Süleymaniye and the Sultan Selim they wait like a holy army encamped. Ramazan ended a month ago but banners of festival lights bearing spiritual exhortations still hang between the minarets. Georgios sighs from the pure splendour of one of the world's great city vistas but also because he cannot remember how long it is since he last looked on this parade of architecture, when he last crossed the Galata Bridge. A tram rolls past and down on to the thronged quays of Eminönü. Not even the car air-conditioning can keep out the smell of frying mackerel. The virtual Istanbuls of Georgios' white library have no smell. Down and hooting through the crowds and on to the ferry. It is only twenty minutes from Europe to Asia but Georgios huffs and hauls himself up the companionways on to the deck. The driver insists on coming with him. Georgios suspects he may be armed. Everyone is up on the deck in the hope of some respite from the heat but there is not a breath on the Bosphorus this afternoon. Women in headscarves air themselves with little electric fans. A smooth-legged girl in hot pants and a halter top positions herself on the rail where the truck drivers can see her. The ferry breaks out past Seraglio Point and subtly adjusts its speed and course to run in behind a leviathan Russian gas tanker throbbing down the Bosphorus to the Sea of Marmara. Georgios appreciates the ferry captain's constant instinctive calculation of relative velocities. Consciousness is not requisite for intelligence.

Clear of the bridges, the big tanker has run up its kite-sails. Georgios shades his eyes to follow the lines up to where kites the size of a city block billow and strain. A kilometre up there is good wind. To the south, where the crack between continents widens up to the open horizon, the sky is black with kites.

Ariana had left Istanbul as the second wave of arrests came down. Georgios had come with her across this water. He remembers the gulls hanging over them, barely flicking their pointed wingtips as they slipped and slid around each other without ever disturbing the symmetry of the flock. The ferry had ducked in behind that long mole, into Haydarpaşa Station. Then he saw the jandarm truck parked before the station's Teutonic front and faltered at the top of the steps. The police were leaning on a wall and smoking. Police were not part of the plan.

'Don't come with me,' she had said. 'I'll be all right.' Train to Izmir, then the ferry to Piraeus. In the Aegean she would be safe. He had lifted his hand in farewell as she walked past the lounging policemen. They did not even look up. She never looked back. He watched until he was sure she had made it into the station. Georgios realized that he had been afraid so long it had become part of his breathing, his walking, his sleeping and reading and bathing. He understood that what he felt now was not loss, but the end to that fear. Loss would come and it would be terrible.

No calls, no letters, he had told her. Georgios had no doubt that his mail was opened, that there was a listening ear to his home telephone, that the university lines were routinely tapped, but he had expected some word back through the expatriate network. Ariana had disappeared as utterly as death.

The ferry sweeps past Haydarpaşa, no longer the gateway to Asia now the trains bore directly under the black, bone-rotten ooze on the bottom of the Bosphorus. Engines roar as the captain manoeuvres in to the slip. The car carries Georgios along the Marmara coast, under the shadow of the great concrete bowl of the Fenerbahçe stadium, up through an indifferent straggle of apartment blocks and over the ridgeline into sudden wonder. Here, in a narrow valley falling down to the Sea of Marmara, is a hidden place. Its foot stands on the ugly shoreline sprawl and the Bursa expressway but its head is swathed in green glory. Georgios glimpses sensuous, lenticular Ottoman roofs through the canopy of Mediterranean oak and peel-barked limes. A man in a cap swings open black wrought-iron gates three times his height. A second man in a sober suit nods and touches a finger to his ceptep headset. Georgios notices several similar casually arrogant men, with their jackets unbuttoned, along the curving drive. To the seaward side pavilions and kiosks tumble down the valley between landscaped rhododendrons and azaleas. Within this cocoon of cool green there is no sight of the mould-stained white cubes of the houses ranged up and down the ridgelines. Perfumes of cedar and Aleppo pine stray into the air-conditioning.

The house disappoints. The roof is too flat, the eaves too heavy; the balconies lean that little too far forwards, the effortless harmonies of classic Ottoman architecture are spoiled by over-emphasis. It is a good late-empire recreation of a minor Imperial Palace, the kind of place petty paşas were secluded in when their brothers ascended to the throne in those more polite times when rival siblings were no longer strangled on accession. Some late-era businessman will have built this, nostalgic for the brighter, clearer days when the empire was strong.

A woman in a suit samples Georgios' scent with a wand, checks him against her list, issues a security tag and escorts him up the stairs to the main salon. All is European high kitsch; man-high golden sconces crusted with gold leaf fruit and foliage, picky-spindly furniture in the French style. Cherubs, angels, Roman gods and minor members of the Christian pantheon tumble together in the painted ceiling, easy and ecumenical among the sunbeams. They are rendered as one might expect in a culture with no tradition of figure painting.

The upstairs salon is a miniature Versailles Hall of Mirrors. Gilding flakes from the mirror frames, the glasses are blackened and patchy where the silvering has oxidized. Cheap. A waiter offers

Georgios coffee and a few cubes of sweets. The salon is full of groups of men in good suits. They talk comfortably and familiarly as if they see each other every week, they balance their coffee and baklava with ease. Georgios circles around them, old and fat and self-conscious in his greasy-elbowed jacket and too-tight good shirt.

Another singleton catches Georgios' eye and loops around the constellations of confident men. His suit is grey and mall bought, his shirt collar uncomfortable and his cuffs caught over the ends of his jacket sleeves. Identifying a fellow in social distress, he stands by Georgios in the deep window bay that looks down across the gardens with its shrubs and kiosks, over the scum of strip development to the sea. The kite-sails of ships clearing the strait fill the sky like a flock of dark migratory birds.

'I could do with something to wipe my fingers on,' the man says.

'I think there are napkins by the door,' Georgios says.

'I meant that by way of apology for a sticky handshake,' the man says. He's in his late twenties, with a suspicion of beard, neatly trimmed in a way that suggests a more natural growth for normal working life. He has bright animal eyes and a brown face that has seen a lot of sun. His handshake is sticky but firm, outdoorsy. 'Emrah Beskardes.'

'Georgios Ferentinou.'

'It would be dishonest to say that I'd heard of you.'

'Oh, no one's heard of me. Not for a long time.'

'I can guarantee no one's heard of me at all.'

'What do you work in?'

'I'm a zoologist.' Georgios is not one to sneer at another's field of knowledge. All learning interests him. True wisdom leaks from the joins between disciplines. 'I specialize in how signals communicate across animal populations.'

Georgios raises his eyebrows. He hasn't lost that tell-tale of intellectual curiosity. 'I can see how that might be very useful.'

'To be honest, I'm not entirely sure what I can contribute,' Emrah Beskardes says. 'The money's good though. Do you mind if I ask?'

'Not at all, not at all. I am ... I was ... an economist. An experimental economist. I've been out of it a few years.'

A sudden ringing pierces the high-grade chatter; not the chiming of some fanciful ormolu clock but a man in a suit banging his spoon on the rim of his coffee cup.

'Ladies and gentlemen, if you'd like to follow me through.'

'I suppose we'd better do our part for the motherland,' Beskardes says. He quickly and discreetly slides the nozzle of a nano-inhaler up his nose and gives a short puff. He offers the tiny cone to Georgios. Georgios declines. It fascinates him that etiquette buttons up its gloves while technology waltzes around the world.

The merchant who built this little palace spent his money on the public facade. The salon at the rear of the house is unadorned, almost dowdy in its flat pilasters, cracked cornicing, peeling paint faded from old gold to nauseous mustard. The windows overlook storerooms and garaging, the solar plant and a power line dipping down between the built-over ridges into this hidden valley. The organizers have laid out a horseshoe of tables with an old-fashioned smartsilk screen on the wall at the open end. No ceptep downloads here; nothing to take away. There are two types of water on the tables but no notepads or pens. Emrah Beskardes draws a house on the child's magic slate set at his place and then erases it with evident pleasure.

The delegates seat themselves. Georgios notes that they stay with the same social clusters they had formed in the main salon. Only three women. A tall, thin man with impossibly long hands bustles through the double doors to take up a position at the open end of the court of faces and Georgios experiences two sensations, both linked, he never expected to feel again. One is a tightening in the base of his belly; muscles long-buried there remember their duty to armour the body against threat. The other is slow, prickling contraction of his balls. Georgios knows this man. The last time he saw him was across an arrangement of tables like this, with bottled water sparkling and still, at the meeting that forced him into retirement. His name is Professor Ogün Saltuk. He is Georgios' eternal enemy.

Age has been kinder to you than me, Georgios thinks as he watches Professor Saltuk slowly scan the room. *We were skinny young men, wiry on work and theory. Your hair went first but you were wise enough to shave it off entirely and your beard still holds some black.*

'Ladies and gentlemen,' Professor Saltuk says. 'Thank you all for coming today to this inaugural meeting of the Kadiköy Group. I'm sorry if it's all seemed rather James Bond, but undertakings of this kind – as experimental as this – of necessity must be carried on behind closed doors, in secret, on a need to know basis. I appreciate that some of you have come at short notice and from a considerable distance today, I hope your hotels are comfortable. I assure you we will sort out that billing issue. Well now; introductions: I am Professor Ogün Saltuk of the University of Istanbul School of Economics.' He pauses for a small sip of water. Emrah Beskardes is already drawing him as a lizard on his magic slate. Saltuk continues. 'We've been deliberately chosen from a wide range of disciplines: experimental economics, materials physics, epidemiology, political and economic analysts, historians, a psychogeographer, even our very own science-fiction writer.' He nods to a stocky, middle-aged man with a greying beard, who manages to look gracious.

'Zoologists,' Beskardes whispers and erases his reptile-Saltuk.

'Many disciplines and backgrounds; you'd wonder if we could possibly have anything in common. I'll not be so gauche as to say, love of this great country, but I will say, we all care about it. We care about it very much. Each of us, in his – or her – own way is deeply concerned about this great nation; its past, its present and yes, its future. Whatever other political entities claim our loyalty, first and foremost we are all good, concerned citizens of Turkey.

'In our five thousand years of civilization, our history has often been the handmaid of geography. We lie exactly midway between the North Pole and the Equator. We are the gateway between the Fertile Crescent and Europe, between landlocked Central Asia and the Mediterranean world and beyond that, the Atlantic. Peoples and empires have ebbed and flowed across this land. Even today sixty per cent of Europe's gas supply either passes down the Bosphorus or runs under our very feet through pipelines. We have always been the navel of the world. Yet our favoured location by its very nature surrounded us with historical enemies; to the north, Russia to the south, the Arabs; to the east, Persia and to the west, the Red Apple itself, Europe.'

The Red Apple, the myth of Ottoman imperialism. When Mehmet the Conqueror looked out from the parapets of his fortress of Europe at Constantinople, the Red Apple had been the golden globe in the open palm of Justinian's statue in the Hippodrome, the symbol of Roman power and ambition. Mehmet rode through the crumbling Hippodrome, the decaying streets of dying Byzantium and the Red Apple became Rome itself. The truth of the Red Apple was that it would always be unattainable, for it was the westering spirit, the globe of the setting sun itself.

'Now we find ourselves caught between Arab oil, Russian gas and Iranian radiation and we found that the only way we could take the Red Apple was by joining it.'

This is poor stuff, Georgios thinks. *You would not insult under-graduates' intelligence with this.*

'This group has been convened as an informal think-tank working in parallel with the Haceteppe group in Ankara. I had been working with MIT on the idea of a pure blue-sky group for some time but circumstances have forced our hand. As you know, there was a bomb attack yesterday on a tram in Beyoğlu. We're in possession of additional information that has led MIT to raise the general security level to red one. I'm not going to tell you what that information is; that's the idea behind the group. You may have heard of my work; I published a book ... *Great Leap Forward: How Ignorance Really is Bliss?* No? It was an English-language publication ... Anyway, the thesis is that intelligence, working on minimal information, can make leaps of intuition far beyond those achievable by directed thinking.'

I know this theory, thinks Georgios Ferentinou. *I know it very well indeed. And you've learned the second part of it equally well; that the prerequisite for this creative Great Leap Forward is a sufficient, rich and diverse ecology of information, with no data outweighing any other. Not perfect information, that economic lie, but a landscape in equilibrium.*

'We've gathered a group of the most diverse and original thinkers in Turkey. We've cast our net very wide; we've aspired to the eclectic. I believe that this diverse group, working on minimal information, may reach insights and intuitions that the Haceteppe group never will. Thinking is allowed here; everything is permitted. These are big wide blue skies. One thing I would say is; in sessions, don't depend on your own strengths. Allow yourselves to play, to be surprised.

'You'll be relieved that we don't require any mental heavy lifting, not today. This has been an introductory session; a chance to get to know each other and your diverse fields of work. I'd encourage you not to hurry away, to stay around and talk. We are on a government tab.' Small but appreciative laughter from the older academics. 'We'll run four sessions over the course of this week. You'll appreciate that I can't give you any documentation or briefings to take away with you, but I will leave you with one thought. Just play with it, kick it about, let it roll around in your head.' Saltuk makes television presenter gestures with his figures. He has also had his teeth whitened. Georgios now notices their perfect occlusion. Exactly meeting teeth are false and vaguely terrifying. Georgios finds his own gritting. 'Don't censor yourself, don't be afraid. One word. Gas.'

The bell rings up and down Özer's trading floor. The Artificial Intelligences shut down around Adnan like butterflies folding their wings. The market is closed. A quarter of a million after margin payments, in tight trading. Adnan has been riding the Iron Condor, trading options on the twenty-four-hour delivery market. It is part of the foreplay to Turquoise, trying to subtly tickle up the market to maximize the value of his hot Iranian gas. Adnan loves options, the quick-buck ballsiness of the short-order market, hedging strategies changing minute by minute as the market price hovers around the strike price. Straddles and strangles, butterflies and that Iron Condor; Adnan's shifted strategies constantly, anticipating market moves. It's not about the gas. It's never about the gas, carbon credits, oranges. The gross material is irrelevant. The deal is the thing. It's trading deals, contracts. There are even derivatives markets in onions. The market is money in constant motion. The market is endless delight.

When Adnan returned to Kaş in his first Audi and bespoke suit the boatmen along the harbour jeered him, the bar owners and restaurateurs threw one-liners but behind the barbs and the banter was the realization that you could make it out of Kaş, make it all the way to Istanbul, make money.

No one could understand how he had made that money. 'You sell things you don't even own, so you can buy them back cheaper when the price goes down?' Adnan's father had said. 'How is that right?' They were on the boat. It was moored firmly to the quay. Some day Adnan might brave it out into the turquoise sun-dazzle of the Mediterranean. Not this day. 'Short selling,' Adnan said. 'It's a way of hedging your bets.' His father had shaken his head and thrown up his hands when he tried to explain derivatives, options and futures and that every day contracts worth ten times the economic output of the entire planet changed hands.

'It seems to me that you people don't need us,' Adnan's father said. 'Banks and funds and companies like Özer, all you need are your contracts and your tradeables. You don't need a real economy. It gets in the way, a real economy.'

'It's just buying and selling, Dad.'

'Oh I know, I know. All the same, when they ask, I'd like to be able to tell people what my son actually does.'

Adnan strips off the red jacket and throws it to one of his junior writers as he strides off the floor. The thing is saturated with per-spiration. He's occasionally tried to calculate how much liquid he sweats out on the floor. At least a football match worth; probably more. They only play ninety minutes, with half time. They can wear shorts. Adnan is almost permanently dehydrated. He enjoys the little edgy glow, the vague spikiness. It works well with the nano, and the first drink always hits like a hammer.

Behind the glass in Settlements, Kemal looks up. He frowns at Adnan, grimaces strangely.

'Where are you going?' Kemal asks.

'I've a meeting.'

'Meeting? Who are you meeting?'

Adnan bends kiss-close. 'White. Knight.'

'I thought that wasn't until tonight.'

'It's not until tonight, at the hour of seven o'clock when a very fine speedboat will take us out to the Princes Islands. In the meantime I am going to get possibly the best shirt available in Istanbul from my tailor and spend maybe an hour at my barber because I don't want to look like a bloody student and the inside of my nose is hairy as a dog's ass. And I may very well buy Ayşe something silver because she likes silver and she is hot in silver. And by the time I've done all that, it will be time for the speedboat.'

'So you're not looking over it this afternoon.' Kemal chews his bottom lip. He's been doing that more lately but Kemal is always jittery. He's been taking ever-larger doses of concentration nano. He's the edgy one at the Kebab Prophet's, the pop-eyed war-movie grunt who'll run amuck with the chaingun: Twitchor: Ultralord of Nervy.

'Not today.' It's a point of professional honour to Adnan to be there when the accounts are settled. The Sarioğlus pay their way. 'So if you've any awkward little bodies to bury, this would be a good day to do it.' Adnan claps Kemal hard on the back. The guy almost rattles.

'Go and fuck our White Knight,' says Kemal but the humour is uncomfortable, like grit in an eye.

'I certainly shall. I'll call.' Not for the first time Adnan wonders about the staunchness of Kemal, of all his partners. He's thought through every detail of Turquoise; the shell companies, the financial instruments, the subtle market manipulation and the hedging strategies; everything except the exit strategy.

Great-Aunt Sezen has lived so long on the balcony that she has become part of the architecture. No one can remember when she first dragged her bed through the family room on to the little iron balcony hung with a Turkish flag but at least two generations of Gültaşli males handy with welding torches and power tools have put up screens and roofs and added extensions and annexes so that Great-Aunt Sezen's balcony is a second apartment clinging like a spider to the first. Summer and winter, she will be found there. She believes that it is bad for the lungs to sleep indoors. Great-Aunt Sezen claims not to have had a cold in thirty years. And she can watch Bakirköy flow beneath her, and the aeroplanes coming in to land, which she loves precisely because she has never been on one and never will. She watches them as wildlife, a branch of ornithology.

She is a lioness of a woman. From the outside of the building her presence fills the apartment. She is a big woman, of rustic build. She is crowned by an animal-thick, pure grey shock of hair, combed and styled every day by the women in the house. She speaks little; she has little need. Her eyes are bright, penetrating, see all and understand more. She can still barely read, the world comes to her through her sprawling, brawling, ever-expanding family and the radio, which she adores, especially now it has been connected to a solar panel. She has no time for television. She is the mater familias of a real life soap opera. She is universally adored.

Sub-Aunt Kevser is her Vizier. She consults, conveys and commands. She interprets the will of Great-Aunt Sezen. She issues fetvas. If Great-Aunt Sezen is in favour, it is halal, A-Number-One, approved with the highest possible authority. If she says that Great-Aunt Sezen does not like it, it is haram, condemned, with no hope of appeal. Sub-Aunt Kevser frequently does not deign to trouble Great-Aunt Sezen with trivialities; all that is necessary is whether, out of Kevser's long and deep knowledge of the matriarch, Great-Aunt Sezen would or would not approve. Sub-Aunt Kevser is wire-thin, of indeterminate middle-age, short-haired and square-spectacled, itchy with constant nervous energy. She never seems comfortable on a chair or a divan. She has never married, it was never expected that she ever would. She is Vizier and Gatekeeper.

'He kidnapped my car,' Leyla Gültaşli says.

Yaşar raises a finger. Sub-Aunt Kevser insists on parliamentary proceedings for family councils. Great-Aunt Sezen approves of proper order.

'Point of information. I think you'll find that it is Ceylan-Besarani's car.'

'What I mean is that I took this job on the assumption that I was to put together a funding strategy for a nanotech start-up company,' Leyla says. 'Nobody said anything to me about hoods holding the company car to ransom, or about dodgy relatives who seem to have been grey nano dealers and disappear owing a lot of money, or about using half a family heirloom as a loan certificate.'

The Gültaşli/Ceylans look at her. The council consists of Sub-Aunt Kevser, Chief-Uncle Cengiz, In-house Cousin Deniz, Aunt Betül, Yaşar and Great-Aunt Sezen on her balcony, the radio burbling like a little singing bird.

'I'm a professional, I expect a little professional respect.'

Silence around the table. The Honda engine still stands under it on a layer of motorsport magazines.

'I'm not doing anything until someone tells me what's going on.'

Aunt Betül breaks the silence. She is the family genealogist.

'Mehmet Ali is on the Yazıcoğlu side of the family, in that his great-grandfather Mehmet Paşa is also your and Yasar's great-grand-father, so you're all second cousins. Mehmet Paşa is Great-Aunt Sezen's father, his eldest son Hüseyin was head of this branch of the family until his death twelve years ago – taken before his time, much missed – his third son is Mustafa Ali your grandfather who was a bus driver in the 1940s and married into the Özuslus of Demre, whereas his youngest daughter Fazilet married Orhan Ceylan in 1973 and set up a branch of the family in Zeytinburnu. So you are related and there is a claim of kinship there.'

Family first, family always. Since she arrived off the bus from Demre, Leyla has feared that her escape to Istanbul was permitted because it had been agreed that it was temporary. One day her mother would have a fall, her father a mild stroke. In Istanbul the ceptep would call, a call of kinship would be made and she would spend the rest of her life spooning food into her father's mouth, helping her mother up and down the street steps into the road. Her brothers would add an extra floor on to the leggy house, she would be comfortable with her own kitchen and bathroom and a little balcony from which she could look across plastic roofs like rolling waves to the unobtainable sea. But she wouldn't be free. Women of Demre didn't have freedom. They had responsibilities. Career, what does a woman want a career for? Women don't have careers, it's against nature. As a girl it had always been implicit that Leyla's career was to be the carer. Her sisters would have the husbands and babies.

For her sister Rabia's twelfth birthday Leyla bought her a wonderful wonderful present, a thing she had seen online that had filled her heart with amazement: Magic! Sky! Lanterns! As the sky darkened everyone had gone up on to the flat new flat roof – Aziz had just finished a newlywed floor – and her father had lit the little wad of fuel-soaked cotton wool. They stood in a circle around the glowing tissue paper balloon, holding it carefully as instructed, doubtful that so flimsy and flammable a thing could do anything other than catch fire and blow on the wind. Then, wonderfully, wonderfully, her father had let go, it had bobbed toward the concrete, then lifted, climbing high and fast, a globe of light receding into a purple sky streaked with indigo cloud: the Magic! Sky! Lantern! going higher and higher until the wind from the mountains caught it and swept it over the top of the tallest of the Russian hotels and out over the dark sea.

Again, again! Rabia had cried and they had sent the rest of the pack of four aloft, one after another but the magic only works the first time and as Leyla peered to make out the tiny shining dot against the banded clouds she had thought, *I shall be like that. I shall rise so high and brilliantly I can never be pulled back down to the tomato fields of Demre.*

But family pulls and family ties and family binds and if she has called this conference in the Gültaşli family living room, it's partly because she hasn't been told everything she should about Mehmet Ali and the Koran contract, and partly to tell them not take her for granted or assume the liberties to which family feels entitled. She is here today as Leyla Gültaşli, professional marketing consultant, not Little Tomato with her nose in books. *Take me seriously.*

Chief Uncle Cengiz is the senior male and rules the outdoor world of business and dealings as the women rule the indoor world of home and family.

'He was always trouble that one, from the day and hour he was born. His father was a truck driver, so he was never there to give the boy the right discipline and then when he was thirteen his mother upped and walked out with his little sister. This is what's wrong with this country; nobody sticks with anything, as soon as there's any trouble or effort or they hit a rough patch they get up and walk away. When the going gets tough, the tough get out. Well, his Dad couldn't mind him, not with the hours on the truck, and at the time I was working with his uncle Aziz Yazıcoğlu in the parts shop. He hadn't the room for the lad so he came to me, I'd space after Semih got married, so I took him in. Worst thing I ever did. I was never done with the police coming round. Your Aunt Esma's head was turned. I minded him until the army would take him, in the idea that it might knock a bit of sense into him. Well it knocked something into him because whenever he came back he moved straight out into his own apartment. None of us saw hide nor hair of him for six months until he turned up in a very flash suit and a sportscar and some Russian Natasha on his arm. From tapping everyone and his wife for cash to wads of money in six months? There's no way you do that righteous and sober.'

'How long ago was this?' Leyla asks.

'Three years.'

'Did anyone ever ask him where all this money came from so suddenly?'

'A bit of trading, a bit of property development, migrant worker deals. Every flash bastard was coining it after we joined the EU,' Uncle Cengiz growls.

Sub-Aunt Kevser clears her throat. Great-Aunt Sezen does not approve of salty language. Leyla is making Cengiz Gültaşli look like a fool in his own living room. She forestalls her next question: *And you believe that?* But she has to ask, she has made him look like a fool.

'Whose idea was it to go to this man for a loan?'

'None of the commercial banks would touch us,' Yaşar said.

'What about Aso? Did he not have contacts, or relatives who could have helped?'

'There are Kurdish regional development funds for high- and emerging tech start-ups. The problem is, they're based in Diyarbakır.'

'Are you saying that you didn't apply for regional funding because you didn't want to go Kurdistan?'

'I work with a Kurd. A Kurd is my business partner. And he's more than that, he's a friend. What I'm saying is, I didn't apply because they don't have the infrastructure. Istanbul is a nano town, Ankara's a nano town, Diyarbakır's a . . . town.'

'I made the decision,' Uncle Cengiz says. 'No one would touch the boys, or they wanted impossible securities or too much of the company or the rates they were asking were sinful. Family rates and the option to buy back the fifty per cent when they made proper money. You go to your family first.'

'He was people trafficking then,' Yaşar says. 'Smuggling in migrant workers from the Stans.'

'Well he's doing nano now,' Leyla says. 'The kitchen was full of plastic vials. Does anyone have any idea who this man is who hijacked the car? The one he owes money to? Can we do a family thing and ask around? Someone must have an idea. It's important, he said he was going to keep an eye on me. If he's keeping an eye on me he's keeping an eye on everyone. He scares me a lot.'

The men at the table mumble.

'And does anyone know anything about Mehmet Ali? All I'm told is second-cousin Mehmet Ali has half a Koran that gives him half the company: find the Koran. Am I looking for a Holy Koran or am I looking for the man? Is he alive, is he dead, is he in Istanbul, is he in Turkey?'

'He's alive,' says Aunt Betül. 'I'd know if he wasn't. It's a gift.'

'Well then, help me. You wanted to keep it in the family, then I need the family to help me.'

'We will help you,' says Sub-Aunt Kevser. 'We're your family, we will always support you.'

From the balcony comes the voice of Great-Aunt Sezen, like the voice of the holy book itself, 'The Koran wants to be one.'

Let there be no doubt, Ayşe Erkoç is wearing the best shoes on the Galata Bridge. Not that anyone but her will notice; the trams are too relentless; the traffic too dense and male; the tourists too dazzled by the revelation that Istanbul, close with its vistas and wonders, suddenly spreads itself to them against a cloth of gold sunset; the pedestrians too intent on home; the teenagers sneaking out of the informal nano-bazaar that has grown up in the underpasses and tunnels and gun shops at the Beyoğlu end of the bridge too paranoid and inarticulate; the thieves and pickpockets and phoney shoe-shines too focused on their scams to notice a pair of shoes flashing past them. As for the men and very occasional women leaning over the rail, rods bristling the air like whiskers, no shoes could disturb their concentration even if they were on the feet of the Mahdi himself. Ayşe momentarily imagines that the hundreds of rods are oars and the bridge is a fishing-galley, unmooring itself, as the old iron pontoon bridge had been unmoored and sailed upstream to Bal-atkarabaş, a *dromon* swinging out into the Golden Horn bound for high adventure. Between the stools and the plastic buckets of catch and bait and jars of maggots and mackerel heads and the plastic tool boxes of hooks and flies and the butts of rods resting on the ground are many traps for fine shoes. But Ayşe passes lightly and fleetly. God, they are good, these shoes.

'What is the dress for, darling?' her mother had asked as Ayşe once again stripped and clothed herself in the museum of her childhood.

'I told you last night,' she said, pulling on the shoes.

'You were here last night?' Ayşe had seen Fatma Erkoç look over to her diligent daughter Güneş, who had nodded. 'Oh yes. Of course you were. Lovely dress. Is it new?'

'We're having dinner out on the Princes Islands with Ferid Adataş. He's a financier, very rich. Multi-millionaire. So, will I do?'

'You'll do for a multi-millionaire,' Fatma had said. Ayşe kissed her lightly on the lips. She left a molecule-thin whisper of lipstick. 'Oh, darling, no, the shoes,' she called after her departing daughter. 'Red is no colour for a lady.'

Red the shoes. Red the man. *You can't miss him*, Selma Özgün. Red the fisherman, Master of Mellified Men, is dressed head to toe in his titular colour. Red and gold Galatasaray baseball cap, red zip-up jacket, zipped to the neck despite the heat trapped up on the bridge, red track bottoms sagging at ass and knees. Only his shoes fail; fake Converse All-Star sneakers going at the welts and the eyelets, in standard denim blue. *You can get those in red*, Ayşe thinks. He leans against the rail beside the Eminönü-side stairway, cigarette in hand, sea-eyed, gaze drawn out along the line of his rod, beyond where Golden Horn opens into Bosphorus, beyond the passage-ships, beyond Asia. There is nothing in his bucket. There doesn't need to be. Ayşe wonders how, in her many crossings of the Galata Bridge she could have failed to notice the fisherman in red, so garish among his demure, old-man-coloured colleagues. How many times has she been the fast one, the busy one, the preoccupied one, not raising her head to look? The invisibility of red. You see the colour but not the man.

Ayşe finds a place at the rail beside the fisherman. Odours of barbecuing fish rise from the restaurants on the lower deck.

'Any luck then?' Ayşe asks.

'Not a whit. The weather's all wrong. They're all staying down where it's dark and cool. Sensible fish says I.' Ayşe cannot but wonder if the reason he isn't catching, the reason all the buckets lined up along the footpath are empty, is because the mackerel have all been fished out long ago. The legendary gold of Byzantium, sunk in the Golden Horn to keep it out of the hands of the conquering Turks, would surely have long since been hooked up piece by piece by generations of Galata fishermen. It's a recognized Istanbul profession, fishing lives away by the water's edge.

'Selma Özgün sends her regards.'

'And how is the bold Selma?'

'Working for the government.'

'I hope they're paying her a lot.'

'It's a government think-tank.'

Red suppresses a smile. His face is thin and dark from elements and seasons, his chin stubbled. His fingers are yellow from cigarettes he never smokes.

Ayşe says, 'I am ...'

'Ayşe Erkoc.'

'Have we ever ...' Ayşe tries to picture him shaved, suaved, suited and scented.

'No. I'd remember. It's a small city, is what. We all live in small cities.'

'Selma says that you're the man to ask about Hacı Ferhat.'

Red taps the fisherman next to him and points to the lower level. He puts a newspaper on Red's stool and repositions the tackle boxes. Territory at the rail is fiercely contested and tightly time-shared. It is only as Red passes the giant Turkish flag that covers the stairway and pier head that Ayşe realizes why she has never noticed him on all her crossings of the Golden Horn. A man in red beside a red flag. Hiding in plain sight. He raises a finger to the maitre d' of the first landward-side restaurant. The maitre d' flicks a finger; teenage waiters set up a table and two stools by the footpath.

'These are the worst restaurants in Istanbul,' Red says. 'The prices are outrageous, the fish is dreadful and the coffee execrable but I can keep an eye on my line.' He nods at the weft of lines dropping from the upper level past the restaurant front into the water. Ayşe wonders how he can tell his from the hundreds of others. This may be part of the legend. Coffee is brought, with water and roasted pistachios. Close to the water, in the shade of the bridge, there is respite from the heat. Cool eddies spiral in across the water.

'Before I tell you anything about the Mellified Man of Iskenderun, I must first ask you to take a look at me. What do you see? Do you see a first class honours graduate? Best in his year? Do you see a promising local historian, a writer for magazines on the secret delights of Istanbul life? You see a tramp and a bum, a man who stands with a line in his hands in all weather, a man with a face like an infant teacher's handbag, a ghost of the Galata Bridge. You see a wasted life. This is the face, this is the life of a man who pursued the Mellified Man of Iskenderun. Do not ever let the scent of honey seduce you.'

Too late, Ayşe thinks. *Selma Özgün already dripped that on to my tongue.*

'It's not for me, it's for a client.'

'Has he paid you?'

'A retainer.'

'As long as he's happy seeing his money thrown to the wind and the gulls.'

'My clients tend not to entertain such worries.'

'Good then. Here's how you will waste time, money and happiness on the Mellified Man. If Selma has sent you to me then she's given you the basics; the Ferhats, the curse and the Hairy Man of Cappadocia. After that, stories diverge, and stories become theories.

I mistrust theories. They're poor foundations for belief.'

Red lights a cigarette. He moves it like a baton, beating the rhythms in his words.

'Theories on the subsequent history of the Mellified Man of Iskenderun fall into three main categories, all of them geographical. By that I mean, they derive from which way the Hairy Man of Cappadocia turned. Thus we have the Northern School, the Eastern School and the Western School. The Northern School posits that Hacı Ferhat was brought to Trabzon on the Black Sea Coast, and thence to Crimea to the summer palace of the Putyatins, a princely family descended from the former kings of Kiev. Of course, the story is that it wasn't Rasputin cured the Tsarevich, it was honey from the coffin of Hacı Ferhat. When the Putyatins fled the revolution, they brought the Mellified Man with them in their exile to Istanbul. Depressingly, it's become tied in with Anastasia-hunters and Tsarevich theorists – if there's one thing worse than Mellified Man bores, it's Romanov theorists. Theories. Always these theories.'

Red leans forward, glowers at his fishing line, sits back and takes a nonchalant sip of coffee.

'The Eastern School posits that the Hairy Man of Cappadocia didn't come from central Anatolia at all but was a wandering dervish from Persia who had temporarily joined one of the anchorite communities around Nevşehir. He went back east with the coffin. This is where the story gets untidy, which interests me because real history is never tidy. The Northern School is one consistent theory, albeit embellished. The Eastern School is an entire bouquet of theories. Most agree that the dervish lost the coffin – died of disease, was assassinated, set upon by robbers, strangled by a rival, strangled by a lover, gambled it away. Some say that a renegade order of Alevis took it and that it passed down family lines and it only came to Istanbul in the 1970s when people started to migrate from the east en masse. Some say that it passed into the hands of Syriac Christians, or the Armenian Church, or older, primeval forms of Christianity like Nestorianism. Others say that the Kurds murdered the holy man, stole his coffin and took it to what is now Iraq to use as a centrepiece of a blasphemous Yazidi rite. Every ten years they draw off some of the honey and use it to cure ills and work wonders. People come from all over, both sides of the border. In this version the coffin only came to Istanbul in 2003, after the American invasion, and the Kurds brought it because it was the last place their enemies would look for it, in the Turks' greatest city. Another version has it that CIA special operations agents bought it in later 2001. They'd been working up there on the border for years – the place was a virtual dollar economy. It got impounded at Izmir when we refused to let the American fleet load and resupply just before Operation Restore Freedom. Customs has it, allegedly. Now, I particularly like these stories because I like the way that fable evolves in parallel with real world events. Unfortunately, I can't give them any credence. They're too public, and the Customs Secretariat is way too corrupt for the Mellified Man of Alexandretta to lay undisturbed in some warehouse for twenty-five years. Hacı Ferhat's been to Mecca – again – and Medina and St Catherine's monastery on Sinai and Jerusalem and even as far south as Ethiopia, to Axum, where he's been conflated with stories about the final resting place of the Ark of the Covenant. You'll note there isn't a Southern School; there used to be southern stories but they merged with the Eastern interpretation about fifty years ago. He's even been as far east as the Fire Temple in Baku.'

Red flicks the burned-down cigarette end into the water and lights another. A ferry sweeps through the gap between the lower tiers. It's good to be close to water, close to ships, low down on the waterline, Ayşe thinks. It's a fresh way to see. Were she wearing less formal shoes she would kick them off to curl her feet up beside her on the seat. This is story hour.

'Now we come to the Western School. These are particularly clever. The common base is that, after obtaining the coffin, our hairy man of Cappadocia passed west through Istanbul to the Balkans to join a dervish order in what's now Bosnia. It became a local relic and focus of pilgrimage after the dede of the tekke noticed honey leaking from the coffin and the legend developed that this honey, applied to the lips of soldiers, gave them the courage, strength and invulnerability of the Hacı himself. Wounds would spontaneously heal, bodies regenerate. It's obviously a variant of Hızır legend, but that didn't stop anointed partisans fighting off the Ottomans in the 1890s, the Germans in the Second World War and the Serbian militias during the 1990s. At the moment of the Bosnian people's greatest need, the tomb of Hacı Ferhat will again exude miraculous honey. Now this is far too good a story and of course every embattled Muslim from Sarajevo to Islamabad appropriated it. Pashtun mujahadin, Palestinian *intifada* stone-throwers, Chechen suicide bombers, even Kurdish fighters have claimed the protection of Hacı Ferhat. What interests me is how once again the Eastern School is slowly absorbing another tradition. In twenty years or so I expect it will have subsumed the Western School entirely. So, those are your three options. In two of them the Mellified Man of Iskenderun ends up in Istanbul, in one of them in a tekke in Bosnia.'

'I notice you're not telling me which one of them is correct.'

'No, I'm not.'

'Well, are there any which are demonstrably wrong?'

'The Tekke of Hacı Ferhat does not exist. There are several Nakshabendi Hakkani Golden Chain tekkes in Bosnia, but they are a sober order and not given to the veneration of relics. The Kadirilik are well established throughout the Balkans but their record keeping is fastidious and nowhere is there a mention of anything like a Mellified Man. Likewise the Rif'ai, though their main centre is in Albania. However, they are close to the Bektaşis and the Alevis, so a Mellified Man might have made his way back to Anatolia. The possibility remains that Hacı Ferhat could persist as a localized saint or have even passed into the Christian Church but given the weight of legend – invulnerable soldiers of matchless courage do attract attention – we would have heard about it. Certainly it attracted the attention of the Serbian Army in the latter days of the Bosnian War.

As the Serbians were being rolled back by NATO's Operation Deliberate Force, a small group of Serbian Special Forces under Major Darko Gagoviac was sent to locate and loot the body of Hacı Ferhat.'

'Loot a legend?' Ayşe asks.

'But it's not legend, is it?' Red says. 'He and his unit worked their way indiscriminately through dervish houses all across Bosnia. Hacı Ferhat was an excuse. Their mission was to kill as many Sufis and burn as many tekkes as possible. They found nothing – which doesn't mean there was nothing to find. As word of the destruction spread, the dervishes would certainly have hidden their treasure. You see? Nothing is known. Nothing is knowable. So I have to conclude that, much as I am charmed by the Western School, I ultimately find it unconvincing.'

'Tell me about the Russian School.'

'I find Russian involvement unpersuasive, for opposite reasons to the Western School. Any number of old white Russians claim to have the Mellified Man. This instantly makes me suspicious. Why Russians, why not Poles or Kashubians or Bulgars or Armenians? The funnel of history in the form of the Russian Revolution is too convenient – it smacks of historical engineering. It's the kind of story you would make up looking back from the present day. Sloppy thinking. If Hacı Ferhat had been in Crimea, he was much more likely to have been dislodged by the Crimean War, and so would have reached Istanbul sixty years earlier, or even France or England. Typical Russian self-aggrandizing, I fear. What kills it for me is that none of the Northern School stories existed at all before a book published in Moscow in 1992, just after the White Revolution, it's called *The Honey of God: The Romanovs and the Mellified Man*. It was written by an ex-Black Sea Fleet helicopter carrier captain called Dmitri Lebvedev, who obviously had too much time on his hands.'

'My late father was a commander in our Black Sea Fleet,' Ayşe says.

'I did my military service in the navy.' Red shrugs at his fishing line. 'Too much time on my hands.' He rises from his seat to check the line. Weighted hooks cast from above hurtle past Ayşe to plop into the languid water. A ferry swells out of ship-scape, in bound for Rüstempaşa.

'So it's some variant of the Eastern School,' she says.

'This is a labyrinth in which entire lifetimes can be lost. Selma will have warned you, I will warn you again. There are people who have given years of their lives – their entire – lives to studying the Mellified Man. Many of them were searchers like you, but they gave it up when they realized that if the Mellified Man were ever to be found, it would almost certainly not be from their theories, and the finding would prove that their theories were worthless and their entire lives manifestly wasted. Istanbulus can happily waste whole lifetimes on trivialities as long as reality is never allowed to intrude. Theories. Never let your theory be exposed to vulgar empiricism. If you wish to search further, I can point you in the same direction I have pointed all the others. Make of it what you will. All I have are stories. Perhaps stories are all there are – and that would be enough. That would be a colossal edifice of creativity. But if you want to talk to a direct descendant of Hacı Ferhat – or who claims to be – then you must go to Beshun. You can find her in the Egyptian Market. She only works mornings. Look for rabbits. Rabbits and vegetable seeds. As dear Selma told you, tell her, Red sent you.' He gets up from his chair, lights a fresh cigarette and peers down the length of his line into the water. 'Come on up, you bastards. The sun's off, it's the cool cool cool of the evening. Oh. By the way, you don't mind getting the coffee, do you?'

As he promised, it's overpriced. As Ayşe rattles off a grudging few cents as a tip, she notices a smaller, nimbler, faster craft come up alongside the ferry and then dashingly cut across it to curve in towards the landings at Eminönü. She hadn't noticed the time, the slant of the light, the length of the shadows, the deep gold of the hills of Asia. Her boat has arrived.

*

'We much prefer online applications,' says the smart man from the European Emerging Technologies Investment Board. He is quite handsome but knows it, which is a flaw in Leyla's book of smart men, and wears a nanoweave fabric tie that changes pattern every twenty seconds. That is a lesser flaw. The office is full of little nano toys and gewgaws; a sheet of nano-weave silk folds and refolds in restless origami while a pile of smart sand in a tray on his desk builds itself into endless pagodas, no two the same. Nano-impregnated liquid runs uphill to fall over a little water mill, a floor rug changes texture from pile to fur to quills to bark. Nothing holds its shape for more than thirty seconds in this twitching office

'I think I was in this place on an early acid trip,' Aso had whispered as they seated themselves at the itchy, compulsive desk while Mete Öymen retrieved his notes on Ceylan-Besarani. In his suit and shirt Aso is much more presentable as ambassador of Ceylan-Besarani than Yaşar. He has the presence of height and he's not fat, a thing Leyla dislikes in a pitch. It's not hard to tighten up a good look for your business. There is still room for Aso to improve: shoes for a start, and ironing.

'Online doesn't give you the immediacy of a face to face meeting,' Leyla says. 'You don't get the passion.'

Mete Öymen looks as if he might vomit at the thought of passion face to face. He studied his silkscreen.

'Nano. Yes. Eighty per cent of our applications are for nano start-ups.'

'We're not a start-up. This is development funding to build a prototype and market test.'

Again Mete Öymen studies his screen. 'You haven't come to us before.'

'We've had private funding so far. You have a fast-track fund.'

'It generally takes six to eight weeks.'

'We've got maybe four days.'

'I would have to say it's unlikely.'

'At least an expression of interest.'

'The next funding decision meeting is on Friday. It might be possible. How much are you looking for?'

'A quarter of a million.'

'Applications for funding over one hundred thousand go through the European Regional Technology Infrastructure Development Fund.'

'How quick is that?'

'Fast Track is quicker. There is an Accelerated Entry level for the ERTIDF and because it's a structural fund it doesn't attract as high a percentage of match-funding.'

'Friday?'

'Doubtful. It might be possible to split your EETIB Fast-track fund into two or even three separate applications, as long as none of them are over one hundred kay in value.'

'At least take a look at our presentation.'

Aso handshakes the code to Mete Öymen.

'It's best on your ceptep.'

Byzantium's not dead, he whispers to Leyla as Mete Öymen watches the pretty crawling molecules. The patterns stop playing on his eyeballs.

'I don't get it.'

Leyla feels Aso twitch. *Keep cool.*

'It's a universal bioinformatic read-write head. It stores information on non-coding DNA – junk-DNA as you call it. It turns every cell in the body into a computer.'

'Why would anyone want to have such a thing?'

Aso is shaking with suppressed anger. Leyla touches her hand to his arm.

'This is a world-changing technology,' she says. 'Revolutionary. Nothing will be the same.'

'There's little market for revolutions, I'm afraid. I'm not convinced it's commercially viable but throw in an application and it'll be judged on its merits. I'll need your most recent audited accounts, articles of incorporation, a statement that there are no financial encumbrances on the company and some indication of match-funding, in cash or kind.'

'We can get that to you.'

'If you want us to look at it in the next round it would need to be on my desk first thing tomorrow. I don't know if that gives you enough time.'

'We'll make the time, Mr Öymen.'

His handshake is as shapeless and indefinite as his nano.

Aso doesn't speak in the elevator. He doesn't speak in the lobby or on the street as they stomp through the evil heat to where Leyla has parked the car, cursing the virused autodrive that means she can't leave it to run around town by itself and come when called. He waits until they are belted in, engine running and pulling gingerly out before shouting 'Bastard!' so loudly that Leyla almost swerves into a kid on the way home from afternoon school.

'"Little market for revolutions, I'm afraid". Bastard! "I'm not convinced it's commercially viable": why is that, Mr Mete Öymen? Is it because you can't imagine everyone having the ability to store every piece of information they'll amass in their entire lives? Or is it because you can't see why people would want to be able to swap in talents and abilities and whole other personalities like ceptep apps? Or is it that you just can't see the advantage of personalized brain-to-brain telepathy? "But throw in an application and it'll be judged on its merits." You wouldn't recognize its merits if I carved them into your forehead with a laser, you snivelling, cowardly, patronizing, smug, jobs-worthy little Turkish bureaucrat. Apologies to any Turks here present. Sorry. I get passionate about it. I get angry about it. I'm not asking him to understand it down to the last detail; just see the bigger idea, see the possible, be awed by it. It excites me. This is total human makeover, man! This is humanity 2.0!'

'I'm trying to drive here,' Leyla says. It's cram-hour, Istanbul hot and impatient to get home, into the cool of home, shoes off jacket off air-conditioning on. Aso's is not the only anger on the streets.

She creeps the citicar forward through the stalled, sweating traffic. Truck wheels loom over her, crushing orbs.

'I come from a passionate people!' Aso cries. He is lucid with his arms when excited. Leyla ducks. 'I tell you something, we're a people who know injustice when we see it – and we've seen a lot – and that was an injustice. A fat, monstrous shit-stuffed injustice.'

'Don't kid yourself it's personal,' Leyla says. She threads the little silver three-wheeler between two dolmuşes. The packed passengers look more miserable even than Aso. 'It's nothing to do with you, or the project and it's certainly not eight hundred years of prejudice against the Kurds. Even if Öymen had thought it was the most brilliant visionary thing he'd ever heard in his life, even if it was the biggest evolutionary leap forward for humanity since we got up on our hind legs, we still wouldn't get it. We couldn't. Aso, we don't have the articles of incorporation.'

'We've got our half of the Koran.'

'Oh yes? And he's going to look at this and say, how is this an article of incorporation? And you'll say, well the other half of this gives ownership of fifty per cent of the company to a small-time grey nano dealer who's at best disappeared and at worst might be at the bottom of the Bosphorus. And he will say, don't waste my time. And this is why you need to do it professionally from the get-go. From the start.'

'Just as well he hated the project then,' Aso says. Against herself Leyla giggles. Wedged into a tiny shitty citicar like segments of an orange, oppressed by tall trucks and big buses and arguing about the evolutionary future of nano-enhanced humanity. She could be drawing up marketing plans for kids' toys.

'Is this a Kurdish thing?'

'What?'

'Being deliberately contradictory?'

'It's an Aso thing.'

Again she giggles.

'You do good giggle,' Aso says.

'Ah,' Leyla says, cutting him off. 'You assume too much Mr Besarani. Do you need to go straight back to the office?'

In her peripheral vision she sees a wide smile break like a new season.

'Why do you ask, Ms Gültaşli?'

'Because I want to call in somewhere and introduce you to some new friends called Mr Shoes, Mr Shirt, Mr Haircut and Mr Manicure. And while we're on that, I still need that employment contract.'

'Children, here's a surprise for you,' Pinar Hanım says. Can looks up from his desk. He had let his gaze wander. He doesn't need to lip-read and so doesn't always keep his eyes on Pinar Hanım's porcelain-perfect face. Not paying attention enrages Pinar Hanım. She's not allowed to hit you now everyone's in the European Union but she wields ostracism, personal hurt and sarcasm like a three-rod nunchuk in a kung fu video. Can pays attention now. A surprise. Now that every eye is on her, Pinar Hanım says, 'A very special visitor, come back to see us. Come on in, Bekir.'

Can sits straight upright at his desk at the back of the class. Bekir, best of friends and rivals, the only one who Can recognized as a match and a brother, the only one in Yildiz Special School who showed any curiosity about this teeming city that spun around them, the other cities it contained and the other worlds beyond them. They'd been buccaneers, criminals, superheroes and pains-in-the-ass. They'd always had their hands up first with the right answer, the answer that was more than right because it went outside Pinar Hanım's lesson plan; the too too clever boys at the back of the class. Three months ago Bekir got into his parents' car at the gates and never came back. When that happens there is only one place he could have gone to: Gayreteppe Clinic. It makes the deaf hear, but it takes them away from the family of Yildiz School. Can is the hearing boy in the deaf school who can't leave that way. They fix hearing, they can't fix hearts.

'Bekir has come back to see us all,' Pinar Hanım announces. Bekir twists his foot uncomfortably. He knows he is a traitor. He has given up his identity in the nation of the deaf. 'Say hello, Bekir.'

'Hello,' Bekir speaks weakly.

'Bekir has something special to tell us, don't you, Bekir?'

'I've been to the doctor's.' He still hasn't lost the alien croak of the profoundly deaf who have never heard the sound of their own voices. Everyone knows where he's been.

'And what happened?' Everyone knows what happened.

'They made me able to hear.'

'Isn't that great, everyone? Let's all clap hands for Bekir.'

The loud applause is like a soft wave running over Can's toes. Bekir peers at the back of the class, looking for Can, a message to him, hey, are you there, it's all right isn't it? Still friends? It's all right. *You're the same as me now*, Can thinks. *Not deaf.*

It's too hot today for recess outside so Can and Bekir sit at the back of the classroom and tap away on Can's laptop. The stream of cool, kind air from the air-conditioning rattles the torn foil lid on his cup of ayran.

'What are you doing?'

'Solving a murder.' So, it's not a murder, but someone died.

'Cool. Can I see?'

'If you like.'

Bekir stands over his shoulder

'What are you posting?'

'A bit of a robot.'

'What robot?'

'The robot that chased me.'

'You got chased by a robot?'

'Yes but I got away but it fell and broke a bit off and I have got a number.'

'You're going to post it on bot dot net?'

'I have a lot of friends on bot dot net.'

'All they do is talk on bot dot net. They're fan boys. They don't know anything. You want to know if anyone knows what the serial number means. Here.' Bekir leans over Can and rattles keys. A new page opens.

'Gladio dot tee arr. That's like Deep State conspiracy wonks.'

'And what do you know about the Deep State?'

'Mr Ferentinou tells me.'

'Your Mr Ferentinou is Greek and probably a traitor. And even if they are conspiracy wonks, that doesn't mean they don't know anything.'

'About bots?'

'About everything.'

'Where do I register?'

'Here.'

Tippy tippy tap. He's in. Two minutes later the photograph is posted from his ceptep on to the forum. Can's a conspiracy theorist now.

Strapped into the Gas Bubble as Mom whirls him home from Yildiz, Can presses face and palms to the window. Istanbul whirls past in a kaleidoscope of colour and movement and tiny revelations; the cascading domes of a mosque in the shifting perspectives between two modern glass and steel towers, a man pushing a hand cart up a steep alley overhung by balconies, the poster of pop-star Semsi in those tight-tight glittery red pants that never fail to thrill Can. He touches lips and tongue to the glass to touch the vibration of the engine, the bass rumble of the city. People stare at him, Look! It's the Windowlicking Boy! That's what you think, but what none of you know is, he's really the Boy Detective, in disguise.

His ceptep vibrates. A reply to his post. A conspiracy wonk, a Grey Wolf, a bot freak, has identified his shard, right down to the shipping number.

'Would you look at that?' Adnan Sarioğlu says to his wife on the private quay at Sedef. 'It's got a little sling under its ass to catch the shit. Does it shit pearls or something?'

The boat was a vintage Italian Riva; polished mahogany and green leather, effortlessly luxurious and fast. As it rounded the harbour beacon and dropped down into the water to burble up to the mooring, Adnan and Ayşe could see the caleche waiting under the antique Ottoman gas lamps.

'What's the nag and cart about?'

'It's the law out on the islands. Motor vehicles are banned.'

'What do you mean "the law"? He owns the island. If he wants, he could have a Lamborghini sitting there.'

'Only two seats in a Lamborghini,' Ayşe said.

Now the driver helps her up in her deadly heels on to the small and perilous step and up into the carriage. Adnan slides his hand down her calf.

'I feel a seam.'

'Of course.'

Adnan climbs in beside her. The four-wheeled caleche bounces on its C-springs. Adnan settles back into the upholstery. He breathes in old leather and horse and the herbs and musks of the island. Gas lamps curve away from the harbour in a zigzag up the unseen hillside to the greater congregation of lights high up against the airglow: Ferid Adataş's house. Adnan can make out vague music. Billie Holiday.

The driver mounts the box seat, clicks and flicks his whip. The matched pair clop forwards. The sudden jolt sends Ayşe into Adnan. They giggle. They've giggled since the Riva pulled away from Eminönü. Adnan hates boats and dark water. Ayşe knows he would only giggle if there was something of which he was more nervous.

I'm with you, Ayşe thought. *You're not alone here. I'll look out for you, guard your flanks, take out the snipers. We're a team.*

Folded in the caleche's skin-soft buttoned leather, Ayşe whispers, 'The left side horse has got a hard-on.'

'He's not the only one.'

'I believe it's called Coachman's Lob,' Ayşe says. 'It's from the particular rhythm of a horse-drawn carriage. It's an occupational hazard, so I'm told.'

Adnan falls sideways, helpless with suppressed laughter.

'Look at the fucking size of that. It's like a fire-hose. Imagine trying to trot with that slapping between your legs. Now this, however . . .'

Adnan takes his wife's hand and moves it toward the erection in his tailor-made suit pants. Ayşe laughs, then her eyes widen at the sudden touch of Adnan's fingers on her thigh, high up inside her skirt, light and shocking, an electric butterfly.

'What are you doing, you Anatolian savage?'

'Just checking.' Adnan traces the line of the seam up the back of Ayşe's leg. Leather, silk, finger, silk, skin. Layers, sheers and veils. She's always found the tiny denials of silk, of sheer nylon and lace and butterfly gauze, so much more arousing than simple skin on skin. Silk mediates, sheer nylon turns every touch into a caress, an opportunistic slip of the hand into romance. She feels Adnan's hand tense at the thrill zone where stocking ends and bare, warm thigh begins. He's more direct, the transition from one state to another, from veiled suggestion to promise, exciting. 'You know, that seam really does go all the way. That's proper quality, that is.'

Yes, and a proper turned heel, but I don't expect you to notice that. The heel of Adnan's hand is hot and hard against the silk triangle stretched over her pubis.

'When the deal's done,' she whispers. By the time he gets into that dining room, Adnan will be a pillar of constrained energy and charisma. Every eye will be on him, every ear tuned to his least word. This isn't dinner, it's war.

Ayse snuggles close to Adnan in the embrace of the skin-warm leather.

The caleche stops and sways. Hooves stamp on cobbles, harness jingles. The house is a subtle geometry of intersecting planes and elevations, presenting many facades, hard to grasp as a first impression. It offers no welcome, no obvious means of entry; windows are narrow horizontal slits. From the terrace cantilevered out from the hillside comes a suggestion of movement and conversation and vagrant Billie Holiday. The driver unfolds the carriage step. His antique Ottoman style uniform, the carriage and the horse with their faintly ridiculous fly fringes over their eyes, are magnificently incongruous against this aggressive modernity. Adnan takes a deep breath of the night air. Thyme, sage, dust and salt, honey and sweat.

'Smells like Kaş.'

A small black rectangle appears on the unbroken white wall.

'Adnan!' Ferid Adataş's handshake is freely offered and as firm for a woman as a man. 'Mrs Sarioğlu; how lovely to meet you.'

'Erkoç,' Ayşe says. 'I go by my maiden name.'

'Of course, forgive me. Well, welcome welcome. How was your trip?'

'Very low carbon,' Adnan says. He nods at the caleche.

'What you gain on the carbon you lose on the methane,' Ferid says. He laughs at his own joke. As they cross the cobbled courtyard Adnan whispers into Ayşe's dark hair,

'I'm just going to say, you look un-fucking-believable tonight. Absolutely stunning. I don't care who's in there; nothing – no one – is going to come within a whisper.'

Ayşe squeezes Adnan's ass.

Drinks are served on the terrace. Ferid Bey's other guests are Mr Munir Güney and his wife Nazat, General Barçin Çiller and his wife Tayyibe, Professor Pinar Budak and her husband Ertem. Munir Bey is a prominent bureaucrat in the European Commission in Brussels. He specializes in trade and tariffs. General Barçin Çiller is a field commander with recent active service on people trafficking patrol along the Iraqi border. Pinar Hanım is Professor of Literature at the Boğazici University, specializing in women's divan poetry of the eighteenth century. Ayşe memorizes each name and face as Süreyya Adataş introduces them. Women introduce women, men introduce men. It looks like etiquette but Ayşe senses a more strategic game: isolate her from Adnan. Süreyya Hanım has her trapped in the corner of the terrace. Across the dark water of the Sea of Marmara, Istanbul glows, veils of lights drawn about her. Ferries are fast-moving constellations on the black sea; the big ships slow-moving clusters of red and green. High above, underneath the stars, the riding lights of sky sails wink slowly.

Ayşe rests her glass on the stainless steel railing. Air eddies across the terrace and for the first time in weeks she feels cool. She leans over the rail, attention seized by small shapes in the low brush. 'Are those bones?'

'Dogs, Mrs Erkoç,' Süreyya Hanım says. 'The island has an unusual history. Back in the 1920s, the new Istanbul Municipal authority was concerned about the huge population of feral dogs terrorizing the streets. Old women were being savaged, babies dragged from prams, drunks found half-eaten in the gutters in the morning. Once they rounded them all up they realized there were far too many to terminate in one go, so they brought them all here, dumped them and let dog nature sort it out. Within a year not a single dog was left. The gardeners are forever turning up bones.'

The meal is served in a long, elegantly minimal dining room. One wall is smoky glass that softens the lights of the Marmara shores to glow-worms, the other is worked from the raw rock of the island. Ayşe runs her finger surreptitiously along the grain of the table. It confirms the evidence of her eyes and nose; the table is one single piece of Lebanese cedar. Glass mosque lamps hang overhead; at first the arrangement seems uncharacteristically design-free, then Ayşe's long unravelling of the meanings hidden within elaborate Arabic scripts unlocks the concealed pattern. The arrangement of oil-flames mirrors the spring constellations.

The seating plan has placed her as far as etiquette will permit from Adnan. Ferid Adataş presides at one end of the table, Ayşe to his left. Opposite her, Mrs Çiller, the general's wife. She has wide country hands and a wise light in her eyes. Ayşe thinks she will like her. To Ayşe's left is Ertem Bey, himself a well-regarded reviewer and poet. Onwards, clockwise around the cedar rectangle; the elegant and disdainful Mrs Güney, then General Çiller himself. *What is it about the military*, Ayşe thinks, *that they can carry the stiffest of uniforms with grace and bearing but when they are put in a suit, no matter how well cut, they rumple up and crease?* Süreyya Hanım, all charm and skill, is at the opposite end of the table from her husband. To her left, across the long diagonal from Ayşe, is Adnan. To his left, the professor. Beside Professor Budak is Munir from the EU Commission, and back to Ferid Bey's coterie of ladies. Eurocracy, military, liberal arts and an unapologetic capitalist.

Ayşe twists her water glass ninety degrees. Adnan doesn't miss a beat as he charms hostess and general but she knows he saw it. Just testing. She had devised the code with just such a seating plan in mind. She had rehearsed Adnan on the boat over. Glass, earlobe stroke, ring twist, necklace touch, ear-ring flick.

'And this one?' A finger touched almost absent-mindedly to pursed lips.

'Shut the fuck up right now.'

'I must admire your jewellery, Mrs Erkoç,' Ferid says. 'Is that a Greek cross?'

'It's Armenian, twelfth century,' Ayşe says. Mr Güney and Mr Budak sit upright, sharp as meerkats, their political sensibilities alerted. 'Probably from the workshop of the Church of St Hripsime.'

'It's very lovely,' says Mrs Budak. 'I do so love old, traditional pieces. How did you come by it? I never have any luck with things like that. They have either long gone by the time I get to them or they're Bulgarian or Kurdish fakes.'

'A good place to start is with the grape bunches at the base of the cross.' Ayşe leans forward. 'See? There should be six on one bunch, five in the other; for Christ's Apostles, minus Judas the Betrayer. The points will always end in three loops, for the Holy Trinity, so they say, though it has much older roots than that, all the way back to old solar religions, when these were sun discs. If it doesn't have those, then it certainly is a fake. Then again, I do have an unfair advantage when it comes to pieces; I own a gallery.'

'What, antiques?' says Güney.

'No,' says Ayşe carefully. 'A gallery. I specialize in religious art;

miniatures and calligraphy mostly, but it's hard to resist a good cross when it comes, and they don't come half as often as I'd like.'

'Well, if that cross is anything to go by, I shall certainly come to call on you,' Mrs Çiller says.

The first course is served. It's small and exquisite as brooches. Ferid Bey leans confidentially over his plate. He's a toucher; his fingers rest lightly on Ayşe's wrist. 'What Tayyibe doesn't say is that she deals in religious curios herself.'

They're not curios, Ayşe is about to say, *they're the words and aspects of God*, but Mrs Çiller breaks in with an exasperated, 'Oh Ferid!'

Mrs Çiller raps the back of Ferid Adataş's hand with a spoon. 'We're moving into property, is all. Buying those new apartments in Mecca. It's a boom business; you wouldn't believe the number of people who want to retire to a quiet and pious life with a balcony view of the Grand Mosque. We can't keep up with demand.'

After the plates are removed by the silent and swift waiting staff, General Çiller leans forward and says across the table to Güney, 'What's this I'm reading in *Hürriyet* about Strasbourg breaking up the nation?'

'It's not breaking up the nation. It's a French motion to implement European Regional Directive 8182 which calls for a Kurdish Regional Parliament.'

'And that's not breaking up the nation?' General Çiller throws up his hands in exasperation. He's a big, square man, the model of the military, but he moves freely and lightly ' The French prancing all over the legacy of Atatürk? What do you think, Mr Sarioğlu?'

The trap could not be any more obvious but Ayşe sees Adnan straighten his tie, the code for, *Trust me, I know what I'm doing,*

'What I think about the legacy of Atatürk, General? Let it go. I don't care. The age of Atatürk is over.'

Guests stiffen around the table, breath subtly indrawn; social gasps. This is heresy. People have been shot down in the streets of Istanbul for less. Adnan commands every eye.

'Atatürk was father of the nation, unquestionably. No Atatürk, no

Turkey. But, at some point every child has to leave his father. You have to stand on your own two feet and find out if you're a man. We're like kids that go on about how great their dads are; my dad's the strongest, the best wrestler, the fastest driver, the biggest moustache. And when someone squares up to us, or calls us a name or even looks at us squinty, we run back shouting 'I'll get my dad, I'll get my dad!' At some point; we have to grow up. If you'll pardon the expression, the balls have to drop. We talk the talk mighty fine: great nation, proud people, global union of the noble Turkic races, all that stuff. There's no one like us for talking ourselves up. And then the EU says, All right, prove it. The door's open, in you come; sit down, be one of us. Move out of the family home; move in with the other guys. Step out from the shadow of the Father of the Nation.

'And do you know what the European Union shows us about ourselves? We're all those things we say we are. They weren't lies, they weren't boasts. We're good. We're big. We're a powerhouse. We've got an economy that goes all the way to the South China Sea. We've got energy and ideas and talent – look at the stuff that's coming out of those tin-shed business parks in the nano sector and the synthetic biology start-ups. Turkish. All Turkish. That's the legacy of Atatürk. It doesn't matter if the Kurds have their own Parliament or the French make everyone stand in Taksim Square and apologize to the Armenians. We're the legacy of Atatürk. Turkey is the people. Atatürk's done his job. He can crumble into dust now. The kid's come right. The kid's come very right. That's why I believe the EU's the best thing that's ever happened to us because it's finally taught us how to be Turks.'

General Çiller beats a fist on the table, sending the cutlery leaping.

'By God, by God; that's a bold thing to say but you're exactly right.'

The main course arrives. It is small and dark and sculptural. Adnan catches Ayşe's eye. She turns a fork upside down. *Don't push it.* The general and Mrs Adataş have drawn Adnan into an intense debate which consists mostly of Çiller talking fast and low and jabbing a punctuating finger. Mrs Çiller is asking Ayşe about her gallery.

'The gallery is in an old converted tekke in Eskiköy in Beyoğlu. I'm sure there are a few of the old Mevlevis still hanging around, and any amount of djinn. What's a tekke without a few resident djinn? There's definitely something about the place, sometimes when I catch sight of the Sephardic Kabbalist pieces out of the corner of my eye I see the text moving around, rearranging itself, rewriting itself. I'm always very reluctant to sell them.'

'Oh, how can you work there?' Mrs Çiller says. 'It would scare the wits out of me.'

Mr Budak cuts in. He is a tight, snippy man who loves an argument.

'But sell them you do. You're not a museum, you're a commercial enterprise.'

'I have a bespoke network of collectors.'

'Yes yes yes, I'm sure they're all the most refined and cultured of connoisseurs, but, ultimately, it's about treating religious art, sacred writing – precious cultural artefacts to the people who made them – as nothing more than supermarket goods.'

'There is a huge difference between a Koran cover and a pot of yoghurt.'

'That's my point. You see refined connoiseurism, I see cultural appropriation. You say you have Sephardic texts; what gives you the right to sell them? Have you considered the wishes of the Sephardic community, of any of the communities and cultures whose sacred things you sell in your gallery? Have you even thought of asking?'

The table's attention is all on snippy, hectoring Budak, but Ayşe keeps Professor Budak in her peripheral vision. This is another setup. Ertem Bey goes in with the shock and awe; then Budak Hanım comes after and Haliburtonizes the place.

Budak Hanım says, 'Historically, under the Ottoman millet system, where each religious and ethnic community was to a certain extent self-governing under the over-arching Sultanate, the idea of ownership, of property was much less clearly defined, isn't that the case? In local communities, property was based on a sense of utility, not on an absolute market value for a commodity or service, but on its social value, its benefits over its life span to a group. What I believe economists call fundamental value, as opposed to "mark to market"? Isn't that right Mr Sarioğlu?'

'I'm a trader, not an economist,' Adnan says. 'I don't talk about money, I'm too busy making it.'

'Indeed. I'm no economist either. In fact, the point I'm making was that, historically, there was a third way between fundamental value – which can be value to an individual – and mark to market: which we could call the social market; value as a shared asset and as something that binds together and gives identity to a community. So, say a Greek icon, or an Armenian cross, has a social market value which the retail market values simply can't reflect.'

Careful Adnan, Ayşe thinks. *I see you bristling to my defence, hero, but I'm not the one under attack here.* Professor Budak is a natural communicator. Her low, quiet-but-carrying, self-deprecating but confident voice has quashed all other conversations. She commands the table. No one notices that the main course has been cleared away and small spoons of refreshing between-course foam have arrived.

'It seems to me that this historic third way, of looking at economics in the social sphere rather than as a mathematical abstraction or a product of individual psychology, may be more fruitful for the real world. After all, a market is ultimately a social construct, isn't it? I can't deny the tremendous energy of Western individualism, but it's not without a price. The shadow of the great crash hangs over our generation, yet here we are in a booming market utilizing even more complex and subtle and interlinked financial instruments. At some point it will inevitably crash again: as weapons of mass destruction go, unrestricted market economies are among the more subtle but sure. I can't help but think that a socially mediated economy, one that costs-in common value, trust and mutual obligation, might be the model for the twenty-first century. Neither big finance nor small-is-beautiful, but something in between, something human scaled, something like the shared cultural identity and ownership of the Ottoman empire's many cultures. Value is identity. What do you think, Mr Sarioğlu?'

Ayşe knows that shade of pale in Adnan's face, the thinning of the lips. She twists her glass. *Be cool, trader.*

'What do I think? I'll tell you what I think. I am the money. As simple as that. I am the money. More money than the entire gross national product of our country passes through my accounts every day. Every single day. More money than you can imagine. Because I'll tell you a thing about money. When it gets to that level, it stops being just money. It becomes something else. Something bigger, wilder, stronger and more beautiful. A storm of money. A hurricane of money. I don't own it, I don't control it, no one can control it, no one can master it. I close my eyes and I step into it and it takes me up and I ride it for a while – for a few moments because no one, no one can take more than few seconds without being cut to pieces – and then I step off again and when I open my hands, I've grabbed something out of it. Profit. It's not a dirty word, it's the only thing you can take from that storm of money. A single handful. You think I work the markets for that handful, that profit? I do it because it's beautiful. It's beautiful and it's terrifying and it will cut you to pieces but for those few moments that I'm in it; I am the money. So you can talk about your fundamental value and your mark-to-market and your social markets and they mean absolutely nothing because the money doesn't care. Simple rules, kids' games – you give me that now, I give you this later – all play off each other and whirl up into something no one can totally grasp and no one can predict and no one can ever, ever hope to control. I think that is magnificent. Money. Raw money. That's all there is. And you should be glad of people like me and Ferid Bey, because we face that every single day; we put our hands into it and we pull out the stuff that makes your world work. And if it ever stops, if it even slows down, if it ever shines a little less brightly; everything you know will end. So your theories are good and fine but when it all comes down, the money doesn't care. And I don't care, because I am the money. I make your world turn. I am the money.'

Silence around the table. The waiters take the opportunity to whisk away the untasted spoons of palate cleansers and deftly serve the final course.

The sound in the alley is tremendous, alien, terrifying. Necdet comes down the steps on to Vermilion-Maker Lane and it's a physical force. It pushes him back into a shuttered shop doorway. Hızır is master of djinn and it is not beyond the old Green Saint to have some mother-of-djinn the size of a cloud squatting over the dervish house. He presses his cheek to the red-painted plaster. The sound creeps along the wall, waxes and wanes, eddying on the stifling air through Eşkiköy's labyrinth of alleys and fountain-fed squares, reverberates from the steel shutter and Coke machine chained to the wall and the balconies leaning close over Vermilion-Maker Lane. It's huge, it's strangely familiar, it's hair-raising. It's real.

Hızır is not a tame saint. The Green Man took everything, every memory, every grace and vice and gave him back something he now remembers as his life. He burned his sister. Ismet took him to the dervish house to save him from his family.

'What do you want me to do?'

The Green Saint had closed his eyes and turned his face away. Necdet thinks he may have been crazy then. Corridor opened on to corridor, tunnel on to tunnel, drawing him ever deeper, ever darker into vaults and cisterns older than any of the three cities whose names stood over these stones. He found himself by a pipe, thick through as his body, running from darkness to darkness. It thrummed beneath his hand, and when he pressed his ear to it he imagined he could hear through the tick insulation the scream of speeding gas. What was real, what was fantasy, what was the world between; he could no longer tell. When Mustafa finally tracked down the banging on the never-opened firedoor and broke the security seals, he found a Necdet dirty dusty bloodied but his face was as radiant as the Prophet's. He was touched, he was changed.

The noise booms louder, focused and amplified by the alleys as Necdet comes cautiously up Vermilion-Maker Lane. Adem Dede Square is filled with people. Most are women in headscarves with a scattering of young men with leather jackets, smart hair and polished shoes. They all face the dervish house. Necdet sees Ismet's head above the headscarf-horizon. He must be standing on the gallery steps. Now he picks out the rest of his brother's study-group. Their jackets are snappy, their shoes smart. They're a well-dressed tarikat, of men with jobs. A high-toned expectant murmuring rises from the crowd. This is the sound that has haunted him through Eşkiköy.

Bülent and his enemy Aykut watch from their respective doorways. Tables and chairs are safely folded away. The Greeks who drink tea at Bülent's have wisely taken themselves elsewhere. Aydin closes up his news and lotto ticket stall, apologizing his way around the women in headscarves and respectable coats. The last of the day's simits, stale now, feed the pigeons. The neighbourhood watches from their balconies. Even the deaf kid's family have thrown open the shutters and look cautiously down, wary of being seen. There's the kid, peeping over the railing. Necdet looks up; there's the boy's pet robot, the bird, circling over the square. Some windows are shut. The fat old Greek, of course. The Georgian woman, who everyone thinks is a prostitute. Does he see a flicker of movement at the curtains, gone as soon as he focuses on it? Details. It's like he has been given new senses. The world is sharp, the world is detailed, the world is connected. Words are painted on the gallery door. Something idolators. Yet there is the girl from the gallery, the one whose karin he saw underneath the earth, at the back of the crowd. She mustn't want the crowd to know she works there. Necdet quite fancies the woman who owns the gallery. He likes the boldness of her boots and skirts. She would be classy and make a lot of noise.

A movement to his right. The crowd parts as the women pack into a denser configuration. Hızır is there, perched on the lip of the fountain. In the same instant the gallery girl turns and sees him. Her point and simultaneous shout silence the square. Everybody turns towards him. Necdet doesn't try to run. This is why Hızır is waiting for him here in all of Istanbul. You can't outrun the will of God.

Ismet pushes through the crowd. His tarikat boys are close behind him, they form an honour guard around Necdet and guide him between the bodies to the porch of the art gallery. *Burn Idolators* is what's written in silver paint. Heads faces, heads faces, heads and faces and scarves. On the balconies, more faces. No scarves.

'Listen, listen, listen!' Ismet shouts raising his arms. 'God has given us a great gift, right here in Eşkiköy. In our days, in our own streets, God is still at work. I followed God and set up his study-group here, to bring justice – proper justice, God's justice, to Eskiköy, and God has blessed our work. He has given us a gift: a shaykh, our own shaykh!'

The deaf kid at Apartment Four is almost climbing out of the balcony. His mother has hold of the back of his football shirt. From his place at the fountain Hızır watches. He might be amused. Ismet keeps his arms up. Necdet is expected to say something.

I'm not a shaykh, I'm a skunkhead. I'm not a saint, I'm a slacker. I'm not a Sufi, I'm a sister-torcher. I am the Black Sheep.

Necdet remembers where he saw this before. The crowd on Necatibey Cadessi, the wall of faces as he fled from the police drones, the man in the white T-shirt who was videoing him, just before he turned and saw the woman's head with the light pouring from it.

Hızır casts his eyes upwards. Necdet sees the smoke pour into Adem Dede Square, hears by djinn-sense the mosquito shriek of micro-fan engines.

'Get out of here!' Necdet shouts. 'The police, the police are coming. They've sent robots!'

The headscarved faces look up as the faint smoke of swarmbots clusters together into insect-scale crowd-control drones. The crowd breaks up into fleeing women, hands over their heads and faces, protecting themselves as the police-bots buzz and strafe, hunting for exposed skin to tag with their RFID-seeded dye sprays. Headscarves flutter to the ground, long modest street coats are cast off, the women shedding anything that might have picked up the betraying orange stain of an RFID-tag, that could draw the police to their front doors. There's a different noise in Adem Dede Square now, a high-pitched panicked shrieking. The square is deserted in seconds. The balconies are empty, the shutters locked tight. Cobbles, walls, shop fronts, cars are polka-dotted orange with tagging-dye. Ismet drags Necdet away as a salvo of dye pellets splat against the gallery shutter. *Burn Idolators*; orange-flecked silver. The swarm of insect-machines spirals high into the air above Adem Square and explodes into its component smart-dust. Sirens approach. Necdet glances over his shoulder as the Tarikat boys hustle him down Güneşli Sok. Hızır is gone. In his place a solitary robot creeps like a spider in a relentless nightmare from beneath the lip of the bowl and scurries up the orange-pocked wall. It's not the police; it's not the deaf boy's bird-toy. It's an alien watcher.

Adnan has a theory about cigars. Cigars are the amputated cocks of your foes. They are the businessman's equivalent of the cum-spurt of champagne on the Grand Prix podium. I chew up your penis, enemy.

The Budaks had barely outwaited coffee. The caleche rattled off down the hillside at the fast-trot-verging-on-a-canter. The Güneys took their leave, Güney tight and over-formal, his wife smiling, twinkling even. Did Adnan hear her whisper, *Tremendous fun, darling*, to Ayşe? Mrs Adataş was skilfully guiding Ayşe, the general and his wife to her collection of Byzantine mosaics in the day room. The result was imminent. Nothing could be read. Everything hung suspended. Adnan felt no fear. 'Come on back out to the terrace,' Ferid Adataş said.

The night was still and incredibly, infinitely clear. Everything seemed poised, on the edge of falling. Adnan felt terribly terribly afraid, terribly terribly alive; present in every cell, every flake of skin and hair. The slightest movement, the least breath, the very touch of the lightest thought would shatter this moment of pure being.

'I wouldn't be at all surprised if you got an invitation to dinner,' Adataş said.

'What, who?'

'Pinar .'

'You think?'

'Oh, I think. She loved you. She's an old Trot but she respects someone with an opinion. Doesn't matter what it is, as long as they can argue it. Nothing she likes better than a good row. All that poking and prying was to test if you were solid or just Özer corporate balls. You'll get an invitation to dinner. She's got a fabulous cellar. She won't be so easy on you next time. She'll take you apart. No, she's wonderful fun, Pinar. Her husband now, he's a sanctimonious shit. Have a cigar.'

That was when Adnan knew he had it. It felt like every star in the sky was falling through him, a vertigo, a rush of fire.

The smoke spirals down into the hollows of Adnan. This is the greatest thing he's ever felt.

'Your hand, Mr Sarioğlu.' Data jumps from palm to palm, coded on to the natural conductivity of the flesh. 'That's your deal memo.'

'I'd like to take a look at it.'

'I'd be offended if you didn't.'

Adnan deftly slips the ceptep out of his breast pocket and behind his ear. The writer drops over his eye.

'Due date the sixteenth.'

'Take it or leave it.'

'Twenty-five per cent.'

'You'd expected more.'

'As you say, that's the contract . . .' But it's the full two million. It's everything he asked for.

'How soon can I draw down the credit line?'

'Just as soon as you get this back to my lawyers with an account.'

Accounts are not Adnan's terrain. He is Ultralord of the Deal.

Kemal in the back office will set up the nested folders of paperwork, the payment schedules and transfers and dummy account names.

'It's not securitized.'

'Hedging is what I do, son. What's two million here and there between me and Özer? It's a good bet. A thousand per cent return? We're not standing on my terrace here because I didn't know a good gamble when I saw one. Your figures check and your contacts are legitimate – as legitimate as this kind of business allows. I told you I was impressed with your balls – passing off hot Iranian gas – and I value Pinar as a judge of character but the bottom line makes sense. Everything follows from that.'

A hollow knock of steel shoes on cobbles; the caleche has returned, the horse in its fringed eye-wear stands with one fore-hoof raised.

'That'll be for you. The general and Mrs Çiller are staying. They're old friends. Don't think me an ungenerous host, but you do have to work in the morning.' Ferid Bey laughs like a detonation and claps Adnan mightily on the back. 'And please don't throw the cigar butt. We're on a brush fire alert.'

In the hall, Adnan and Ayşe exchange the final codes of the evening.

Ayşe: hands upturned in a small plea. *What*?

Adnan: a small clench of the fist. *Yes*.

He is quite quite lost. These are the streets, the sudden flights of steps and darting alleys, the hidden gardens and lost cemeteries, the shops and small lycées and slimy drinking fountains of Georgios' childhood world, yet he stands paralysed in the middle of Soğanci Sok with the girls huddling together in their short summer skirts and bright shoes and the boys pushing past with their dangerously-gelled hair and sleeveless brand-name T-shirts. Barkers call: *Come and have a real good time in our bar*. Neon and plastic signs, awnings and street tales, young men smoking fashionable-again şiş; tiny gas-powered citicars and mopeds. A dozen musics assail him, snatches and snippets of private beats. Georgios walked up this street every morning for six years with his bag on his back like a soldier's pack on the way to Göksel Hanım but the buildings look different, their faces are harsh concrete not the soft, too-flammable wood of old Cihangir. The lights hang wrong, the gutter down the centre of the narrow street is too deep, there should be a narrow sok with a low green double door at the end of it; everything is cartographically correct but nothing is familiar.

Georgios stops a pizza delivery boy on his way to his moped. He holds out the hand-drawn map Constantin gave him that morning at the çayhane.

'I'm trying to find Maç Çok.'

Pizza boy takes the map and frowns at it.

'Three up on the left and then down past the April Mosque.'

'Thank you.'

The boy has removed the muffler from his moped engine; when he drives off, pizzas stacked and bungied on the parcel shelf, the roar is like gunfire among the windowed walls. Still Georgios stands petrified on Soğanci Sok. A few steps and he will be there. On her streets, at her door. It's all too sudden, too quick, too close.

Every Tuesday the New Thinking Group met at the Karakuş meyhane in Dolapdere. Monday was poets, Wednesday was experimental film-makers, Thursdays was singer-songwriters with proper musicians on Friday and Saturday but Tuesday was New Thought: politics, philosophy, feminism, critical theory. Economics.

'Darling, you really have to have this young man,' Meryem Nasi had said as she disengaged Georgios from the coterie of politicians and pundits on her terrace and dragged him to where Ariana Sinanidis kept her court of dazzling young men. 'Most brilliant economic thinker in thirty years. Shake up all those dreadful tired old lefty dogmas, what?'

'An economist?' Ariana said it as she might have said, *torturer*.

'Experimental economics,' Georgios apologized. 'Evidence based economics.'

Riot troops were disembarking from trucks and forming into

columns up in Taksim Square, though Georgios could not see anyone abroad more dangerous than home-bound salary men. In the weeks since the generals had ousted Süleyman Demirel, random troop deployments had been the order, the better to sow a sense of omniscience, that the army knew its opponents' minds before they knew them themselves. He scurried past the phalanx of riot shields, head dipped. Martial law scared him.

The Karakuş café was a smoky brown bar with old photographs of French intellectuals and Turkish poets on the walls. A new, large portrait of Atatürk hung behind the bar; beside it a scarcely smaller picture of General Kenen Evren. There were tables crowded together with a mishmash of chairs, there was a raised dais at one end with a microphone. Loud English ska music played from a DJ booth in a broom closet. The bar was crowded, all the tables full. Young men in German combat jackets and denims, young women in tapering jeans and cavalry-style jackets pressed against the walls. The cigarette smoke was solid. Georgios faltered as he opened the door and every head turned to him. He would likely have run but Ariana Sinanidis detached herself from the table nearest the stage – more handsome, intent young men – to welcome him.

'You made it, come on in. There's a seat for you up here. We're all dying to hear what you have to say.'

Self conscious in his suit, Georgios nervously drank coffee which only made him more edgy, and oversmiled at Ariana's attempts to bring him into the conversational circle, which was all about the coup and who had been disappeared and how the army had finally turned on its Grey Wolf stooges who had been stupid to have ever believed they were invulnerable but what could you expect from the Grey Wolves and the CIA was behind it, and their Deep State running dogs.

Georgios heard his name called from the DJ cupboard and he stepped up through the sparse applause on to the stage and blinked into the tiny spotlight fixed to the ceiling that turned the cigarette smoke into a wall of luminous blue and it was all of a sudden deadly

deadly quiet. He started stammeringly, shuffling his careful notes on the postcards, reaching for words. The room was far away, the room was cold and closed. Then the passion kindled in him and the cards in his hand went ignored and he talked about what he had found in economics and how he was trying to take the subject out of the dead sea of mathematical modelling into an empirical, experimental science – a true science of hypothesis and proof. It was the most human of sciences because it was the science of need and value and cost. He talked about the new subject of non-linearity, of how mathematical predictability can cascade into randomness, into chaos; and Thomian catastrophes, where one state of behaviour suddenly collapses into its antithesis. He talked about the irrationality of rational actors and experiments in economics, of expectation and paradox and non-zero sum games. He talked about his hopes for a future economics that more closely modelled the human world than modelling itself, that nestled into a new roost between psychology, sociology and the emerging physics of non-linear systems. He talked well past the ten o'clock curfew. He thanked them for coming, he thanked them for their attention.

The questions started. He was deep in an argument with a Marxist with a Che beret on the inevitability of class war when the police came in through the door. Tear-gas grenades rolled between the chair legs leaking vapour. The door came down, the police came in with riot shields and sticks and gas masks. A girl in a Lady Di frill-necked blouse went down spraying blood from a hideous head wound. Patrons stormed the stage. The Marxist bravely turned on the assailants, chair raised. A policeman knocked him off balance with his shield and smashed him to the ground with his heavy black riot baton. CS gas turned the air opaque. There was constant screaming. Outside, a tinny, distant voice shouted unintelligible orders through a bullhorn. The surge pushed Georgios hard against the wall. Photographs of Sartre and de Beauvoir cracked in their frames behind him. The audience stormed the bar, desperate for the back entrance. A dull roar came from the kitchen area, the crowd checked momentarily. The police were at the back too. In the second of indecision, Ariana dived through the crowd, seized Georgios by the hand and hauled him toward the DJ booth.

'There are stairs up to the roof.'

She pulled him up three storeys of boxes and stores and decaying rooms to burst out on to the gently sloping asphalt. Others followed, seeping away between the water tanks and television aerials, roof to roof to roof. Ariana did not seek safety but went to the parapet to look down into the street.

'They'll see you,' Georgios said.

'I don't care.'

Army trucks and vans blocked the street in each direction, their backboards down, their doors open. Soldiers wrestled men from the meyhane into the trucks; hands cuffed behind them, bent over, head down. Up and in they went. It was done with skill and ease. They went quickly and quietly. The women went to the vans. They were allowed to stand up, but they shrieked and shouted more. Army dogs on short leashes barked, lips curled, at them and that quieted them. The women who went to the Karakuş café had heard of females stripped and thrown into a room with specially trained rape dogs. You could only kill yourself if that were to happen. You could never be clean after that kind of defilement. Four soldiers carried the Marxist with the Che beret. His head hung loosely, like the Christ taken down from the cross. Blood gleamed on the cobbles. There was a light in every apartment window both sides of Şirket Sok. Silhouettes behind the shutters and net curtains.

'Go on, I see you, I see you!' Ariana raged at the lighted windows. 'Tell what you see, I dare you, tell what you see. But will you? Oh no. Not Şirket Sok. You probably called them in the first place. Bastards! Bastards!'

She drew herself back and spat full and furious into the street.

'Ariana, you have to come!' Georgios shouted. 'It's only a matter of time before they make it up here.'

But she stood hurling curses down into Şirket Sok, her dress billowing in the Meryem Ana Fırtanısı, the wind of September. To Georgios she was magnificent, she was the proud, fierce heroine of Greek legend; she was mad Electra, she was Nemesis. But the soldiers had heard her and were breaking out hand-held searchlights from the trucks while others were unshouldering their guns and he was paralysed by dread until he seized Ariana and hauled her away from the edge.

'Take my hand.'

The spell was broken. Georgios closed his fingers around hers and rushed her over the cracking roof tiles, under the leaking water tanks, through mazes of washing and gardens of pot geraniums, over the roofs of Dolapdere.

He was on Taksim Square two days later. The body of a young man had turned up down at Karaköy in one of those black Bosphorus currents that trapped suicides and extra-judicial execution victims in private, endless whirlpools. His face was so badly broken neither his mother nor his father could recognize him. The props, the police said. Bodies that go into the water get chopped up pretty bad, with all the ships going up and down. His parents identified him by his German Army surplus combat jacket and the crimson revolutionary's beret folded neatly into his pocket.

Three hundred people were in Taksim Square that October Saturday in defiance of martial law. Six weeks before it would have been thirty thousand, raging in the aftermath of the coup. Anger has a half life. Generals become just another government. Ranged against the three hundred were phalanx after phalanx of soldiers, twelve deep around the Atatürk memorial, always the goal of protestors; yet Ariana slipped Georgios' hand to surge forward among the leaders. They were lovers by then. The square was huge, the sky the flat blue of judgement and the forces against them were monstrous and implacable, but Georgios felt an unfamiliar cry go from his throat and tears of huge pride in his eyes at Ariana's righteous ferocity, in his city, in what he dared to do and plunged after her. He was never so truly in love again.

Pizza boys are the truest guides. Maç Çok is a shallow entry off Maç Sok, one frontage deep, no wider than its green double-front door. The shuttered windows zigzag up four storeys. He can't go up there and knock. He can't cold call, he can't turn up into forty-seven years of exile and silence. What if she answers? What if she takes him by surprise before he knows what to say? What if she speaks first? What if she says nothing? What if she doesn't know him? What if she's become like this building, crabbed and pressed, staggering and lines untrue?

Opposite the mouth of Maç Çok is a tobacconist's, neon-lit, radio-murmurous. A teenager squats on a low stool reading a football magazine by the glow from the Coke machine. Georgios fumbles through the newspapers and magazines on the rack. He looks ridiculous and mildly criminal.

'Do you know if a woman has moved in here recently? Not from the east; European, a Greek woman from Athens.'

The shopkeeper shakes his head but the boy with the football magazine looks up. Whatever he might say is now irrelevant for Ariana Sinanidis is there, walking down the middle of the street with two bags from the local mini market in each hand. It's her, so her; there can be no doubt; how could Georgios ever have feared that he might not recognize her? Older but not aged. Thinner but not wizened – and not coarse, not thick and waddling. She moves with grace on the treacherous cobbles, her heels are high. No blue veins in the hands gripping the plastic bags. She has not changed her hair in forty-seven years. It falls straight and long as shining as he remembers it. Her face – he daren't look at her face too long for fear she might catch his eye and see him watching her. She looks tired. Georgios wants to step out and take her bags from her. The urge is so strong it feels like sickness. Then the moment is gone, Ariana turns into the short entry to the narrow, slanting apartment.

The teenager stares at Georgios when he buys the legitimizing bottle of water he has been turning over unconsciously in his hands. Then he realizes tears are running down his lapels.

*

The Riva powers through the dark waves, bounding and slapping hard on the troughs. Deep night, black water, swift machine. Ayşe stands in the cockpit, bracing against the brass trim of the windshield, ecstatic in the engine throb and the lash of spray in her face and the salt stiff in her hair.

'Can you make it go faster?'

The pilot nods and opens up the throttles. The computer synchs the engines, the boat lifts its nose harder out of the water. The surge of speed is immediate and atomic. Ayşe imagines tracing two radioactive wakes across the water behind her. Light. It is a blazing night. Beneath a sky-glow dome, the city spreads on either side of her in wings of light; rank upon rank, tier upon tier, the hills mounting one above the other, the individual lights blurring layer upon layer into glow and sparkle. Ayşe glances over her shoulder. Adnan sits in the centre of the rear seat, arms spread wide along the seatback in what he imagines looks like nonchalance, but Ayşe knows he is clinging to the leather-work.

I love you, man, this bright night, Ayşe thinks. *You were brave and brilliant and thrilling and beautiful – all the things I've always loved about you.*

'Let me drive.'

The pilot frowns at her.

'I've driven one of these before.' How could the daughter of a naval father not know how to handle powercraft? He had taught her, on those summer weekends when the city grew too stifling and they moved lock and stock along the Dı̇o to the summer house at Silivri on the Marmara shore. Ayşe lays her hands on the throttles and the smell of summer childhoods returns: barbecue lighter fluid, salty dust and after-sun lotion. Theirs had been an unglamorous old fibreglass double-outboard, nothing like this pearl of wood and carbon fibre and fat carbon-greedy engines, but Captain Erkoç had shown her how to make it stand up out of the water. Ayşe taps off the auto synch and pushes the throttles forwards. She tunes the engines by the throb of her body. It's all vibrations. The boat leaps forwards. The tuning is breathtaking. Ayşe shakes her hair out, shakes the speed-tears from the corners of her eyes. In a long, roaring curve she takes the hurtling, bouncing boat in around Sarayburnu Point with its monster Turkish flag, carefully spotlit. The Golden Horn opens before her; Istanbul's hills, carpeted with gold, fall on either side. This, this is the way to enter the Queen of Cities. She glances back again at Adnan. She's got him scared now, but he's excited. What, trader; am I hot, trader?

She flashes between the ferries and the cruise ships moored in at Karakoy like a wall of light and drops down into the water, mortal again. She nudges the Riva gently in to the mooring, barely kissing the tyres. Engines gurgle to silence, the water goes still.

'Who taught you to do that?' the matelot asks as he gallantly hands her up on to the quay.

'My dad was a destroyer captain.'

The boatman salutes. On land Adnan is the hero again. He adjusts the drape of his jacket, the reveal of his cuffs. Then he swoops and scoops up Ayşe, crushing her to him, her heels scraping the concrete, their faces breath-close, kiss-intimate.

'Didn't I?' he roars. Ayşe can taste the wine he swallowed. 'Didn't I, by fuck?' Adnan spins her around. Caught up in his arms, Ayşe feels boats, buses, buggies, minarets blur around her. 'Come on!' Adnan shouts and she slips back to earth but he has her hand and he dashes through the night-time strollers, through the close-laid tarpaulins of shifty ware, straight out into the traffic, dodging and dancing and stopping the trucks and tour buses with an out-held hand and the grace of lovers. A tram sweeps down upon them. Ayşe shrieks, then Adnan's hand pulls her clear of the killing monster, between the scooters and the Volkswagens and into the alleys between the shops that shoulder up against the New Mosque. There, in a doorway against a red painted roller shutter overhung by a curl of urban wisteria, Adnan pulls her to him. Ayşe slams hard against him, a declaration of war as of love, wanting him to feel the power of her belly, the strength, the perfection of her thighs. A youth in a leather bomber jacket jeers up the alley at them. Adnan bellows with filthy laughter but pulls her on, deeper into Sultanahmet. It's no city for lovers, this old Ottoman capital.

On Hoca Paşa Sok at the back of a tiny neighbourhood mosque she backs him into a doorway. His good pants, his deal-making pants are open, his half-hard, heavy cock is in her hand. She has a bad bold idea what to do with it, then lights go on in the grille above the door across the alley. Ayşe shrieks with laughter and spins away, running and laughing up the maze of cobbled alleys that run up to Cağaloğlu. Away from the main streets Sultanahmet is empty. The shuttered shop faces radiate the memory of the day's heat. Ayşe stops in the middle of a steep cobbled lane overhung by dusty almond branches to step deftly out of her panties. Adnan catches her, prises the gossamer triangles from her hand and presses them to his face.

'Now that's what I call a fine bouquet. Exceptional vintage.'

Ayşe grabs the pants and forces them into Adnan's mouth, laughing hysterically as he munches with great woofing chomps like a monster. A woman late home, shopping bag in hand, coat pulled discreetly around her, crosses the top end of the alley. She stares at Adnan with the pants hanging from his mouth.

'Waugh!' he roars. He waves his hands. The woman flees, coat pulled tighter against the immoral night. Ayşe and Adnan are still aching with laughter as they tumble into the elevator in the multistorey car park. Ayşe's dress is up around her waist, her legs wrapped around Adnan's waist and her back jammed against the emergency call panel when the elevator pings and stops on three and the door opens on a sick-faced man in bad-cut suit and bad-cut hair. He blinks. His little mouth is open.

'Going up,' says Adnan. Adnan and Ayşe fall out of the elevator and into the Audi. It's the only car on the entire level. 'Two million euro!' Adnan shouts. The chipped pillars, the tyre-polished concrete return it to him. 'Two million euro!' No one is so corrupt, so insensitive to the malign spirit of place, as to fuck in an empty multi-storey car-park. But Ayşe keeps her hand on Adnan's cock as he third-gear spirals down the exit ramp, one hand keeping the wheel on full lock. Tyres shriek, the ghosts of old multi-storeys. *If we hit a random drip of oil we're dead*, Ayşe thinks. *No, that can't be. Not this night.*

Out in the street Adnan clicks in the autodrive. Ayşe wiggles close to open her thighs to his touch. She frigs him gently, more a tease, all the way through the shuttling dolmuşes on O1. On the bridge approach she feels Adnan take his thumb away from her clitoris. The auto drive snaps off. The gas turbine whinnies like a proud horse. Acceleration pushes Ayşe deep into the seat. This is a thrilling car. The bridge to Asia is an arc of light. High over the black water, between continents. There are ships down there. Floodlit Turkish flags stand like beacons along the hill-tops of the Asian shore. Moons and stars, hanging limply. Night is no respite from the heat. Down there, where the dark water abuts the bright shore, is the yalı of Adnan's dreams. Your secret deal will buy it for us, but my secret deal will take us to the yalı of which you really dream, the one behind me, on the European shore.

She smokes. The night traffic never ceases. The Audi burns past truck after truck after truck rolling up from the east into the maw of great Istanbul. Ayşe rolls sideways to gaze out the window at the blur of cheap housing and strip stores. She opens her lips a syllable; smoke falls from her mouth like water. Spindly minarets, tinny silver domes, cheap Saudi-built mosques, alien and thoughtless. Youths hanging around. Sports fashion. The police have pulled over a truck. Three cop cars. The truck carries Armenian characters; the five-o'clock-shadow men in mud-coloured clothes standing listlessly have come from farther east than that.

They seem the only passionate things in Ferhatpaşa as they cross the still-warm concrete from the garage to the lobby. Speedboats, horse-drawn carriages, glittering previews over as the night of lights, good suits and high shoes and million-euro deals: Ferhatpaşa does not believe in these. It's still urgent, she still wants him; he's hungry for her but every second dry, drab Ferhatpaşa wears away at it.

He's kicking his shoes off in the hall; strewing jacket, tie, shirt across the living room floor. A man should undress from below the waist. She's never been able to teach him that; lazy Kaş beach boy.

'One minute. Keep it hard for me. I am going to fuck you until your balls are like dried apricots.'

Quick pee. Needs doing. By the time she is clean and sweet and out of everything but the stockings he loves so much and the killing heels, he's face down star-fished across the bed, snoring.

Wednesday

5

From early light Adem Dede Square has been busy with mops and buckets, hoses and scrubbing brushes, multi-surface cleaners and paint-stripper. Up ladders, hanging out of balconies, on chairs, working painstakingly on the details of carved doors with tooth-brushes, bent over cars dotingly dabbing away the orange bug-bursts with T-Cut. Hafize mops the front steps and dabs at the woodwork of the Gallery Erkoç, working the graffiti out of the floral scroll, sleeves and trouser legs rolled up immodestly in the heat and effort; Mrs Durukan, leaning out of the balcony screens freely and enthu-siastically hosing down the front of her apartment and treating the angry shouts of the splashed in the street as if it is their fault. Kenan's roller shutter has spared him the worst of the paint-bot attack; even that shameless Georgian woman is on her knees on her balcony, hair tied back in a headscarf. There is a temporary truce between Bülent and Aykut as they scrub at their chairs and tables and splattered windows with nylon dish scourers. Orange-tinged streams of water run across Adem Dede Square, merge, vanish down drains and through unexpected sinkholes between cobbles, pour down the steps on Vermilion-Maker Lane in a bright cascade. If you had a police frequency scanner, you could map the hidden watercourses of Eskiköy, Georgios Ferentinou thinks, sitting at his recently cleaned table outside Bulent's çayhane. Another secret Istanbul. His own section of the dervish house remains resolutely freckled. The first rain will wash it away.

'I'm thinking of suing,' Bülent says, wringing out his mop and pouring another bucket down the street drain.

'The police? Don't waste your time,' Lefteres says.

'No.' Bülent nods over at Güneşli Sok down the side of Aykut's meyhane. 'Him.'

The old Greeks keep a moment of uncomfortable silence.

'You don't want to be starting something,' Lefteres says.

'Well, something is started, whether we like it or not,' Father Ioannis says. A great dark presence in his beard and robe, he is even more quiet and brooding than usual. Georgios notices his hands busy knotting and unknotting his prayer rope. 'They were at the church again last night. Spray paint. God is Great. Infidels will burn. Greek paedos.'

'Have you tried talking to Hüseyin Yaşayan?' Hüseyin is the imam of the small Tulip Mosque and a brilliant amateur historian of Beyoğlu types and characters. Georgios has frequently drawn on his prodigious store of community knowledge to help chart his alternative maps of Istanbul.

'I called him. There's not a lot he can do against Hızır.'

'The Green Saint? We are in trouble.'

'Hüseyin'll make some mention about community relations at Friday prayers but it's not his people doing it. This is grass roots, popular religion. God preserve us from young men with religion. He's as scared of them as we are. He's duty bound to report this kind of thing to the Ministry of Religious Affairs, but if he does, Tulip Mosque would burn right after St Panteleimon. This will not end well.'

'You know,' says Lefteres, stirring his tea, 'I'm thinking of taking that commission.'

'The lampoon?'

'Against your woman.' He nods at the Georgian woman pausing in her industrious scrubbing to mop her brow.

'I thought you said you had to be satisfied there was just cause and a clear social need,' says Bülent.

'I can be flexible on the just cause if the social need is clear enough,' Lefteres says. 'Right now it couldn't be clearer.'

'God save her,' Father Ioannis mutters. Everyone around the table understands a minority fingering a yet smaller minority. Show which side you're on.

'I'm writing a new contract,' Georgios Ferentinou announces to crack the bad silence. 'There will be a terror attack – actual or thwarted – involving gas at some point in the next ten days.'

'I'll buy that,' says Bülent. 'Is this what you've been talking about in your think-tank?'

'They've had information,' Georgios says. 'It's an interesting group. Lots of experts in diverse fields. I was put next a zoologist who specializes in how birds manage to communicate a threat across an entire flock in a split second. Isn't that fascinating? Might terror groups unconsciously communicate signals to each other? If we could just recognize that language. There's Selma Özgün the psychogeographer. She's interested in how over centuries city architecture affects the social and mental spaces people inhabit. I can see how that might give insights into where terrorists might preferentially strike, or where they might live and meet. There are legacies in these things. They've even recruited our one and only science-fiction writer. That's clever.'

'The big fear's always been blowing up one of those gas tankers in the Bosphorus,' Bülent says. 'I saw this programme on the television; Istanbul's particularly vulnerable: the hills on either side of the Bosphorus contain the blast. The programme said it could locally reach the intensity of Hiroshima.'

'God forgive you for knowing too much about this sort of thing,' Father Ioannis says.

'Well, when you've a three-year-old you watch a lot of Discovery Asia,' Bülent says. 'It's good; you learn stuff.'

'You see, I think that's what Ogün Saltuk will be thinking,' Georgios says.

'Ogün Saltuk. Wasn't he the one . . .' Constantin says.

'He was,' Georgios says quickly. 'The same man.'

'Yes,' says Constantin, frowning as if the tea spoon he is twirling is the very axis of great Istanbul, 'The one you once said never would have an ideal academic career, untroubled by anything like an original thought.'

'I said more than that and the man is fool and a plagiarist,' Georgios says. 'But it interests me. I want to see how it develops.'

'So you don't think it's a tanker,' Bülent says.

'It's too obvious.'

'Ten to one Ogün Saltuk suggests it,' Constantin says.

'So what do you think, before you float your terror contract?' Bülent asks.

'I don't know,' Georgios says. 'There's something; there are forces moving, patterns I can't quite see but I can feel.'

'You'll be seeing djinn next,' says Lefteres. 'Hey! Maybe that would do it.'

'Well, I'll take a few of your gas contracts,' Bülent says. 'Never steered me wrong yet.'

'Well gentlemen, I'll be taking my leave.' Lefteres rises painfully from his place. 'I have a lampoon to write.'

Next to rise from his low stool is Father Ioannis. 'I'm going to call round with Hüseyin, though there's bugger all he can do. If anyone's interested, I'm saying a vespers tonight.'

Georgios and Constantin sit in comfortable silence as men can enjoy silence between them without the need to fill it with words. The Alexandrian lights a cigarette and slumps into accustomed ease behind it, trickling a thin ribbon of smoke up into the warm air. Around them the cleaners and scrubbers and swishers of Adem Dede Square come to their independent, but simultaneous truces with the tag-paint of the Istanbul security police. It's too damn hot out there for work.

Georgios studies his smoking friend. Cynical, manipulative, gossipy as a widow and vindictive when wronged, opaque of motives and closed of heart, Constantin is far from the kind of man Georgios would choose for a friend. Constantin's family claimed to be as old as the city of the delta's name; sons and daughters of Alexander himself. He speaks seven languages, including Classical Greek, and nods to five religions while believing none of them, has studied at three universities in the capitals of three former empires. Nationalism, then Islamism, both twentieth-century political inventions, destroyed the Greek civilization in Egypt that had endured for three thousand years; in Cairo first, ever the political crucible. But cosmopolitan, decaying Alexandria could not remain aloof to the forces surging through the Islamic world. The Pig Riots, the Alexandrians called them: a government health purge to eliminate potential vectors for the H1N1 Swine Flu virus had led to a mass swine cull and, by implication, a purge of the non-Muslim communities. In Alexandria the Copts were still strong so the religious fervour had turned on the small, weak Greek community. In ten days they were erased from history. Constantin had seen the flames leap from the broken dome of St Athanasios and taken the next flight out. He still owns properties in the city, managed through shell companies, trickling rent through middle men and civil servants on the take; enough to keep him in Istanbul. From one dying Greek community to another. Decay; the slow drawing in of the world; hüzün, that uniquely Istanbulu sense of melancholic nostalgia.

'I saw Ariana,' Georgios says.

'Did you talk to her?'

'No'

'Well, you need to buck yourself up, Ferentinou. She leaves on Friday.'

'How do you know this?'

'We are not the only Greeks in Beyoğlu. I can give you her number.'

'Call her?'

'You have business that has gone unfinished for over forty years.'

'Long before you ever landed in Eskiköy,' Georgios suddenly snaps. 'You think you know everything, you know nothing; a gossiping fool is what you are.' He rises from the table, throws down a scatter of euro coins. There is business forty-seven years unfinished, but Constantin, cosy as a flea on a dog in his own self-exile, thinks it must be something as simple as love unrequited. Love it was, but time and politics have turned it into a need for absolution: Georgios Ferentinou fears that Ariana Sinanidis blames him for the death of Meryem Tasi.

Necdet can't remember the last time he set foot in a mosque but the body never forgets. Wash the feet, the hands, the face and the neck, the ears. Wash with water from the heart of Hızır. The Green Saint has taken himself away and the djinn have withdrawn to the edge of their world but he hears their whispers like wind turning leaves on a tree. They have always been drawn to mosques, mescids, shrines, sacred stones. He leaves his sneakers in the alcove. From the beauty of the tile work to the solid brass lamps Necdet can see that Tulip Mosque was once richly endowed but its fortunes have faded with its neighbourhood and can no longer afford a pensioner to watch the shoes. The carpet beneath his soles is thick and soft, he curls his toes into it. The djinn hang back at the mosque door, fluttering and rustling. By God's law they are not permitted to enter.

The tarikat has gathered under the loge, the raised platform where the aristocracy would pray, a few metres closer to God, but Necdet does not join them yet. He remembers other, engrained responses. Necdet places himself on the carpet facing the mihrab. He kneels, performs the prostrations. The body never forgets the moves; the tongue never forgets the Arabic. The ritual works him, stretches his muscles. He kneels, hands on thighs. The peace is immense. He looks up into the tiled dome. There are words up there, stretched and concealed by the geometric patterns of the tiles, hidden words. If he concentrates he can make them out. The ninety-nine beautiful names of God, intertwined with stems and leaves and flowers. A Paradise garden blooms in tile across the dome. What kind of flowers are those? Tulips. This is the Tulip Mosque. Necdet realizes that this is a beautiful building and that he knows nothing about it. How old is it, who built it, why? It's glorious and he's ignorant. The place he lives, the dervish house; he never thought about it as more than a place to sleep, smoke, escape but it has a history, it has lives woven through it, it has holy men. He understands suddenly that it is very old. Which came first, mosque or tekke? Who were those dervishes, what decided them to build their house there? What brought Ismet and his new dervishes; the building, the history, God, something else?

'Peace be with all here,' he says and sits down on the carpet among the brothers. The dervishes mumble greetings in reply. Many of the faces he knows from their visits to the tekke, some better than others, but there are men here he has never seen before. Necdet looks at each in turn; details, distinctions, personalities. These are people, individuals.

'In God's name you are very welcome to the Adem Dede group,' Ismet says. 'You know many of us already, but this is your first proper induction to the tarikat. We've seen things that can't be rationally explained, we've seen you do and say and see things that seem like prophecies from God. What we want to do here is test those, gently, in the spirit of brothers, to discover if they are Islamic or not.'

The big man across the circle in the striped shirt speaks now. Necdet knows he is a garage mechanic in the everyday life. His name is Yusuf and he is second in the order.

'God willed that we set up this group to explore how God's justice worked out in a modern, urban society. God's will is timeless and there can be no division of it, but like a diamond, changing light can cast changing reflections from its facets. While we revere the lives and example of the Hadith, we've gone back to the Koran as an unshakeable foundation. In the Holy Koran the light shines brightest. In every word we're shown the right society – God's society – the true shariat. Our divine task, thanks be to God and his prophet Mohammed – is to apply that perfect law at the level where people need it. On the street; between families, between people, between small businesses. People need justice. Our judges are aloof at best, corrupt at worst. They are distant and they judge by man's values, not God's.'

'Immoral values,' big Yusuf murmurs.

'Always it costs. The law is a rich man's game. Lawyers get fat on writs and contracts and divorces. They spin cases out and out and out so they can wring every last cent in fees. Why should the law cost? Why should it only be available to those with deep pockets, or influential friends? This is corruption. God's justice is pure and God's justice is free. This tarikat, God willing, is about training holy men to be judges in a system of community justice. There are examples all over the world of community micro-credit schemes, why not community micro-justice? We offer a new shariat to those who agree to be bound by its judgements. We seek to judge quickly, fairly, transparently, and in accordance with the Holy Koran.

'Now we have a case that will really test our faith and abilities: your visions and prophecies can give us an enormous foothold in this community, but first we have to judge, are they Islamic or are they not? Now, what is it you claim you see?'

'I see beings, creatures, living things that aren't from this world. I've seen things made from living fire, I've seen people's doubles, their exact doubles, upside down inside the earth.'

'Do you see any here now?' Yusuf asks.

'Not now.'

'Djinn are forbidden entry to mosques,' Ismet says. 'Djinn are Koranic. Sura 6, the whole of sura 72 ...'

Yusuf raises a finger. 'Brother, we haven't established that these visions are even djinn.'

Ismet sits back, fidgeting. Necdet feels an immense still calm rise up through him, anchoring him to the marble.

'I had a vision of a burning baby,' Necdet says. 'In the toilets at work. I saw spirits inside the computers.'

'My brother works at the Levent Business Rescue Centre,' Ismet interjects.

'I saw streets filled with them,' Necdet says and hears again their rustling, rattling, clattering fistle; flocking over and around and through each other. 'I saw them on every car, every street, I saw them on people's shoulders, I saw them in the earth . . .'

'We have to allow for contemporary interpretations,' says Armağan, an older dervish, grey-haired, with glasses and a peering, inquiring air.

'Of course,' Yusuf says. 'Go on.'

'And I saw the one who masters them.'

Involuntary straightenings, stiffenings, small intakes of breath.

'Could you tell us more about this vision?' Yusuf asks.

'Yes,' Necdet says, and knows this is the time to tell because he can smell green verdure blowing through this Tulip Mosque, a perfume of flowers, a scent of deep waters. 'Something led me out of the office, through a service door. There were corridors, tunnels that went down deep, way way deeper than anyone knows, down deep right under Levent. There's a fountain down there, an old old fountain, from the old pagan days. But there was still water in it. That's where he was sitting, by the fountain.'

'Who?' asks Ismet.

'The green man,' Necdet says. *Hızır, Hızır;* the name runs around the circle. *The Green Saint. God is great. God is great.*

Yusuf raises his hand again.

'Brothers, please. Brother Necdet, would you mind describing this green man?'

'He was an old man in a green robe, like he was older than everything but at the same time, the youngest thing in the world. He had a hook nose and a big beard like an old Ottoman and the greenest eyes. He smelled of water, old water, deep water, very very pure water. He could smile and be terrifying in the same look. He felt very dangerous, very old and very wild, like he could upturn the roots of the city just because he felt like it. I was very very afraid but, at the same time, how could I be afraid? Of him?'

'God be praised,' Bedri cries, a boy from the east who works in a Taksim hotel.

'The Holy Koran . . .' Ismet says quickly.

'*The Cave* does not directly name Hızır, Al-Khidr,' Yusuf says.

'He is *the unknown* who met Moses, and that is all the sura says. And that he is vizier to Dulkarnain.'

'He's here,' Necdet says. Consternation erupts among the brothers, praise and fear alike. 'I see him, he's right beside you, Hasan.' The kid with the vague moustache tenses. The mosque lamps on their long chains sway to a sudden air. Necdet bows to the figure in green, cross-legged on the carpet. Yusuf raises his hands, stills the circle again.

'Brothers, a saint may be among us, but God is in us. Brother Necdet, I've a question for you. You were caught up in the bomb on Monday morning on the Levent tram.'

'I was, yes.'

'Only the bomber died, I won't say martyr as no one has claimed the martyrdom. These visions, they only began after the bomb?'

'That's right. I was trying to get away from the police, and I saw the head.'

'A head? What head?'

'Her head. The bomber woman. I saw her head, in mid-air, and there was light coming out of it.'

'But these visions, you never had anything like them before the bomb? We need to be very clear on this.'

'Never.'

'Do you think it possible that these djinn, even Hızır himself, might be some kind of … illusion, hallucination, brought on by being too close to the bomb?'

'I had a friend who was caught in a Kurdish IED on his service down in Gaziantep,' says Necmettin, a skinny, bad-skinned man in his twenties who has always seemed to Necdet the closest to him in personality and temperament. 'He was a mess. Nothing physical, all in here.' He taps his head. 'Horrors; thing you wouldn't believe. Things eating him alive. He met himself going up the down stairs. Post traumatic stress disorder. They all know about it but they don't want to admit it.'

'I was in this place way out east called Divrican,' says Big Şefik, a huge, docile bear of a man with a strange red beard. 'Serving my time. There was a whole village there suddenly started seeing djinn and angels and ghosts. They were Kurds; Yazidis. Demon worshippers.'

'My brother saw that the girl from the Art Gallery was pregnant,' Ismet says. 'Necdet could tell her she was pregnant because he saw her karin inside the earth.'

'Which we have already agreed is not Islam!' Yusuf thunders.

The imam, an elderly, scholarly man with heavy glasses, has been moving around under the women's balcony, checking a wall tile here, a frayed piece of carpet there, a dead light bulb elsewhere, but always with an eye on the tarikat. He looks up and glares at the raised voices.

'Brothers, this is a prayer hall,' Ismet says but Necdet sees him stare the imam down. The old man turns away.

'Brother Necdet, I'd ask you now about yourself. How did you come to be with your brother in the dervish house?'

'This is not relevant,' Ismet says.

'There are some of the brothers here who don't attend your meetings in the dervish house.'

'I set fire to my sister when I was out of my head on drugs,' Necdet says. 'I was not a good man. I was idle, I was rebellious, I was immoral and disobedient to my parents, and I had no respect for Islam. I used drugs, I dealt drugs, I stole cars, I stole money from my neighbours, I broke into their homes and robbed them, I started fights and beat people because I liked it, I was angry all the time.' As he speaks Necdet holds Hızır in his eye. The Green Saint draws words out of him like water from a well. 'I set fire to my sister because she looked at me wrong. My father would have killed me but Ismet saved me and brought me here, to look after me, get me away from the people I knew there. I was worthless. Ismet gave me a safe place and found me a job.'

'All I did was offer a safe haven,' Ismet says.

'Do you profess that there is one God and Muhammed is his prophet?' Yusuf asks.

'It's like I've been asleep, or buried, or that my eyes just haven't been able to open wide enough, but now I am awake and I can see things. I think I was pretending at playing a person, until now. How can this be?'

'Yes, but do you profess?' Yusuf asks again.

'God's power is not to be constrained,' Ismet says.

'We are judges, not mystics.'

'I don't see any distinction. We are judges, and we are mystics. If people are to trust our judgements they must see that they are God's not man's. This is God's power.'

'Cheap showmanship degrades our work.'

'This is God's will at work. God has given us a rare and precious gift; we don't have to understand why and how and to whom he gives it. We can't. All we have to do is accept that it is for us.'

'This is superstition.'

'It brings people.'

'It brought the police,' Armağan mutters. Ismet rounds on him.

'Let them come! It only shows how weak they are, how afraid, how distant and remote from what people really want and need. If they persecute us, it means we're doing God's will. Let them come, we'll show them who's strong. Vote. What do you say brothers? I say, from God.'

'Haram,' Armağan says.

'Halal,' says the young man next to him, the one with the almost-moustache, whose friend had been caught in the roadside bomb. The vote goes around, the pattern is simple to see. The young vote yes, the older ones vote no.

'No,' says Yusuf, 'This is haram.' But he knows he has lost the vote and his influence in the group.

'This is Islamic,' says the final dervish in the circle.

'Let there be no disunity,' Ismet says, holding out his hand to Yusuf. 'God is one.'

'God is one,' Yusuf says and takes Ismet's hand. The tarikat breaks up with a brief prayer, the circle rises. The young men crowd in around Ismet. Already they're calling him Dede, grandfather, the honorific of a dervish leader. Ismet Dede. Shaykh Ismet.

Hızır remains seated on the carpet. *What have you done?* Necdet thinks. Hızır answers in a laughing voice like spring: *Who ever said I was a tame saint?*

Ismet has a word for each of the tarikat members as they leave the mosque, a handshake, a touch on the back, an embrace. When they have all put their shoes back on and gone to their garages and banks and stores and metro trains and taxis, Necdet says to his brother, 'What would have happened if I had lost the judgement?'

'How can we be respected as kadıs if our judgements carry no weight?'

'I don't understand.'

'Half the law is its enforceability. Even the infidel judges will tell you that.'

The imam looks over. He wants these zealous young men, these troublemakers, out. He wants his beautiful, historical mosque back. Ismet gently turns his brother to one side, shielding himself from the imam's view, and casually slips back the waist band of his jacket. Tucked into the waistband of his trousers is the butt of a gun. Outside, in the brilliant light, the djinn flock and storm like starlings.

'Red? So?'

Beshun Ferhat sits enthroned among rabbits and birds. At her feet are mega-packs of vegetable seeds, the photographs of aubergines and peppers and fat tomatoes faded to near-monochrome. To her right hand is a small table on which sits a glass of tea, a Sobranie Black Russian in an ivory holder balanced on an ash tray filling the air with its glorious louche incense and a white rabbit on a lead. Beshun Ferhat is a mountain of a woman, sloping outwards from the top of her head to her floral patterned harem pants and her clumpy country-woman's boots. She smells of rose water and the body-warmed, oily musk of menopause. In the gloom of the animal market she wears round-eyed dark glasses, as if she wants people to think she is blind though Ayşe knows she is not. She seems immovable among her cages of pet rabbits and puppies and singing birds, a pillar of the market. Ayşe has detested this place from early memory. The smell of piss-sodden straw and unclean animal bodies whirls her back to the age of five when her father brought her here as a Sunday treat. She had cried at the sight of the poor puppies six to a cage and tried to pester her father into buying them all to set them free. They hadn't stopped at this stall. This terrifying woman would have branded herself on Ayşe's memory.

'He's not catching any fish,' Ayşe says.

'No one is,' Beshun says and takes a long draw on her Sobranie, an affected, theatrical gesture that involves the most delicate of fingertip holds on the ivory, an upward tilt of the head, a trickle of smoke up through the birds' cages to the minarets of the New Mosque. She notices Ayşe's noticing. 'Would you like one, love?'

Ayşe lights, inhales, savours the pungent, exotic, Russian flavours. It reminds her of wooden Riva speedboats, horse-drawn carriages, exquisite verbal duelling, almost sex in the empty streets just above this mosque-shadowed market. She issues a stream of tiny smoke rings from deep in her throat.

'You know, I should buy these more often.'

'I used to smoke Samsun but none of the Turkish brands taste of anything since we joined the EU.' The rabbit twitches its ears. 'So, love, my family heirloom? Red told you his stories, did he? All you'll get from me, love, is another story. Stories are all there are. Yes yes yes, I am Beshun Ferhat and I am the ten-times-great-granddaughter of Hacı Ferhat. My people are Hatayis, we are the veritable Ferhats of Iskenderun though none of us live there now. None of us have lived there for five generations. The Ferhats have been in Istanbul since 1895 but as you know, love, it takes much longer than that to be accepted as a true Istanbulu. Who are your people?'

'Erkoç of Şişli. It was an old naval family. My mother is a Çalışlar of Meşrutiyet, her sister married the Justice Minister.'

Beshun rolls her head.

'Old stock. Here. Let me show you something.' She gropes for her bag. Ayşe refuses to find it for her. *You can see, old woman.* Beshun takes out a sheet of yellowed paper in a plastic sleeve. 'This is my family tree.' Her fingers trace the trunks and branches. 'See how I can trace my lineage back to Osman Fahir Ferhat, the oldest of Hacı Ferhat's sons, the one who supervised the sealing of the coffin.' Her fingers skip down a drastic narrowing of the trunk. 'This is where we came to Istanbul. See how many of the branches die off here? We suffered a great reversal of fortune in the late nineteen hundreds. Death in war, death by drowning, murders, vendettas, plague and disease. Male heirs died young; some were not suffered to live, if you understand what I mean. God was hard on the Ferhats, but fair. He pruned out the dead wood, the diseased and inbred. He gave us an opportunity to start afresh and renew our fortunes.'

Which is why you are managing a pet stall at the cheap end of the Egyptian Bazaar, Ayşe thinks. God but these Sobranies are nice.

'This was long after the curse of the Hairy Man of Cappadocia.'

Beshun stamps a booted foot and rattles the side table with a fist. The rabbit starts, eyes and nostrils wide but its leash is harshly short.

'Do not pollute my ears with the name of that charlatan! There was no curse, there was no hairy-assed dervish from the wilds of Anatolia. Listen if you'd be wise. My family were renowned in Iskenderun as great magicians. That was always the source of our fortune. Hacı Ferhat himself was the founder of our family school: he was a merchant, a traveller and also a student of the mysteries and magics of the countries that he visited on trade. His interests knew no bounds, he conversed with shaykhs of Aleppo and Damascus, the djinn masters of Cairo, the Jewish Kabbalists of Tripoli and the angel summoners of Jerusalem. He was on first-name terms with the greatest magicians of Persia and India. He studied with ritual mages in Rome and the star magicians in Milan, he regularly visited demonologists in Prague and Vienna, he corresponded with the great Etteilla in Paris and the London disciples of Enoch.'

A middle-aged man wanders in among the cages from the throned alley, asking about guinea-pig food. Beshun leans heavily over in her chair and hauls a packet of vacuum-packed hay from a box underneath the puppy cages. *Men of voting age should never have anything to do with guinea-pigs*, she thinks. One of the pups manically scratches its ear. Ayşe fears fleas.

'Where was I, love?'

'Your family of magicians.'

'Oh yes. Hacı Ferhat. Like any good father, he wanted success for his sons in life and business so he taught them what he could of his magic. They've passed it down the line to this very day.' Beshun heavily pats the rabbit. It flinches from her hand. 'But at the same time he was also a member of a secret tarikat. Its father-house was here in Istanbul but it drew brothers from all over the empire. It wasn't exactly a magician's circle – it was very respectable, there were shaykhs and dervishes in it as well as many prominent men from all parts of Thrace and Anatolia – but it was interested in the more bizarre aspects of religion. Not only Sufism, they also studied Buddhist teachings from Japan and Tibet, Hindu belief, Christian mysteries. They believed that there was a holy language – not Arabic, not Hebrew, not Latin or Greek or any language people speak – God's language, and that it was a written language, and that each letter in its alphabet had control over a different part of the universe. They got in trouble with a few imams because of oaths and allegiances and things like that but they had enough money and the right political connections to buy them off. Well, love, you know what Hacı Ferhat did and what he turned himself into, otherwise you wouldn't be here. And you know that the Mellified Man of Iskenderun disappeared. This is how it really happened.'

Beshun lights another Sobranie. Ayşe accepts the offered cigarette. Smoking in a pet market is not smoking in the street. This is acceptable for a lady.

'You see, the stories of the curse of the Mellified Man have it right enough to be wrong. Yes, my family did fall on hard times, but that was not because of the Mellified Man. Yes, there was a dervish, but he was not a wandering Sufi. He was a magician. What happened was, my great-great-great-great-great-grandfather Ahmet decided that the only way to restore our fortunes was to sell the Mellified Man. There were bids from all over the empire and Russia, Egypt and the British Raj and as far afield as China. Then a letter arrived, oh! Like a thunderbolt. We had forgotten all about the secret society, the Tarikat of the Divine Word, but they had not forgotten about Hacı Ferhat. It said that a man's first allegiance was to his tarikat, that oaths had been taken, that Hacı Ferhat had never stopped being a brother and the Tarikat of the Divine Word had an iron claim on the Mellified Man. Now, as you might imagine, it was not exactly legal to sell a Mellified Man, even in Ottoman times, so we could not go to a judge. The tarikat offered a solution: let God decide through a duel of magic, our family magic against theirs. Now, no one knows what happened, no record was ever made, all the participants were sworn to secrecy and no one has ever spoken, but my great-great-great-great-great-Uncle Nihat Ferhat, who had never married and had dedicated himself to studying Hacı Ferhat's writings, met with the greatest magician of the Tarikat of the Divine Word. It was a battle of words: the old magic of the spoken word against the magic of the written word. We lost. We surrendered the Mellified Man. All was lost, we sold up what we held in Iskenderun and came to Istanbul to rebuild our fortunes, the ruins of a proud family.'

The two women slowly exhale fragrant smoke.

'And the Tarikat of the Divine Word?' Ayşe asks.

'It would have been destroyed by Atatürk at the time of the Revolution along with all the other orders,' Beshun says.

'Yes, but we all know that the orders were never destroyed, they merely went underground,' Ayşe says.

'This order was singled out in particular. It was popular with members of the Sultan's family and high-ranking government officials and members of the Committee of Union and Progress were members. There is a story that the other orders were suppressed to cover the total destruction of this one.'

'No trace remains?'

'You're very far from the first to try and find the Tarikat of the Divine Word, love.'

But ideas buzz in Ayşe's imagination like fleas on puppies, flies around cage-cleanings wrapped in newspaper, song-birds fluttering in cages. The trick is not to let story seduce in a city built from stories, tale upon sedimented tale. Istanbul is an oral culture. The old magic was charmed into being by spoken words. Historians, columnists, writers, curio-hunters, even psychogeographers, their primary sense is hearing, and so they are deceived by their ears. Ayşe's sovereign sense is vision. Truth is always in the eye.

Beshun strokes her rabbit.

'The magic hasn't gone away you know.'

Here I pay the storyteller, Ayşe thinks.

'It still passes down through the family in the direct line from the Iskenderun brothers. I have some limited power to foretell the future. Would you like?'

'Go on then,' Ayşe says.

'I usually charge . . .'

Ayşe already has a twenty-euro note in her hand.

'Maashallah, forty-one times.' Beshun grunts with the effort as she lifts a shoebox from under the table. It's filled with file cards glued to cardboard backings, each of them hand-lettered with a Koranic verse or a proverb or a line of poetry. Nashun clears away the tea glass and the ash tray under her seat. Ayşe worries about the proximity of Sobranie to so much guinea-pig food. Beshun sets the box on its side so the cards spill a little way from their confinement, then releases the rabbit's leash, lifts it and presses her nose to its wiffle-nose, her lips to its rodent-y mouth, whispering and muttering rabbit-charms. Ayşe shivers.

'This is Süleyman'

'Should I ask a question or something?'

'No need, love. Süleyman knows.' Beshun turns the rabbit head-over-paws three times. 'Hippity-hoppity lippity-loppity, by the swop of my ears and the lop of my feet and the wiffle of my nose, tell me tell me tell me.' Süleyman the rabbit shakes the dizzy out of its ears and sniffs along the line of cards, three times up, three times down. It pokes at a card with its nose. Beshun lifts the card and sets it face down on the table. Twice more Süleyman prods at cards. Beshun sets them carefully aside and gives Süleyman a kiss between his ears before confining him again.

With great deliberateness Beshun turns the first chosen face up. *Al Ba'ith.* The forty-ninth beautiful name of God, written in a circle in fat felt-pen Arabic.

'God the sender from this world into Paradise, the raiser from death; God the resurrector,' she says. She turns the second card face up. Ayşe holds her breath. Theatre is more than half of any oracle. It is an old card, the paper yellow and torn at the edges, the corners patched with yellowed Sellotape. A verse from Rumi.

'A strange sweetness, never felt before, spreads through the flesh,' Beshun recites. 'And the mouth revels in the luscious taste of the reed flute and the player's lips.'

Beshun flips the third card. A garden of messy Arabic, poorly versified. Bees in coloured felt-marker and crayon draw little buzz-lines around the words. Some carry little buckets full of honey. Sura 16.

'As Your Lord has taught the bee, saying, "Make houses in the mountains and the trees and in the hives which men build you.

'"Moreover, feed on every kind of food and walk the beaten paths of your Lord." From its belly comes a many-coloured liquid, which gives medicine to man.'

Beshun pushes the cards to the centre of the table.

'Well, love? Are you answered?'

'What do you think?'

'You won't find it. Istanbul has too many secrets, too many stories.'

Ayşe leaves an additional twenty-euro note on the little table. As she slides on her sunglasses against the glare-after-gloom of Yeni Cami Cadessi she is struck by the stomach-muscle twinge of not being alone. She doesn't know how she knows, but she's certain a car is following her. Ayşe sets down her bag on a pedestrian crossing call button on the side of a lamp-post and uses the excuse of hunting for a ceptep to scan the street. Cars driven by men. It could be any one of them. Does the driver of that silver Skoda look at her a moment longer than normal Istanbul street-staring? Fortunes and conspiracies. Hidden histories. Magical thinking. She has a bookstore to call on and lost dervishes to find.

The Boy Detective and his Monkey Robot Sidekick go dashing along dusty abandoned corridors and up and down lost staircases. Over the century since the tekke was dissolved by Ankara's decree, developers and residents have partitioned and repartitioned the generous spaces of the dervishes, walling in a balcony here, connecting a pavilion there, boxing in that staircase and subdividing rooms and levels, in the process mislaying whole architectures that lie close as a kiss but forever apart from the inhabited parts of the dervish house. Here are ways known only to the rats, the famine-thin cats that hunt them, and nine-year-old boys. Usually in the tunnels and shut-off corridors Can will run his fingers along the wall, feeling the thrum of the outside world, its traffic, its people, its shouts and voices and musics, amplified through the wood. Today he's too excited, bounding down the stairs two steps at a time. Monkey at his side spontaneously breaks into a swarm of scuttling components, forms into scuttling Snake, flies a few wingbeats, breaks apart again, shattering and reforming, picking up its master's excitement. The Boy Detective has a lead, a real, proper like-it-is-on-the-television lead.

First the formalities. Can takes out the earplugs, carefully cleaning off the wax and skin flakes and ick that's gathered there. The heard world rushes in; always his heart thumps, not in panic, chaotic patterns of sodium ions polarizing and depolarizing across its surface, but in the pure thrill of what he had only felt through his fingers filling up its proper sense. Mr Ferentinou makes tea. Can doesn't like tea but he likes to be offered it. It's a man-to-man thing.

Mr Ferentinou is a bad mood this morning. He answered the door in it, he's making tea in it, he bangs down the saucers in it.

'Are you all right, Mr Ferentinou?' Can asks.

Mr Ferentinou is taken aback by the directness of the question. He bristles, harrumphs, then softens.

'I've had an argument with someone,' he says.

'People your age can have arguments?'

'People never stop having arguments,' Mr Ferentinou says. Can thinks about the vibrations he feels through the bedroom wall some nights, the soft, rhythmic syllables, high and low; his mother for a long time his father for a short time, his mother for a long time again. Parents arguing when they know their son can't hear. 'It's worse at my age, there's the possibility you might not be able to put it right again.'

Can knows that this has to do with death. Can knows about death. He is forced to think about it every day.

'What will you do?'

'I'll put it right before the stubborn bugger dies. I'll call him. Oh, stupid man.'

Can sets his plastic evidence bag on the table. He can barely contain himself, squirming in his seat.

'I found something out. A lead.'

'What have you done?' Mr Ferentinou asks.

'That bit of robot I found, I put it out on a conspiracy wonk site.'

'Conspiracy wonk?'

'Gladio dot tee ar.'

Mr Ferentinou rolls his eyes and says something in his own weird language that Can knows can't be good.

'You do know, young man, that MIT watches those Deep State sites.'

'I got a lead,' Can says doggedly. His BitBots have reconfigured into Rat and sit on his elbow, tasting the air with silicon whiskers. 'I found the robot, the robot that chased me.'

'We're in this anyway it seems. Tell me what you found.'

'The number is from a chassis, khassis . . .' Can fumbles over the alien word, 'chassee number. It's a factory ident. I know what it is and where it's from. It's a version of a Nissan A840 Precision Manoeuvre robot. License Number NPM21275D. They're made for difficult inspection areas, like working at heights or in tunnels or in high-energy environments like power lines n-plants.'

Mr Ferentinou nods his head. He's impressed.

'So we know where it was made.'

Now Can bounces up and down on the bench seat.

'But I know where it went, I know who bought it! Botsearch dot tee ar. It's an English language site but some Turkish fans have done their own Turkish language pages.' Can taps on the silkscreen, the book that holds all books. He turns the displayed page to Mr Ferentinou. 'Look, see? Built in May 2024, leased to TIK to June 2026. What's leased?'

'It's like a kind of renting. TIK are a big infrastructure company.'

'They work on bridges and the Marmaray, I know that,' Can says. 'Then Huriyet Cable and Transmission. They're a big electricity company, they run power lines and those big pylon things. That's infrastructure too, isn't it?'

'Very much so, Mr Durukan.'

'They have him until last October, when he's retired because he's picking up too many faults.'

'He, him. You said *him*.'

'I did?'

'You did. I find it interesting that we assume robots are male. Carry on.'

Can often can't fathom Mr Ferentinou's wanderings and ramblings and diversions. He frowns in concentration. This is Detective stuff.

'He goes quiet then until he turns up in a sale, here, in April.' Tap, drag, windows open and slide across the i-paper. Samast Auctions, over in Kayişdaği.

'Do you know who bought him? It?'

'No, they paid cash, like you always say. Cash is king.'

'It's the first lesson any self-respecting terrorist – or freedom fighter for that matter – learns. Your detective work is very good, Mr Durukan, but the trail seems to go cold here. It's quite a distance from Samast Auctions to lying in pieces on the street outside here.'

Now Can is boiling with excitement, and he almost squeaks with pleasure and he snatches the screen away from Mr Ferentinou and opens up new pages with his fast young fingers.

'But remember, I said it was a fan site.' The page is titled *Spottings*. Two thirds down the list of registrations is NPM 21275D. Him. And times and dates. 15:30 January 18th 2027. 09:25 February 22nd 2027. 14:04 March 2nd 2027. And places. Dereboyu Cadessi. Meriç Cadessi. Evren Sok.

'Is this crowdsourcing?' Can asks. He learned the word from Mr Ferentinou. He likes the idea; throw a question out into the world, someone – or everyone – will answer.

'It's the modern word for it.' Mr Ferentinou frowns, then drags out the addresses on to a map. The stork's eye view of Istanbul swirls, then swoops down to the eastern suburbs. Stars appear among the flat roofs of the housing blocks: the places where Kayişdağı's bot-spotters, its nine-year-old boys and old men with nothing to fill their mornings, spotted the robot NPM 21275D.

'See how close together they are?' Mr Ferentinou says. 'Terrorists tend to form small world networks, with strong local bases and occasional global connectors.'

'Terrorists,' Can breathes.

'Oh, I am sure so, Mr Durukan.' Then Mr Ferentinou does one of those pieces of mind magic that Can loves to see but can't quite understand. Keeping the pin-marks, he pulls up maps of his other Istanbuls, the ones made from how long it takes to get to work, how far people travel to buy food, where the power lines are, where the dolmuşes run. Bus routes, levels of debt, water supply, ages of mosques, gas pipes. Here he stops. Can follows his finger down on to the map. In the centre of the constellation of robot sightings is a small knot of blue lines.

'Kayişdaği Compression Station,' Mr Ferentinou says. Fingers to map, Mr Ferentinou and Mr Durukan follow the blue lines. Can remembers winters filled with puzzle books his dad bought him from Aydin's news stand. Join the dots, that was connecting, the pleasure found in anticipating the final shape as the line grew more defined from point to point. Mazes: finding the centre was easy, the reward poor; a chocolate bar or an angel or a statue. The real pleasure came in following the seeming dead ends and imagining what greater treasures might lie hidden beneath the pages; secret doors, other worlds.

Fat veins run away to all cardinal points; north and south to connect with other pipe nodes, east towards Anatolia and ultimately the Caucasus, the gas lands of Central Asia, west to Istanbul, under the Bosphorus to the Balkans and southern Europe.

'Blue Stream, Nabucco . . .' Can cuts off abruptly. Mr Ferentinou has shut off the silkscreen. He snatches it up to his chest.

'No, that's enough. No more. It may already be too much. No no. You have to go now Mr Durukan.'

Can's head and heart reel from the sudden shock. He might cover his face, then he might cry.

'But Mr Ferentinou . . .'

'No no, don't talk to me any more about this. You have to leave this, do you understand, Can? I am beginning to see something and it makes me very very afraid. We're not detectives, this is not the television; great crimes and terrorist plots don't get solved by old men and boys; they're solved by police, the security forces, with guns. Promise me you won't have any more to do with this. Promise me. You must promise me this or you can never come here again.'

'But that's not fair,' Can begins to say and bites it back because that's the sort of thing a kid shouts and the rules between him and Mr Ferentinou have always been gentlemen's rules. Misters both. Mr Ferentinou means this. So Can looks at him in the eyes, which has always made the old man uncomfortable, and says, 'All right then, I promise.'

But it's a lie. No, not a lie, something else, a Does Not Apply. Rat perches on his elbow and as everyone knows – everyone in Yildiz School – no promise made in the presence of a rat is ever valid.

The conversation with Türkan Bey, Landlord of Felicity Apartments, takes place entirely through the street door intercom.

'Mehmet Ali Yazıcoğlu,' Leyla repeats.

That low-life rent-boy-mongering Georgian-trafficking failed-moustache homosexual transvestite wife-beating bet-welching tax-dodging money-laundering free-loading Besiktas-supporting little pathetic nonentity of a wannabe hood, who, if there's still a God in the seven heavens, will end up some day soon in the foundations of an overpass on the E018 . . .

Leyla steps back to the grille to interrupt the gale of invective.

'The kapici said you'd sold on the contents of the apartment.'

A pause.

'You're not family, are you?'

'Not directly.'

'Well, someone owes me two months' rent. Two months!'

'Mr Özkök, where did you have the personal effects sent?'

'Bugger all I got for that pile of shite. Do you have money on you?'

'Mr Özkök, the name of the dealers?'

'Some place in Seyitnazam. I'm coming down. I'll see to this personally. Stay where you are. I'm coming down.'

Leyla bolts. She runs perilously on business heels. She left Yaşar circling in the Peugeot – parking was a patent impossibility around Türkan Bey's Inebey office. Where is he, where is he? Don't have crashed, don't have started a fight at traffic lights, don't have got into anything that involves police. There, bouncing in over the tram lines. The car doesn't stop as Leyla opens the door and drops in to the passenger seat.

'Go go go!'

Yaşar pulls into the traffic. Leyla sees a big man with a sloping forehead, heavy jowls and a big moustache at the door of Özkök Properties looking up and down the street. As the car passes Leyla drops down in her seat but the movement draws his eye. He recognizes her from the intercom camera, thinks about giving chase, settles for waved fist and roaring.

'Let me guess, he still wants his back rent.'

'Just keep driving, he might still follow us.'

'They probably taught you different in marketing, but renting property, it's never seemed an honourable way to make money to me.' Yaşar says. 'Using money to make money.'

'Isn't that what this is about, getting finance to make more finance?'

'This is getting finance to make something that will change the world. Notice the two little extra words in there? "Make something."'

'Auction houses in Seyitnazam,' Leyla says as she takes over the steering wheel at a gas station.

Hazine Auctions, Yaşar says almost immediately and blinks the location to the navigation system. Driving, driving, constant driving, whirling around this huge, hot city between low rent apartments in new-build suburbs and by-the-week-offices and black marble lobbies and Bosphorus view business suites. How many of the drivers and passengers around her swirl endlessly along Istanbul's arterials and circulatories and interchanges, never reaching the centre, never reaching anywhere? This afternoon it's a meeting with CoGo Nano!, brand leaders in mass market nano. After that it's more calls to nano companies and private equity firms and venture capital funds. Leyla can't imagine when she will crawl back up the creaking wooden stairs of the dervish house. Thinking of the afternoon meeting reminds Leyla of a question that has been rattling around in her head.

'How do you come to be working with Aso?'

'I met him at Ankara U and then we went on together to Bilikent University. It's the only place if you've any ambitions in nano.'

'It seems a bit of an odd pairing.'

'Odd? What do you mean odd?'

'Well, I mean, you don't think of . . .'

'Kurds.'

'Yes, Kurds. You don't think of them as scientists.'

'Why? What do you think of Kurds as?'

'Well, I've never heard . . .'

'Kurds herd sheep, commit honour killings and like nothing better than a good vendetta.'

'No!' She hasn't thought that, not in those words or images or clichés, but the prejudices and presumptions are a watertable, dripped into her like the irrigation of the polytunnels through family, friends, television and news and mosque and school: Kurds are conservative and insular, Kurds keep their own ways and customs, Kurds aren't really proper Turkish citizens. They form a level on which everything she has ever thought about the Kurds has rested. She's a down-home Demre racist. It's an ugly truth.

'The guy is a genius,' Yaşar says. 'I just do the grunt work; design the molecules, do the mathematics, compute the folds. He sees big. He's the visionary. He's the one looking ten, fifty, a hundred years into the future at what we'll all be. He sees that, as clear as day. It scares the hell out of me, but he sees it, he looks right into it, like the sun, and it doesn't blind him. Or is that something else that Kurds don't do?'

'Yaşar, I'm sorry . . .'

A call comes in from Uncle Cengiz to swing out to Bakirköy to pick up Cousin Naci.

'He's a good lad, a big lad. He does Taekwondo.'

'Why do I need a cousin who does Taekwondo?' Leyla asks.

'I had tea with the Big Man and asked if he might have any idea who is in charge of things over by Felicity Apartments.' Every town, every neighbourhood has a Big Man. He goes by various names and honorifics but they all mean Big Man. He sits, mostly. Outside, preferably. He drinks a lot of tea, and may smoke. People greet him and he has a dog that never gets indoors. He knows everyone and sorts things. He accepts small considerations and local protection. 'I gave him your description. He said that sounded like Abdullah

Unul. He used to work with Russians on the usual Russian stuff: vice, people trafficking, nasty stuff like that. The Big Man said that he'd heard Abdullah Unul was in money-lending now.'

'So we've got Abdullah Unul's money.'

'Leyla, he also said to be very careful; Abdullad Unul did things for the Russians. Russian-style things. Leyla, I don't think it would do any harm for you to have somebody with you. That's why I'm sending Cousin Naci with you.'

'Did you never think that at some point it might have been a good idea to call the police?' Leyla asks.

'The police?' The shock, the shame in his voice over the tyre-noise. 'Not with family, no no.'

Cousin Naci is loitering under the ten-metre revolving plastic dervish that advertises the Çelebi Travellers' Restaurant far across its dusty, electric smelling edge-of-expressway industry park and the Gordian Ataköy Interchange. He's a big, broad, slightly frowning twentysomething in track pants and a very clean white Adidas top. He smells of fabric conditioner. He moves sweetly and with effortless muscularity. Yaşar clearly hates him so Leyla can't help but be predisposed to like him. Two men in smart pale blue overalls and sweet little rubber boots wash the car while Yaşar ransacks the shop for snack food and soft drinks. Leyla looks up at the slowly whirling dervish, one hand held up to the God, the other turned down to earth. The line of unity runs through the heart. Here the nanotech revolution was born, she'll tell them when they interview her for the *People Who Shook The World* segment on the news.

The back seat of a 2020 model Peugeot Citicar was never designed for Cousin Nacis. Even with his knees almost under his chin he looms over the front seats. Leyla's certain the car steers light at the front.

'What belt are you?' she asks Cousin Naci.

'Black,' he says.

'What dan?' Yaşar asks.

'Fifth. I'm licensed as a deadly weapon.'

Hazine Auctions is a roll-shuttered industry unit on a business lot at the back of an apartment park off the D100 expressway. Cheapness and meanness hang in the air with the dust. The balconies are already pulling away from the apartments; rust traces little ochre fans beneath the wall mountings. Grafitti on the shutters, invocations of God and Atatürk and football. Toyota pick-ups on the street. Hazine Auctions is the bazaar of final resort. Buy from those who need to sell, mark-up affordably. Ceiling-high shelving racks of mini-motorbikes and electric guitars and weddings dresses; music systems and bicycles and designer shades. White goods, priced in felt marker on gaudy orange stars. There is a whole bin of cepteps. Each item a failed aspiration. A hope too high. It's not a pawn shop, never a pawn shop. Pawning is usury. Pawning is haram.

Turgut Bey is very proper, in a flash suit and smile

'House clearances, yes, we do those. The way we work is we pay a flat fee, sight unseen, then I send my boys to sort everything and box it up – I get a lot more if it's all tagged and sorted, especially the bric-à-brac. Dealers specialize: books, china, curios.'

'It's this address.'

Leyla has written it down. She doesn't like the idea of flesh-to-flesh data transfer with this man. Turgut Bey shrugs.

'You'd have to talk to the boys.'

Boys they are, sons and cousins in leather jackets, drivers of vans and tappers of keys. In the glass box that is Hazine Auctions back office Turgut Jnr drags and taps spreadsheets across his silkscreen.

'Twenty boxes sundries, sorted,' Turgut Jnr announces. It's hot and dusty in this concrete warehouse. It smells of small sorrows.

'We're looking for a specific item,' Leyla says. 'It's a family heir-loom, one of those miniature Korans, but there'd be only half of it. You might have noticed it.'

'To be honest we get so much stuff,' Turgut Jnr says, flicking itineraries across the screen. 'We wouldn't catalogue anything so small as that. One box assorted religious paraphernalia. You're in luck.'

'Could I ask who bought it?

'Now that's commercially confidential.'

The first of the day's petty cash twenties leaves its silk harem. Zeliha had handed over the cash grudgingly. Leyla must remind her again about that contract.

'It was bought by this guy. He's one of our regulars. He likes the religious clutter.'

Turgut Jnr swooshes the receipt across the screen. The box went for twenty euro, what she has just paid out. Of course, there is no guarantee the hemi-Koran was in the box, or that if it was, that the buyer hasn't sold it on again. That Abdullah Unul isn't prising it from Mehmet Ali's fingers with a claw hammer. The Taekwondo Black Belt Deadly Weapon is looking at scrambler bikes. Leyla hopes he'll be enough.

Topaloğlu Art and Antiquities. Kavaflar Sok, Grand Bazaar. Leyla's hopes wilt. Miniature Korans are just the kind of souvenir – authentic, oriental, portable, vaguely transgressive – tourists love to buy. Half a koran might be a less appealing buy. So unattractive this Topaloğlu might have thrown it out. She could go head-spin crazy second-guessing motivations and possibilities. The certainty is that she and Aso have a meeting with CoGoNano! in two hours and she needs a shower, a change and a pitch rehearsal.

She's getting used to Cousin Naci filling the rear-view mirror. Fabric conditioner is a preferable odour to the car's natural fug of nanotech designer and mouldering food. The driver's footwell is carpeted in a layer of pulverized snacks. This is not good for her shoes. Leyla accelerates up the inbound on-ramp and drops the Peugeot into a gap that wonderfully opens between a taxi and a tow truck. Until she took this commission she'd never noticed how many tow trucks there are out on the roads.

When the bus took Adnan Sarioğlu in his uniform away from Erzurum after six months in the Land of Opportunity, he had sworn on his father's honour, his mother's life, his brother's masculinity, his

sister's purity and his prophet's beard that he would never set foot
there again. God, knowing people, thinks little of honour or purity
or even life, but vows made on his prophet he loves to confound. So
it was by the direct will of Allah that Adnan Sarioğlu found himself
back at Erzurum seven years after finessing a transfer from there to
the tourist police at Dalaman: why risk an idiomatic English speaker
to an IED? Not *in* Erzurum, *at* Erzurum. At Erzurum Airport. On
the bare tarmac in the peeling wind of early March, with sleet
threatening by the squall and three men in Istanbul suits and shades.

'What the fuck are we doing here?' Kemal said, hung-over and
oppressed by the hugeness of the sky.

'I want you to see it so you understand it,' Adnan said. 'I don't
trade in something I haven't seen.'

'You trade in natural gas,' Oğuz said. 'And little packets of digits
you call contracts.'

The story they had told their colleagues in the back office, in the
compliance department, in pipelines, on the trading floor, was that
it was a bonus-week lad-about, a city-boy stag weekend; trail-biking
in the Wild East. The flight arced them high over ochre, desiccating
Anatolia and the painfully blue lakes of the Tigris and Euphrates
dams. There were eight seats in business class on the little Embraer
city hopper. The Ultralords of the Universe took them all, shouting
across the tiny curtained off cabin to each other. Kemal drank the
entire flight and tried it with the hostess. Her face was stiff with
disapproval and perfect foundation.

'They have a water melon festival here,' Kadir said as they trudged
across the wet, wind-whipped apron from the plane to the waiting
charter helicopter. 'I read it in the in-flight magazine.'

'Doing what?' Kemal asked. 'Sticking them up each others asses?'

'Never judge a place by its airport,' Adnan said, sliding his shades
up his nose. There was ice from Ararat in the wind and he had
forgotten to tell everyone to bring a coat.

'Only judge a place by its airport,' Oğuz said.

There was no drink on the helicopter. Kemal sat out the flight with his forehead pressed against vibrating window, gazing down at the sparse hugeness of the east. The glass rubbed a red weal on to his forehead.

'You look like a Shi'ite at Ashura,' Oğuz said. Then Adnan picked out the first silver shine of the feeder pipeline, bestriding ridge and valley, village and hard-scrabble field, throwing itself up mountain-sides and swooping across high snowfields. He motioned the pilot to fly in over it.

'Can you take us down?' Adnan shouted.

'This is a military secure-fly zone,' the pilot shouted back. 'There's a low-altitude restriction.'

'How low can you go?'

'Well, I wouldn't want to get much under thirty metres.' Adnan grinned under the aviator shades he had made all his co-conspirators buy at Atatürk Airport so they could look like hoods and jabbed his finger downwards.

'Take her to the ground.'

Çaldıran Transfer Station was an alien outpost, an invasion base of silvery tubes and corrugated iron cubes, chain-link fences and yellow hazard signs, solar panels and heavy-metal valves, set down in a long sculpted valley of winter-browned grass and sheets of naked rock. Mountain ridges stood on either side, ice-capped, snow-dusted. One helipad, a two-rut road cut straight as a wound down the valley, sheep paths on the hillsides. Three pipelines, a steel Y, a triskelion.

'What a shit-hole. You were stationed here?' Kemal asked.

'I was stationed at Erzurum. We came up here on exercises. You should see this place in the spring. The flowers are incredible. You can stand here for hours and hear . . . nothing.'

'This is the spring,' Kemal said, pulling his jacket around him. The alcohol, the high-altitude, low-pressure mild-delirium, had crept into his blood and chilled it. 'And what I'm hearing is a little voice saying, *hypothermia, hypothermia.*'

'Does anyone actually work out here?' Kadir said.

'I see a guy with some sheep,' Kemal said squinting up the valley. 'And an AK47.' The light was actinic and harsh, sharpened by high snow.

'The station is automated,' Adnan said. 'A maintenance man will come out from the main Özer office in Erzurum maybe once a month to check everything's working and the locals haven't sold the pipework off for scrap.'

'Does he come for the wild flowers and the beautiful silence too?' Kemal asked.

'Kemal, shut up,' Kadir said. 'I see pipes. Show me how you work the trick.'

'Oğuz is Ultralord of Pipelines,' Adnan said.

'Simple. It's a shell-game with a natural gas,' Oğuz said. 'Çaldıran was originally built as an intake plant from the Marand field in Iran to the Nabucco pipeline. It was only after the Green Line was shut down that Özer and its partners in Nabucco realized Çaldıran could act as a bypass around Erzurum in case of an accidental shutdown or political problems.'

Kadir turned his airport shades to the flanking mountains. He had always been the aloof one, the lofty one, duly diligent. He pumped the blood of old Ottoman paşas. 'That would be Azeris, Georgians, Armenians, the Kurds and half a dozen Islamist groups who want us out of Europe and in with the mullahs where we belong. Not forgetting the Iranians themselves.'

'The folks around here are mighty friendly, yes. But this set-up allows us to do a simple swap. Lord Draksor didn't waste his time out here. We arrange a shut-down of Nabucco in Erzurum. The gas is diverted here, but we have control of Çaldıran. We're already running gas from the Green Line up to the station at Khoy.'

'Won't they notice a time lag?'

'Oğuz can time it to the minute,' Adnan said. 'It will be seamless.'

'The computers handle the fine details,' Oğuz said. 'No one will ever notice.'

'And the Baku gas?'

Adnan shrugged. 'Keep it in the tube, outgas it, burn it off, run it the other way down the Green Line and let the poor widows of Marand have three months of free cooking. What matters to me is I'm selling Iranian gas on the Istanbul market at Baku prices.'

Again Kadir looked long to the hills and the high, flat clouds streaming across the hammer-blue sky.

'This is theft.'

'We're simply exchanging one supply of gas for another,' Adnan said. 'Özer keeps the profit on the Baku gas, the Iranians get the cash price, we keep the differential. This is not a zero-sum game.'

'You have any Iranians in mind?'

'I've got a contact,' Adnan said.

'Well, I suggest you cosy up to your Iranian, and get me the fuck back to Istanbul before something else blows out of Iran and fries my balls,' Kemal said, jigging from foot to foot, shoulders hunched and hands thrust deep in his pockets.

That Iranian is a whey-faced, soft-worded, dodge-eyed, wisp-bearded, nail-manicured, cheap-shoed effete Ayatollah-follower who has feed from his kids' social network sites on his ceptep, and not tits or sports like a proper Turk, but he's a Sepahan fan who can name the entire 2025 IPL championship team and their positions so Adnan can work with him. When the deal's done, when Turquoise goes down and everyone is divvied up; they'll get him up around Taksim. This isn't some pious piss-hole with sand up its ring like Esfahan, or Tehran for God's sake. This is Istanbul, Queen of Cities. You sit there in your Islamic beige suit and no tie sipping your ayran, but anyone who's prepared to divert thirty-three million cubic metres of embargoed gas through the Green Line can't be too serious an Allah-botherer. Out on the town with the Lords. Then we'll really see Seyamak Larijani.

The Iranian's only public vice is his taste in accommodation. The Anadolu is a boutique hotel in the New Ottoman style, so fresh Adnan's shoes leave prints in the carpet. Small, bespoke, it effortlessly advertises expense in every carefully sourced artwork and piece of furniture. Adnan wonders, Does Ayşe's stock feature among the over-framed miniatures? She wouldn't mention it to him, she wouldn't think it worth it. The gallery is her business; Özer his, that has always been the contract. Men's world, women's world. Except for Turquoise. Turquoise breaks all the conventions.

The rooftop bar is a glass box, high over Beyazit, extravagantly climate-controlled on this hottest, heaviest day yet. *Money and high places*, Adnan thinks.

The other three Ultralords of the Universe have already arrived and are comfortable in the over-sized leather chairs, ordering coffee from the staff; handsome Russians in faux Ottoman frock coats. The Iranian rises from his seat to shake Adnan's hand.

'So the contract is finally in place,' Larijani says. The air-conditioning dews the side of his glass of chilled yoghurt ayran. A waitress with heartbreaking cheek-bones brings Adnan coffee though he doesn't need it. He's still buzzing from last night. 'I had been concerned at the lack of . . . clarity.'

'Adataş didn't get where he is by not spotting a good deal,' Adnan says. The thrill of the close glows still, a deep, red throb at the base of his belly, in his balls, in the bulb of his prostate. He should have fucked last night. Why the hell did he let himself fall asleep?

'I look at it,' Kemal says in his bad English. The contract came through to Adnan in a ceptep chime as he was spinning, yawning but glowing, down the snake of pre-dawn taillights into Europe. White Castle lawyers know no sleep. Flesh and blood lawyers would have drawn it up; this was not the sort of contract you could entrust to Artificial Intelligences. In a blink he flicked it across to Kemal, on the Bağrantı Yolu. He would have put the car on autodrive and gone through the heads of the agreement while his last season Lexus was swept along, a corpuscle in Istanbul's concrete arteries towards Beyazit. The Lexus 818: the car of the executive who lives with his mother. You talk dirty but you get your underwear ironed, Adnan thinks. Kemal is uncharacteristically clean-mouthed and restrained this morning. Adnan doubts that it's out of respect for the Iranian's sensibilities. 'It's pretty much a boiler-plate short-term loan agreement, with some non-standard clauses.'

'Non-standard?' Larijani asks. His voice is soft but carries enormous presence. His English is precise and distinctly English, unusual for that nation with a long mistrust of the British. He commands rooms.

'With a deal like this, I'm sure you can understand that Mr Adataş needs to protect himself,' Kadir says.

'I had assumed that Mr Adataş would cover his investment by hedging. That is what White Castle does.'

'We mean, protection from identification as being involved in any part of Turquoise,' Kadir says.

'It's a question of multiple layers of Special Investment Vehicles and Special Purpose Entities,' Adnan says. His English is the best of the four UltraLords; Kaş English, beach-boy English.

'I'm familiar with those financial vehicles,' Larijani says. 'What is true for Mr Adataş is doubly true for TabrizGaz. I remind you that the terms of our agreement stipulate once the monies are paid there can be no recourse to us in case of loss to yourselves or Mr Adataş. Everything must be deniable.'

'Oversight, compliance and due diligence are all my department, Mr Larijani,' Kadir says.

'What he means is, as soon as the deal's done and we've all got what we're due, we'll close Turquoise down, roll it up and wipe its ass so clean you could eat figs off it,' Adnan says. 'Until we all decide we had so much fun we'd like to do it all again.'

'We shall see, Mr Sarioğlu.' Larijani meets his eyes for a moment. 'Now, concerning payment. I require the funds to be in a special purpose secure account by seventeen hundred today.'

Adnan looks at Kemal. His English is the weakest of the four Ultralords', but this is his fiefdom. Kemal sits forward in his chair, hands folded, softly chewing his bottom lip. He says nothing. Adnan says quickly, 'The funds will be transferred as soon as the documents clear Ferid Bey's legal department.'

'Yes, quite. Nevertheless, my deadline stands. It's a security issue. Oh yes, I'd almost forgotten.' Larijani slips his hand into the breast pocket of his jacket and sets a plastic vial across the low, Iznik-tiled table. 'Who is making the transfer?'

'I'm the named signatory on the SIV,' Adnan says.

Larijani slides the vial towards Adnan.

'You're fucking joking.'

'I assumed use of nano was commonplace in Özer?'

'Yes, mass-market general performance-enhancing products.' Plus an internal market of greyware from the bazaars of Fenerbahçe and the pressed aluminium start-up sheds on the bleached hills outside Ankara. 'That's . . .'

'Iranian?' Larijani smiles. 'What do you think it's going to do, turn you into a raving mullah? It's a one-shot optical security ware. It will imprint the account code on to your retina in a form that the lasers of your eyewriter can read.'

'This is military grade technology,' Kadir says.

'We are not so backwards at TabrizGaz as people think.'

'Balls,' Adnan says, snatching up the plastic container. 'I'll take your Islamic nano and run a fucking mile.' Kadir's hand stays his as Adnan prepares to twist off the seal.

'Maybe you should wait until Ferid Bey's people have signed off.'

'As long as you are aware of my terms,' Larijani says.

'Here are mine,' Adnan says. 'I call Turquoise. The quants have forecast an eighteen-hour minimum, ninety-six-hour maximum for the twenty-four-hour spot market to peak. Quants couldn't find their dicks in the dark. I say the market peaks on Thursday morning. The gas will be in Istanbul twelve hours later.'

'You can foresee when a market is peaking?' Larijani, 'Truly you are a latter-day prophet.'

'I'm the fucking Gas Prophet, you'd better believe it.' Adnan sits back easily and comfortably in his chair. *Yes, I know the markets;*

yes. I make the deals; yes, I call in the money, yes, I am never wrong. Do you know why, you no-ass, beige-suit, cheap-shave, wife-hiding, ayran-sipping Sepahan supporter? Because it loves me. The money fucking loves me. 'So keep your cellphone charged, you wouldn't want to miss that call.'

'I await it eagerly, Mr Sarioğlu,' Larijani says. 'You'll find Tabriz-Gaz and the Green Line ready.' He raises his glass of ayran. The white yoghurt has coated the inside of the glass and dried into cracks and crazes. 'My friends.' The Ultralords raise their coffees. Coffee and yoghurt; that's no toast for the gods of money. 'To Turquoise, to success, and to profit.'

'Turquoise,' Adnan mumbles.

As the other three Ultralords fold away their cepteps and unhook their eyewriters, Kemal calls over the handsomest Russian to settle the bill. Larijani leans across the table to whisper discreetly to Adnan, 'I say this to you because you are a married man. When this is done and we've made our money, you must come and see us in Isfahan. It's really rather a lovely city, and I have do that executive box season ticket to Sepahan.'

'Only after you've seen Cimbom.'

'That sounds reasonable. But my wife would very much like to meet yours.'

'Of course,' Adnan says. 'Your hospitality honours me.' Meaning: I *would sooner see Ayşe doing the splits naked at half time in the Aslantepe Stadium than hide herself in one of those ugly, woman-hating coat things.* 'When we have money.'

'You wait thirty-one years for a prophet and then another one turns up.' Mustafa raps the flat screen with the back of his hand. The first thing he does every day is to read the online papers, at length, over tea.

The djinn have been quiet since the judgement in the Tulip Mosque, orderly. They are still present, thick in the air as pages in a book, and as rich. Bound, disciplined. Necdet doubts that it's his own doing. Do they obey God's shariat, as ordered by the Adem Dede dervishes, or the mastery of Hızır?

'Did you hear that? Do you listen to anything I say? I said, you're not the only one.'

'What?'

'There's a woman out in Ereğli. She sees into souls. Peri and all kinds of fairy folk are speaking to her. People are coming from all over for cures and healings and fortune tellings, all that sort of thing. It's all in *Cumhuriyet*.'

Necdet cranes over Mustafa's shoulder to read the article. He flicks down the article, stops abruptly at a bad photograph of a motherly woman.

'That's her.'

'The Prophetess of Ereğli. I think that's slightly over-egging it.'

'No no, her. Her. I need to go there. I need to talk to her. I know her. I've seen her before. She was standing right beside me on the tram when the bomb went off.'

DEFENDED BY ROBOTS says the sign on the door, right above the one that says CLOSED FOR LUNCH. Ayşe pushes the door. She knows it will be open. The bell tinkles.

'Can't you read?' a voice shouts from further than the architecture of the shop should allow. 'Defended by robots! They have stingers. Three days of pain and a permanent unsightly rash.'

'You can't afford a cleaner, let alone robots,' Ayşe calls.

A bark of laughter from deep in the impossible perspectives.

'Ayşe! Buttercup! I'm down the back.'

To go down the back in the Sultan Mektep Bookstore is to journey through Istanbul's architectural history. The nineteenth-century Ottoman frontage, original wood, opens on to part of an arcade from early post-Conquest which in turn, through a home-brew knock-through, gives on to a Byzantine era vault. Burak Özek-mekçib arranges his stock accordingly. Set textbooks – the Sultan Mektep is close enough to the university to be the official Subversive

Bookstore – contemporary fiction and non-fiction fill the street face of the shop. Towards the rear, political texts, banned books and underground magazines, some of them dating back to when the Sultan Mektep was a landmark on the Hippy Trail. Tickets from the Pudding Shop, travel books and Herman Hesse from the Sultan. Burak's father had owned it then, and been prosecuted many times for sedition and insulting Turkishness. Burak is the architectural adventurer; armed with ranging sonar, GPS and ancient maps of Beyazit, he has expanded his legacy into three millennia. Under the arches of the old Han are, in the first bay, translations, English language in the second and the third, fourth and fifth for Arabic volumes. Burak is down in Byzantium. Here the old, the forged, the perplexing, the visionary, the insane; the occult and the revelatory and the hallucinatory. The pornographic, the prophetic and the profane lie together on the stone-cool shelves.

'Someone is going to clear you out some day.'

'What? Steal books?' Burak peers over his glasses. Floppy, thick, dark hair; inadequate glasses, check shirt, corduroy pants with suspenders, hand-made brown brogues; Burak Özekmekçib is every inch the antiquarian bookseller.

'Someone like me, Burak. Who knows what they're worth.' For all his affected bookish style, Burak Özekmekçib is an exact contemporary of Ayşe's. They met at university on a course on Classical Persian Nastaliq Calligraphy. Adnan would hate him on sight. He would think Burak was gay when the truth is that Burak just didn't like the idea of sex with anyone or anything.

'So, flower, what can I do for you?'

Old Sezen Aksu songs smoulder on the audio. *My mother loved these*, Ayşe thinks. They are the soundtrack to her childhood; autumn evenings in the Samanyolu Sok watching her mother put on make-up to go out with the dashing Captain Erkoç, summers in the house by the sea dancing around on the patio waiting for the barbecue to heat. Burak kisses Ayşe in the French style. After graduating he spent five years in Paris, returning to inherit the shop on his father's death. In Paris he claims to have learned kissing, anarchy, red wine and the concept of the leisured lunch.

'I need information.'

'It's always something with you, rosebud. Here, come up the front, I've a lovely bottle already open.'

Ayşe follows Burak up through time. It is a lovely bottle: a 2022 Madiran, standing on Burak's gargantuan Ottoman era desk. Burak produces dusty glasses from a drawer and wipes them with a hand-kerchief. He takes the swivel chair, Ayşe the old rocker. Madiran is shared.

'So?'

'The Hurufis.'

'Created by Fazlallah Astarbadi aka Naimi born Astrabad Iran 1340 Christian Era. Started preaching fairly orthodox Sufism around Persia and Azerbaijan circa 1370. Moved towards more esoteric beliefs which he incorporated in the *Jawidan-Al-Kabir*. Tried to convert Tamurlane the Great and was executed for his presumption, which caused his followers to rebel, for which they were put down with proper Mongol efficiency. They struggled on as a sect for a couple of decades before fizzling out or being incorporated into other more orthodox orders. The Balkan Bektaşis and Shataris in India are the guardians of the legacy. How's that for WikiBurak? The Hurufis are dead, rosebud, dead and long gone.'

The Madiran is very good, tannic, then deep and soft, thrillingly dehydrating. The pleasure of lunchtime drinking, to sit back in a cave of books air-conditioned by Byzantine architecture, glass in hand and watch perspiring Istanbul pass the window.

'Well that's the official history, but I come to you for unorthodox history, Burak. If there were Hurufi orders still operating today, you would know.'

'Well, of course there are any number of wannabes calling them-selves Hurufis, petal. Every half-baked occultist and kabbalist and Letterist and crossword compiler calls himself a Hurufi or a neo-Hurufi. The order is dead, poppy. If you want I can point you to a couple of Bektaşi shaykhs who have copies of Naima's original text and maps of the correspondences of the *zuhur kibriya* on the human face. Then there are people like the Meru Foundation who claim connections with the Hurufi tradition and claim to have a universal alphabetic motif in the first line of the Hebrew Genesis, but that is principally an American Kabbalist project. About twice a year you'll get an article in *Toplumsal Tarih* about the sacred geometries of Sinan mosques or the Seven Letters of Istanbul . . .'

Ayşe lifts a finger from her wine glass.

'Tell me more about that.'

'The Seven Letters? It's a legend put around just after Sinan's death, that the seven letters omitted from the opening verse of the Koran spell the secret name of God and are written on the geography of Istanbul in the alignment of his architecture. The man who reads it whole and entire will unlock the heart of the Holy Koran and see the unveiled face of God. To me it's clearly a piece of clunky propaganda put out by the Kalifate to justify the the profane sums they spent on Sinan's building spree, establishing Istanbul as a pil-grimage to rival Medina and Mecca – which would rake in the money – and reinforce the Ottoman claim to be the head of the Islamic world. Of course, no one has ever found the seven letters.'

'Man?'

'I beg your pardon?'

'You said, "the man who reads it whole".'

Burak tops up the Madiran. *He is a dangerous drinker*, Ayşe thinks, *the kind with whom your glass is never empty*. When this is done, when she has the money, she must go out with him and talk art and old Istanbul and university and all those things she can't get from Adnan.

'What are you up to, meadowsweet?' Burak says, frowning in suspicion.

'I'm following something.'

Burak throws up his hands in caution.

'You be careful, I've heard Antiquities is cracking down again.'

'Burak, you insult me. These articles about the Seven Letters, do you remember who wrote them?'

'I do indeed. Most of them are by a chap by the name of Barçin Yayla. I get books for him. Arabic stuff, Persian theology, Sufi and Kabbala stuff. I'm surprised he hasn't called on you; he's forever harassing me for calligraphic panels.'

'He couldn't afford me.'

'Too true, too true. Lovely guy but completely barking – now there is a man who considers himself the last Hurufi. Lilac, are you thinking of talking to him? I must insist you let me talk to him first. I'm sure he'll agree, it's just that, well, he's a touch brittle.'

'I'd appreciate it.'

'Give me a moment.' Burak slips on his ceptep eyewriter. It looks supremely incongruous, like a ray-gun, or a turban. Ayşe watches digits flicker over his eyeball. Sezen Aksu belts out torch songs of lost love and hüzün. A movement at the foot of the stack of Turkish pulp thrillers almost sends Ayşe's wine glass to the floor. Rat! No, even more surprising – a rat would be no surprise at all in the Sultan Mektep: a little domestic robot, the size of two hands together, assiduously vacuuming around the piles of books. Burak frowns at her from behind the eyewriter.

'It's ringing now. Did you think I was making it up about the robots?'

Within ten steps of the Anadolu Hotel's front door Adnan's shirt is saturated and clinging. The heat on Yeniçeriler Cadessi is like a blow, a burden on the back of the neck. Only fools and teenagers in almost no clothes brave the solder-hot pavement. Even the English hide from the sun, red faces burning at the backs of shady cafés. Trams slide past, windows packed with weary, heat-drained commuters. Buses manoeuvre clumsily, lumbering away from stops, wedged to the door with hot, irritable, drained Istanbulus. Car drivers have long since given up any hope of forward motion and sit resigned in their inching traffic jam, windows wound down, T-pop and talk radio blaring. The heels of their hands rest permanently on the horn. One word, one spark to the vehicular tinder, and this whole street could erupt into a death-fight. There are no buyers for the Fresh! Squeezed! Pomegranate! outside the bar on the corner of Çemberlitas. It looks to Adnan like the greatest thing in the world, a plummet into bottomless cool. The bar's air-conditioner has a fluttering rattle. As he identifies it he becomes aware of another, deeper, more breathy pitch from the ceptep store, then, as he attunes to that, a third voice chimes in, a high-pitched, asthmatic whine from the cheap fashion shop, then the overheated shush from the second-hand bookstore, the insect buzz from the long-distance bus, the whistle of the car air-cons. Last comes the bass drone of the big roof fans. Adnan is at the centre of a symphony for air-conditioners. Best fucking tune in the world.

'Are you going straight back to the office?' Kadir asks.

'I'm in no hurry.'

'The Beyazit Mosque is supposed to be good for the contemplation. It's designed to be cooling in summer. All that marble.'

'What do you know about mosque architecture?'

'Walk with me anyway.'

Frantic Beyazit Square has surrendered to the heat, its crowds driven into shade and down alleys and soks under the shadows of balconies and leaning walls. The step through the arch of the mosque gate into the courtyard is a step across worlds and times. The growl of the street is pushed away. Adnan can hear the water dripping from the brass faucets into the marble trough of the fountain at the centre of the court. The cloisters are deep and domed, shaded and sheltering. The marble invites the touch of bare feet. Suddenly crazy in the heat and the escape from it and the excitement of the deal, Adnan kicks off his hand-made shoes and peels off his socks. Half-millennium old marble under his soles. Geological reflexology.

'You should try this.' Adnan flexes his toes.

'I wish you hadn't done that,' Kadir says. 'It's so much harder holding a serious conversation with someone without footwear.'

Adnan's arches flex, tense with a foreshadowing of cramp.

'Tell me.'

'Kemal may not be staunch.'

'Kemal is a shit-talker.'

'Kemal assuredly is. Kemal has also lost something in the region of two hundred and eighty million euro over the past four weeks' trading.'

The marble beneath Adnan's feet is suddenly ice cold, clammy as corpse skin. The courtyard, the colonnades and fountain and the cascade of domes, a waterfall in stone from the crescent moon finial of the mosque, all sway and swoon. Bare feet are very bare, very silly, very exposed.

'Kemal's not a trader. He's back-office.' Adnan's cool has fled like startled starlings. He is jabbering, ranting, saying the first obvious thing in his head.

'As well as you he's working with Haluk and Hilmi.'

'The Cygnus X boys? That's not finance, that's voodoo.' Buying and selling, finding advantage, opportunities for arbitrage, the breathless, stratospheric domain of derivatives; behind the abstractions and the minutiae of timing was a physical commodity, whether heat for the widows of Marand or cool for the citizens of Istanbul. Dark liquidity, the so-called dark pools, the blind game where buyers and sellers hid their intentions from the gaze of the market, was black magic. It was a minimum information grope, it was trawling on the sea-bed. It was cold, pitiless entropy. The theory was sound and simple as a boat. Large institutional investors; pension funds; investment funds; managers who moved mega-shares, geological blocks of stock, wanted a way to buy without signalling their intentions to the market and finding hedgers and smaller, sprightlier traders taking positions against them. Dark pools allowed traders to post a desire to buy or sell anonymously – no price, no quantity, no names. Buyers and sellers groped towards each other.

To Adnan, dark liquidity would always be an abandoned cinema in Eskişehir.

'I don't do cinemas. Allah was good enough to give us FlickStream, why should we turn our noses up at it?' It was his third date with Ayşe, the one where they Introduce you to Their Friends. Her friends were bloody art students but on the whole they were better looking than MBA students.

'It's not a movie. It's an installation.'

On a Third Date you're allowed a refusal – only one, you don't want to look like a whiner – to show that you're not a complete pussy. He should have held on to it. I don't do cinemas, but I do installations even less.

'It's more like a game,' Ayşe said, using her Third Date First Flicker of Telepathy.

The art students weren't as good looking as he'd expected but they handed them each a laser pointer and told them to spread out through the stalls. There were already a few dozen scattered across the auditorium, crouching down in the rows, behind the curtains, the speakers, the sound baffles.

'Is this like the army?' Adnan asked loudly because it irritated the liberals.

'Sort of,' Ayşe said. Then the lights went off. Someone not Ayşe brushed past Adnan, from across the auditorium a laser beam sparkled through the dusty dark, was at once answered by five others, and Adnan got the rules. It was duelling lasers in the dark. Every shot might find a target, but it immediately flagged your location. Within fifteen seconds Adnan has tactics: listen, stick your head over the scalloped row of chair backs, shoot and move. Shoot and move. Shoot and move. The dark was velvety, dusty, warm and complete as the secret places of a body.

'Adnan.' He turned his laser on the whisper at his feet, then recognized the voice and took his thumb off the trigger. 'Are you enjoying it?' Ayşe whispered. A web of lasers criss-crossed the humid vault of the cinema.

'More of this kind of art, please.' Then he said, 'It's like the market. I never thought. You signal your intent, you take a shot, everyone knows where you are and moves against you.'

'I would probably never have thought of it that way,' Ayşe said. 'I just came here because it seemed like the kind of place you could do this.' And without any sighting or ranging or the least flicker of laser light she had her hand on his thigh.

'So you can,' Adnan said and pulled her down on top of him.

That has always been the difference to Adnan between the light and dark markets. The light market was the never-ceasing duel of lasers, all signalling to each other, all reacting to each other, like starlings dashing between the minarets of the Blue Mosque or cars on the Atatürk Approach. The dark was stumbling, feeling out the contours of a body, groping, whispering, recognizing, then the stifled exchange of body fluids.

Billions flow daily through pools of dark liquidity, between massive institutional buyers and sellers who risk exposure should the market sense their submarine mass move against them. But no darkness is ever absolute. Every night holds whispers. Analysts run algorithmic programmes of searing complexity, looking for statistical patterns and premonitions in the prices of stock. Raiders mount financial skirmishes into the dark to discern what might be for sale, how much and at what price. Some apply thermodynamics, looking for localized, minute decreases in the overall entropy of the dark market to game the price. The Cygnus X project is a degree of abstraction beyond even those, designed to probe the darkest of dark pools. Two terrifyingly smart quants, Haluk and Hilmi, reasoned by analogy to black holes and information theory. The darkest dark pools, the black holes, give no sign of their presence or mass until a buyer enters their gravitational fields. They swallow all information of price and quantity. A black hole has no hair, the physicists love to joke. Adnan's never understood that. Nor can he begin to comprehend the quantum field equations and Stephen Hawking's own formulae Haluk and Hilmi use to extract price information from the Great Dark Ones. But he can admire it. All Özer was exhorted to praise Haluk and Hilmi. Quantum Field Pricing Theory was bold, was brilliant, was the stuff of Nobel prizes. Adnan can admire it as long as it's in the money. And Kadir says it's not. Catastrophically not.

'The theory gave them beautiful data,' Kadir says. 'They could see in the dark. Then they tried to get clever. They reckoned they could arbitrage the dark market.'

'I'm trying to imagine the amount of processing power you'd need to crunch and arbitrage in real time.'

'The kind of amount that requires sign-off from the fortieth floor.'

'Mehmet.' Mehmet Meral, Chief Operating Officer. Mehmet the Conqueror, he liked to call himself. His office was decorated with Janissary military antiques. He preached martial virtues: swiftness, sureness, discipline, a sipahi's cavalry boldness. Mehmet the Cunt, they called him on the trading floor.

'He specifically put Kemal on settlements to make sure it was covered right and, just for a moment, Kemal took his eye off the ball.'

'Kemal doesn't do that.'

'He does when the ball is Turquoise.'

'Fuck.'

'He passed the Cygnus X account to a group of juniors on the assumption that they would keep each other right. They didn't. They made a small mistake, they tried to hide it. Errors to cover errors. You know how it is.'

Sometimes, in the small, hot, smelly Ferhatpaşa bedroom, Adnan is wakened by a sound in the night. It's not the roar of the highway or the television from next door beating T-pop against the wall or the shouts of youths from down at the petrol station. It's a huge sound that fills the sky around Apartment Block 27 and the earth beneath it, an endless rip as if God were tearing apart the seven heavens and every spirit that lived there, down to the atoms. It leaves him paralysed, sweating, heart pounding unable to find sleep again. It's the sound of the money rending. The deals are so fast, the opportunities so brief and the numbers so huge that a mistake must happen. Such is the pressure behind that hole, that flaw, that the whole thing will go, all the way down. Thousands can escalate into millions, into losses that can stagger entire economies. The money, tearing. When he married, when he bought the nasty little apartment out in Ferhatpaşa and realized that he had shamed Ayşe before her family though she would never say, that she would sleep in a gece-kondu if his arm were her pillow, he heard the heavens tear almost every night. He was a junior trader, an order filler, always running, never a moment away from the indices to make sure, to check he hadn't made a fatal flaw that could run up the side of the Levent tower and shatter it into dust. He can't remember when he last heard that shriek but he knows he will tonight.

'How did you find out?'

'He told me. He thought maybe I could edit the records. I've looked at it. It's terrifying. Moving losses off the balance sheet and reporting them as profits, setting up error accounts inside error accounts, using margin payments to make trades on his own account to cover losses, faking hedge trades. All the classics. It's almost textbook.'

'Fucking Kemal. Why did he have to try and cover it up? Just fire the bastards and take it from Mehmet the Cunt. Özer's capitalized to much more than two hundred and eighty million.'

'Mehmet the Cunt has problems of his own. Mehmet, Ercan, Pamir; Özer is rotting from the head. We're overextended in every division to six times our capitalization. We're an accounting fiction. It's a house of cards, but it's Cygnus X that will bring the whole tower down. Pamir may throw Kemal to the wolves to forestall the Financial Regulation Authority launching a wider investigation into Özer as a whole.'

'We're exposed. Fuck!'

The mosque warden, patiently sweeping the court with a besom, looks up and frowns.

'Can we call off Turquoise?' Kadir asks.

Adnan rounds on him.

'If Özer goes down I'm not going to be the one on the ten o'clock news sitting on the steps with everything I own in a cardboard box. Turquoise is my redundancy cheque. There is a way out of this. We can do this. It's our money. We can do this. We're the Ultralords of the Universe; we're still the smartest guys in the room.'

He can't lose it. He won't lose it. Not now, not after all he's done, after all the work and the contacts and the meetings and the careful deals and the planning, years of planning, from that first casual question out in the east on military service, *So where does that pipe go?* To the moment, so clear in his memory, so bright and crystalline, deep as a turquoise, riding up in the scenic elevator with Istanbul's hills and waterways at his feet, when the idea of the most audacious gas scam of the century came to him, made him choke with suppressed laughter at the whole ballsiness of it; Turquoise, whole and entire by the time the door opened on to the trading floor. He can't let his grip relax, see it fall away from him swashing down through the dark water. Lost.

Water drips from the battered copper spouts of the çesme. Adnan stoops, fills his cupped hands, dashes cold water from the deep aqueducts and cisterns beneath Istanbul into his face. Again, it runs through his fingers, he splashes the heat and the tiredness from his face. He gasps at the purity of the cold.

'If we were drug dealers, or even the security police,' Kadir ventures.

'We're not those men,' Adnan says fiercely. 'We're not even going to think like those men. I don't want to hear that again.'

'I had to float it though.'

'Consider it floated.' Beads of cold water run down Adnan's neck and under his collar.

'Have you any better suggestions?'

'Better ones, meaning ones that don't make us murderers and land us in jail? No. How do you silence a man who knows too much?'

'Maybe he doesn't have to be silenced,' Kadir says. Always the well-spoken and educated one, an old Istanbul name from an old

Constantinople family; now he is his most Ottoman. ''Maybe he just needs to forget the salient details.'

'What, designer amnesia?' Water spills have turned Adnan's shirt translucent and glued it to his chest. His body hair makes spiral, animal patterns.

'The nano gives and nano takes away.' Kadir is the Ultralords' dealer, little racks of plastic vials, from the grey market in the underpass at Galata tram station. Adnan's been there once, a piss-reeking tiled toilet of neon-lit stalls selling cigarettes, replica guns and nonprescription nano. 'Designer amnesia, no, that's beyond us. Memories are stored holographically, in multiple locations. The nano would have to locate and bind to the memory locations and repolarize the neurons without affecting any other memories using that architecture. Editing specific memories is maybe ten, twenty years away. However, for every scalpel there is a baseball bat. We all make jokes to the Kebab Prophet that we're the pharmacological front line, experimenting on ourselves, a neurological time-bomb waiting to go off. What if it did?'

'Do you mean, overdose Kemal?'

'No, it's unreliable; we mightn't get the desired effect. Kemal might end up dead anyway. The nanoware designers can't edit specific memories, but general amnesia might be achievable.'

'You're talking about giving him a chemical lobotomy.'

'A moment ago we were floating the possibility of killing him so I think it's a moral improvement. It would be nothing like what you say; the technology exists to target locations in the brain that correspond to different types of mental activity; emotions, smell, short-term memory. Short-term memory I think is the way to go. I can make some enquiries. It will have to be customized, and it will cost, but once the manufactory is programmed they have it for us next day. I think I can guarantee what will look like a massive short-term amnesia. We'll point to his work-load, pressure to deliver, increasing reliance on nano to meet deadlines. Does he have anyone? Apart from his mother? We're even doing Özer some good; who knows what else he'll forget along with Turquoise?'

'God between me and evil,' Adnan says. 'You are a cold fucker.'

'Do you have another suggestion?'

'You know I don't. Temporary amnesia.'

'I can't guarantee it.'

Adnan turns his face up to the cascade of domes. Water every-where in this mosque; in the heart of every mosque.

'If I could see any other option I would tell you to stuff your nano up your ass but I can't. I'm in.'

'I'll tell Oğuz. He needs to know.'

'He'll be staunch.'

'He will. Good then, we're agreed. I will source the nano. I leave it to you to administer it.'

'Wait. I give it to Kemal?'

'I'm in Oversight and Compliance. If I come down there'll be mass pissing of pants. You're on the Trading Floor, you see him every day. I'll source the stuff; it's up to you to get it to him. I'm sure you'll think of something.'

'Fuck you, Kadir.'

'Everybody tries.' He smiles weakly. 'That's the job of Compliance.'

'I'll do it.'

'Good. We know what we have to do. Shall we head back to the office?'

'No, I want to stay here a while. God, this is a nightmare.'

The heat and reviving afternoon bustle of Beyazit Square swallow Kadir. Adnan sits on the edge of the loggia. The mosque attendant comes and sweeps deliberately around him, solicitous of a tip.

6

The ship explodes. White light, a blinding flash, a fireball too hot and pure to be mere flame. The first few seconds of destruction are in silhouette, the dark shoulders of Asia and Europe, the taut bow of the bridge between them, the flecks of ships in the channel. The world blinks back into colour. The blast has blown the centre span of the bridge upwards to tear. It tears, cables snap. The roadbed twists and plunges like an amputated snake. Cars are scattered like leaves. Trucks pour from the severed bridge. They plummet very slowly among the falling road sections. Whole sections of tanker – bulkheads, pieces of superstructure, ruptured tanks, entire engines the size of houses – are blasted into the air and fall to earth, destroying houses, highways, taking out whole columns of suddenly stalled traffic trapped on the approaches to the bridge, tumbling end over end, crushing vehicles like ants. The shock wave capsizes the squat, grubby ferries like toy yachts in a sudden blow. The blazing hulk of the tanker swings across the main channel, collides with an upbound bulk carrier. Together they settle slowly down into the deep black water. The Bosphorus is aflame with burning ships, a fire fleet of carriers and oil tankers and Black Sea freighters. A cruise liner shoots flames from every deck of shattered windows. Along the shore the blast front shatters the houses and apartment blocks of the well to do. Roofs are stripped away, cheap konaks collapse and crumble. The last of the old Bosphorus wooden yalis are swept away like straw. Cars tumble like dice, speedboats are thrown up hillsides and into trees. A fraction slower than the shock wave and the fire, the tidal wave hammers the shore communities, turning shards of roof and smouldering timbers into a rip tide of churning, crushing wood and metal. The blast-tide peaks, then ebbs, drawing cars, boats, shops, houses, clingers to the flotsam of their homes out into the Bosphorus. Sleek and prosperous Bebek and Kanlıca are shattered, lovely old Kuzguncuk burns. Gas flares from broken mains. Marshalled along their hilltops the glass towers of Levent and Maslak are eyeless, every pane of glass smashed, a hail of diamond daggers on to the streets and plazas. In a flash, in a blast, Istanbul is smashed. Finally the twin pylons of the Atatürk Bridge, trailing cable and decking plates and weakened by the fireball, break at the knees and slide into the black water. Only stumps like broken teeth remain.

'It's damned impressive,' Emrah Beskardes whispers to Georgios Ferentinou, 'but I did see this on Discovery Asia.'

The video ends. The screen retracts. The delegates of the Kadikoy Group blink and shuffle and rearrange their papers and sip water.

'Five hundred thousand tons of liquefied natural gas,' Ogün Saltuk says.

He sounds like a Discovery presenter, Beskardes the zoologist writes on his magic slate, then pulls it clean.

'Of course, that's a special effects piece from a television programme you might have seen a few months ago about the particular vulnerability of Istanbul to a concerted terror attack on a Russian gas carrier. I actually served as a technical adviser on that programme ...' (*Told you*, Beskardes scribbles) ' but the details are accurate, with a little televisual licence. But half-million tonners regularly pass down the Bosphorus.' A ship clicks up on the screen, a monstrous floating monolith of a thing, bridge and accommodation units squatting low behind the monstrous, coffin-shaped pressure body. 'This is the *Ararat Star*, the largest gas carrier currently afloat, a Russian three-quarters-of-a-million tonner that began operating five months ago. You might have seen it; it's been through the Bosphorus four times already. It will make a passage through the Bosphorus on April 19th. What you saw in the excerpt was based on a ship smaller even than the half-million tonners that have become industry standard. The *Ararat Star* has twice the capacity. Twice the destructive power. That has to be irresistible to a terror group.'

'To whom?' Georgios hears himself ask. His voice holds a quiver of anger; he can't take much more of this stupidity. 'Who would want to destroy Istanbul? Kill eighty thousand people? What would that achieve? The Islamists aren't blowing up symbols of Western decadence any more. The jihad is on the streets. I know, I've seen it. Tarikats, kadıs, shaykhs; they solve problems, make the peace, keep social order, judge in a dispute. There's a new shariat: street law. It works. People use it.'

Ogün Saltuk chews on his bottom lip. 'Turkey has always had enemies, within and without; even more now that we are the front door of Europe. We're seen to have made a decision, aligned ourselves.'

Georgios Ferentinou would speak but a louder voice talks over him, 'Surely we have tight enough security at the Black Sea and Sea of Marmara; you see them out there every night, waiting for security clearance to enter the Bosphorus. A three-quarter-of-a-million-ton gas tanker can't be that easy to hijack.'

'They are on autopilot through the Bosphorus, to prevent acci-dental collisions. That could be hacked,' a new voice says while Emrah Beskardes whispers to Georgios, 'I think I saw that movie; it was an old one. The cook saved the day. He was good with knives.'

Ogün Saltuk chimes his water glass with his pen.

'If you could just hold on to all that creative energy, we have time scheduled for small group work. We'll break and do some big blue thinking and then come together in circle time to pool our thinking. Remember, imagination allowed.'

Georgios looks enviously on as Emrah Beskardes heads with his group out to one of the airy pavilions in the garden. He is sent to a damp-smelling ante-chamber with cracking cornices and mould stains on the plaster. The ceiling is high, the surfaces hard and echoing. On his gilded chair, Georgios glimpses a turquoise triangle of sea between the tree tops. The other group members are young aggressive men who like talk of megatonnage and megadeaths and the banks of the Bosphorus burning, so he is pleased to find Selma Özgün a fellow group member.

'We haven't met, but I am an appreciator of your work. Georgios Ferentinou.'

She peers at him quizzically. 'Ferentinou of Cihangir?'

'I was indeed, but I moved to Eskiköy. Adem Dede Square.'

'I know a neighbour of yours. Owner of an art gallery, specializes in hooky religious art? Gallery Erkoç?'

'Madam, I live upstairs from it.'

'In the old Mevlevi tekke? How delightful. It's a very interesting place, the Adem Dede dervish house. One of the last few seventeenth-century wooden tekkes not to burn. So you know Ayşe? By the way, I didn't really mean it about the hooky art. What is your line of work?'

'It was – I'm retired – experimental economics. Economics as a real science rather than a set of mathematical conceits.'

'I was interested in what you said about street shariat,' Selma Özgün says. 'You see, I rather like the idea of community justice. It's personal, and I think it works rather better than institutional justice because it sees the parties concerned on a day-to-day basis. When you see not just the other party down at the supermarket every day, but the judge as well, that makes for a well-ordered society. There's a lot to be said for the old Ottoman millet system when every community was free to abide by and be judged by its own social and legal systems; provided they didn't conflict with Imperial law. I think that rather than automatically clamping down on it as some kind of threat to anti-secularism, the government should be looking at ways of incorporating it into the existing legal system. We organize religion on the community level, why not law? No, I'm rather in favour of your street shariat – do you minds if I steal that expression darling? – provided they don't go trying to ban alcohol and make me wear a headscarf.'

'I can't be that hopeful,' Georgios says. 'They have a shaykh. He sees djinn.'

'Now that is interesting,' says Selma Özgün. 'A shaykh in the old Adem Dede dervish house. Do tell, sweetie.'

Georgios Ferentinou talks about Necdet the freeloader who was caught in that bombing down on Necatibey Cadessi and now sees karin, talks to djinn and is the confidant of Hızır the green saint. As he talks he notices that Selma Özgün is not the only interested listener. While the Big Blue thinkers argue about what to write on their flip chart pad an older man on the edge of their clique, a man with the straight bearing, neat moustache, bad suit but well polished shoes of a career military man, has been increasingly leaning to catch Georgios' and Selma Ozgun's conversation, straining to overhear, turning towards them and away from the arguing men.

'I am a connoisseur of spontaneous outbreaks of the marvellous,' Selma Özgün says, clapping her pudgy, be-ringed fingers in soft delight. 'An avid collector of village miracle workers and street seers and latter-day dervishes. It proves to me that the age of wonder is not past. That's the fourth now.'

'What do you mean?' Georgios asks.

'Seers of the strange and marvellous. There's been a fresh outbreak. I read all the local news sites; it's amazing what you find between all the uncredited aggregating and name calling.'

'Others are seeing djinn?'

'Well, not djinn exactly – it all began with this woman in Ereğli who started to see into souls and tell fortunes: the peri were whispering it to her, apparently. Then there's this businessman in Nevbahar: he's very interesting, very up to date; it's not fairies or djinn; it's robots. Those swarm-robots that build up into all kinds of different robots. But at some level it's the same; he finds lost things and gives prophecies.'

'Ereğli.'

'And Nevbahar'

'Eskiköy. And the fourth?'

'Firuzağa.'

The parquet floor seems to drop beneath Georgios. He clutches for the gold braid of his imitation Parisian chair. It's cheap and badly fitted and comes away in his fingers.

'Oh,' he says, the only word his whirling imagination can shape. Ereğli, Nevbahar, Firuzağa, Eskiköy, all within walking distance of the Topkapı-Yesilçe tramline. Can, the boy, the robots; did he get any photographs, can he get any footage of the bomb? A woman, a businessman, Necdet. They should be easy to find.

'Are you quite all right, sweetie?' Selma Özgün asks. 'You look a bit peeky all of a sudden, I'll get you some water.'

'No, it's quite all right, the room, it's very stuffy, horribly musty.'

'Hızır, now; that I would very much like to see,' Selma Özgün continues but an MIT staffer comes to call the group back to the main conference room. She takes the flip-chart pad – they will be destroyed after the session for security. The group files back out of the damp, stifling salon. The military man hangs back to talk with Georgios.

'Major Oktay Eğilmez.'

'I am Professor Georgios Ferentinou, retired.'

'Oh, I know. We have met before. It was a long time ago; the Haceteppe Group? Like this, only in Ankara. I was very junior then.'

'I'm sorry, I don't ...'

'As I said, I was very junior. Interesting stuff there. My thought is; if this is supposedly a think-tank put together to think the unthinkable, surely we shouldn't be limiting ourselves in what we can think about?' He pauses to let Georgios through the door and in the moment of physical closeness whispers, 'I did express reservations about Saltuk's suitability to lead this group.' He glances down. Georgios Ferentinou follows his eyes. The major holds his magic slate at waist height. Three words on it: *Eminönü Ferry: 16:30*. He erases it with one pull of the cardboard tab and slips the slate into the inside pocket of his unremarkable suit.

*

The glass eyedropper contains 36 per cent hydrochloric acid. When Barçin Yayla beholds the Seventh Letter written on the face of Istanbul and sees reflected there the face of God himself, he will uncap it and calmly, religiously, drop half a syringe on to each unblinking eyeball. Having seen the secret name of God, what worldly visions could compare? They can only clog and cloy and confuse the purity. As the last thing Barçin Yayla ever sees, it will be fresh, blazing forever.

The apartment smells. Ayşe had thought it would; a cheap top-floor walk-up next to a light-well into which generations of citizens of Küçükayasofya have casually thrown garbage. Add a heatwave. It must be bad. The smell is worse. It is a many-layered reek, complex and rich, individual odours combining into new, unidentifiable stenches; no sooner has the sense of smell acclimatized to one reek than it discovers a new one to evoke a gag reaction. Dust bunnies man sweat unwashed sheets dirty floor ancient sofa rot mould piss – Ayşe vows never to go near the bathroom – but with them the more esoteric smells of the single male obsessive: fusty books, printer inks, old incense, stale oils, yellowing newspapers, a peculiar phenolic plastic smell with no identifiable source, photographic chemicals, fixatives and preservatives, overheated electrics and hot halogen bulbs. As Ayşe examines the photomontage of aerial shots of pen-insular Istanbul and Üsküdar that occupies an entire wall of the living-room/kitchen, Ayşe slips a thumb-sized atomiser of Chanel 5 – only the classics – from her bag for a surreptitious spritz.

It is a staggering work. Mosques, tombs, baths are outlined, handcoloured and annotated with threads leading to satellite pieces of text, photocopies of newspaper, inscriptions and pieces of tâlik script, photographs and compilations of thumbnails, contact sheets, line-of-sight shots of the minarets of one great mosque from another, and the alignment of the minarets of yet another mosque beyond that; pages torn from old tourist guides, drawings of sacred knots and the thirty variations of cat's cradle, print-outs of multi-dimensional geometrical polygons and topological forms, Persian, Arabic, Turkic,

Nabatean, Hebrew and Greek alphabets and scripts, prayers arranged in magic squares and Trees of Life and sacred ladders, architectural plans, detailed close-ups, with dimensions pencilled on, of the design of domes, numerological treatises, articles in English from *Scientific American* on network theory and graph theory, reports from city surveyors and Marmaray engineers, brief biographies of Sultans and paşas, curling Post-it notes with brief jottings, in a neat, tight hand, written tersely on them. The cloud of annexed material overshadows even the wall-filling map; Ayşe traces threads of connectivity over the door, on to the roof, bouncing along the line of the skirting board through a brief history of the Haseki Hürrem Hamam, marginal verse-counter in decorated Korans in *Sülüs* script and a piece on the Three Utilities Problem in mathematics. The ceiling is a mosaic of articles and photographs, drawing and writings, held up against gravity with Blu-tack, yellowing Sellotape and thumb-tacks from which the connecting lines run back through dozens of ideas to a source on the montage. It is the totality of the sacred geometry of Istanbul. It is the mother of mash-ups.

Among the web of threads and sheer weight of research, Ayşe at first doesn't notice the patterns on the aerial photograph. It's a blue thread following the line of a Byzantine watercourse that draws her attention. Direction, purpose, ignoring street patterns and architecture. She follows it to a pin in the Cistern of a Thousand Pillars, then under Sultanahmet Park to the Haseki Hürrem Hamam. Here she loses the blue thread – a water thread, Ayşe concludes – in the tangle of annotations and drawings – until she picks it up again at Haseki Hürrem Mosque, dedicated to the same wife of Süleyman the Magnificent. Then she sees it, the pattern, the plan, whole, entire. That same gift that makes the letters in the hands of long-dead Sephardim move on her gallery wall lifts the blue line off the streets and and soks and houses and mosques of Istanbul and turns it into a letter, a Kha, floating above the rooftops and domes. A Kha two kilometres on its longest side, written in the angular, blocky, archaic Kufic Arabic script, pinned out in the mosque and turbes and hamams of Sultanahmet. Then she see another connection.

'Sinan,' she breathes. The great builder, the Armenian convert who became the architect of Sultans. His ambition to build a greater dome for Islam than the Christian dome of Aya Sofya would always be frustrated.

Barçin Yayla nods vigorously. As befits a man who attends prayers in the nearby Sokullu Mehmet Paşa Mosque the prescribed five times daily, he is as ablution-sweet as his apartment is detritus-foul. Apart from his breath. He seems not to know of toothbrushes. Ayşe places him in his mid-thirties, but she knows from the many antiquarians, dealers and forgers she meets that it is hard to tell the age of a man with an overweening passion. He is as Burak promised, polite, shy, intense, naïve, dedicated, wary. He is the last Hurufi.

'Sinan surely would never have had any contact with Hurufism,' Ayşe says.

Barçin Yayla nervously touches a finger to his lips, as if to suppress contradiction.

'I think you'll find that Sinan was a military engineer and architect with the Janissary Corps for over twenty years. The official order for the Janissaries was Bektaşi – and as we know, the Bektaşis appropriated much of their theological discourse from Hurufism. I think it exceedingly likely that Hurufism existed in the form of an order within an order, an initiatory secret society for the elite. The military loves its hierarchies and rituals. My work makes it very clear that Sinan expressed Hurufi philosophy in the mathematics of his great buildings. The use of space, the proportions, the ratios of volume, are all numerologically derived from the Holy Koran.'

'It's one thing building a cloister to reflect the 768 of the numerological Bismillah, it's another planning a giant alphabet out of an entire city before you've even built your first mosque.'

'It is, but remember, Sinan was chief architect and city planner at the time of the conquest of Cairo. He practised on that city; demolishing and building where he liked. I have no doubt that he was already forming the idea of a sacred geometry. His first building as

Architect of the Abode of Felicity was the Haseki Hürrem Mosque for the Kadin Roxelana. Not his greatest work by any means, and he was working from existing designs, but it was identifiable as his first mature work. There's a story in his autobiography *Tezkiretül Bünyan* that while he was surveying the site he noticed that children were pulling live fish from a grating in the street. When he went to investigate he discovered an entire Roman cistern down there. Perhaps it was this that inspired him to realize his vision. Hidden water. The never-ceasing stream of Hurufism.'

'He later built the Haseki Hürrem baths.'

'And her tomb, yes. All to the plan, all to spell out the Seven Letters.'

Ayşe traces other threads looped around the pin in the Mosque of Roxelana. Green, the colour of the prophet, reaches across the Bosphorus to Atik Vallide and Mihrimah Sultan Mosques in Üsküdar in a Shin ten kilometres across. Thread by thread, Sinan's buildings are tied into a monumental alphabet. Only in slab-sided, rectilinear Kufic could such a work, drawn in lines of connection between buildings, even be attempted. The insight is that the letters are not sequential, written across the city. They are placed on top of each other, superimposed. One site may form a node in several letters. They are not meant to be read. They are meant to be apprehended whole, at once, by the eye of God immanent everywhere.

Ayşe tries to imagine the years of effort entailed in drawing these letters out of millennia of history of Constantinople, training the perceptions to remove the houses, the streets, the Roman and Byzantine wonders, the works of prior and lesser engineers and see only the buildings of Sinan and their geometrical relationships to each other. Trying out the permutations must have been the work of years. A dark and perversely delicious fear gnaws Ayşe, the intellectual intoxication she experiences from opening a new manuscript or unwrapping an unseen miniature and knowing that she stands on the edge of the incomprehensible, that she holds in her hands a world and a way of thinking alien to her in every way. The past is another universe: a long dead sect drew its truths across whole cities for generations it could not imagine. Yet the Seven Letters traced out in coloured thread on the satellite images of Istanbul confidently proclaim that this is a truth that should stand as long as the Queen of Cities herself. This is dark, occult fruit. Ayşe is dizzy with strange.

She steps back from the wall. 'There's one missing.'

'That's correct.'

Ayşe traces the pattern of the threads.

'The final letter: Fa. I don't see it. It's not here.'

Barçin Yayla bows his head. He sits down at his work table, as rambunctious with cuttings and magazines and prints-outs and photographs as his walls. Ayşe notices that between the piles of paper, the table top is incised with dizzying circular graph patterns, all lines and nodes and vertices, seemingly scratched into the wood with the point of a pair of compasses.

'I can't find it.'

'What do you mean?'

'I can't find it. The last letter. The Fa. It has to be a Fa, but I can't get it to fit. I've tried every permutation on the photographs and maps, I've even got a friend at the university to write me a little programme to try out different topologies, I've even looked at different scripts. I can't get it to fit. Maybe I'm missing something. Maybe there's a clue I'm missing, or a building has been demolished that I don't know about – but I don't see how that could happen; I'm pretty sure I have all the architectural records and copies of old maps. Maybe what happened is Sinan simply didn't finish it. He died before the pattern was completed.'

'He can't have,' Ayşe says emphatically. It's not about the million euro now. It's the puzzle, the chase, the mystery for its own sake. The city still wears a jewel of secrecy next to her heart. Ayşe's theory is beautiful and elegant and fresh and thrilling and she can't bear that it might fall to sand because the Great Architect failed to complete a mystical schema he had set in motion fifty years before. The great Sinan did not work that way. If Barçin Yayla is correct and the Seven Letters were intellectually complete even as Sinan was building fleets on Lake Van to ferry Ottoman soldiers to war against the Safavids, he will have allowed for the vagaries of a career as an Ottoman court official. Sinan won't have left the best to last. 'No, the pattern's complete. It has to be. This is the Chief Architect of the Abode of Felicity. This is our Leonardo Da Vinci.'

'You sound, how shall I say, most certain of that.'

Tell him. You will have to tell him some time. She could lie but Barçin Yayla's manic, monastic dedication deserves better. His apartment stinks like Iblis' shitter but she respects him. He is serious and he is trustworthy. He doesn't care for Mellified Men and million euro deals; all he wants is to finally be able to read the Seven Letters superimposed over the divine geography of Istanbul and burn his eyes out so that the Secret Name of God will remain indelibly branded into his retinas. He's an innocent. He's God's fool. He is the Sufi of chaos. Tell him.

'I believe that the Mellified Man of Iskenderun is buried somewhere inside the final Fa.'

The gallery interests and repels Yayla: his eyes brighten at the mention of her Bektaşi calligrams; letters manipulated into the shape of a pear or a rose or a bird or, most pertinently to a self-proclaimed member of a sect that saw humanity as the perfect image of the divine word, a man. They darken again when he hears this is for commercial gain. They narrow at the story of Hacı Ferhat.

'This is not right action. Only the undying one is permitted to see the Day of Resurrection in his own flesh. The man who dabbles in forbidden practices buys his own destruction.'

They widen when Ayşe confesses that she has a buyer for the Mellified Man.

'Money will break the superstitious hold of this monstrosity. It's a good thing. Sell it, break it up, destroy it, let the soul of this misguided Hacı return to the earth.'

His sits back in his chair, eyes wide as a child's when Ayşe unwinds the thread of reasoning that brought her to his door.

'When I hear of a battle of magics, between the spoken word and the written word, that sounds to me like an echo of a much older battle, between the oral tradition and the written tradition. This Tarikat of the Divine Word – the name itself is deeply Hurufi. If we take Beshun Ferhat's chronology at face value, her family lost control of the Mellified Man towards the end of the nineteenth century, not the end of the eighteenth century. The Corps of Janissaries was destroyed by Sultan Mahmud the Second in 1826 in the Auspicious Incident. At the same time the Bektaşis, who were the Janissaries' particular religious order were disbanded and their shaykhs and babas executed. We know that the Bektaşis were the repository of Hurufi philosophy and theology: it seems reasonable to me that in Istanbul the order went underground, especially if it was an elite group.'

'But Beshun Ferhat claimed that Hacı Ferhat had been a member of this secret Tarikat in the eighteenth century,' Yayla says. 'Before the Auspicious Event.'

Ayşe has always admired the Ottoman talent for euphemism. The Auspicious Event was the massacre and execution of ten thousand Janissaries. Bodies had been heaped in the Hippodrome, rotting in the June heat. The more perfumed the language, the more brutal the repression.

'It was probably a perfectly respectable gentlemen's religious society, with a preference for esoteric alphabetic and numerology games. You know how tarikats split and change and reform. And I don't believe any form of supernatural power was involved, there was no battle of magics. A war of words sounds to me like a clash of legal systems; local, orally-based millet against shariat. They lost the case, and the coffin. But, if they were a secret Bektaşi order that survived the Auspicious Incident, and if Sinan had used Hurufi mysteries held by the military Bektaşis to draw the Seven Letters, it seems altogether reasonable to me that the Tarikat of the Divine Word would have known about it too. When they were threatened with destruction after the foundation of the Republic, they would have tried to hide their greatest treasure, to keep it safe from Atatürk's reforms, and also as an investment should the order ever rise again. They must have known its commercial value. My belief – my theory – is that they buried it where only they could find it, using their esoteric knowledge of the Seven Letters. Why do I think it's the seventh letter? Because it's the one even you can't find. It's the hidden key to the secret name of God. They knew it, but the destruction of the Order was more total than they ever imagined. The society was destroyed. The information was lost. But I believe it's still there, lost for over a century somewhere among Sinan's architecture. Find the final letter, find the coffin.'

'Find the coffin, find the final letter.' When Barçin Yayla is engrossed, his fingers perform a little unconscious trick that Ayşe finds quite disturbing. He flicks the glass eyedropper over the back of his knuckles, round his hand, back again, over and over. She imagines it shattering, spraying hydrochloric acid in her face. 'This is fine intellectual play but it leads us only to where we are already. I have dedicated years to prayer and the study of the Holy Koran and Seven Letters.'

What you won't say because you are polite is, if I can't find it, no one can, Ayşe thinks.

'This is the most complete collection of material on the Seven Letters of Istanbul in Turkey,' Ayşe says. 'In the world. No one has more books, more drawings, more architectural plans, more notes and cuttings and articles. There is nothing to know that is not here. Everything sufficient to faith is contained with these in this room. The answer is here. You've seen it. You just didn't recognize it.' She goes to the bookshelf. She can't begin to calculate the value of the antiquarian volumes on the shelves. Faith, even solitary, maniac faith, can always find money. 'Come on, let's think. You're not the first to have read these books. Which are the key texts? The Tarikat of the Divine Word, what would they have read? Because they've certainly read these. Come on man, come on! You want to see the secret name of God? Books books books. Show me the books. The question is a written word, the answer is a written word. Sinan is the key. The man, not the buildings. Where can I read the mind of Sinan? Where does he betray his secrets?'

Barçin Yayla is dazed by Ayşe's aggression. *This is not how women act in your world*, Ayşe thinks. *If there are any women in your world*. He pulls out three paving slab volumes, leather bound, worked in beautiful gold leaf.

'*The Architectural Archive of the Grand Mufti of Istanbul*, Sai Mustafa Çelebi, *The Book Of Buildings* and the *Tezkiretül Bünyan* of Sinan. Do you read Arabic?'

'I read Arabic.'

Barçin Yayla hands Ayşe the Sinan autobiography.

'Do you read Arabic quickly? One question. What am I looking for?'

'The thing the eye of faith overlooks.'

Lines run. Pages turn. Hours pass. The silence is utter. All Istanbul is outside the window but it seems muted, slowed, suspended in golden heat, mellified. Ayşe glances up to refresh her eyes. Arabic imposes a rhythm, a diction, a direction on the world different from the left-to-right, up and down of Roman alphabets. The room is cut free from time; it could be a hundred years from now, a thousand years ago. Sacred time. Ayşe understands it now. The words run. The words run. Look for what the eye of faith overlooks. See with the eye of the unbeliever, with the eye of the dealer, the merchant. Light moves across the room, another layer of yellow and brittle laid on the stacked newspapers and magazine cuttings. Shadows lengthen, the heat is immense. Ayşe long ago stopped noticing the smell.

. . . the Chief Architect of the Abode of Felicity commissioned a pattern for the Tomb of the beloved Kadina Hürrem with Yakov Assa of the kehalim of the Sephardim.

Ayşe reads the line again.

. . . Yakov Assa of the kehalim of the Sephardim.

She can't breathe. This airless, dusty, stifling, stinking box is suffocating her. She sets the book down.

Yakov Assa. Sephardim.

What the eye of the faithful overlooks. Ayşe hooks on her eye-writer. She clicks in to the architectural image archive. All Istanbul exists here, digitized, eternal, fully explorable. The tomb of Roxelana, built by Sinan in 1558 in the great Süleymaniye Mosque complex. Heart pounding, Ayşe swoops around the tiled interior. Tree of life motifs blossom over niches lined with floral tiles. Above each door is a panel of calligraphic Iznik tiling, gold on blue. This is the only writing. Ayşe focuses on a word, clicks in, refocuses, clicks in; in on the letter, in in. She can't breathe. Each letter is made up of minute individual letters. The resolution is just enough to show the letters are distinct from each other, but Ayşe does not doubt that each letter contains the working of the entire panel in micrography. Fractal geometry. The great composed of the small.

'Micrography,' Ayşe breathes, the first word in how many hours? Ayşe can't tell. The sun is low, striking directly into this attic room. 'The seventh letter, the final Fa, is there. It's always been there. It was just too small for you to notice.'

It's a privilege, Ayşe realizes, one given only to a few, to see a man undergo a spiritual revelation. As she explains the history and practice of the micrography the Sephardic Jews brought with them to the liberal society of Ottoman Constantinople after the Alhambra Decree banished them from Spain in 1492, Barçin Yayla goes from bafflement through amazement to the same stunned wonder Ayşe felt when she saw the answer, whole and entire, written in minuscule in the tomb of Sultana Roxelana. She now understands what Adnan felt when he saw the plan for Turquoise, whole and entire, in a flash of clarity, but Yayla sees something neither she nor Adnan can. He sees a universe closed to all others, unbeliever or faithful alike. He sees his own private revelation. He sees the culmination of his life. He sees the proof of his faith. If God is in every atom of the universe, the Name of God must likewise be written into every stone of the city, every cell of the body, every molecule, every subatomic particle. Reality is woven from the Seven Letters. The name of God is a cat's cradle of superstring. *God is great*, he whispers. *God is great*.

'Elements of Sephardic micrography informed the Bektaşi calligrams. The Sephardim were well established in Istanbul by Sinan's time, he would be familiar with the idea of micrography through the Bektaşi influence on the Janissaries. We know he commissioned Yakov Assa to create pieces of micrography for the tilework in Sultana Hürrem's tomb. The small in the great, the great composed of the small. The secret name of God can only be properly known by understanding that it is written into the heart of everything, every day. We're not looking for something on the scale of cities and landscapes. We're looking for something quite small, something in plain sight, something seen every day that is easily overlooked.'

'In Istanbul? Such a search would take lifetimes.'

'But he wants it to be found. The secret name of God can always be found by the dervish who truly understands. The Tarikat of the Divine Word wanted to bury the Mellified Man where it could only be found by future Hurufis. If the greater letters are formed around his architecture, I think it's a safe bet that the minor letter is also.'

'There are twenty-two Sinan mosques in Istanbul, let alone hamams, mescids, medreses, hans, turbes,' Yayla says. But his fingers have again found the glass tube of hydrochloric acid and toy with it.

'Well it won't be the first piece he built and it won't be last because no one knows what his last work will be.'

'God willing,' Yayla adds.

'I'd suggest we start with the clue we have: the micrography in the Haseki Hürrem Turbe.'

'The interior of the tomb of Roxelana is covered in three thousand tiles. Any one of them could contain the final Fa.'

Yayla's resolve is weakening. Ayşe has seen this in many of the treasure hunters and fixed-focus antiquarians she has met in the small city of Istanbul art dealing. The closer they come to the object of desire the more reluctant they are to grasp it. The search is the thing. The process is the purpose. The final mystery can only be anticlimactic. The story is ended. There will be a day after Barçin

Yayla reads the Secret Name of God and he will need to sleep and eat and excrete like any other day. The search could be over this very night, so quickly, and not by his own effort. He could have wasted fifteen years more and still not found the Lost Letter because he could not see beyond the meaning of letter to letter as art. It took the insight of another. A woman.

'I don't think so. Small things are easily lost. What if that one tile broke or came off? It will be small and inconsequential, but I think it will be in multiple places.' Get him. Grab him. Don't let him waver. 'We can go now. We can go right now. It's still open. Come on. You could see it this very night. This very night.'

Hesitation. Revulsion. Dread. Then exultation.

'Yes, yes we will!' Barçin Yayla cries. 'If it's there, let's find it. Gracious God is good, God is compassionate.' The marching chant of the Janissaries. Yayla disappears into his bedroom to get a backpack. Ayşe sighs. Intellectual exhaustion is the most draining type of tired, and she has far to go yet before she finds the resting place of Hacı Ferhat. It's right. She knows she's right. Rightness is stitched into every cell of her brain. It's all about ways of seeing. She flicks out a cigarette and is about to light up when Yayla catches sight and calls, 'Excuse me, would you mind not doing that? It stinks the place out.'

The lasers write on the eyeballs in perfect synchronization. It's quite beautiful to watch. The beams are micron-width, only visible when dust falls, glittering, through the gap between eyewriter and eyeball. Dust. Shed skin cells. Eighty per cent of household dust is exfoliated, something like that. The truth that we are fountains of dirt and excretion gives Leyla the goose-flesh horrors. Icky. The dancing thread of light draws twining DNA strands on to the retinas of Team CoGoNano! The same animation into which she fell, dazzled, out at Nano Bazaar. The same animation which had baffled Mete Öymen of the European Emerging Technologies Investment Board. He had the soul of a civil servant. These are business people. They chase down cool, they're hunters of the hip.

Leyla tries to read their faces but Mahfi Bey, Ayfer Hanım and Gülnaz Hanım have very carefully positioned themselves with their backs to the wrap-round window with its heartbreaking view down over Beyoğlu to the Golden Horn and the eternal Bosphorus. They are deliberate silhouettes. Leyla has to keep herself from squinting, shading her eyes, being seen to look.

She had kept her cool past security, past the exquisitely made-up receptionist with complexion like an apricot, past the leather-upholstered waiting area of sofas so deep and well-constructed she sank into them as she sank into sleep, up in the elevator with the meet-and-greet from CoGoNano!, into the fifteenth-floor office with its views over continents and empires.

'May I freshen up?'

Certainly.

In the marble washroom, with its rose water and cologne and de-ionized water splashes, she gave the little squeal and skip of excitement. Done it. Made it. Top of the tower. Corner office. CoGoNano! on the swing tag. She thrust a can of deodorant up her blouse, aimed it at her armpits. When will this heatwave ever break? Squirt one squirt two. Leyla remembered that her mother had called it a Kurdish shower. She blushes, embarrassed by the memory. People you love can do bad things. Then she patted down her hair and freshened her lips and straightened her skirt and marched out to battle. New shoes, a shirt sharp from the iron, seemed to have focused and charged Aso.

'You nano-ed up?' she whispered as the PA escorted them to the conference room.

'Just a little HFK-32Gamma, like anyone,' Aso murmured back. 'You mean you're barebrained?'

In the conference room eyeballs go dull and leaden. The sexy animation comes to an end.

'We're talking about a revolution,' Leyla says. 'This is the first day of a whole new world. Information written into the genetic code. All the stuff we store on to flick drives or our ceptep or distance storage somewhere in Tajikistan; that will all be inside you. All the photographs you've ever taken; that's like a fingernail of storage. And you can recall them just by thinking. Ever wished you had perfect, photographic recall? Now you do. Now all you have to do is see something and you will be able to recall it – and not just recall it, show it to others, in perfect detail. And that's only the start. All the music ever written can fit into your appendix. Every book ever written, that's a little bit bigger; that's maybe a few centimetres of your bowel. All those things you wished you could do, like play the piano or learn a language or repair your car or do accounting: you can download that and store it permanently. You want to memorize a play, or you want to review every test case in the law library? It's yours. Home plumbing, programming code, physics, chemistry, you've got them. You can know everything, I mean, everything. Ordinary nano gets purged from the system. The Besarani-Ceylan transcriber writes it into the cells of your body. You can't forget your body.' Leyla's amazed how she's remembered this. Word for word. As a child, Leyla would dress up with her sisters to perform that year's Eurovision song contest entry or the winner on *Turkey's Got Talent* for the big family New Year party. She grew up without fear of an audience, confident to speak to anyone, stand on any stage from a coffee table to a panel of investors, but until now she never appreciated the thrill of performance. The words pour out of her. She's blazing. She loves this. 'You can record and replay every detail of your life. All of it. And that takes up the space of, say, the size of your stomach. Your whole life, inside you. Another you. And you can live other people's lives. They can download all their experiences into you. You can know what someone else really thinks. You can think what they think, you can predict exactly what they're going to do. The next industrial revolution is here. This is more than just nano. This is the moment everything becomes smart. This is the Besarani-Ceylan transcriber.'

Leyla stands a moment, holding their attention for the few seconds it takes for the adrenaline to ebb. Then she snaps shut her case and sits down beside Aso at the big table. Is that the heat of the sun on her face, or the afterglow of the pitch? Team CoGoNano! is silhouetted, faceless.

'Thank you very much Ms Gültaşli, and Mr Besarani too.' The only way Leyla can tell that it's the man speaking is by his voice. 'You've presented your product well and your commitment and passion is obvious to all of us.'

'I'm sure you've questions.'

The man's head turns slightly to the woman on his right. She says, 'What CoGoNano! is really about at the moment is mass market nano apps. We've put money into some entertainment-based products – we're developing some dance-based nano, another big one is a voice changer. A project we're very fond of is a Tourette's Syndrome simulator. It's very very funny; we'll be leaking a viral next month, we'll find out through the hits. We're thinking about celebrity endorsement, maybe some kind of stunt where we sneak it into the Meclis in Ankara. Politicians with Tourette's. That's got to be funny. We're very excited about a product we're market-testing, which is Mind Candy; it's a visually oriented brain-training game that effects real neurological change. So this is absolutely in the right area for us, in that it's non-industrial, but we're really more in the market for must-have lifestyle accessories for fourteen- to twenty-four-year-olds.'

'So that's a no then,' Leyla says, marvelling at the composure in her voice. The third silhouette speaks now.

'It is Ms Gültaşli. Thank you for bringing this to us and we wish you every success, but we're not really into changing the world.'

The approach to the Bosphorus Bridge is grid-locked. The little rattly citicar is mired in traffic, intimidated by walls of trucks. Horns blare. The air-conditioner struggles against the heat. Even Cousin Naci's immaculate white top sports sweat circles under his arms.

'There's no use hooting your horns, it's not going to make it go any quicker,' Leyla shouts at the curve of stationary vehicles sweeping down to the beautiful leap of the bridge. 'What are they hooting their horns for? People are stupid you know, stupid.' She winds the window down and yells up the six lanes of motionless traffic, 'Bastards! Stupid bloody selfish bastards! You just couldn't think of anyone else, could you? Oh no, have to get there on time, have to look cool, and here we are, here's ten thousand people, all stuck here because of your bloody selfishness! Bastards! They should throw you off the bridge!'

A middle-aged driver in a battered old red Toyota stares at the foul-mouthed harpy in the next. Aso also stares. Placid Naci's eyebrows are lifted.

'Are you sure you didn't get a sniff of that Tourette's thing?' Aso says.

Leyla whirls on him.

'And you're no better, Mr Oh-I've-picked-up-this-really-nasty-virus. Fix it. Take the time and fix it, if that's even what it is. Bastards! Bastards! They could have told us before we took all the trouble of going to see them. "We're not really into changing the world." I've only just realized we didn't get to see anyone with real money. They fobbed us off with juniors. "Must-have lifestyle accessories for fourteen- to twenty-four-year-olds." Bastards.'

'I do believe you're beginning to care, Ms Gültaşli,' Aso says.

'I care about being professional, that's what. I was good! I was fucking good!'

There is a sharp intake of breath from Cousin Naci at the dirty words from his relative's mouth. Gültaşli girls don't curse. The Demre branch does.

'Well, we may be down CoGoNano! but we're up a lead on the Koran cover,' Aso says. Naci nods.

'Oh, why do you have to be so bloody reasonable? You were the one in exactly the same place doing exactly the same thing yesterday after we got turned down for the Euro fund. Be angry!' she shouts out to the truck drivers and red Toyota man. They pay no heed, they have their hands on the gear-shifts; from their higher vantage they can see movement ahead, rippling back from the arched back of the bridge.

'Perhaps there is a quantum of anger,' Cousin Naci says.

Leyla and Aso turn in their seats, gape-mouthed. Cousin Naci shrugs and returns to his customary silence. The trucks begin to roll, the little citicar boxed between them. Leyla's ceptep chimes.

'What!' she shouts. 'What now?'

It's Lütfiye Ashik from Special Projects at Özer Gas and Commodities returning her call. Mr Saylan can give her half an hour tomorrow at nine thirty, if that's acccptable.

'Yes, yes, of course it's acceptable. Hello? Hello? It'll be two of us, myself and Mr Aso Besarani. Thank you. Goodbye.'

Now the men are open-mouthed.

'Özer!' Leyla shouts. 'Özer! Özer Gas and Commodities, Special Projects Division!' In the corner of her vision, on the edge of the rear-view mirror, she notices there's a tow-truck eight vehicles behind her.

The ferry slides along the side of the gas carrier and darts across the stern, rocking on the wake. Georgios Ferentinou steadies himself on the companionway rail, breathing heavily. Nimble girls dash down the steps, chattering over their shoulders. He mops his brow in the heat and puffs up the next flight of steps. The gas carrier ploughs on under the bridge, half-submerged screws turning slowly. Georgios imagines it flashing into an annihilating fire. Would he see that flash, would he feel the heat of the fireball and if he did, would it be a blazing, ecstatic agony, or would it be the merest kiss of warmth before incineration? He imagines the girls in their city shorts and sun tops, their strappy sandals, the flesh of their exposed thighs and bare arms turning to boiling black tar. It would be quick, it would be instantaneous. Dead without even knowing. On these stifling nights when the dervish house seems to focus all the stored heat of the day into his small wooden bedroom, his thoughts go often to guessing the shapes and garments of death.

Major Oktay Eğilmez sits on a plastic bench in the shade of the bridge. He lights a cigarette, offers the pack to Georgios as the old economist sits heavily beside him.

'In 2021 I was assigned to military intelligence in Diyarbakır,' Major Eğilmez says without preamble. 'In the run-up to EU accession we decided to conduct a series of strategic strikes against the PKK. The plan was to damage its structure and weaken Kurdish nationalism's bargaining position before European human rights and ethnic minority legislation tied our hands.'

'Militarily eminently sensible,' Georgios says.

'We thought so too,' the major says. 'It was a highly successful unorthodox warfare operation.'

'I wondered why I'd never heard of it.'

The ferryboat turns in the channel and the light dips under the bridge canopy into Georgios Ferentinou's face. The sun is full and generous. He smiles, feeling the skin tighten. Old men should smile in the sun.

'Any action had to be one hundred per cent deniable during the accession process. So it was tactical assassinations made to look like murders or accidents, black ops strikes, special forces operations disguised as wedding massacres; you know how those Kurds are.'

'Somewhat like Greeks, so I've heard.'

Major Eğilmez dips his head. 'My apologies, Professor Ferentinou.' The sun falls on his face now and he closes his eyes in momentary worship. 'For me, the best thing about this frankly ridiculous think-tank is that it brings me back to Istanbul again. Ankara is all politics politics politics. And no one can cook. Dr Cengiz Samast was assigned to our command.'

'I've never heard of him either.'

'I would be concerned if you had. Dr Samast is our country's pre-eminent second-generation chemical warfare consultant.'

'I'm afraid I have very little understanding of military terminology.'

'Killing your enemy is clumsy and, frankly, messy. It creates resentment. How much more subtle, and clever, to turn him into your ally.'

'I should not be hearing this.'

'Operation Euphrates was a project to field-test a second-generation chemical device on an isolated civilian population. It consisted of an airborne nanoscale agent designed to enter the brain and modify dopamine, oxytocin and serotonin uptakes. You're familiar with those neurochemicals?'

Two van drivers in scuffed workboots take glasses of tea to the rail to watch seagulls dipping in the wake.

'I know they're central to behaviour formation and emotionality.'

'The agent was designed to increase passivity, disrupt associational ties and enhance mutual distrust while at the same time expanding receptivity to our information.'

'Propaganda.'

Major Eğilmez is amused. 'Professor Ferentinou, you know as well as I that the Turkish Republic does not engage in propaganda. We *market*. We chose Divrican, a small and isolated village, in Şırnak Merkeze district of Şırnak Province. There were two reasons: the village was known as a base for a local PKK warlord, also, its proximity to the border with Iran meant that any – unforeseen – consequences could be blamed on fall-out from Fandoglu Mountain. You may remember that we implemented an evacuation plan for villages in the border region and that we're still imposing restrictions on livestock and agricultural products from that area.'

'By the same token, I presume the Turkish government does not engage in economic warfare either.'

'Of course not. The package was delivered at three a.m. by a modified Hoodoo stealth drone. Within four hours the entire population was manifesting neurological symptoms.'

'Symptoms?'

'Heightened suggestibility. Visual and auditory hallucinations, of a consistent and persistent form. Belief in the reality of these hallucinations, in the form of schizophrenia-like inner voices, an unshakable trust in the personal nature and authority of these hallucinations.'

'The nature of these hallucinations?'

'Religious visions. Supernatural manifestations. Inner voices that spoke with the authority of God.'

'Jesus and his Mother,' Georgios Ferentinou says simply. He is having difficulty breathing. His lungs, his trachea, are lead.

'Yes. This sounds familiar, doesn't it? People who see peri and fairies, little magical robots. Djinn. Karin. Hızır. I'm a rational man. I don't believe in djinn and karin and the Green Saint. I would say, your shaykh friend has been nanobombed.'

'But what, how?' Georgios flusters. The ferry shudders as the engines throw into reverse. The traffic and quays of Eminönü slide past. Major Eğilmez rises to his feet and straightens his jacket.

'We seem to be arriving. You should probably go back to your car, before your driver gets irritated.' He moves into the crowd streaming out of the cabin down to the deck.

'The people, the villagers, the Kurds? What happened to them?' Georgios calls. Gone. Georgios won't see him again. An empty seat at the table tomorrow, a read apology from Major Ortak Eğilmez. Pressure of work, other commitments.

The ramp is down, the traffic is manoeuvring around the black government limo. The driver stands by the open door, looking up impatiently at Georgios on the high deck.

Mustafa taps the mirrorshades into exact position in the bridge of his nose with the tip of his forefinger.

'Are we in an action movie?' Necdet asks.

Mustafa strokes the starter chip. The little gas car has been sitting in the underground laager for years but starts instantly. The plastic seat covers smell buttery and electric. There's a thin layer of dust on everything. The odometer is in low double digits. Necdet hadn't known that the Levent Business Rescue Centre also maintained a small fleet of cars.

'There's stuff down here I think even the company's forgotten about,' Mustafa says, throwing on the batteries of fluorescents that illuminated the concrete garage and and the twenty VW runabouts parked in neat rows. 'I had thought of setting up a taxi company, but Suzan might notice the kilometrage.'

Mustafa hurtles up the spiral ramp, headlights blazing, like he's Special Agent Metin Çok or the legendary Jack Bauer.

'In answer to your question,' he says as the garage doors open before them in a blazing wedge of late afternoon light, 'Yes, in a sense, it is an action movie.'

Necdet recoils with a soft cry. The sky churns with djinn; billions of them, moiling and boiling through each other like the storm of God himself. Storm grey, liquid slate djinn, ropes and cords of them woven from lesser djinn from least djinn, shouting through the sky above Levent. The strands of djinn are binding together into huge sheaves, the guy-cables of a divine bridge between Istanbul and heaven. The web of cables all tend in one direction: a sky sign. Necdet has no doubt that it leads to an apartment in Ereğli.

Mustafa's face is tight. He hunches low over the wheel, knuckles white. He darts between lanes, cuts up trucks, races executive Audis and Mercs away from lights. He dashes between approaching trams.

'Where did you learn to drive?' Necdet asks.

'The tourist police. I did my service with them. You tend not to get shot in the tourist police. This is police driving, this is what they call defensive driving. You work on the assumption that everyone else on the road is a homicidal cretin and go from that.'

'So that's why you're wearing those prick-ass mirrorshades.'

Mustafa lets out a bray of laughter.

'Do you know how long I've waited for that, Mr Hasgüler?'

'For what?'

'You to make me laugh. I'll tell you how long. Six months, fourteen days and eight hours exactly. There is one rule to working in the Levent Business Centre and it's that if you don't possess a sense of humour you go insane. I love you like a brother, Necdet Hasgüler, but you have never shown anything remotely resembling a sense of humour. All those mad business plans, that Urban Golf shit; I tried my damnedest to get some kind of a smile out of you and you'd just nod like a dumb-ass mule. Whatever those things are, they're changing you.'

'Would it be very dull if I asked you what you meant?'

'You react to what happens around you. Things surprise you. Other people exist. You talk. You have opinions. They may be wrongheaded, but they're yours. They're turning you into a real person.'

The water-deep serenity and certainty Necdet had felt in the Tulip Mosque, the crushing memories the Green Saint had summoned deep under the Business Rescue Centre; until now he had not thought they might be part of a greater process: the reinvention – or was it more, the invention? – of Necdet Hasgüler. What is, who is this Necdet Hasgüler? Yet he feels familiar in his skin, alert, eyes wide open. He is becoming truly conscious for the first time. Hızır, bringer of waters, master of spring and new growth, is growing him.

Necdet glances at the boiling sky as the car speeds over the Halıçoğlu Bridge. The djinn have formed a circling flock over the big intersection by the main bus station. Mustafa drives into the djinn storm. Among the narrow, apartment-gloomy streets of Ereğli, Necdet spies a corner store, makes Mustafa stop the car

'The woman who sees peri, where does she live?' Necdet asks. The shopkeeper shifts nervously.

'We're not journalists,' Mustafa adds. He points to the Levent Business Rescue Centre logo on his polo shirt. 'My friend here is a shaykh. He has seen djinn. He'd like to commune with Lady Peri.'

The storekeeper's eyes bulge, he fumbles at his worry beads.

'God preserve us. Crimea House. Günaydin Sok. You'll have to pay the kapıcı. He runs the operation.'

'I don't think so,' Necdet says with a pass of his hand, the kind that shaykhs and saints and masters of mystery make. 'By the way, your store djinni says you really should check up on your security.'

'Did he?' Mustafa asks back in the stale heat of the street. 'Need to check up on his security?'

'Doesn't every small shopkeeper?'

The concierge has a small tiled cubicle beside Crimea House's elevator shaft. The elevator is a brass and iron cage, a guillotining thing of oily cables and hurtling counterweights, clashing metal gates and flanged wheels. The lobby smells of old tobacco, cleaning fluid and thick gloss paint. It feels like another century. Few djinn dwell here, just furtive spirits around the gas pipes and the cable ducting.

'Günes Koser,' Mustafa asks.

'You have to make an appointment,' the concierge says. He is of the tribe of kapıcıs, round and fat and yellow. He opens a desk diary. 'Consultations with the shaykha are fifty euro. Morning or afternoon? You can have an evening appointment for a twenty euro supplement.'

'My friend here is a shaykh himself.' Mustafa says. 'He would like to meet Günes shaykha as an equal. He is a master of djinn.'

'It's still fifty euro.'

Necdet tenses, leans forward as if sniffing out perfumes of other centuries.

'You have a lung problem,' Necdet says. 'You smoke too much. You're thinking of seeing a doctor about this. You should. It's serious. It's not what you fear, but it will be bad unless you do something now. You don't want to die with a tube up your nose.'

'Apartment 16,' cries the concierge. 'You are bad men. Away from me!'

'We are God's men,' Mustafa says.

The elevator cage sinks an alarming half metre as Necdet and Mustafa step into it. Mustafa turns the brass pointer round to the fifth floor. Heavy engineered objects clank overhead and are answered from below. With a jerk the car starts upward.

'What do you actually see, when you see djinn?' Mustafa asks.

'Burning babies, faces in computer screens, tiny flying people with very long legs, bodies all wound together like rope. The one inside the guy downstairs looked like a lung, with a beak, and tiny hands sticking out the side. What's that thing smokers get where their lungs go hard and they can't breathe?'

'Emphysema.'

'Like that would look like if it was a living person.'

'I wonder if Günes Hanım sees exactly what you see but just calls them peri where you call them djinn.'

'It's never the same thing twice.'

The elevator grinds up its iron shaft. A sudden loud commotion from the ground floor snaps Necdet's and Mustafa's attention from the ceiling to the floor. Doors banging, voices shouting. Feet running. Figures in dark clothing pounding up the stairs that wrap around the lift shaft. Soft-peaked military-style caps. Necdet crouches, pulling Mustafa down beside him as the figures rush past: impact protection jackets, hi-vis tape at wrists and ankles, pants cuffs tucked into heavy boots.

'Police,' Necdet whispers. He tugs at the dial, punches at the finger-polished brass button. The elevator is intent on delivering them right to the police. The police are ranged around the door of Apartment 16. They are armed and armoured for riot, they have shock sticks and a black battering ram. The tops of Necdet's and Mustafa's heads rise above floor level. Then a hand, a hand from nowhere, grasps the floor pointer and wrenches to the left. Without a grate, without a plaint, the elevator stops and starts to descend again.

'Did you see that?' Necdet whispers.

'They're kicking in her door,' Mustafa says. 'They're in her apartment.'

'The hand, it was green.' But the elevator is sinking surely now, taking them away from the shouting and crashing at the top of the stairs. The hand was green, disembodied but not disconnected; there was a person, beyond the elevator, beyond this entire world. Eyes deep as springtime. Help from beyond comprehension. Clattering bootfalls with the clank, clank of an object being taken down one stair at a time. The elevator sinks down beneath the level of the lobby and stops, jammed, its uppermost metre and a half above the marble floor. Necdet and Mustafa press back into the shadows. The police beat down into the lobby. Two of them handle a gurney, the type Necdet recognizes from the Business Rescue Centre for taking sick and injured down flights of stairs. Clank clank clank. A woman wrapped in a silver thermal blanket is strapped into it so firmly she can only flex her hands and feet. Her head is covered by the foil sheet but she tosses it so hard she shakes off the covering and Necdet sees her mouth is taped. Eyes connect. Necdet reels back. The life of another world cracks between them like lightning; djinn, peri, gods, all, none. Creatures of power. Then four police hurry her out the door. The remaining four haul the concierge, babbling and covering his head, out of his tiled office, out of Crimea House. Necdet leaps up to take action, Mustafa tackles him down and holds him down until the sirens have dopplered away. Then the two men force open the lift gates and haul themselves up on to the marble.

'Did you see that? Did you?' Necdet runs down the steps on to the street. Günaydin Sok is stunned to stillness: a photograph, Istanbul Street, 18:25, April 14th 2027. 'It was her, I saw her on the tram, she was right beside me when the bomb went off. That wasn't any old cops, that was security police.'

Mustafa takes Necdet's arm to hurry him away before he attracts the other sort of police, but Necdet tears free from his grasp. He stands motionless as Günaydin Sok resumes movement and noise around him, intent as if straining to hear music at the edge of audibility. He frowns, shakes his head, then seems to catch a thread of melody. Mustafa sees him strike out across the street. Necdet stops outside the Türkcel ceptep store and points up at the dirty yellow-and-black hornet-chevronned robot clinging like a feeding wasp to the plastic shop-sign.

The call to prayer blares out from the four minarets of Süleymaniye Mosque as Ayşe Erkoç enters the southern gate of the enclosure. Ayşe has always had a horror of the azan. Not the austere beauty of the human voice, even recorded and amplified as it is in these degenerate days, nor the counterpoint of many calls from different distances across the city, breaking across each other in waves of sound. It horrifies her because it has no respect for her. It says this is not your city and time. This is God's city, this is God's time and God's time is absolute. Your comings and goings and doings and dealings are hung around these five pillars. Five times a day you must stop what you are doing and turn to God. She fears the azan because to her it is the sound of atavism. It denies change and the hope of change. It says that all works of hands are temporary, all hope of progress is futile. All that is necessary is here. This is the perfect way. Come and pray. She fears it because it says that Istanbul, Queen of Cities, Abode of Felicity, is a man's city. The azan says there is nothing for Ayşe Erkoç.

'I hope you don't mind me saying,' Barçin Yayla says, 'but I did notice the same car pass us three times while we were walking up here from Küçükayasofya.'

'What kind of car?'

'Oh, I'm afraid I don't know very much about cars. A silvery one. Is Skoda a make?' At the door to the courtyard he says, 'You're very welcome to come to the women's gallery.'

Ayşe would sooner drip his acid in her eyes. While Barçin Yayla prays with the men in the glorious prayer hall that is precisely twice as tall as it is wide Ayşe explores the grounds. Families picnic in the cool shade of the trees, rugs spread on the grass, mothers peeling hardboiled eggs, fathers pouring tea from Thermos flasks. Leaves rustle, stirred by the slightest breath of wind. Ayşe is no stranger to the Süleymaniye Mosque with its attendant medreses and charitable külliye arrayed on two sides; its dome and minarets were the daily view from the window of her adviser of studies at the university but today she sees them fresh. Not with the eyes of faith – she has seen its particular blindness in Barçin Yayla – but with the eyes of the architect, the decorator, the pattern maker. There are mathematical rhythms and harmonies in the order of the domes, from great through lesser to least. The span of the arcades, the placing of windows and buttresses under the dome, the heights of pillars and the numbers of balconies on minarets; the geometries of squares, hexagons, octagons: this place is not stone, it's music. She could spend years, decades searching for the hidden sign in these magnificent stone choruses and correspondences.

Twilight gathers under the trees and in the gateways as Ayşe enters the graveyard where the mausoleums of the house of Osman stand. Does she hear bats? She circles the tomb of Roxelana three times. She studies the carvings in the deepening gloaming, she pokes around in the grass, peers at tomb slabs, feels out the carvings in funerary pillars, scrabbles the gravel back and forth with the toe of her boot. Nothing, anything. She could lose a year, visiting every day in all weathers, to this graveyard alone. How could she have imagined that she would find the key at first glance, fly to it straight as a bullet, that it would shine out among the architectural brilliance of this enormous mosque complex to her and her alone? But the answer is here, she is certain of it. As she wanders back to meet Yayla, the floodlights come on one by one, throwing unnatural, infelicitous light on the dome and minarets. Angular shadows could be Kufic letters concealed in the architecture, they could be buttresses, they could be birds. The families are packing up their crumbs and blankets and trying to find places to dump their empty drinks bottles.

She finds Yayla sitting on the steps by the courtyard gate, his backpack at his side. He shines. His face is radiant, his eyes bright, his skin firm. Ayşe has seen this light in any number of miniatures of the Twelve Imams and the saints, the veiled face of the Prophet himself. She wonders if what she has thought of as innocence and naïvety is not in fact holiness.

'We have a task ahead of us,' Ayşe says.

'A joyful task,' he says and she realizes that he welcomes the idea of years of searching, tile by tile, inscription by inscription, cornice by cornice and niche by niche, that the painstaking search of Sinan's greatest achievement, decades long, is the holy task; that the secret letter is cut in every stone and tile. By the time you find it, you have realized the supreme unimportance of finding it. A Sufi lesson.

Picnickers and evening strollers pass in ones and two heading for the gate on to Sidik Sami Omar Cadessi, in Sinan's times, the Street of the Addicted, not merely from the intoxicants on sale there, but from the hospital that compassionately treated the opium addicts.

'We'll make a proper start tomorrow,' Ayşe says. 'Are you coming or are you staying her for the yatsı?'

'I'll go back to my own mosque for the final prayers,' Yayla says.

'If they knew what you were pursuing, if they knew what you believed, they would call you heretic,' Ayşe says as they walk on crunching gravel under the bat-whispering trees. 'That's not a safe or a private matter these days.'

'Every man is welcome at prayer,' Yayla says. 'God's good.' At the gate to Sidik Sami Omar Cadessi he turns to look back at the great Süleymaniye, backlit by a titanic sunset unfurling like the banners of the army of God over Eyüp, eerily luminous in the floodlights. 'This is joy. Joy!'

There is no joy in this, Ayşe. *This is hell. I've become one of the lost.* Selma Özgün warned her. Red on the Galata Bridge warned her. Even Beshun Ferhat's rabbit warned her. Honey lures, honey seduces, honey traps. Don't get involved with the Mellified Man-hunters. But she did. She let herself be seduced. She has become one of the Lost Legion of Hacı Ferhat.

Barçin Yayla steps down on to Sidik Sami Omar Cadessi and stops dead. His mouth contorts as if in pain.

'I am standing on something,' he says. Ayşe is quick to his aid but she can see nothing on the stone cobbles that might damage him. Yayla's left foot is on a drainage grating, a rather beautiful piece of worked stone, of an age with the mosque, carved and pierced. There seems to be some sort of low-relief motif; rather elaborate for a drainage cover. Then she sees. She sees. The pattern is a series of Kufic letters, laid over each other in a complex grid. Ayşe kneels in the street. A citicar hoots past her, the driver shouting. She does not hear him.

'Kha, shin, say, thaw, tha, jim,' Ayşe says. ' Kha, shin, say, thaw, tha, jim! Kha, shin, say, thaw, tha, jim!'

'I felt it through the sole of my shoe,' Yayla says with wonder. He kicks off the shoe, stands one foot bare in the street. 'I have stood on the Secret Name of God.'

'Well, take your foot off the Secret Name of God,' Ayşe orders. She traces the letters. The carving has resisted four hundred years of Istanbul traffic and rain. The spaces between the rectilinear Kufic letters form the drain holes. Ayşe glances up and down the street. Between the feet of pedestrians, the skittering mopeds, the humming citicars she sees that the drain covers are spaced regularly and evenly across the street. In plain sight, in the least assuming of places, small but ubiquitous, overlooked by all but those who have the eyes to see.

'Sinan, you fucking genius!'

Barçin Yayla is breathlessly chanting *Gracious God is Good, God is Compassionate.*

Ayşe kneels and presses her cheek to the grating. A breath of air, cooled by the deep places of old Istanbul. The breath of the Fa, the missing letter, the unique orientation that points to the heart of God.

'Shut the fuck up!' Yayla is stunned into silence. Ayşe fumbles at her rings. Her wedding ring gives easily. No, not that, never that. She twists off a beautiful Tulip Era turquoise she took as part of a settlement from a buyer from Bulgaria. Ayşe Erkoç drops it through the grating. Moments later there is a faint, clear chime.

Can loves the supermarket. Soft neon, the glow of the shelves. The cool cascading from the chiller units and the mysteries stacked on the high shelves beyond his reach. Families squabbling around the trolleys, putting things in and taking them out again, tiny children in kid seats dealing him grave stares as they are wheeled past or abandoned in the middle of the aisles of wonder, the mothers glancing pitying at him as Mum signs to him. Look, little deaf boy. No, I'm not deaf, and even if I were, I could still see you. The Boy Detective misses nothing, including the packets of pantyhose or razors or bottles of Johnnie Walker Blue they slip under their coats. At the check-out he likes to try to guess the personalities of the shoppers ahead from their groceries sliding along the belt. What Can loves about the supermarket is that it is not Adem Dede Square. It is not Kenan winking at him and Asking. Him. In. Very. Big. Mouth. Movements. How he is today?

The supermarket is full of old people this evening, shuffling up and down buying nothing, keeping cool in the air-conditioning. The car park is suffocatingly hot after the chilled aisles. The air smells of hot blacktop. The world is endless and rich.

'Mom,' he says. 'I think this is what California must be like.'

Şekure Durukan makes the sign which says, *What are you on about now?*

'Oh, nothing,' Can says. He loads another bag into the back of the Gas Bubble.

Supermarket night is always treat night; an ice-cream bar that Can eats in the car, not from impatience but because of the sense of sophistication he gets from biting through the dewed chocolate to the creamy cold beneath with the lights of the city streaming past. In the car at night, eating ice cream, his mother drumming her fingers on the steering wheel to the dancing volume-display of the radio, he has a powerful sense of a different life they all could have led. It takes place in a nice suburban house, with a garage, and a red tile roof and some space around it. There's a swing and a trampoline at the back. There's a woman sitting on a verandah reading a magazine. There's a dad inside watching sport with his friends; later they may play cards. There's a boy whirring around on the street on a cool bike. He can go anywhere in the world on that bike. That boy is the Can who doesn't have Long QT syndrome.

'QT,' he sings to himself. 'Cutie. Cutie.'

'What's that, love?'

'Cutie.'

Şemsi flashes her spangly red booty at him from the wall-sized hoarding.

Can is not allowed to lift anything heavy up the steep steps to the apartment because of the strain it might put on his heart. His parents have debated fitting a stair lift but have always deferred the cost against the hope that Can will grow into a fitter and stronger teenager. Şekure calls Osman down on the ceptep. Three bags per hand, waddling up the steep wooden steps. Why don't they just lower a basket over the edge of the balcony? Sometimes you can't tell people these things. Not for the first time Can suspects he may be much smarter than his parents.

Can's left a last little nugget of ice cream, a reward for being left in the Gas Bubble out on the street. Şekure and Osman had pulled him in the moment the police swarm robots descended on the crowd. He had been angry at that, then frightened as soft screams began to penetrate the cloak of silence around him. They should have let him see. Adem Dede Square is still measled with RFID-paint in hard-to-reach places: the undersides of gutters, coamings and cornices, carved woodwork, lines and verticals out of the reach of brushes or long-reach window cleaners, the floral-carved stonework of the fountain. The Improving Bookstore hasn't even tried. Can finds the leopard-spotted steel shutter an improvement: excitement, wild stuff within. Aydin's stall is likewise shut up for the night. There is Kenan in his shop, watching Sky Sports on the flatscreen above the door. Bülent and Aykut are engaged in precisely the same activity in their rival çayhanes, lining up their tea glasses in neat ranks and files, Bülent's gold rimmed, Aydin's crimson. Can smiles. He likes to notice these patterns. It's the way Mr Ferentinou looks at the world. There's Necdet; Shaykh Necdet now, Can supposes, creeping home down the steps of Stolen Chicken Lane from wherever he spends the day. He never looked great but he's dreadful now, face thin and eyes staring like you see in cartoons of mad imams and hunched over. If that's what God does to you you should pick your friends more carefully. There might be a robot watching him. There are so many places in the konaks and old buildings around Adem Dede Square where a robot can hide unseen, spying. Can knows, he's used most of them. He remembers Mr Ferentinou's warning and squeezes down into the seat well, peering over the top of the dashboard.

Necdet hesitates, as if he's scared to go down Güneşli Sok to the squat. Then all the doors open on the little white van parked beside the Adem Dede çayhane, a van Can has not even noticed because it's so ordinary. Three men: young men in bomber jackets and sports pants. They run at Necdet, too fast for him to react and knock him hard to the ground. Before he can recover they roll him on to his stomach, pull his arms behind him and bind them with cable tie. While the wind is knocked out of him and he can't cry out they drag him to his feet and rush him to the van and throw him in through the back doors. Two men follow him in, the third gets into the driver's seat. Doors slam, engine kicks. Can slides down into invisibility as the white van accelerates past him down Vermilion-Maker Lane. All in the single, silent breath held by Can Durukan. So fast, so hard, he's the only one saw the kidnapping. Bülent and Aydin at their glasses, Aykut watching one of the interminable preambles to the Galatasaray cup-tie, all were looking elsewhere. Can is the sole witness.

He exhales. The paralysis is broken. The Boy Detective knows what must be done. Can rushes from the Gas Bubble, up the stairs where his parents are descending for their second, complaining load. Şekure signs furiously at him. Can opens the computer and throws himself on to his bed, squeaking in frustration at the interminable boot screens. So slow so slow! It's up. More endless moments as the BitBot application opens. *Come on*, he breathes at the screen. Come *on*. And he's in. And he stops, hands crossed in the gesture that assembles Bird out of the wasp-nest of BitBots clinging under the eaves. *Promise me you won't have any more to do with this*, Mr Ferentinou said. *We are not detectives. You must promise me this or you can never come here again.*

'But I'm the only witness,' Can murmurs to the screen. 'If I don't do anything, no one will. Only me, Mr Ferentinou.' Can crosses his open hands in the haptic field and Bird forms. He crosses thumbs, waggles fingers. Bird, fly! And he's up, wheeling over the overhanging wooden eaves and cloistered garden and little hushed graveyard of the dervish house. There are only so many ways the white van can go from Vermilion-Maker Lane and Bird can cover them all with its many eyes. Bol Ahenk Sok, no, Alçak Yokuşu. Can has seen people take mopeds down the steps. Desperate and dangerous kidnappers might risk a van. No. Down on to Necatibey Cadessi. Evening traffic, headlight and streetlight dazzle, neons and luminous trams sailing past, hard to make out one white van from the many on the big street. Can reconfigures Bird's eyes and swoops low over Necatibey Cadessi. They have to be here and they have to be going in this direction, towards the bridges. But there are so many white vans. You never notice how many until you need to look for one white van. There. There. Five back in a line stopped at traffic lights. Bird glides up over the line of cars.

'Size of rat!' Can whispers and brings his fists together. Bird explodes into a rain of BitBots. Millimetres above the road, they configure into fast, street-smart Rat. But the lights have changed, the traffic is rolling. White van is drawing away. Can hisses with concentration as he steers Rat in and out between crushing car tyres and dodging mopeds, faster faster! But White Van is getting away from him as he frantically scampers through the taxis and the trucks. By a silicon whisker he escapes the guillotine of tram wheels as he follows White Van across the tracks where the line curves up toward Beşiktaş. Two car lengths, three car lengths. Can rolls his tongue in fierce concentration. Every neuron is focused on this ultimate street-driving game. They're getting away, they're getting away. And then the traffic lurches to a halt in one of those inexplicable Istanbul slow-downs that freeze whole districts for no obvious reason and just as unreasonably clear themselves. Rat dives under crawling cars, dashes between wheels. There there! Less than a metre to go and the traffic speeds up again. They're moving off, getting away. One chance and one chance only: Can stabs his hands forward with a sharp cry even he can hear through his plugs. Rat leaps, seems suspended forever in midair, latches on to the rear licence plate.

'Yes!' Can pipes but the robot magic isn't done yet. 'Go go rat baby!' Down on Necatibey Cadessi, Rat splits open from the head. A tiny ratling, a thumbnail-sized clone of its parent, locks on to the back of the White Van. It's a little app he got from the BitBot forum: BitBot MiniMe. Like most apps, Can had played with it once, shown it to his friends once and then never looked at it again, unable to find a use for it. But now is the bit for which they can't write apps.

'Rat, home.'

Rat Daddy drops off the van, rolls into a ball and goes skitter-bouncing down Necatibey Cadessi, tumbling like an empty plastic cola bottle between the crushing wheels and the growling engines. Now. Again Can brings his fists together. In mid-bound Rat reforms, dodges away from a water truck and scampers to the safety of the gutter.

'Good Rat, clever Rat,' Can says and sets the robot into homing mode. It will slowly but inevitably find its way back to the Durukan balcony, crawling on minimum power. Rat's job is done. Now the task is Rat Baby's and Can opens up its window. The view from its tiny cameras is fish-eye distorted; the device is little more than a tracking device and that is all Can Durukan needs. Rat Baby will ride the White Van all the way to its destination.

'I know where you live,' says Can Durukan.

The bedroom door opens. Can's father stands there in the wedge of light. Can can see his jaw tighten in frustration.

'What do you do in there?' he asks with wonder. Can pretends not to be able to lip-read him. Osman Durukan closes the bedroom door. Can returns to Rat Baby and opens up his location on a map. Heading for the Atatürk Bridge.

'I so rule,' says the Boy Detective.

*

You are an icon of the Virgin Mary, Mother of God, Theotokos. You are small and crude; the eye and hand of faith shaped you but devotion was not enough to overcome want of skill. Your hands are painted from three different perspectives, your eyes are wide but flat; turned away from the world. Your face is brown and long and has in its gaucheness captured your ineffable sorrow, dyed in the melancholy of this city long before it was called hüzün. No precious gilts or crushed mother of pearl went into the making of you, your frame is painted wood. You are small and dowdy. The casual eye glances off you, hanging among the bolder and brighter and more outwardly radiant paintings on the iconostasis of St Panteleimon's Church. The eye of faith sees deeper. There is something ineffable, numinous, about this small, faded, grubby work. It's not the face, the hands, the fingers raised in clumsy blessing. It's the blue veil that drapes the Virgin's head. How could the same hand have produced this? It seems to float free from the wood, light and luminous, almost sparkling with light. You are the Icon of the Little Virgin of the Protecting Veil. You have hung among lamps and images of the divine for fifteen hundred years. Your painter set pigment to wood the same year Justinian dedicated the great church of Aghia Sofia. You were too humble and clumsy for that basilica of emperors; lesser churches, the churches of the people were your proper place. You gained their veneration. You earned their love. You attracted a mythos as a worker of small miracles: lost things found, soldiers kept safe, travellers protected. You escaped the razing of the Iconoclast Era because a widow, thankful for a son returned safe from the eastern borders of the empire, hid you in her bosom for a year and a day, ever after bearing the rectangular mark of the Little Virgin pressed into her flesh. When the Mother of God appeared in a vision to the Holy Fool Andrew and spread her mantle over Constantinople to defend it from Saracen invasion, your beautiful shawl became part of that greater protecting veil. When Mehmet the Conqueror released his armies on defeated Constantinople for three days of looting, you were hidden, face down, in a horse manger as blood ran in the streets and the last memory of Byzantium burned. Now Muslims as much as Christians venerate you and come to leave small offerings for a lost thing found, a stubborn bureaucrat charmed, a son on military service kept safe.

Fourteen hundred years, four empires, a dozen churches; now you rest on the sanctuary screen of St Panteleimon, neither ancient nor venerable, a hidden treasure among the dozens of images that adorn the iconostasis. This is the trick of it: the profane eye can't recognize you, the eye of faith must seek you out. You teach that everyday miracles are found in everyday places; hidden, unassuming, vanishing into the crowd as soon as they're performed. The divine is in the faces you see every day, all around, covering you like a veil.

This evening Father Ioannis has honoured the Little Virgin of the Protecting Veil by lifting her from the iconostasis and setting her in the stand in the narthex, a special icon for special vespers. There is already a small pile of euro and cents under the stand.

The cosmic blue of the veil shines out in the stifling shade on Havyar Sok and calls Georgios Ferentinou in. He has been wandering, thinking, shaping thoughts about faith and chemistry, when old faith catches his eye in a kingfisher flash. He has not intended to go anywhere near St Panteleimon, but the cool of the protecting blue veil seems to infuse the little tiled vestibule. The growl of Istanbul is pushed away. Georgios Ferentinou can breathe, breathe deep without catch or tightness. The air smells sweet, not of incense, or the cleaning liquids Father Ioannis used to cleanse the urine, but an older deeper fragrance; the perfume of the Virgin, and older than the lady of Christianity, to the old gods of the Greeks and the Hittites, the fecund Venuses of primeval Anatolia.

Father Ioannis chants the Prokeimenon. He has a fine, basso voice, deep as a cistern. Bell-true. Georgios murmurs the lines of the liturgy. Never forgotten. Teach a child in the true way. He's never fought with religion; what is the point of railing against such beauty, such intimate theatre, such a chime of eternity? He can treasure it without believing it. He stands by the corner of the narthex door, in the shadows where he can see and not be seen. Candles and oil lamps burn in rows before the iconostasis. The agony of St Panteleimon is all the more brutal in the flickering light. His martyrers nailed his hands to his head. There is the gap usually inhabited by the Little Virgin of the Protecting Veil, surrounded by nailed skulls, flayings, cruel executions, those art works so coveted by Mrs Erkoç in the gallery. Russians pay ridiculous money for them; gas lords and mineral oligarchs fill walls with the martyred. Dark and enigmatic people, the Russians.

Father Ioannis steps into Georgios' view and takes a position before the sanctuary gates. The old man draws back. The occasional prayers. Father Ioannis' voice commands the space beneath the star-painted vault of St Panteleimon. It's not the first time he has celebrated divine office to God alone. But he is not alone with God. A movement, a shadow in the intimate gloom of the nave. A worshipper; a veiled head: a woman.

Georgios' heart catches in his chest. He steps away from the door, doubly terrified of being seen. But he must see. He moves carefully around the door until both Father Ioannis and the woman worshipper are in profile. Her head is bowed. The veil hides her features. A strand of silver hair escapes over the collar of her blouse. Georgios hardly dare breathe. It is her. It must be her. The Song of Simeon ends, the woman looks up. Her face catches the light. She is perfect in her unselfconsciousness, smiling in delight at the ringing resonance in the old church's acoustic. Father Ioannis' basso toll begins again. *Let it last forever*, Georgios thinks. Let it be the unending threnody of the Mother of God for the broken world, outside time. His hands shake. This is voyeurism; he is a Peeping Tom of the soul. The incense is suddenly cloying. He must leave. He has to leave. In his haste he catches the icon stand. The Little Virgin of the Protecting Veil, aloof for fourteen hundred years, tips towards the tiles. Georgios sets her back in her position but the scrape and rattle of the brass stand has turned Ariana's head to the narthex. Georgios whirls away, hunches his shoulders and pulls his jacket close around him. *Don't hear me, don't see me, lady draw your veil around me.*

Behind his wooden door, in his wooden kitchen, Georgios sets the kettle to boil. There is his tea, a Black Sea blend prepared specially for him. There are the tea glasses, winking in the down-lighters. Georgios Ferentinou hurls the tea glass at the wall. The tiny bulb of delicate glass explodes. Another, then another, all of them, Georgios roaring now in wordless rage and loss. All of them. He can't breathe, is there nowhere to get away from the heat in this house, this terrible house? He hates it; he always has hated it. He only came here because he couldn't afford anywhere better, after Ogün Saltuk told him his career as a tenured professor was over. Decisions he was not conscious of making chipped his life away to leave this splinter of a man. There should have been friends beyond a few old Greeks; there should have been family, there should have been children. There should have been Ariana Sinanidis.

Economics was not always the dismal science. For half a season, the early autumn of 1980, economics was thrilling, economics was revolutionary. Economics was, for a few sweet weeks at the rag end of summer heat, cool. Georgios Ferentinou had never been cool. He had never spent the night in Taksim bars and Beyoğlu cafés with people who could talk ideas long after curfew, who were as excited about new ways of thinking and looking at the world as he. He had never marched beside names and faces he knew from the newspapers and realized that they were just people. He had never turned his back to police water cannon or learned how to scoop up a CS gas canister and lob it back at the armoured ranks, then run madly through the alleys and soks of old Beyazıt and Eskiköy to stop in a doorway, breathless, wide-eyed with the sudden realization of danger, breath-close to Ariana Sinanidis and have that breathlessness break into the hugest laughter. He had never even known he could run. He had been thin and pale and abstract. He became ever so quietly, ever so modestly, political. He fell in love.

Love blinds you most to the times. The lectures he gave, the rallies he attended, the flyers he ran off at midnight on the department Gestetner, it was not socialism or communism or islamism. It was romanticism. There is no more incandescent passion than love in a time of revolution. Even when the faces from the newspapers were no longer at his shoulder in the demonstrations, when more bodies without faces turned up in the prop-wash at Kadiköy and Eminönü and remote laybys on the Bursa highway, nothing like that could happen to him. Love protected him like the word of God.

'It's us it will all come down on,' his mother said. 'I saw it in '55. It always comes down on the Greeks, and the Kurds and the Armenians. And the Jews. You think you know it all, running around with that Sinanidis girl, that they can't touch you, but they have long memories, the Turks. All those great research posts, those big academic promotions, you'll just never quite make the grade. There'll always be some Turk who's better qualified, has a better publishing record, fits the position better.'

'They won't be here,' Georgios said. 'We'll have swept the generals away and proper socialism in.'

'What do you know about socialism?' Georgios' father said.

The arrests began three days later with the Armenians; prominent members of the community, socialites, professionals, fourth estatists lifted from their places of work, from their family tables, from their beds. Most were released within twenty-four hours. Some subsequently stood trial and were jailed, to be returned to their homes and hearths years later when a democracy acceptable to the military took control in Ankara. Some never returned at all. The Greeks read the signs. Within a week eighty families had moved out of Cihangir. Georgios' family finally, desperately, contacted their son by a telegram sent to his department concierge.

'Oh son, don't say you won't, you can't stay,' Georgios' mother had begged. He remembers that night at the house as the first time he had seen her old, so small, her legs terribly thin and frail.

'I've work to do here.'

'Work, you mean running around with those Young Socialists,

whatever they call themselves, that Sinanidis girl? She thinks too much of herself, she does.'

Georgios bit down anger.

'No, I mean work. I have a doctorate to finish.'

'You can transfer that to an Athens university.'

'Which Athens university would that be?'

'Now son,' his father interrupted but Georgios' mother went down on her knees then and wept without shame.

'You break the family, you break my heart, why won't you come? It's only for a year or two, and maybe then everything will different and you can move back.' Knowing, as everyone in the cramped, stale-aired living room into which the cooking smells wandered to die, that they never would, that none of the Greeks piling their lives into cardboard boxes and fruit crates ever would.

'Tell me at least you're not doing it for her,' his mother implored. It was an underhanded, unclean blow, the type only a mother can hope to deliver.

'I have a doctorate to finish,' he said in a voice of stone.

He helped them load Mr Bozkurt's delivery van. He was careful not to carry any of the boxes holding his childhood things. He let his parents take them, mutely; he would have to come for them some day. No son could give away his childhood. What he would not watch was them drive away in Mr Bozkurt's white van, turn out of Somuncu Sok on to Cihangir Cadessi, to the new highway west, through Edirne to the border. They went down into Greece, a foreign country, and rented a cramped, overheated apartment in Exarcheia, which they hated for the rest of their lives because no one could understand their accent and called them Turks.

He went back to his university room and ignored Ariana's phone calls. Three days after the Ferentinous left Cihangir, where they had lived since Hellenic times, the government moved into the university, breaking up sit-ins, beating students, arresting agitators, detaining academics and researchers. Then the black car came to take Georgios Ferentinou over the Bosphorus Bridge.

Three times Georgios finds the ceptep in his hand, three times he sets it down. He is sick with fear. He tries to imagine how she will sound. He's forgotten her voice. He has rehearsed what he will say, but he can't anticipate her answers. She may not even want to speak to him. She may just disconnect. He couldn't bear that. He has spent his professional life estimating risk, how people assess it, judge it, accept it; now he can't face it. Georgios snatches up the ceptep. The number is on speed dial. It's calling. A voice answers in a foreign language. Greek, it's Greek. Georgios stumbles for words.

'Hello? Hello?'

'Hello, who is this?'

It was the strap on the front and the back of each hand for anyone Göksel Hanım caught speaking Greek in her class.

'Hello, is that Ariana Sinanidis?' Georgios hears the waver in his voice.

A pause. Georgios holds his breath. The voice speaks again.

'Who's calling?' She's spoken six words but the voice, that voice, floods back to him in every syllable and nuance.

'It's Georgios Ferentinou,' he says.

Thursday

7

It is Deal Day.

The weather on Deal Day is bright and hot hot hot. Shimmering off the highway at six in the morning hot. Tarmac glossy and melting. Turkish flag hanging like a dead bird from the pole on the top of the hill across the highway hot. Adnan has been up since the dawn azan. Prayer is better than sleep. Profit is better than either. There are Deal Day rituals to be observed. Shoes to be shined: he sits in his jockeys on a kitchen chair with a newspaper spread on the table; flecks of stray polish clean off skin more easily than fabric. The trousers are working up a cut-yourself crease in the press. Brush lint stray hair dandruff from the jacket. A Deal Day shave is like you see in the ads, close, closer, closest yet. Five blades close. Hasan would do it better, do it the proper way, with a long open razor. Afterwards. Treat yourself. Relax back into the big chair when the deal is done and let Hasan kiss your face with his steel. Adnan exhales a long, slow gasp at the stinging splash of kolonya. Adnan doesn't believe in those magazine-marketed aftershaves with macho names like Blue Steel and Hugo Man or worse, the names of football players and golfers. Kolonya is the proper smell of a man. Doubly so on Deal Day.

Does the DJ know something, or is the music on the dawn patrol show particularly rocking? Confirmation bias, like when he bought the Audi and every other car on the road seemed to be an Audi. Adnan is ironing his Deal Day shirt when Ayşe emerges from the bedroom in just her pants.

'You look hot,' she mumbles, pushing at her pillow-hair.

'Hottest one yet, the radio says. Up to thirty-eight.'

'I meant you, in your pants and nothing else, doing your shirt. Men ironing. It's very delicate, like men doing ballet.'

He wonders she can see him at all through the blear. Ayşe's a hard waker. She rolls into the kitchen and fills the kettle. The pipes whistle and bang and make that strange animal roaring but at least there is water at this hour of the morning.

'That's only because you don't do them right.'

'It takes a lot of practice not to do them right.'

But she does make coffee right, wonderfully good coffee, the kind you only learn from growing up with a cook in the house. Deal Day coffee. Adnan drinks it well away from his still-iron-warm shirt. How much better will it taste on the sun-deck of his waterside yalı with the big ships sliding past? They might have to wear more clothes then. An eyeful and then some for the ship crews and the nosy neighbours. They should be so lucky. God, but she looks good, squatting down to take clothes out of the washer-drier, thighs spread above petite, balancing feet, the divine peach of her ass. Her back is incredible. He's never really noticed it before, the perfect shapely symmetry of the muscles around the valley of the spine but it astonishes and arouses him. Everything is sharper and sexier on Deal Day morning.

'Sorry I was late in last night, I was setting a few things up with Ahmet and Mehmet.'

'Are you chasing something?'

He can tell she is smiling from the play of her muscles.

'I certainly am.'

'Are you going to tell me?'

Again the muscle-smile. 'Certainly not. I'll tell you when it's done. You do your deal, I'll do mine.'

Ayşe takes her coffee into the bedroom. By seven Adnan is dressed. Deal Day shirt, Deal Day suit, Deal Day tie and socks and shoes. She was right. He is hot. He fastens his cufflinks.

'Right. To battle.'

Ayşe steps out of the bedroom to see him off. She's pulled on her Japanese silk kimono.

'I preferred you as you were,' Adnan says. Ayşe swats at him with the sleeve of her kimono.

'Come here you.' Her kiss is long with a promise of fierceness and tastes of coffee. 'Go and do it and come home a millionaire'.

'I'll call you when it's done.'

The usual boys are hanging around the garages. They must loiter there all night. As always they cast glances and make small, animal noises ostensibly among themselves as Adnan opens up the Audi. Look-at-me noises are all they ever do. Adnan considers winding down the window and telling them to fuck off and go and get a proper fucking job, fucking layabouts. This time next week he'll be out of here.

The car pulls out of the garage on autodrive but once Adnan is on the highway he flicks into manual. The discipline of driving prevents him thinking too long about what he must do to Kemal. The traffic is already heavy; the heat-haze thick as a curtain beyond the climate-controlled windshield, the radio bouncing with prophecies of temperature records for May smashed by eight o'clock. He blinks up audio of the closing prices in London and Frankfurt, the Henry Hub in Louisiana, the Vienna Hub and the mid-morning prices from the East Asian markets. Central Asia is already spiking; Baku just about to open. The big Audi thrums through the silver traffic. Ultralord coming though.

Kadir calls five minutes out from the bridge. The world asserts itself again. Adnan taps autodrive. Kadir's face appears on the windscreen.

'Hail Hydror.'

'Hail Draksor. I've got the materials. Where are you?'

'About half an hour away.'

'I'll wait for you in the main lobby.'

'I'll see you there.'

'It's looking good, isn't it?'

'Yes looking good.'

'I mean, looking hot. Hottest one yet.'

'Yes, hot.'

Up on to the bridge approach. Down there to the left is his yalı. That's the way to think of it. Adnan distracts himself by calling up the real-estate agent's brochure on to the screen. That balcony, that terrace, watching the traffic arc over the bridge knowing you don't have to be one of them.

The car is slowing. The car comes to a halt. Gridlock on the Bosphorus Bridge, a place Adnan hates to be caught, suspended high above water on slender engineering. Large numbers of cars on autodrive sometimes fall into lock-step, stymied by over-anticipating each other's relative motions. He knocks off the autodrive: let the sheep clear before him. Emergency braking kicks in immediately: something other than herd computing has caused this jam. Now the horns begin. Adnan scans across the drive-time channels. Reports of an incident on the Bosphorus Bridge. Highways Department report . . . an incident . . . incident. Incident to Adnan means human agency.

Adnan steps out of the car to get a better look at this incident. At once he is engulfed in blaring horns. To his immediate right a woman yells silently at her windshield, bouncing her hand repeatedly on the horn. The centre of the disruption is close, no more than eight cars ahead. Beyond, the summit of the arching roadway is empty. A lock is forming on the Asian-bound lanes as drivers slow down to gawk.

'Can you see what's happening?' Adnan shouts up to a heavily moustached truck driver beside him.

'There's a car right across both lanes,' the driver calls down.

'Is he hit?'

'Not as far as I can see. He's just sitting there. What's odd: whenever anyone tries to edge past him, he moves the car to block them. Whoa. Metal on metal there.'

A long distance coach is stopped behind the swearing woman's car. Passengers pile up at the front of the bus, craning to see. Swearing woman steps out of her citicar on to the bridge.

'Can someone tell me what's going on?'

A man two cars ahead turns and shouts, 'It's a jumper!'

'A what?' the woman asks.

The truck driver swings down from his cab. The coach door gasps open, drivers and passengers weave up between the parked vehicles.

'Maybe if we left him alone we might all get in quicker,' Adnan says but people are moving, pushing past him from behind and it's the football moment, when you just let fall and become part of the crowd.

'Will someone please tell me what's going on?' Citicar Woman asks one final time, then the crowd pushes her forward. 'My purse!' she cries. The crowd is four deep between the cars at the front of jam. Adnan squeezes to the front: a suit is authority. No one wants to get too close to the mad man in the red Toyota pulled at right angles across the highway. The damage he has done to the cars that tried to sneak past him is obvious: fenders bashed, lights smashed, paint and carbon fibre splintered. The driver is a middle-aged man, curled haired, grey at sides and temples, with a country look to him. The Toyota is a ten-year-old Istanbul registration, an old gasoline job converted to gas. He sits with his hands on the top of the wheel, very straight, looking forward. Now that the orchestra of horns has ended with everyone leaving their cars to see the drama, the sound of his engine is very loud.

'Here come the cops!' a man two cars to Adnan's right shouts. It's an impressive sight; motorbike cops coming four abreast over the curve of the bridge and down the empty road. They park in the same smart line; the officer in charge dismounts, draws off his gloves one at a time and walks towards the red Toyota. The driver flicks his eyes towards the policeman. His fingers flex on the steering wheel. As the motorcycle cop comes up to his window he slams the clutch in, floors the pedals, smokes the tyres and blasts forward to ram the crash barrier. A great cry goes up from the onlookers. The Toyota reverses fast, the policeman just makes it out of his way. Again the driver glances at the cop, again he smokes forward and smashes the barrier. The metal is buckled and flattened. Again the driver reverses back to his position across the bridge. Adnan can see him breathing fast through his mouth. He is very very afraid. The officer in charge backs off to consult with his colleagues. Police frequencies crackle and spit.

Then a voice shouts, 'Aren't you going to do something about him?' A second voice joins in, 'Move him, get him out of there or something!' Citicar Woman now, with her purse left on the front seat, cries, 'You know, some of us have jobs to go to. Jobs that pay your wages!' A passenger from the coach, for whom this is excellent drama at the end of a long, tedious bus journey, shouts, half-joking, 'You've got a gun, can you not just shoot him and get it over and done with?'

The officer in charge turns at that. He takes off his helmet to stare out the crowd but his attempt to cow the onlookers only stokes their defiance. Adnan has smelled this kindling, pheromonal mob-sweat at matches just before a fight breaks out in the stands.

'How long do you expect us to stay here?'

'It's your fault, we'd've had it sorted by now.'

'Haul him out!'

'Come on, get on with it.'

'The man's right, shoot the bastard.'

The Toyota driver looks deeply scared now and revs his engine. Silence on the bridge, then a single voice behind Adnan shouts, 'Hey you, yes you!' The driver looks around, terrified. He can't find the face accusing him. 'Yes, you! Why don't you give us all a break and just do it? You want to, so why not? Do it!'

Other voices in the crowd take up the cry. *Do it! Do it! Be a man, for once.* At Adnan's side the mightily moustached truck-driver mumbles, 'God be merciful; what are we doing?' *You're right*, Adnan wants to answer the truck driver, *this is monstrous, we are beasts.* But the rhythm of the crowd pulls him. He sways, his heart tunes to its beat. He knows what is happening, he has felt it many times at Aslanteppe. Go on go on. Cimbom Cimbom. Go on go on. Cimbom. And he is shouting with them, *Go on go on. Do it. Do it!*

A roaring wall of voice, not hatred, not cruelty, nothing emotional, just the mind of the mob.

The man in the red Toyota shakes his head. He looks up as if he can see heaven through the roof of his old car. He reverses back. The crowd raises a cheer. The man smiles in surprise, delighted. The audience love him. He spins the wheels, screams the tyres, smokes the blacktop, then pops the brake. The car shoots forward so fast the front end slides sideways. The crowd's guttural cheer falls starkly silent as the red Toyota hits the flattened crash barrier obliquely and flips up in a spinning twist. The car seems to sail a long way out over the Bosphorus. It hangs in the air. Its arc down to the water is very slow and theatrical. Still turning belly-up, the roof makes a huge splash where it hits the water. It goes straight down.

There is a silence beyond silence, where all sound is dead and the air is dumb as lead. Adnan's eyes throb, his breath flutters in his chest. He has just seen a car drive off the Bosphorus Bridge and plunge into the water. That can't be. He egged a man on to kill himself. Him and a hundred others. The exoneration of the mass. No one voice is to blame. But his voice was there. *Go on go*, he shouted. He would have done it anyway. Yes, the crowd was just giving him what he wanted. Why choose the middle of the Bosphorus Bridge, the middle of the rush-hour to suicide if you don't want an audience? He smiled, he waved at his audience. You couldn't have done anything to stop him. Go on. Drive on. Have your day. Everybody else is making their way back to their vehicles. You have a deal to make. And a neurological beating to deliver. It seems not so bad after goading a man into killing himself.

The truck driver shakes his head and climbs back up into his cab. The coach passengers file back on to their bus, not looking at each other. Citicar Woman is tearful and swearing again, a soft, edge of breath *bastard bastard bastard*, as if Red Toyota man is the one at fault, not her.

We jeered a man into killing himself.

Engines fire up all around Adnan. The police now have something that requires their authority, officiously waving cars forward. A heli-copter stoops over the bridge tower and drops down beneath the level of the roadway towards the water. You'll find nothing there. The Bosphorus, with its double currents and dark eddies, swallows all indiscriminately. There are whole civilizations down there, in the ooze. He'll be settling down there into three thousand years of history, Red Toyota man. Get it out of your head. It's Deal Day. Put it away. Concentrate on the work you have to do. But he feels dirty, dirty between the toes, dirty between the teeth, soil under the skin. Dirty in the blood, like he imagines heroin addicts must feel, like there is ash swashing around inside their bodies. A policeman brusquely waves Adnan forward. He flicks the Audi into autodrive and lets it take him up over the bridge into Europe.

The lampoon is a single sheet of A4, laminated, thumb-tacked to the street door of Ismet Inönü Apartments. Lefteres considers himself almost as skilled with the brush as with the pen and has illuminated the three verses with a frame of intricate floral design. It is his finest work in many years, not only in a difficult formal style, but an acrostic; the initials, emboldened in red, spell ROXANA WHORE. It is those that attract the eye of the passing morning pedestrian, a double-take that draws them out of their routine to read, remark, wonder what piece of local drama they have tripped against. But the good women of Eskiköy, the Hanıms and the long-standing residents of Adem Dede Square are delighted by it. Since Bülent put the shutters up and lit the gas burners and Aydin took his delivery of simits from the little Japanese micro-truck, the old women have flocked around Ismet Inönü Apartments like starlings, peering at the art, reading the verses out to each other, scattering in a flutter of scarves at the sound of the street door rattling. Lefteres has been at the çayhane since opening, very much contrary to his habit, watching reactions, basking in approval.

'Of course, the difficult part was using the style of Attar in the context of a lampoon,' Lefteres regales his morning tea colleagues.

'Maybe I wasn't paying attention in class, but I missed the "Georgian sucker of donkey dick," in the *Parliament of Birds*,' Bülent says gathering up empty tea glasses. He alone of the patrons of the teahouse disapproves of the lampoon. Georgios Ferentinou waddles across the street from the dervish house. 'Hey! Georgios! What do you think of Lefteres' lampoon?' Lefteres scowls: he wanted the honour of the reveal himself. Georgios frowns, puzzled. Bülent pushes a copy of the lampoon into his hands. Georgios scans it, pushes it away from him.

'Yes, very good. Very clever.'

Before Lefteres can angle for further praise, Bülent cuts in, 'Tea, or maybe coffee this morning, Georgios Bey? It's just you seem a little distracted this morning, and one of my good coffees would just cut right through that.'

'That's because he saw Ariana last night,' Father Ioannis says. 'She was at my vespers.'

'I did more than just see her,' Georgios Ferentinou says. 'I called her. I talked to her. And I am going to meet her tonight, in a restaurant.'

Now Lefteres and his lampoon are truly eclipsed.

'Then you would have missed all the action here last night,' Bülent says. 'That Hasgüler boy got lifted.' Small consternation; tea glasses upset, spoons knocked to the ground. 'And they weren't police either. I don't know who they were but they were in like a knife, out of the back of a van, grab the man, in the back, close the doors and away. Right up the side there.'

'What what what?' Georgios Ferentinou asks. Bülent's news has cleared his bewilderment better than any coffee. 'Who was taken? What, where?'

'Djinn-boy,' says Constantin.

'Necdet Hasgüler? What happened? It is most important that you tell me.'

'Well, I didn't exactly see it,' Bülent says. 'The only one who saw it all was the deaf kid.'

'He's not deaf,' Georgios says. The Greeks chorus, *It's a heart condition*. 'If Can saw it, I must talk to him.'

'Whoa, whoa whoa, hold on there,' Lefteres says. 'I have just written a superlative lampoon, not only witty but literary as well, with the express purpose of diverting the attention of the Turks, who get mightily exercised by this kind of thing, away from us Greeks, and an old, single Greek man wants a one to one with a nine-year-old Turkish boy? No no no.'

'You don't understand, this is hugely important,' Georgios cries. 'I feel it may be a matter of national security.' But Lefteres has succeeded in diverting conversation back to his lampoon, and now he has spotted a young man in a good leather jacket with a courier bag slung over his shoulder shooting it on his ceptep.

'I will bet he is one of my fans,' Lefteres says, 'the ones who run the websites and fan groups.'

Bülent is still not impressed with the lampoonist and his work and when he sweeps Georgios' empty tea glass up on to his tray he asks quietly,

'This national security, is it anything you can tell me?'

'I believe that young Mr Hasgüler, and others on that tram, were deliberately infected with nanotechnology agents, that the group responsible monitored them with surveillance robots, and now they have taken him to observe at first hand whether their experiment has succeeded.'

'What experiment?' Bülent asks.

'To see if religious belief can be artificially created.'

Bülent's mouth and eyes widen but his verbal response is never made for at that moment the street door of Ismet Inönü bangs open and the Georgian woman herself rips off the lampoon. She shouts at the photographer. Her words are almost unintelligible, lost in a scream but the tone is clear. The young man backs away, *whoa, I mean, hey, no offence, relax*... He was only ever a rehearsal.

She storms across Adem Dede Square, her flat-heeled slippers slapping on the cobbles. She is dressed in three-quarter-length leggings and a loose yellow T-shirt. Ornate silver ear-rings, tiered like pyramids, swing and glitter. She has put on make-up for the street.

'You filthy men, you filthy men!' she screams. Her Turkish is weak and heavily accented. 'What filthy things you say? Me, a poor woman, a woman who work hard and never say a bad thing about anyone. I come to Istanbul, I come to strange city of strange people, no language but I work hard, I never say a bad thing about anyone, but you call me whore and dirty, you call me a dirty Georgian whore. Filthy things, filthy things. Look at you, old men, only brave when you are together. And you have a priest with you. Hide behind his robes, old men. Hide like children under your mother's skirts. Hide behind your piece of paper, can not say this to my face, no; you must put up a piece of paper, in the night, when no one looks. And look at you: a priest! Aie! This I cannot believe, a priest of God. This maybe I expect from Muslims, but Christians! I am good woman, I work hard, what have I done to you Christian men?' Her rage breaks into tears now. This is shaming. Georgios cannot look and cannot look away. The Georgian woman slaps the laminated sheet down on the table. 'I am not ignorant, I can read Roxana Whore. Oh you bad, filthy men. To say such this of a poor woman on her own in a foreign city. And you, Father.' In the end the tears and the words run out and all that remains is her anger and humiliation and dignity. She turns. Halfway across Adem Dede Square she stops and shouts up in a sobbing, torn voice to the balconies and shutters, 'Bastards! I know you all, filthy bastards.' She closes the street door behind her with barely a click.

There is an Ottoman bearing, Adnan observes. A firmness, an uprightness, yet elastic, born lightly. He's seen it most in old military and civil service families who understood that their country would always need them. Kadir is instantly recognizable on the floor of Özer's cavernous, sun-showered atrium. Straight, graceful, easy.

'You're late,' Kadir says. No Hail-Draksor-Element-of-Earth-assist-me shit.

'You know when they say on the traffic feeds that there's been an incident? I found out what that means.'

'You could have called. If Kemal's already prepped for the day . . .'

'He won't. Everything that got backed up on the Bosphorus Bridge will have been diverted on to the Fatih Sultan Bridge. Kemal will have been caught up in that.' Adnan couldn't have called. He couldn't do anything other than he did. He can still see that car, elegant as a competitive diver, twisting in the air. He'll be seeing it for a long time. Kadir moves his hand the slightest fraction and like a conjuror there is a plastic nano vial between his fingers.

'What will it do?' Adnan asks.

'It was the best they could come up with in the time. It puts holes in your medium-term memory and then fills them with random junk. Pseudo memories, false memories. The theory is that it puts so much noise into the system no one will be able to tell what's real and what the nano put there.'

'Theory.'

'Stuff like this, you can't test it. You have to trust the designers.'

'How much were these designers?'

'Eight thousand euro.'

'For an untested product that has to work first time. And not kill anyone. No, not anyone, Kemal. Or turn him into a psychopath, or just plain brain-mezze.'

'Now you have scruples. It's money, Adnan. That's all it's ever been. The market opened twenty minutes ago. Are you going to do this or not?' Kadir has the magician's touch, the vial disappears with a flick from his fingers, reappears.

'Give it to me,' Adnan says and snatches away the vial into the safekeeping of his fist. It's still there, folded snug against the lifeline of his right palm, as he leaves the elevator and takes the short walk – hellos, good mornings, how-the-devils to the usuals he meets in those few steps – to the back office. Kemal sits at the coffee table, a saucer of tea in front of him. Beside it is his vial of enhancement for the day's work. It's his morning ritual; tea and nano. Beyond the glass the Money Tree is as brilliant with lights as a tree in the orchard of Paradise.

'I wouldn't mind a drop of that tea.'

'You never drink tea.'

'Today's different.'

'Fuck, it is. Tea for Lord Draksor.' It's instant cay, powdered piss; Adnan can't drink it but Kemal at the kettle is all the distraction he needs to make the switch. Open the palm, close the palm. Done. So simple. He takes his red and silver trading jacket from his locker. The ceptep writer hooked over his ear, the laser-head positioned a centimetre in front of his right eyeball, that's the finishing touch. Ayşe's right: accessories do make the outfit. He slips the stolen nano into his pocket.

'I presume you got caught in that thing on the Bosphorus Bridge,' Kemal says, boiling the kettle. 'What was it, some old dear deciding she'd left the gas on and throwing a u-turn?'

'No.' Adnan says. 'It was a suicide.'

'Fuck,' says Kemal.

'A guy drove his car off the bridge. Straight over the edge into the air.'

'You saw this?' Kemal stirs in sugar. The crystals swirl in the bottom of the glass.

'I told him to do it. Me and about fifty other people. We all stood there and shouted at him, go on, do it. And he did.'

'Fuck,' says Kemal again. He sets down the tea glass on the coffee table, beside Kadir's pirate nano. 'I mean ... fuck.'

But Adnan's no longer in the back office of Özer's trading floor. Neither is he on the bridge, watching the red Toyota spin its wheels on air. He's in Kaş, at summer's end, on his father's gület. In the gentle eyebrow of coast beneath the Taurus Mountains, the season dawdles into October. Kaş has always sold itself as a sanctuary, a hidden place, moving to a subtler rhythm than the dance-beat of the Aegean resorts. Kaş has seen their mistakes and resolved never to make them. The rag-end tourists, blowing in on the first fresh wind of coming autumn, bring with them a particularly easy, undemanding attitude. They have sun, and warmth and turquoise water as deep as time. Adnan's just turned four. He's on his father's boat taking snorkellers out to dive the drowned Lycian tombs. He wanders between the bikini women and the speedo men sprawling on their mats on the foredeck. The women coo and cluck at him, the men smile. He's a cute kid, with the enquiring frown-smile of children who grow up in the sun.

The swimming snorkellers look like great pale starfish. The tombs are jumbles of pale stone, shimmering under long drowning. Adnan's father cooks köfte on a little gas grill that hangs over the side of the boat; then it is time to rendezvous with Uncle Ersin's gület, who will bring more beer and vodka for the snorkellers and take Adnan back. Adnan's father doesn't like him being around drinking people. Uncle Ersin brings his gület in alongside; the two boats bob an arm's length apart, rocking gently on the cat-tongue sea. Close enough to pass the crates of beer and vodka one way and Adnan the other. Maybe it's the cat-tongue wind gusting up as it can, capriciously, along this mountain-fringed coast, maybe it's Adnan's father and Uncle Ersin careless from long habit. Maybe Adnan's a heavier four-year-old than they think. But, as he's swung out over the side, a grip is lost, a hold fails and he drops into the water.

He can't swim, he's only four. Even if he could, the shock, the splash, the sudden cold would paralyse him. He goes in, he goes down. Adnan can still see the water over his head, looking up at the concave lens of light between the two boat hulls. He can still feel his legs kicking, but still going down, the bubbles rising around him and how strange they were. Bubbles. The line of light dwindling, narrowing to a thread as that unpredictable cat-sea pushes the hulls together. To blackness. He remembers kicking, kicking down in the black water, lungs, head buzzing with motes of a black darkness, head humming, chest spasming with the need to breathe but he can't but he must but he can't but he must. Kicking kicking but he can't see the light, is he going up or is he still sinking.

Up in the light, screams from the bikini women, *Oh my god the boy he dropped the boy*. The speedo men jump to their feet but the crew are already pushing the gülets apart with boat-hooks. As clear water opens, Adnan's father and Uncle Ersin dive. They pull him out cold, limbs flopping. Uncle Ersin pumps his chest, Adnan's father picks him up by the ankles and swings him like a cat. Adnan chokes, coughs, spews up seawater and phlegm and bile. The doctor is waiting on the quay as the gület ties up. It's a dash in the doctor's car to the emergency room at Olu Deniz. He's released the same evening. Four-year-old boys can take a lot of water without drowning. It's the dive reflex, primeval behaviour hardwired into the brains of the very young that adults learn to forget. Children go calm and limp, their heart rate slows, blood is diverted to their brains. They can survive up to twenty minutes under water. Adults panic and drown. For the next three days aunts and other generous relatives come to visit the miracle boy and bestow sweets and kisses on him. But Adnan never forgets that slit of light closing down to darkness, going down into the black water. He remembered it on Ferid Bey's boat, bounding across the riffles towards the lights of the Golden Horn. He remembers it every time he drives across the Bosphorus Bridge, over that slot of deep dark water between the hills. He remembered it, remembered it so well when he saw the red Toyota spin out into the air, and drop with a diver's subtle splash into the water. He felt what it would be like to go down in that car; the black water pressing hard against the door, jetting in through the cracks and vents and loose seals; filling up the footwell, the compartment, the light dwindling in the water dazzle and going out.

'Two to three on Arsenal?'

'What?'

'Tomorrow, you know? Bookies are offering two to three on the English fuckers.'

'Oh, yes, ah, yes. Arsenal.'

'Sorry, you've other things to think about.'

'It's just a deal.' Adnan pats his pockets. 'Shit. I've left my gear in the car. Any chance I could use yours?'

'Your need is greater than mine.'

Adnan lifts the betraying vial and tosses it in his hand.

'I owe you.' He twists off the cap. Now is the trader's sense of timing. He closes a nostril, prepares to inhale, then bursts into a spasm of coughing. The nano sprays from him in iridescences; fractured rainbow. 'Fuck. Sorry about that. Fuck. I'll just balls it out bare-brained. Could you call someone in health and safety to clean it up?' Under Brussels regulations, nano spills are toxic disposal, like energy saving lightbulbs.

One car over the Bosphorus is enough for any day. It's enough for any lifetime. He'll go and make the money and work out later how to get it clean, get it safe. He always does.

'Fuck me a million,' Kemal calls.

'Oh, considerably more than that. Element of Air assist me!'

As he steps on to the trading floor, Adnan twists off the cap of Kemal's stolen nano and snorts it down. There's ballsing it out, and there's buck stupidity.

EQUIPMENT LIST FOR BOY DETECTIVE ON COOL MISSION

1. Large backpack, at least 30×40×15 centimetres. Internal capacity for item 2 (below). Lots of side/front pockets with zips. Black, red, grey. No pink, purple of branding for kids' TV/movies/toys. School backpack by default/necessity.
2. Computer. With charger. Computer battery at full charge; battery life, eight hours. Computer contains all known information about Case of the Mysterious Robot/Case of the Vanishing Shaykh (title undecided).
3. Ceptep. With charger. For emergencies only. Ceptep will remain switched off until absolutely completely utterly needed as Boy Detective can be traced through the positioning system. Utility doubtful, but better safe(ish) than sorry (very).

4. Headphones, small, in-ear ear-bud style, for monitoring item 2.
5. Packet of sticking plaster.
6. Water, two seventy-five centilitre bottles, sports tops. Can be refilled from public fountains: Istanbul drinking water (historically) pure and fresh and sweet.
7. Antiseptic wipes, for chafing from backpack straps – the Boy Detective estimates he will be carrying the backpack for at least eight hours – cleaning fingers after eating hand-food, cleansing toilet seats, general hygiene needs.
8. Underpants, change of socks.
9. Waterproof; nanofibre, v. good. Rolls up in ball the size of fist. Rain not forecast but it could get chilly later.
10. Rollerball pens, three of.
11. Small journalist's notebook, black bound with an elastic strap to hold flip-cover open/closed: v. professional.
12. Sun block. Factor thirty. Boy Detective doesn't get outdoors as much as he should/would like.
13. Sunglasses. Ditto. Also, can't be detective without sunglasses.
14. Antiperspirant spray, footspray: cooling peppermint. Chewable toothbrushes (four) from vending machine at Tesko. Why does a supermarket need to sell chewi-brushes? Comb for hair.
15. Money. One hundred and twenty euro, in small denomination notes, in three rolls secreted in different locations for security. Roll three, in highest value notes, curled up in the space between the toes and ball of right foot. The Dire Emergency Get Me Home Fund. It's enough for a taxi from any part of Istanbul to Adem Dede Square, by Eskiköy Taksis online booking prices. Phone cash is find-me cash. Cash cash is safe, anonymous. Cash cash is king.
16. Tourist map of Istanbul with transport lines clearly marked. Less detailed then the ceptep map but secure. Home-printed map of the Kayişdağı district, with the GPS readings from

the Rat Baby flagged. The last reading is a business park off Bostancı Dudullu Cadessi.

17. Pants with lots of pockets, cotton socks, comfortable trainers well-worn in, no rubbing, with lots of wiggle room for toes. T-shirt in dull, anonymous colour, no logo. Spare in backpack as padding for computer.

18. BitBots, in Snake incarnation, carried curled around the left wrist and up Boy Detective's arm, hard pressed to his warm pulse.

Say what you see.

I see ... I see the world of djinn, the creation of fire, where nothing is fixed and form flows into form, spirit into spirit, everything flickering, everything changing and budding and being swallowed up, creatures of living flame.

Say what you see.

The words ... he doesn't know how he knows these are words, they flow from and merge into the ceaseless creative fire of the creation of the djinn. But now they take a permanence, a visual echo, a shadow that lingers on the fire even as it's consumed, something that's more than vision: *sound*.

'Say what you see.'

Necdet hears the words.

'I am in a room with white walls and a grey carpeted floor. I am lying on a mattress. The mattress is covered in a floral print. The door is open. In front of the door I see a woman kneeling on the ground. She is wearing jeans and square glasses. She has green scarf over her head. She has the sleeves of her sweater pulled over her hands. There's a man next to her with big hair and a leather jacket. At the back of the room is a third man ...'

'Enough. He sounds lucid enough,' says the man with the big hair in the leather jacket. Necdet struggles to keep him in focus. Otherworldly flames flicker around him.

'Do you know who you are?' the woman asks.

'I'm Necdet Hasgüler. Who are you? Where is this?'

'We can't tell you,' the woman says. 'If it helps you can think of us as Divine Engineers, and you are our experiment.'

'You took me. You lifted me from outside the tekke, I was on the way home, where am I, what time is it?'

'It's later than you think. It's morning, you've been here since last night. You're unlikely to remember much of what happened.'

'We subjected you to targeted suites of nanoagents,' the big hair man says. 'We know quite a lot about you, Necdet.'

'You're not the police.'

The man with the big hair laughs.

'Oh no, but I can see why you might think that. The police were moving against our subjects, they forced our hand, we had to take you before the police did.'

'We are God's Scientists,' the woman says. Her face is familiar to Necdet but he can't place it. The square glasses and the green scarf make her look older than she is. Every body, every line and edge flickers with the invisible fire of djinn, like heat haze.

'Could I have some water?' Necdet asks. The other man passes him a fresh bottle of Sirma, flipping the sports cap. He's a big square guy in a green shirt. The green moves, flows, coalesces on the edge of Necdet's field of vision as he sucks like a baby on the water.

'What do you want from me?'

'Your vision,' the woman says. Now Necdet sees through the flame-edged outlines that Big Bastard Square Guy has a gun, a big military service assault rifle.

'I see djinn,' Necdet says simply. 'This room is alive with them. Your bodies are crawling with them like lice.' Big Guy twitches but Green Headscarf Woman says,

'We know that.'

'I see Hızır,' Necdet says. The three look at each other. 'He's in the room. He's in all places at once. That's why he's the eternal traveller. You say you're God's Scientists; they're not from God, the djinn. My brother thinks they are, but they're not. They're not even from the creation of fire. There is no creation of fire. They're from my head, from all the stories and ghosts and movies and saints and medreses and comics I ever heard. I see djinn, some see peri. But I don't know where Hızır comes from.'

Big Hair and Green Headscarf exchange glances. *Are they together?* Necdet wonders. They leave the room for a moment and through the swirling vertigo Necdet hears them talking. It can only be about him but it's too much effort to concentrate to try to listen through the aural fire-roar of djinn. When they come back they resume the exact positions and postures they held before.

'We interviewed you under nano partly to draw an accurate picture of your life. We don't have time for lies and evasions. We know who you are and where you come from and what you do and what you did.'

'Kizbes?'

'Yes. At the time you felt no guilt, no remorse, no emotion of either pain or pleasure at having left your sister permanently disfigured with third degree burns. Your motive was that she was bugging you. In the act itself, you showed no rage or aggression, you carried out the act as if you were a robot. These are symptoms consistent with massive dissociative disorder.'

'I don't know what that is,' Necdet says. 'But believe me when I say, that wasn't me. That was another me. That was someone who looked like me and sounded like me, but he was just dust. In the head. Dust. I was in so many parts, so strung out, so far apart I was like dust. Nothing connected to anything. Can you understand that?'

'So your personality has changed.'

'Yes, no. I don't know. There's another person I remember being ... It's like all the dust in my head has blown out and turned into djinn. And then there's Hızır. You did this, who are you? Some kind of tarikat? Some kind of Salafis?'

'We are God's Engineers,' Green Headscarf says. 'We are spiritual people, we burn with divine fire, we are on a jihad but we are not Islamists. We come from different religious traditions. There is a

Sunni, an Alevi, an Orthodox, a Nestorian. Jihad is the eternal struggle towards the divine. All faiths know it. One of us was the bomber on the tram. She was not a martyr, she was a researcher. She was my sister. She was ... she had ... No. That's not for you. The press commented that no one else was killed. This was the plan: the bomb was designed to deliver a package of nanoagents. You and several others received the payload.'

'These djinn, they're just, chemicals?'

'You said yourself that you knew they were not from God,' Green Headscarf says. 'What is important to us is that you are another Necdet Hasgüler. The old Necdet Hasgüler is dead. Killed in the nano attack. The question we want to ask you next, what is Necdet Hasgüler now? We'll give you some time to think about that. Our brother here will keep an eye on you and get you anything you need. Rest. Reflect.'

Green Headscarf and Big Hair get up to go to the other room. Necdet calls after them, 'The djinn, what happens? Are they going to go away eventually?'

Big Hair frowns. 'Why should you want that?'

The nano fountains up through Adnan's Sarioğlu's brain like a representation of the Money Tree, hanging out there in the centre of the trading atrium, sculpted from neurons. This kung-fu of Kemal's is strong. His sight is brilliant and penetrating; the lights brighter, the colours stronger, his focus clearer. His peripheral vision is diamond sharp, he feels he can see right round the back of his head. He can see a little way into things. Details, geometries, lines of connection and intention are all clear in Adnan's sight. He hears every sound, every voice, every hum and click all at once, entire and yet specific; with the least flick of concentration he can unpick a conversation from the weave and know without seeing where and who the speaker is. He can hear the plastic click of his swing-badge as he strides to his customary place by the Money Tree. The hot wetsuit smell of money envelops him. This is what Ayşe's mystics and beloved dervishes experienced when they spoke of the oneness of things. Everything, all at once, connected yet discrete. This is how we are meant to be, at our best and greatest, Adnan understands. The nano is just a different dervish dance.

Element of Air, assist me. Adnan taps his ceptep and the AI come in a rush that takes his breath away, market windows swooping down out of the high roosts of the Money Tree like starlings, flocking, swirling around him so that in his enhanced vision he walks wrapped in a cloak of shifting information, a living mosaic. The traders in their coloured jackets nod to him, intent on their own businesses, wrapped in their own insulations of information.

Adnan looks up into the canopy of the Money Tree, lifts his hands and the symphony begins. He summons, analyses and flicks away pricing screens. Summon weather: he pulls down three different forecasts from the Ankara, Moscow and Tehran weather centres. Change has always come from the east. The spot markets are juddering, a fractal Brownian motion of tens of thousands of AIs automatically placing and filling orders. The spots have always been the natural home of the speculator; get in, make the money, get out quickly.

'Right then, let's go to market,' Adnan orders his Artificial Intelligences. The Baku Hub opens before him. It's a beautiful, intricate flower of traders and contracts, derivatives and spots, futures and options and swaps and the dirty menagerie of new financial instruments; micro-futures, blinds, super-straddles, fiscalmancy evolved in quant computers so dark and complex no human understands how it makes money; all folded like the petals of a tulip around Baku's fruiting heart of pipes and terminals and storage tanks. Istanbul is a barker's tent, a street hustle by comparison. Baku is where the gas goes down.

'Ali, my adipose friend.'

'What does that mean? Fat I bet. Bastard.' Fat Ali's English will never be the equal of Adnan's, and is heavily accented. 'Where have you been?'

'Ever seen a car fly, Ali?'

'What are you on about? What is this nonsense?'

'I have. Now, I want to sell some gas today. Who's buying?'

A news AI opens a blinker in Adnan's peripheral vision. Adnan flicks it to centre and front. The Greek government is readying Athens Emergency Rooms for an influx of the elderly as the Turkish heatwave heads west. When Yunanistan perspires, the Balkans sweat. The migrating storks lead the way. Time to lay out the stall.

'Ali, one hundred and twenty contracts for Baku Caspian, twenty-four-hour delivery.' Prices are edging upwards. Adnan opens his hands, creating a window into the Belgrade and Sarajevo exchanges. The value of the big Serbian and Bosnian-Croatian-Slovenian gas companies are placing orders. The Balkans are in the market.

'They're with you now.'

Adnan places the contracts. Immediately the bids flow in. He sells quickly to Beogaz the big Belgrade energyco. It's not the best price. It's a good opening price for Adnan. The market will adjust to the sudden influx of so much gas. He'll buy them back through an Özer SPE, watch the price rise, sell them on again. He'll sell and resell his gas many times before the closing bell, at each stage extracting value. Turquoise has only just begun.

Two hours into trading and Adnan's gaming of the spot markets has pushed the price to $450 per thousand cubic metres. It's getting into the money. Adnan's jacket is soaked with sweat; the concentration is total. The sleight is to keep Turquoise moving through a whirl of other trades on the spots and the derivatives markets. His feet ache and swell inside his shined shoes. He's in danger of losing track of time; this shit of Kemal's is a rough horse to ride. Savant levels of attention coupled with a Sufi's grasp of the whole pattern. He sees Kemal glance at him nervously through the back office glass. Adnan flicks his head. Do you know that I know? I saved you, man. They would have taken you out of here strapped into a gurney. You owe me but you'll never know. But the hole is still there, the pit beneath the Money Tree that goes all the way down to Iblis. Throw all of Turquoise in there and watch it flutter like confetti. We must face that. When we're in the money, that's when we'll face it. Everything is easier when you are in the money.

The Balkans are out of the game. The money has moved west. The Hungarians and Italians are placing orders, anticipating heat in the streets of Budapest and Roma. The Vienna Hub, through which Mittel Europa's gas is sold and distributed, is at four sixty. Adnan's reading the same meteorology feeds as they are and he knows it can go higher. Four eighty in Vienna. Adnan buys back the Turquoise consignment. Kemal is on his feet behind the glass. He can read the prices on the Money Tree as clearly as Adnan. What he can't read, what no one else can read, are Adnan's aggregators; thousands of tiny barely-intelligent bots that crawl the regional news and community networks. All knowledge is local. The market is not some lofty, abstract edifice of pure economic behaviour. At every point it is connected to the world of people and their values. It is made of human hearts and dreams.

The price on the Vienna Hub edges to four ninety-four. The aggregators open a shattered mosaic of windows around Adnan. Ice-cream sales are down in Izmir. In Cappadocia the fruit growers are moving less stock to the cool underground storage caverns carved from yielding tufa. Cocktail of the Day at the Mardan Palace Hotel is the pure white-winter Tsarina's Pearl. Yesterday it was the Tropical Caipiroshka. The Şaş restaurant in Kaş is taking its tables indoors. Eken Domestic Gas has a two-day wait on deliveries for patio heaters. Turkey has spoken. Foretold by a thousand fingers held up to the wind, weather eyes cast to the horizon, the heat wave is breaking. Perfect information is a rumour, perfect rumour is information. Adnan bows his head, lifts up his hands as if in prayer and banishes the swarming aggregators.

Adnan Sarioğlu offers four hundred and ninety five dollars for ten thousand cubic metres of twenty-hour Caspian on the Vienna Hub. Two seconds later MagyaGaz buys at his price. Adnan sells and bales. Turquoise is sealed. As he turns away, the prices on the Money

Tree screens peak at four nine-seven. Then the market learns what Adnan scryed from his hoteliers and fruit growers and cocktail shakers, the people whose livelihoods depend on the weather, and goes into free fall.

Kemal applauds silently through the glass as the figures tumble. Adnan nods. *Book it*. Turquoise isn't complete yet. He taps up two com screens on his ceptep. One is to Fat Ali, who will arrange delivery from the Baku end. The other is through a remote server on an encrypted channel to Seyamak Larijani. Adnan reads anticipation, excitement, delight, guilt all written on his face.

'Mr Sarioğlu?'

'Fire up the pumps,' Adnan says. As he closes the connection the account expires. Second call is to Oğuz down in the land of pipes.

'Hail Terrak.'

'Hail Draksor. So what did we sell for?' Oğuz asks. Adnan tells him. 'Fuck yeah!' says the Ultralord of Earth. He will make the calculations and the flow rates and the transit times and send his little software peris to cause mischief out at Erzurum.

'There's something else I need to tell you,' Adnan says. The rush ends so soon. Truth is, it was not that high a rush. It was nothing compared with the brilliance of the conception, the daring joy of setting up the deal with TabrizGaz, the frustration and ultimate triumph of the hunting of the White Knight. The dramatic climax of Turquoise was the action of a split-second, over before human consciousness could register it, an AI carrying out an order at computer-speed.

Oğuz's face clouds.

'You're alarming me. What have you done?'

'Not on this line.'

Dead air. Then he sees through the glass Kemal raise his hand to take a new call. Kemal nods, then turns to Adnan out on the trading floor, grins and mouths the name *Oğuz*.

Oğuz is back on the line.

'You didn't do it.' There is a special hissing shriek tone of voice for muted screaming in public. Oğuz has it very well.

'I said, not on this line. Let's go down early to the Kebab Prophet. I have a plan. Say about twelve thirty.'

The market has over an hour until close but Adnan has nothing out there that his AIs can't handle.

'Fuck. We are so fucked up the ass. Does Kadir know?'

'I'm about to tell him.'

Kadir's reaction is more reserved. They have clean asses and mouths up in Oversight and Compliance.

'You say you have a plan,' he says in that measured, reasonable tone practised by Compliance managers and security police interrogators. Adnan would hate to be on the end of one of Kadir's investigations. The bastard knows Adnan doesn't have a plan. But Adnan can see the beginning of a plan, like a line of light on the horizon.

'Twelve thirty then, and I'm sure your plan will be brilliant.'

There's one more call he has to make before he leaves the trading floor, the one that means most to him,

Ayşe's ceptep goes to message. Adnan should not be surprised but he is disappointed. To have told her while it was still hot on him, that would have been triumph.

'Hi, love. It's done. Four nine-five. Start picking interior designers.' He takes a breath, feels a shudder in it, partly nervous tension evaporating, partly the come-off – and it will be a terrible one, it's always bad with new nano – from Kemal's Horse. 'Love, let me know if you're going to be late. I'd really like to see you. You know? Okay. Love you. See you.'

Buy at sixteen dollar fifty. Sell at four hundred and ninety-five. The come-off is starting; evil flashes of another paisley-patterned universe, but he loves it. He fucking loves it.

The white van has been parked on Sidik Sami Omar Cadessi since the early hours. It's an old Türk Telekom Mercedes Sprinter, the logo painted out but still visible, a corporate ghost. The workmen have erected plastic barriers with red and white chevron warnings to keep pedestrians away from the work. People have become litigious about health and safety since the EU. Mistrustful days. There is a little awning with a seat and a gas-hob for a tea-maker. Men in T-shirts, multi-pocket workpants and hi-vis vests stand around sipping tea and and contemplating the hole they have made in the cobble-stones of the Street of the Addicts. A radio burbles Talk Sport. The Galatasaray-Arsenal Cup Tie kicks off at two.

Ayşe Erkoç learned long ago that the secret of doing anything illicit in Istanbul is to do it in full public gaze in the clear light of day. No one ever questions the legitimacy of the blatant. Mehmet and Ahmet are the Sufi Masters of Blatancy. They're the guys who would walk into your office and steal your computer away by telling you it needed a warranty service. They're the guys who will sell your apartment while you're still living in it. They move things, they store things, they hide things, they source things. They have a pantheon of Greek Gods lifted from classical sites from the Hellespont to Olympos in a warehouse out in Zeytinburnu. They have Alcahöyük antlered bronzes and Hittite hunting reliefs, Byzantine mosaics and Orthodox frescos, Selcuk mihrabs and Tulip Era minbars in some place off the O3. They have entire temples, each stone RFID tagged and coded, boxed up and ready for shipping. Ayşe has never con-tracted them before – her work so far has been too light-weight, too flimsy for these lifters of stones and shifters of sarcophagi – but they are on the speed dial of every antiquarian in Istanbul. They are big bull-headed guys, rolls of fat at their necks, stubble-scalped, built like wrestlers from Edirne. They were wrestlers from Edirne. They're not quite brothers. They get things shifted.

They set up their van and cordon, erected a fake Türk Telekom sign and nonchalantly prised off the drain cover and scraped it across the cobbles. Barçin Yayla, camouflaged and anonymized in a hi-vis jacket, let out a howl of protest.

'Who is this?' Mehmet asked.

'He's the last Hurufi,' Ayşe said. Mehmet and Ahmet looked at each other.

'Best keep him out of the way.'

Ayşe looked at the hole, the opening, the gateway, the portal.

'I go first, that's the deal.'

'Whoa whoa whoa whoa,' said Ahmet. 'First, we have some tea. That's what's first.'

'Tea?' Ayşe yelled.

'How is anyone going to believe we're Istanbul workmen if we don't take tea every half-hour?' Mehmet said. 'Get the pot on.'

Now the tea-boy collects the glasses and excitement shoots up strong as bile in Ayşe's stomach. She feels weak. She tries to breathe deeply, slowly, through her nostrils, deep centring breath. Her breathing shakes. Her hands shake. She feels nauseous. Last night, when she finally slipped into bed beside Adnan after hours hurtling around Sultanahmet making the deal with Mehmet and Ahmet, she had deliberately tried to push this moment from her mind by thinking of trivialities, necessities, contingencies, emergencies. In the morning too she had thought about Adnan and his deal and the kit and attention he would need for that, to keep the excitement from paralysing her. It's now. Now. In a very few minutes she will go down into that hole on a rope with a torch on her head. What will she see? Ayşe pushed her imagination away from imagining. Be here, be present. But before that, a necessity and contingency. She takes Ahmet and Mehmet round the back of the van, draws them into a huddle.

'Do you think you can handle our Hurufi friend?'

'Why, is he likely to get violent?' Mehmet asks.

'Only to himself. After he sees whatever's down there he plans to burn his eyes out with a vial of acid he carries with him everywhere. He's convinced it's the Seven Letters, the Secret Name of God.'

'Is it?' Ahmet asks.

'What?'

'What's down there?'

'It's what he believes. I need you to take it off him before he can do any damage to himself or anyone else.'

'If he's that insane, he can do it the moment he goes home.'

'What he does in his own home is his own business. I just don't want to be around anyone pouring acid in their eyes.'

'Acid,' says Mehmet.

'Nasty,' says Ahmet. 'Okay, let's get you roped up.'

As they fit the harness around her and tighten the webbing, Ayşe wishes she had not worn a dress this morning. It rides up altogether too high around her thighs, and her boots are altogether too urban for subcity exploration. Her hi-vis bunches up uncomfortably, and the hard hat is an affront. Ahmet and Mehmet's unspeaking assistants have set the tripod over the open drain and hitched the harness cable to the winch in the back of the white van.

'You'll swing a bit when we get you up so we'll steady you,' Mehmet says. And now here comes Burak Özekmekçib sauntering up, hands in pockets, nodding to Mehmet and Ahmet.

'I see you're dressed for action, primula,' he says pulling on a hi-vis.

'The security on this project is ridiculous,' Ayşe says, standing on the edge of the metre-wide hole.

'My my, Ms Erkoç, whatever could you have found at the bottom of that big dark hole?' Burak says. 'I want to see it, buttercup. I want to see you find a legend.'

Mehmet mans the winch. Ayşe is lifted and swung over the hole. Even as the sun lifts high over the many-domed skyline of the medreses, it reveals nothing in the darkness of the hole. Ahmet steadies Ayşe and switches on her lamp. She is perfectly at peace now. She will do what must be done. It is all ordained now. The winch starts.

Coriolis force reaches out and slowly sets Ayşe spinning as she drops into darkness. Her head light flashes across columns, columns beyond columns beyond columns. She is being lowered into a vast underground cistern. When she dropped the ring the previous night she heard no sound of water but Ayşe sends her beam down to be sure. No sign of water, just a gently angled stone pavement with a half-metre deep channel – the sewer into which these gratings fed – running from south to north. Her ring catches the light and glints. Good. Tulip Era turquoise is hard to find. Dust dances in the beam. Ayşe glances up. Her eyes have dark-adjusted, the open drain is a blinding circle of white. Are those faces? Shattered light beams down through the roof vaults from the other drains; shafts of absence, the inverse of calligraphy. Two metres to the floor, one metre. Her heels scrape stone. Ayşe picks up the ring and pushes it back on to her finger. Complete. She unhooks the line and taps up her ceptep. The signal is acceptable, barely.

'I'm down, stop winching,' she says, 'I'm about ten metres down on the floor of a large cistern, about twenty metres by twenty metres. It doesn't look Roman, I'd say it's contemporary with the rest of the mosque. I've no idea what it's for – there's a drainage channel in the floor, maybe it was supposed to supply water to the mosque şadirvan. There are pillars maybe every four metres. I'm looking around, there's no sign of the . . . oh.'

The extremity of her beam lights up a stone coffin standing on a low plinth next to the northern wall of the vault. Ayşe is speechless, thoughtless, actionless.

'Ayşe, are you okay?' Burak is at the end of Mehmet's phone. 'Is everything all right.'

'Yes. Oh yes. Oh yes yes yes. There's a coffin here. It's not Islamic, it's definitely earlier than that. It could be Lycian – it's definitely Lycian. I'm going over to it. Wait, there's something on top of it.'

Ayşe runs her hands and beam over the massive stone sarcophagus, tracing satyrs and fauns, bacchuses and naiads with her fingers, casting shadows of ancient warriors and horsemen, naked athletes, discus throwers. The lid is guarded at its four corners by lions, the head covered by the solar flame-haloed, sensual face of a goddess. Her lips are sealed with lead. The sarcophagus alone is a treasure. The object set on the top is from a different era, a different race, a different civilization, a different faith. It's a stone flag, roughly chipped from the floor and set over the heart of the sarcophagus.

Ayşe picks it up and turns it in the beam of her torch. The light casts the dusty, low-relief shadow of a Kufic letter. Fa.

Ayşe sits for a while on the edge of the drainage channel. She is exhausted. She pants as if she has run a race. Elation, dread, superstitious fear, crowing pride, sex, energy, power, towering achievement surge and clash. Ayşe calls up Burak.

'I've got it. Get down here.'

Ahmet and Mehmet go into action. Extending ladders are sent down into the vault and made fast. Power cables are run down, lights, power tools, ropes and hawsers. Ahmet plugs in the floods and the cistern is filled with the clean clear light of the twenty-first century and sixteenth-century shadows.

'So what have we got here then?'

Ayşe looks up at Mehmet.

'Hacı Ferhat the Mellified Man of Iskenderun.'

'Lady, your fee just went up.'

Ahmet squats down on his hams to study the sarcophagus.

'I'm wondering how they got in,' he says.

'I'm wondering how we're going to get it out,' Mehmet says.

'Doesn't matter,' Ayşe says. 'My contract is to find the Mellified Man of Iskenderun. I've done that. Getting it out is the client's problem.' She blinks up a number. It rings for a long time before being answered.

'Akgün? Ayşe Erkoç. I have your artefact. You can inspect it at this GPS location, minus about fifteen metres. I'll accept payment by draft or cash.'

A figure descends the ladder into the light, Barçin Yayla.

'You have it?

Ayşe nods wearily at the stone slab propped against the side of the drainage channel by her feet. Yayla rushes to it, dust flying from his scuffing feet and goes down on his knees, head bobbing in adoration. Ayşe looks at Mehmet. The big men are fast for their size. Mehmet seizes Barçin Yayla in a wrestler's pin-hold while Ahmet deftly goes through his pockets.

'Sorry brother.' Ahmet slips the eyedropper into the palm of his hand but Yayla struggles, knocking into Ahmet who, momentarily unbalanced, drops the glass tube of acid. Ayşe crushes it under the heel of her boot. The limestone paving hisses and fumes, acid-scarred. Barçin Yayla whimpers. Mehmet releases him.

'Barçin, I couldn't let you do that.'

Barçin Yayla sits down, the Fa slab clutched to him like a child. The acid seethe has been neutralized.

'I wasn't going to use it. Don't you see? Finding the letter is the part, not the whole. The whole is seeing the pattern entire. All I have are letters. This is only the beginning of the work. Here is a tiny stone with a letter the size of my hand carved on it. Up there is the greatest mosque in Istanbul, which is still only one tiny part of a Zay, a Thaw and a Jim the size of a city. Big, little; little, big. How do I fit this with this? How do I see the infinitesimally small and the inconceivably vast at the same time, in the same vision? But that is Sinan's plan. This is the true work. God is great.'

'That acid always scared me.' The leather has peeled from the boot heel that crushed the vial. The metal tip is corroded. Ayşe does not want to trust too much weight or sudden movement to it.

'You collect art, you must know that the miniature artists, at the end of careers spent painting the tiniest, most exacting details that no one would ever look at, would often put their eyes out with needles. Too much beauty, yes, but also too much seeing. They were tired of seeing. The dark was safe and warm and comfortable. Blindness was a gift. I still have seeing to do.'

Now Burak Özekmekçib descends the ladder. He peers down into the light and stark shadows.

'Well lookie at that.' Burak slides the last three metres of ladder. 'Well, aren't you going to open it, rosebud?'

Breaking the lead seal is a slow, painstaking process. Equipment must be lowered into the vault, a generator set up, a rig built around the sarcophagus and levelled and aligned with micrometric precision. Mehmet hands out masks and goggles.

'There's going to be a lot of lead vapour,' he says. 'And lasers.'

Dust and metal sparkle in the beam and Mehmet and Ahmet, demented, demonic figures in their goggles and respirators guide the beam millimetre by millimetre along the line of the seal, boiling away the lead seal. The achingly slow work gives time for Ayşe's triumphalism to decay into doubt. What if the coffin is empty? What if it is just a Lycian coffin that has stood here for two thousand years while vault and drain and the entire Süleymaniye complex, tens of thousands of tons of masonry, were built over it? A piece of historical flotsam that has attracted legends, story upon story under the accumulated mass of myth solidifies into a popular truth: the Seventh Letter, the tomb of Hacı Ferhat.

The beam flicks off. Mehmet and Ahmet push up their goggles. 'That's us.'

A new figure descends the ladder. Ayşe identifies it by its aftershave: Haydar Akgün. He wears a yellow hi-vis vest over his shimmering nano-weave suit. His shoes are shiny.

'Your timing's good,' Ayşe calls. 'We're just about to open it up.'

She tries to read Akgün's face as he runs his hands over the sarcophagus. Amazement is there, awe, disbelief. Reverence, humility. She doesn't see proprietorial pride. His forefinger explores the lead dimple that fills the stone goddess' mouth. Akgün presses his fingers together as if in prayer, touches them to his lips.

'This is a treasure,' he says. 'A treasure. You found it. I can't believe it. This is legend.'

At Ayşe's sign Ahmet and Mehmet gently move Akgün to one side and work the ends of the pry bars into the crack between sarcophagus and lid. Ayşe stands between them, hands raised as if conducting an orchestra. She lifts her hands.

'Gently.'

The pry bars lift the massive stone lid a fraction of a centimetre but that is enough for Ahmet and Mehmet to slip in the wedges of the lifting rig. Again, on the other side of the coffin. Everyone is on their feet now, casting immense shadows across the vault. Silence is absolute. Ahmet passes the control pad to Ayşe. Three buttons; up, down, stop. She presses up. Very slowly, the rig lifts the lid off the coffin. Acrid, fireworky metal fumes still hang in the air but Ayşe rips off her respirator. She wants to smell it. The lid is now half a metre above the open sarcophagus. Higher: a metre. Stop. A musty sweetness, ancient yet fresh, fills the vault. It is the smell of honey.

Ayşe goes to the open coffin of Hacı Ferhat. It is filled with a golden, translucent, sludgy slush of granulated honey. Too much to hope that it would have survived centuries transparent, but Ayşe can see far enough into the congealed honey to make out the dark shape barely submerged in it. A human figure, arms by its side. It's intact.

'Light,' she commands. Ahmet and Mehmet drag lamps across the stone floor of the tomb and adjust them to better illuminate the thing in the coffin.

Ayşe looks on the face of Hacı Ferhat. The degree of preservation is obvious even through the crystallized honey. The body is unclothed, the flesh is sunken and pulled away from the orifices and extremities, the bones jutting like tent poles but the skin, a deep mahogany, is folded and wrinkled, swollen up with sugar, and looks as soft and fragile as gold leaf. The body has exuded a sepia halo that extends a few centimetres into the enclosing honey. Bubbles of gas have become trapped in the human-honey matrix. Fine detail is hard to distinguish through the crystalline mass, hair, beard, nails seem intact, the eyes are mercifully closed, the teeth long and brown, rat-teeth. Ayşe has never seen a thing quite so extraordinary. She has seen mummified bodies, this is nothing like them. They are dry and rattling, more dead than death. There is nothing of death and desiccation about the Mellified Man. It's a man spun from sugar. It's a work of confectionery. For an instant Ayşe imagines plunging her fists into the heart of the Mellified Man, bursting him apart. Would he be gelatinous, or would he be soft and grainy, like halva, or is what she sees merely patterns, hues in the honey left by his slow dissolution over centuries?

Ayşe dips her finger into the coffin. She tastes it. The Mellified

Man is sweet, musky, earthy; there's a crunch from the crystallization, a slightly phenolic tang, a hint of old leather and peat, salt, a touch of urine.

Haydar Akgün gazes into the coffin.

'You have done a remarkable job. This makes this all the more regrettable.'

As he speaks, Ayşe hears the distant sirens. Akgün takes a wallet from his inside pocket and holds it up.

'I am Inspector Haydar Akgün of the Anti-Smuggling and Organized Crime Bureau working with the Directorate of Antiquities and Museums. Remain where you are, police officers are positioned above ground. You are all under arrest on charges of procuring historical artefacts for illegal sale outside the Republic of Turkey.'

A policeman descends the ladders, then another. Ahmet and Mehmet are taken up into the light, Burak Özekmekçib, Barçin Yayla are already under arrest.

'I should have known!' Ayşe shouts at Akgün as two officers take her arms. 'That cheap *Arslan* aftershave!'

'Yes.'

'Can you imagine living other people's lives? We can. Can you imagine knowing what someone else really thinks, being able to predict what they're going to do? We can. The next industrial revolution is here. This is more than just nano. This is the moment everything becomes smart. This is the ...'

'Yes, Ms Gültaşli.'

Deniz Saylan is the smartest-suited shiniest-shod cleanest-shaven neatest-hairstyled best-manicured sweetest-smelling man Leyla Gültaşli has ever seen. He is polite and strong and radiates power and confidence and has a higher, bigger, handsomer more-corner-respecting office with wider views than the CoGoNano! drones – what kind of name is that for a corporation? Three offices on three afternoons and they're all beginning to blur. At least he doesn't have shape-changing toys. Men shouldn't have toys.

'Pardon?'

'I said yes. We're interested in this. We'd like to get involved.'

Sometimes when the coyote runs off the cliff and hangs that cartoon moment in mid-air, he doesn't wave bye bye and drop. Sometimes the coyote makes it back again to solid rock.

'The Besarani-Ceylan transcriber.'

A high-speed elevator streaks up the side of the building.

'This is precisely the kind of project for which Özer Special Projects was set up. I'm sure you've looked at our company profile and history.' Leyla was reading it up on the train to the dolmuş to the Nano Bazaar. Five a.m. she was down in the station, with the platform sleepers and the home-wending partyers and the people who ride the metro all night and the early workers and Leyla the only one in a suit. She had drilled Aso: established 2012 as Özer Gas Distribution. Consistently among the Top Five IBT companies. Share price ... Profits posted last fiscal year ... know your market know your market know your market. 'Our edge over our competitors is that we're completing the transition to a truly twenty-first-century company. Ten years ago we were Özer Distribution, today we're Özer Gas and Commodities, ten years from now, when the pipelines have stopped pumping, we'll be something else. We may even be Özer Cellular Transcribers.'

No, Leyla thinks. *Don't try and be witty. Men are beautiful when they are serious. Aso is best when he is serious.*

'Our strategy is to seek new centres of profitability and pro-gressively abandon business areas as their value drops or competition increases. Özer isn't a gas or a commodities company, it's a profit-generating nexus. We get in at the start, make a lot of money and when the resource peaks, when the market gets crowded, when we get bored with it, we sell and move on. So we throw a lot of seed money at start-up projects we think have the potential to create markets. We hunt for emerging technologies and new business trends. If this can do even twenty per cent of what you say it can, this is the biggest new technological breakthrough since the integrated circuit. This is the equivalent of getting in on the ground floor with Texas Instruments. Have you even thought about the IP and licensing potential. We cannot not be involved with this. We'll draw up a standard development deal to work up a prototype. How much are you looking for?'

Aso is about to speak, Leyla stabs her heel into the toe of his twice-worn shoe.

'Half a million euro,' she says boldly. Saylan doesn't even blink.

'You have to understand that to a company like Özer, that's pretty much small change. Our standard terms are eighty-twenty.'

'Seventy-thirty?' Leyla ventures.

'No, Ms Gültaşli.'

Firm but mannerly. Aso has the mannerly but not the firm. But firm is mannerly. An inability to make your no no is the worst possible manners.

'How soon can you move on this?'

'We can have the contracts with you by tomorrow. Now, we will need audited accounts and certificates of ownership and clear indication where intellectual rights are vested. This is lawyer stuff. From you I will need a detailed technical dossier that we'll put before an adjudicating panel. Nano's not our current area of expertise so we'll hire in specialists.'

'Can I ask who'll be on the panel?' Aso asks.

'For nanotechnology we regularly call on Professor Süleyman Turan of Ankara University and Nevval Seden from Bilikent University. Do you know them?'

'Nevval Seden was my adviser of studies.'

'That's not a problem. We may ask you to a *viva voce* with them. That can be online. Now, we will go through your accounts very very thoroughly. We will insist on due diligence and we will appoint a project director. Can you live with this?'

'Yes,' Leyla says. Saylan ignores her.

'Mr Basarani.'

'I need to talk with my business partner.'

'Of course you do.'

'So, what is on the table here?' Leyla asks.

'Half a million euro development funding to work up a prototype of the Besarani-Ceylan transcriber, in return for Özer Special Projects taking an eighty per cent share in the IP and future profits.'

'Seventy-five,' Leyla interjects.

'No, Ms Gültaşli.'

'And after the prototype?' Aso asks.

'There'll be separate funding for market testing. If that's successful, we go to full production and global marketing. This is a long-term project, medical safety testing alone could take five years.'

'It's been five years in development already. This is our life's work.'

Saylan seems pleased by that answer.

'Good good good. So, get your people to call my people.' Saylan's handshake is, of course, perfect: correct firmness, correct length, correct vibrato and with the crackle of contact details passing palm to palm. 'Thank you very much Mr Besarani, Ms Gültaşli, this is a very, very exciting project. I'd love to talk more with you about it but I do have another appointment coming in. We will talk very soon.'

'You were flirting with him,' Aso says as they wait for the elevator dropping like liquid tar down the face of the tower. They are high as spring storks, giggly as schoolgirls, dazed and drunk on victory. Yes. He did say yes.

'I was not,' Leyla whispers. She was mining him, stripping him of suit and style and grooming and manners. She was taking makeover notes. Not for her, she realizes; for Aso. She feels a new, unfamiliar kick in her belly at that thought.

'But, half a million?' Aso says as the elevator car arrives.

'Small change to Özer, he said. It can be as big a mistake asking for too little as too much.'

'Don't you think ...' Aso begins but the doors open and Leyla ushers him into the full elevator. *Ssh*, she mimes. The elevator drops them down the side of the Özer tower. Men come and go from floor to floor. Aso wants to talk. *I want you to talk*, Leyla thinks. *I want to shout and run around like an aeroplane and splash in that fountain in the plaza, but for the moment, ssh.* In the atrium among the suits and the money men – are there no money women, are there any women other than Leyla? *Ssh.* Handing in the passes at the front desk: *ssh.* The desk is a slab of black marble designed to awe with the power of Özer, intimidate with the stone impassivity of its receptionists. Leyla smiles as she slides her swing-badge across the black mirror marble. I beat you. You big men, I've got your money. Me, the girl from Demre, Ms Have-Your-Little-Career, Ms You'll-Come-Running-Back. Little Tomato. And you Yaşar and all you Yazıcoğlus and Ceylans and Gültaşlis and everyone sitting around the table in Bakirköy, Uncle Cengiz and Sub-Aunt Kevser and even you Great-Aunt Sezen out on your balcony but most of all you, Zeliha, sitting there behind your desk with that pureed-aubergine smirk: me. Me. Brilliant me.

Out on the plaza she turns to face the forty storeys of corporate glass and titanium and throws her arms wide to the seven heavens.

'Özer! Özer! Özer! Love you!'

'Don't you think he agreed a bit quickly?' Aso says. 'One guy in an office says, very good, I like this, here's half a million euro?'

'For eighty per cent. I'm calling Yaşar.'

'I'm not thrilled by that. Back home, you mention Özer in the same breath as "Satan". They run the east like their own private empire. I'm the local lad made good, the only guy from the town got further than secondary school, and the first thing I do is sell my soul to the evil empire.'

'What is this, some kind of anti-capitalist lament? You needed a deal, you got a deal. I'm calling Yaşar.'

'I'll tell you what I think. I think someone else did the spadework for us. I think we ran in second. I think those İdiz boys were in that office maybe three weeks ago looking for funding for their version of the transcriber. That was the difficult sell. That was when Saylan was persuaded. Then we breeze in with the same thing and he sees an opportunity to cover all the bases. Özer gets a virtual monopoly on transcriber tech. For half a million, that's cheap.'

'But their version won't work.'

'It has at best sixty per cent of the functionality of ours.'

'So they'll go for the clearly better product. You've got the money. This is party stuff! Hey! Naci!'

Across the main road stands an incongruous tin kebab wagon. Naci has taken a stool at the counter and sips tea. Hearing his name across the traffic he looks round; seeing Leyla's unconcealable delight he smiles. *You have a glorious smile*, Leyla thinks. *You have a smile that turns you into another person.*

'Before you go off celebrating, I think I should say, there is that small matter of the Koran. The money is only half of it.'

Big Naci dodges into the traffic, raising his hand to stop cars. *He could taekwondo them away*, Leyla thinks. But the brightness of the possible is fading. Aso has deflated her. But God has been merciful to her today, God can be merciful again. It's God's nature.

'Okay, okay okay. Half a celebration.'

Naci is running down the pavement waving his arms in delight.

'Call Yaşar then.'

Necdet drags himself vertical from the mattresses to use the pot. Whatever they gave him, their 'suites of nano' have left his muscles shaking and his joints aching and the room spinning with a vertigo beyond the heat-flicker of djinn, but a man should stand to piss. He sets the pot in the corner and rests one staying hand against the wall.

'Do you mind not watching me while I'm having a piss?'

He startles Big Bastard from his stone-stolid meditations.

'What?'

'Not you, him.' Necdet nods to where Hızır sits cross-legged against the opposite wall. The piss is scanty and dark. Necdet is very dehydrated. What chemicals beyond his own is he excreting into the pot? 'Okay, finished.' Big Bastard throws a cloth over the pot and raps the door with the butt of his gun for Surly Fucker, the fourth member of the group, who has yet to speak a word to Necdet, though he can still feel the bruises of his hard fingers on his biceps. Big Bastard is a different proposition. He practises silence but in the end he always has too many questions.

'When you talk to Hızır, like just then, what do you see?'

'Do Alevis revere Hızır?'

'We revere all saints and imams.'

'How do you picture him?'

'He's old but he's young at the same time, like a man but sometimes like an animal or a bird. He has a halo of green flame.'

'Then that's what you would see.'

'What do you see?'

'Nothing I can explain. Something that comes before the animal or the bird or the man, those are just different shapes we put on something ... unconscious. Something that comes before shapes and seeing and even thinking. Something that exists before we're conscious of it.'

Big Bastard nods.

'Everyone sees their own Hızır.'

'No, you don't get it. Yes, how else could it be?'

'That's what they said too. Yes and no. Nothing that could be explained.'

'They?'

'The ones after Divrican. I'm from the next valley over but everyone knows someone who was affected. The valley of saints and shaykhs.'

'What's this?'

'It was just over five years ago. The Turks launched a final assault on the Kurds before the EU put a stop to it. One night a drone appeared over Divrican, a village in the next valley over. It circled for half an hour. The next morning, everyone was like you. Djinn and angels. Demons. Peris and spirits. Some saw Hızır, some saw Melek Tawus, some saw the Prophet Himself.'

Big Bastard bows his head, as if he fears he has said too much.

'What happened to them?' Necdet asks. In his captivity he's learned that humans possess a huge talent for normalizing. This room, this mattress, this big man with a gun, he's used to them now. He's not scared of them. They are the architecture of his life. Big Bastard's words open a fear inside that comfortable fear, a hole within a hole. 'What happened to them?'

He's assumed too far. Big Bastard bares his teeth, jabs at Necdet with his assault rifle. Necdet backs down again on to the mattress. Hızır sits by the wall, forms and manifestations folding through him like convection patterns in a pan of boiling syrup.

Green Headscarf and Big Hair enter from the next room, where Necdet can make out styrofoam clamshell containers, plastic tidy boxes and cardboard cartons.

'Everything all right here?' Big Hair says. Big Bastard defers in everything to Big Hair. Green Headscarf kneels in front of Necdet. She always assumes the same position, kneeling demurely, knees together, sleeves pulled over her hands. This may be part of her strategy.

'In this session we'll talk about the nature of faith,' Green Headscarf says.

'I don't have any,' Necdet says. 'I don't need it. I can see. Faith is what you can't see. If I can see it, it's not God.'

'There are other definitions of faith. You can have faith in a person, or an object, that it's trustworthy.'

'That's faith in the future,' Necdet says.

'Another way of considering faith is that it's the method by which we hold our reasoned ideas.'

'That doesn't mean they're true,' Necdet says. 'Why should faith only hold true for reasoned ideas and not unreasoned ones?'

Big Hair takes a note.

'Faith is submission to the will of Allah,' Necdet says. 'What are you testing me for?'

'Tell me about the nature of your faith in Hızır.'

'Not the djinn?'

'You insist they aren't from God, that they are manifestations of your own mind. How does Hızır differ?'

'He's other.'

Again. The exchange of glances.

'Religious experience is a universal human trait,' Big Hair says. 'God is hard-wired into us, into the brain chemistry, into the neurons. At a fundamental level, all human religions share common experiences and a common language.'

'The mystics all agree,' Green Headscarf says. Big Hair is annoyed by her words. Disunity among God's Engineers? Necdet wonders.

'We don't believe in a supernatural God beyond the rules of the universe,' Big Hair says. 'We believe in God, in here. God is part of us, God has always been part, God is the part of us that is beyond consciousness. We believe that up until a thousand years or so, human consciousness was quite different from what it is today. We were not one self, we were many selves, one of which was our God self. This was a divine age when God spoke to men and women, when we saw visions and wonders, miracles and saints. God spoke to us in parables and prophecies and allegories and poetry. We've lost that. We've become too conscious. We need to reconnect to our personal Gods.'

'This is no different from the djinn, that's what you're saying. Hızır is from my mind as well.'

'You said he was other. We have reason to believe he's from somewhere different from what you think of as your mind. From somewhere before your mind.'

'I could be mentally ill,' Necdet says. This talk scares him. Fear within fear through fear. 'You said before I had dissociative disorder, something like that. Maybe I wasn't ill, maybe I'm ill now. All this is sickness.'

Green Headscarf tilts her head to one side, pondering.

'Necdet, listen to yourself. Do you think you sound like a sick man?'

'How would I know?' Necdet cries.

'You were ill. We've brought all those conflicts and confusions and anger together in one place, and given it a shape and form and you seem happy to me. They have a voice and a body. They are your God within. They are your Friend. We're delighted with the results so far. We'll talk later Necdet.'

Again they leave. Through the open door he glimpses Surly Fucker's feet next to those of Big Hair and Green Headscarf. He's not getting out. He knows that now. They'll keep him until they have all the answers they need and no longer. He knows what happens to laboratory animals. Yet Hızır flickers from evanescence into a smile. Big Bastard is still twitchy but Necdet senses that he's the weak one. Surly Fucker is enforcer and executioner, Big Hair the technocrat, Green Headscarf the theorist. For Big Bastard it's personal.

'Man, tell me. Those Kurds, the ones from the next valley, I have to know. What happened to them?'

A transparent plastic cylinder of green slush churns on the shelf at the back of the Kebab Prophet's stall.

'What is that fucking shit?' Adnan asks. 'It looks like stuff kids drink.'

'That fucking shit is granita,' the Kebab Prophet says. 'Lemon and lime. You mix it up from powder, the machine does the rest. It is considered highly refreshing. Want some?'

'I've got a bad enough headache without sucking ice through a straw,' Adnan says. 'I tell you this as the man who's putting your kid through college, I hope you didn't pay much for it, because you wasted your money on that heap of scrap. This'll break by tomorrow.'

'I got it on trial loan anyway.' The Kebab Prophet considers a moment. 'So you're in the money then.'

Adnan can't resist a self-satisfied smile.

'Got out at four nine five.'

'What's it down to?'

'Four twenty-two.'

The Kebab Prophet nods his head. He is impressed. 'I've other kids need putting through college.'

'Adana kebab, by three. Like you'd make them for the President. I want meat juice running down my chin.'

'Three?'

'Lord Ultror will be joining us a little later.'

The Kebab scoops up handfuls of meat and starts shaping it around the skewers. He gets them thin as pencils, just shown to the fire; browned and sweet on the outside, bleeding in the heart. The way they should be. Kadir crosses the plaza with Oğuz. No ritual exchanges, no Hail Draksors.

'You didn't do it,' Oğuz shouts. 'Man, we are so fucked. We are fucked every way.'

Adnan sits on his stool at the counter and does not take his eyes from the kebab, which he turns and studies, seeking a point of attack. The meat is fragrant, cumin and garlic tempering the mild rankness of the lamb. The tomatoes are warm and filled with sun. The Kebab Prophet keeps his breadmaker secret – such genius could only be spoiled by commercialization – and treats him like a favoured son. The bread smells like life. 'I have made you a millionaire this morning. So, sit down, eat this exceptional kebab which I have bought you, and then, when you've finished, I shall tell you why we are not fucked.'

The Ultralords of the Universe form a line at the Kebab Prophet's gleaming steel counter. 'Truly, you have exceeded yourself,' Adnan says wiping fingers and mouth on a moist towellette. 'God himself could not make a finer Adana kebab.' The Kebab Prophet bows in acknowledgement. Taking the cue he busies himself at the back of the stall cutting salad.

'Why didn't you give it to him, he's got all the account numbers, everything.' Oğuz picks up without a break.

Adnan turns on him.

'I'll tell you why. Because I'm not Lord Draksor and you're not Lord fucking Terrak. We are not the Ultralords of the Universe.

There are no Ultralords of the Universe. They're cartoon characters. Do you remember how every show used to end? With a big fight. Superpowers, the whole shebang. Big explosion. Bad guy beaten again for another week. Well, if we blow up the bad guy, he stays blown up. He's dead. We killed him. And we don't have superpowers. We work for a finance company. We're not cartoon characters. We're men. Men don't do things like that. Not to a friend. Not for money. I don't need you to understand why I didn't slip Kemal the nano. I expect you to accept that I was right, like I've been right about everything else in this operation.'

'What I understand is that when the shit hits, and it's only a matter of time before that Cygnus X account pulls us all in, they are going to take the top off Kemal's head and go in there with something that makes Kadir's nano look like popping candy,' Oğuz says. The Kebab Prophet's knife moves like death, fast and precise and unfailing.

'We keep our nerve. We hold our fire. We turn up for work, we do our little jobs diligently and efficiently. In the background we roll up Turquoise like a carpet, like we planned. We keep our heads down. We follow through, step by step, just like we rehearsed it. Twenty million euro in two hundred million, in two billion which is probably closer to what Özer owes: what's that? They're not looking for us. They're looking for Mehmet the Cunt.'

'You say, we keep our nerve,' Kadir says. 'I could say back, you don't have a plan.'

'I have a plan. Who says I don't have a plan? I always have a plan. We liquidate right away. Because as soon as the first crack appears in the glass, we need to able to walk out of the Özer tower with it in our back pockets while that place comes raining down behind us. Liquidity works every time. I fancy bearer bonds, they're neater than cash.'

'And Ferid Bey?' Kadir asks.

'He gets his in cash. Cash cash cash. Cash is king, always was, always will be.' Adnan raps his knuckles on the cleanser-scratched steel counter. 'Lord Kebab-or! Another Adana for our fourth member.'

The other Ultralords look up. Kemal is crossing the plaza, skipping around the delivery scooters and mopeds. Adnan holds the kebab up like a trophy. 'Hail Ultror! Take this, eat and walk, because we have a football match to get to, and I'm not turning up at Aslanteppe dressed like this.'

When the Kebab Prophet turns back from adjusting the temperature on his silo of viridian granita there's a hundred euro bill tucked under the napkin holder and four men in dark suits are loping in unconscious lockstep toward the taxi rank like fine criminals.

8

High afternoon sun pours into the white concrete bowl of Aslanteppe Stadium. Cup Tie! Cup Tie! Galatasaray versus Arsenal, Semi-Final European Champions League. Winner to meet Barca in the final in Munich! The biggest prize in Europe! The stands slowly fill, body by body, obliterating the massive CIMBOM written in red seats on white along the home stands. The Arsenal fans have been admitted early to the visitors' end of the stadium where they have draped their banners over the crash barriers and rehearse their songs in the ebb-and-swell oceanic chant of English football supporters. Some have already stripped off their shirts. Turkish drummers and horn sections blare back. The Arsenal fans stab their fingers at them and bellow: you you you! Advertising scrolls up the pitchside hoardings and across the big screens in the stands. The media is here; television trucks parked up along the main road, celebrity pundits half visible in the glass tank of the gallery, a dozen different commentators down on their benches, photographers lolling around the goal-line. Cameramen practise sending their flittercams on strafing runs across the stadium while the touchline cameras shriek up and down. Supporters cheer and wave as they see themselves and their friends ten metres tall on the screens. A blimp manoeuvres overhead: Turkcell. The club DJ blares T-pop over the PA at seat-shaking volumes. Mascots in oversize foam costumes caper along the touchline and try to whip up the crowd.

Adnan Sarioğlu pauses at the top of the stairs. He squints up into the blue dome over the white dish of Aslanteppe.

'See that? A cloud in the sky.'

The Ultralords of the Universe descend the steps to their

season-ticket seats on the middle bar of B of Cimbom, squeezing past and exchanging greetings with well-known regulars. Kemal pauses a moment to take a message from his ceptep, then leans across his friends to whisper, 'It's through. You can take it out any time you want.'

He's officially rich.

They're screening that great Galatasaray motivational video, the one where they storm the walls of Constantinople from the *Mehmet the Conqueror* movie. And here comes the first Mexican wave: there are enough in the stadium for it to work. Adnan surges to his feet and feels himself soften into the atavistic spirit of fandom. This is the Kingdom of Cimbom. People are different here.

'So where exactly is our gas?' Kemal asks, on his feet, arms raised.

'Coming up from Çaldıran into the main Nabucco line right about now and heading towards us at forty kilometres per hour,' Oğuz says, settling back into his seat as the wave passes.

The motivational video, for all its shameless plagiarism and metal powerchords, is working. Oblivious to the heat, the foam-mummified mascots turn handstands and leap and point. Then the stadium PA kicks in at full volume and Adnan feels a shudder run through him. This is where he ceases to be Adnan Sarioğlu, gas trader. This is where he becomes fan. Arsenal run out holding the hands of little children, dazed and tearful in too-large team strips. A distant cacophony from the Arsenal end. Boos and whistles and jeers from the Cimbom seats. It's not about sport. It's about football. The DJ screams an introduction, fire-fountains shoot up along the touchline and Here! Come! Cimbom! The crowd rises and Adnan rises with them, a roar in his throat, his fist clenched. The eyes of the tiny child mascots in Galatasaray cream and red are wide in terror. The DJ announces the team; each player nods or glances at his feet or at the sky or rolls his beads as he is called. There is a cheer for every name, and a seismic thunder for Volkan: fit at last. The teams run to their positions as the captains shake hands, exchange pennants and watch the toss.

'Russian ref,' Kadir shouts up the line.

'Ah no, they fucking hate us,' Kemal says.

'They hate the English more,' Adnan says.

'That's true,' Kemal concedes. Arsenal win the toss and take the ball to the spot. The referee blows his whistle, the players start to move, the captain kicks off and the Aslenteppe Stadium is a hemi-sphere of noise. Arsenal push forward, playing a long passing game that exposes Galatasaray square at the back but Gündüzalp the big ox of a central defender heads the ball sweetly out to Ersoy and it's the break back, Galatasaray going forward and Adnan's ceptep rings.

Ayşe's calltone.

Adnan glances at the display, then notices the location. GPS is on. Bibirdirek Police Station in Sultanahmet. The headset is hooked over his ear in a moment.

'Ayşe.'

'Adnan, I've been arrested.'

Against the green pitch, the blue sky, the mosaic of brightly dressed fans, the words seem impossible. Ayşe. Arrested. They can't fit with each other, with this reality of men in short pants kicking a ball around a grass arena.

'You've what?' Adnan asks.

'Been arrested. They're holding me down in Bibirdirek. It's stupid really, they'll realize they've made a mistake and have to let me go.'

Almost he asks, *Who's holding you, why were you arrested, what's the charge?* But he's not alone in this crowd. Galatasaray under pressure in its own half pass the ball to Aykol who sees space open before him and runs into it, half the pitch. Aslanteppe surges forward with a vast unison inhalation of anticipation. Into the crowd rumble, Adnan says, 'I'm coming down. I'll get a lawyer. He'll be with you by the time I get there.'

Kadir catches threads of conversation drifting like spider-silk. He leans forward, mouths *What? Ayşe*, Adnan mouths back, then, before questions can be asked, he pushes along the line to the stair, fans frowning and cursing and craning to see past him. He is the lone figure moving against the thrilled thrust of eighty thousand Cimbom fans. As he trots down the concrete stairs that smell of piss and new paint he hears Aslanteppe erupt behind him. Goal to Galatasaray. Out on Cendere Cadessi Adnan whistles up the car. He'll drop it at the police station and send it to find a parking space, or just orbit until he needs it again. As he hikes up the road, looking for the driverless Audi seeking him through the traffic, Adnan realizes the prime incongruity, the keystone that holds the arch of improbability together. He has always assumed he would be the one to be arrested.

Gold with silver; plaster-peeling domes. Yellow-roofed soks refuse to run true; every cross-way reveals new alleys and corridors that slope unpredictably between coffin-tight shops and stalls before opening into dome-roofed plazas and bedestens. Turkish flags in all conceivable geometries. Red and white, crescent and star. No home for the starry coronet of the EU here. A painted finger-board points to a tiny mosque, tucked up a twisting flight of steps. Men hurry high-stacked trolleys along the stone-flagged passages. Water spills down the tiled face of a fountain. Everything is very small, packed, wedged together. The shopkeepers are too big for their tiny stands, oppressed by their piled merchandise. The glare of white neon never changes by day or by night. The Grand Bazaar keeps it own time, which is time not marked by the world's clocks or calendars.

Aso navigates Grand Bazaar by ceptep. Yaşar is busy with lawyers and accountants and spreadsheets so Aso has been despatched with Leyla to seek the treasure at the heart of the labyrinth. Leyla knows she would be lost in an instant. Some distracting glint or glitter and she would be wandering. That, say the merchants of Grand Bazaar, is the point. It's only when the mind ceases seeking that true discovery is made. Serendipities: entering the same little bedesten from four different directions and thinking it a different square each time. Stumbling on that quirky little wooden Ottoman coffee stall, a building within a building, knowing that you will never be able to find it again. One footstep taking you away from the pushing, thieving alleys into a dimly lit sok where a solitary cobbler sits by a rusted last and you wonder if he has sold anything in this century or the one preceding it.

Leyla had loathed the Grand Bazaar on first visit. The tat, the fake, the overpriced, it's all still piled high and pushed in your face and shaken, but Leyla sees the line that runs from Capalli Carsi through Hazine Auctions and Nano Bazaar into her. Everyone is huckstering, to everybody all the time. She's no different from these troglodyte men behind their walls of merchandise. The sell is all.

'Aso.'

He has been wandering, following the glowing djinni-dust like the ceptep navigation system drawn on his eyeball.

'This is going to sound like a silly question. I can sell the Besarani-Ceylan transcriber backwards and forwards, I can tell you its functions and its features and it benefits, I can tell you it's the new nano revolution, that nothing will ever be the same, that this is the future today but I can't see that future. I can see fancy graphics of DNA but I can't connect it to me, to people, to somewhere like this. You have these things called Thought Experiments? Here's a Thought Experiment: in fifty years' time, what will I see here?'

'One question: why here?'

'Because it seems the most conservative and resistant to change. It seems the last place a nanotech revolution would conquer.'

Aso gives an odd, ugly-cute little smile and nod of the head as he follows the light only he can see.

'Well, this place will look pretty much the same. Tea shops and antiques and Turkish Delight will still sell. Authenticity will be big. What won't sell is all this domestic tat and consumer electronics. That kind of stuff you do at home, or in specialist plants for the big things like cars. Everyone will have a fab, a home fabrication plant, like a 3D printer only much more sophisticated. As electronics and biology move closer and closer together, we'll print things from proteins and semizotic plastics. When you're tired of that jacket or want new shoes, you just let the old ones die. The fab will recycle them. Everything will be designer. When commodities are cheap, people pay for the label. Take the Donna Karan off the T-shirt and it's just a 2-euro rectangle of cotton. Status won't be measured by product but by styling. Designers will be the new footballers. They'll have cult followings. That's why I said about authenticity being big. Anything that hasn't been fabbed, that is genuine and has the provenance to show it, will be the thing of value. People will pay for authenticity, people will pay for experience. A good cup of coffee will be more valuable than a new ceptep – because a ceptep you can just fab up at home, and we'll be way post-ceptep anyway. Good coffee, that's an art.'

The life of the Grand Bazaar streams around Leyla and Aso. Leyla tries to impress Aso's pictures on to the faces; that good-looking youth lounging against his father's stock of kelims, that yellow-toothed old man in the trinket stall, those two German tourists, that scurrying woman in the full hijab.

'Everyone will be gorgeous, glorious, dazzling. It will be an age of style and colour. People will remember how the Ottomans dressed, it'll be back to robes and turbans. Maybe we'll be surrounded by clouds of free-flying microbots that can assemble into any shape we want, like djinn. Nobody will wear glasses. No matter how bad your eyes are, your vision will be internally corrected, like autofocus on a camera. Nobody will have money, it'll all be credited by the shake of a hand or the blink of an eye or the transfer of a thought. It'll be quieter than it is now. A lot of communication will be done directly, mind to mind. Voices will be reserved for the public world, and for performance. We'll have two ways of speech, like some languages have two ways of talking to people, the formal and the intimate. Verbal speech is broadcast, everyone in earshot hears you. Direct speech is intimate, you have to be invited to it, only the people to whom it's addressed can hear you. You can tell secrets in direct speech. You can be in a crowded room and have a conversation in direct speech without anyone else overhearing. Or you can have that same conversation with someone on the other side of the planet.

Direct speech is not limited by distance. It will be an age of gossip and intrigue and little conspiracies.

'Old friends will meet and sit down here in this çayhane and recall conversations from ten years before, word for word. They'll be able to recreate the scenes in their heads, because the DNA never forgets. It'll be like time travel – a shared illusion of the past. Or they could go to another world entirely, maybe a designer secondary world, a social networking world, that will seem as real to them as this world. People will slip casually between worlds. There will be shared, socially networked worlds and there will be private worlds where you can do whatever you like.

'We'll have extra sensory organs. We'll need some way of getting the information inside out, and outside in. We need to be wired. I sort of like the idea of horns or little antlers, maybe at the back of the head. Or maybe antennae. But I reckon we'll be shy about them, they'll be a private body part that's shameful to show in public or to strangers. They're the gateway to your soul, you don't go showing that to everyone. We'll cover them up. So turbans will be back! I can't wait.

'Then, pretty soon after this, we'll stop covering up. We'll go in exactly the opposite direction. It'll be bare skin everywhere. Why? Because we'll have learned to photosynthesize. We already have photosynth panels for domestic electricity, all we have to do is couple it with a nano transcriber, bind it to the ATP cycle and make like the plants: get naked and soak up the sun. Places like this will be dark and scary. Roofs? No light? Perverse. After photosynthesis, it's anyone's guess. The graphs all go vertical.'

'I wonder if I'm helping you build a future I wouldn't want to live in,' Leyla says. 'I grew up under roofs. Demre was a roofed city. All plastic greenhouses and polytunnels, kilometre after kilometre after kilometre. They go right up to the edges of the road. The houses and the mosques stick up in between. The land's too valuable to build on so the houses go up, whenever someone marries they build a floor on top of the one below. Some of the old houses in Demre are like mini skyscrapers. I remember when the Americans were talking about going to Mars and putting a base there and growing food thinking that it should look like Demre. We know how to keep the air in and let the light through. Maybe if they'd asked us it would have worked. We pump in waste CO_2 from the hotels along the beach; the tomatoes go up to the roof. They're like jungles of chillies and aubergines. Some people have low CO_2 tolerance so they can't work in there and there was one kid was allergic to tomatoes so he couldn't go near them otherwise his face would swell up and explode. I can still smell the tomatoes, and the plant food. We processed it from the sewage from the hotels. We ran it through a digester so we got methane for power and the plant food was clean. My dad wasn't a grower; he was a service engineer for drip irrigation systems. That's all you'd hear in the tunnels, drip drip drip, and the hiss of the misters to help them set fruit. Why am I telling you about Demre? Because people wonder how anyone can live there with no open ground and plastic roofs over everything, but do you know? I loved it. I was so happy there as a kid. So I guess what I'm saying is you can get used to anything. People adapt.'

Topaloğlu Antiques is a brassy cubby of old mosque finials and sanctuary lamps and Greek censers, of framed Hebrew texts and fake icons and illustrations of the Parliament of Birds. And miniature Korans, a display case of them, rank upon rank, gleaming in the light. Topaloğlu himself is a rotund man of middle age, with prominent teeth and male pattern baldness. He wears a cardigan, even in the heat of Grand Bazaar. The shop smells of metal polish.

'You like the miniature Korans?'

'I'm looking for one in particular,' Leyla says. 'It's a family heir-loom.'

'There are a lot of places in Istanbul sell miniature Korans,' Topaloğlu says.

Leyla comes clean.

'Turgut of Hazine Antiques might have sold it to you.'

Topaloğlu looks suspiciously at Aso, who is poking around among the brass lanterns.

'We're not police.'

'You look like police.'

It's the suits.

'I'm in marketing and he's a scientist. We are genuinely looking for a lost family heirloom, a miniature Koran. You'd remember it if you saw it, it's been cut in half.'

'The other half of this.' Aso offers the Ceylan-Besarani half of the Koran on the palm of his hand. Topaloğlu pushes on glasses and peers.

'Oh yes. That I do recognize. It did indeed come in a job lot from Hazine. They keep an eye out for the religious stuff for me.'

'You have it?'

'Ah, no. I sold it on.'

Gleams and glints of highlighted brass swirl around Leyla like wheeling stars. She feels sick, sick in the pit of her belly.

'I sold it last Monday, part of a job lot of surplus stock. I can tell you where has it. I'll write it down for you, I don't do with that handshake business.' He takes a ballpoint to the back of a business card. 'Here.'

Leyla reads the address. She reads the address again to be sure she got it right. No mistake. True journey is a circle, a dervish's turn. God is good, God is very good indeed.

A single jackdaw, black of head and bright of eye, struts up and down the balcony rail of the second floor salon of the Kortanpaşa Palace watching the delegates of the Kadiköy group shuffle forwards in the coffee line. Georgios Ferentinou watches it with pleasure, He has always liked jackdaws. They are urbane, purposeful creatures.

'A corvidae man, so,' says Emrah Beskardes, behind him in the line.

'I like intelligence,' Georgios says.

'That's why I did my dissertation of small-world networks in rook social systems. Did you know they mourn their dead? And they have courts. They identify social transgressors, gather a group of rooks – a jury – isolate and punish them. You've probably seen it without knowing what it was, a group of rooks in mid-air, and all mobbing a single rook. That's a punishment. They go for the tail and pin-feathers. You sometimes see rooks or magpies scrambling around with no tails, trying to fly. They broke the law. I've seen children try and help what they think is a poor lame bird, and the rest of the court will set up an outcry – they sometimes even try and mob them. They're smart but they are bastards.'

Georgios Ferentinou cocks his head, intrigued, an unconscious mirror of the stalking jackdaw outside.

'You seem disenamoured with the objects of your study.'

'You don't love crows, you admire them. They exploit our capacity for chaos. Forget polar bears or whatever kind of tuna we're supposed to care about this month; crows are the bellwethers of what we're doing to the planet. The bigger the mess we make, the better they like it. New behaviours are spreading through crow populations like wildfire. Ten years ago Japanese crows learned to drop hard nuts at road intersections for cars to crack with their tyres. And not just that, they'd wait for a red light before picking them up again. Now crows in London are doing that. Ten years to cross Eurasia. There's an evolutionary pressure, and if it's working on crows, it's working on us, we just haven't seen it yet. Now those same Japanese crow populations are showing behaviours that simply could not have had time to evolve. They can count up to ten. They're making marks in mud on roosts. Rows of mud dots. Now, if that doesn't scare you . . . Do you want to hear the theory? It scares the shit out of me: they're picking up waste nano from the environment and it's rewiring their brains.'

'God save us,' says Georgios Ferentinou and in the coffee queue he feels the clutch of intellectual excitement and fear that comes from the realization that the universe needs nothing from humans.

'Watch the crows,' Beskardes says. 'The crows are surely watching us.'

Georgios knows crow parliaments. He has stood where the accused rook stands. It had been a spring that year too, a late spring made later by the conference in Moscow. Georgios had shivered and huddled through a week of papers and seminars on Imperfect Information, Rational Irrationality, Groupthink, Bubble Behaviour; the fashionable topics of pop-economics; the subjects that earned deals for books with titles with colons and over-explanatory subtitles. He had avoided the mandatory drinking to stupefaction by pleading a touch of flu. He was never certain how deeply his paper on Mental Mappings and Desire Lines: the Psychological Geography of Economic Landscapes had penetrated the vodka hangovers in the lecture hall but citations of it turned up in papers for the next eighteen months, until the next new fashionable theory. But it was a grim week of linger-winter and all the more of a surprise when he emerged from the air-conditioned marble of Atatürk Airport to find spring bursting across Istanbul. There was perfume on the air, clouds of almond blossom delicately screened the minarets and domes of Süleymaniye's huge complex of mosque and tombs and hospitals as Georgios Ferentinou crossed the park to the Department of Economics. A note in his pigeon-hole. Meeting of the faculty. Two p.m.

Georgios can still recall the room's every detail. The flask of university coffee, the jar of powdered apple tea beside the flask of hot water. A plate of small sweets and Western-style biscuits. There was blossom outside the window. He can still recall the seating arrangements. Ogün Saltuk was to the left of Emine Arin the Vice Chancellor.

They asked about the Moscow trip. How was the weather? Not like here. Shame. The delegates? Cosmopolitan. Good. The quality of the papers? Mixed. Good. Professor Ferentinou's offering? Well received. Excellent. Then Vice Chancellor Arin looked to Ogün Saltuk and Georgios knew that everything had ended.

'Professor Ferentinou, your contribution to the Department of Economics, and to the field of Experimental Economics over the past twenty-five years . . .' Ogün Saltuk began. Georgios cut him off.

'You're making me redundant.'

'This is the University of Istanbul, we don't make respected academics redundant. However, there have been funding issues with the Durmuş Yılmaz Chair.'

'It's my chair that's redundant, not me,' Georgios said but he was falling, the world was air, there was nothing to grasp.

'Now that's hardly fair,' said Vice Chancellor Arin. 'There have been funding shortfalls across all faculties.'

There were six around the table, all known to Georgios, all stone-faced. Only Saltuk had lacked the propriety to look ashamed.

'Effective from when?'

'The new academic year,' Saltuk said.

'I'm due six months' notice . . .'

'If it were up to me, but it's a financial matter.'

Georgios sat with his hands loosely curled in his lap. The bravado was blowing out of him, two small sallies of defiance was all he could muster.

'I, I don't know what to do.'

'Professor Ferentinou,' Vice Chancellor Arin said, trying to avert a shaming, uncontrolled emotional scene.

'I won't get anything, I'm not young, I'm not a young man. What will I do?'

'Professor Ferentinou.' Such unction in Ogün Saltuk's voice. 'I'm sure the faculty could consider this more an early retirement than closing a chair, don't you think, Vice Chancellor?'

This is decided already, Georgios thought. *This is rehearsed dialogue. All they are concerned with here is that I don't throw them from their script.*

'My postgraduate students . . .'

'I will take over as their adviser of studies. We do work in parallel fields.' Georgios hated Ogün Saltuk then, hated him with Hellenic depth and passion for now the years of academic abrasion, of simmering tension, of barely contained resentment, were laid open like upturned cards. Every single sniping and carping and snipping and tiny questioning of his ability, his authority, his originality, his loyalty, all were steps to this grubby coup. 'There is one small thing,' Saltuk added. 'You've a number of government and MIT clearances to politically sensitive information. We will have to review those, I'm afraid.'

'Why not just call me a Greek traitor and be done with it?' Georgios stormed out of the room. There was a tight singing in his ears as he raged down the airy corridors, across the quadrangle, a shuddering tightness in his chest. Foolish hopes, vain fantasies surged and crashed in his mind, a visiting lectureship, tenure in the United States or Germany or Britain, a best-selling book, a career as a lovable pop-economist, a Nobel Prize nomination. As well wish for superpowers, as well hope for a god to reach down from the muscular, glorious clouds rushing across spring Istanbul. He was finished. The wind blew and sent almond blossom flurrying around Georgios Ferentinou's head.

It was the leaves that were in flight when the University of Istanbul Department of Economics announced the creation of a new post, the Tansu Penbe Çiller Chair of Economic Psychology, first incumbent, Professor Ogün Saltuk.

Georgios' coffee cup rattles in remembered rage against the saucer. Dark and strong, the long-maturing anger of old men. He must do it now. He has the opportunity, he has the armament. Not for revenge. For the truth. For what he has deduced, perhaps vainly, perhaps foolishly, perhaps with the insight that only an outsider, an exile in his own city, can bring. When he confronts Ogün Saltuk, his motivation will be justice.

Coffee-equipped, the line rotates back into the main salon with the dismal view over the gas tanks. It's a working break; the opening Blue Sky session has over-run and Ogün Saltuk is keen to wrap it up and move on. Georgios suspects that his MIT masters are not getting what he sold them. Fatih Dikbas is blathering on about macro-economic terrorism as a geopolitical instrument, drawing on Russo-European gas diplomacy in the first decade of the century. He is a dreadful, dreary speaker. Ogün Saltuk fidgets and glances at the clock. Finally Dikbas meanders into an inconclusive silence and after a few hanging seconds Ogün Saltuk says, 'Any further comments? No?'

Georgios Ferentinou's arm is flat out before him on the desk. Now he raises it slowly to the vertical.

'I'd like to say something.'

'We are hoping to move on from this part of the programme,' Ogün Saltuk says, making a winding-a-skein-of-wool gesture with his arms that is at once childish and patronizing. 'There will be another opportunity for Blue Sky thinking at the pre-wrap session tomorrow.'

'I do believe that what I have to say demands immediate action,' Georgios says. The whole room seems to draw breath at once. The silence hangs. The jackdaw is at this balcony window now.

'I'd like to hear Professor Ferentinou,' Beskardes announces.

'So would I,' declares Selma Özgün. 'His voice has been lacking in these sessions.' Heads nod in agreement around the tables.

'Very well then,' Saltuk says, chewing at his bottom lip. 'Do share with us, Professor Ferentinou.'

Georgios clasps his hands and leans forward. He finds faces among his peers.

'At the start of these sessions Professor Saltuk asked us for leaps of intuition. Wide blue skies, everything is permitted. In that spirit I would ask the group to consider the possibility of a terrorist attack on the Balkans, Central and Southern Europe using nanotechnology agents delivered using the gas pipeline system.'

Rumbles, mumbles, sittings-up around the horseshoe of tables. Georgios glances at the edges of the room. As he suspected, Major

Oktay Eğilmez is not to be seen. Beskardes has written *cool* on his magic slate.

'At my age I find I think a lot about sanctioned fears. The sanctioned fear of nanotechnology is what the press calls the "grey goo scenario", the runaway replicator that reduces everything to its own matrix. However, as any biologist will tell you, we live in that world already; the overwhelming majority of the biomass on this planet is bacterial: biological replicators. If we're told anything about the nanotechnology revolution, it's that it is the convergence of the biological and the artificial.

'We are the scum on the surface of that bacterial world, we are the survivors. No, what is much more interesting to me, and, I suspect, to a so-called terrorist group, is nanotechnology's potential to reprogramme our personalities. The ultimate victory in any conflict is hearts and minds. In the past it has always been easier to kill than to convert, but this is the age of ideological conflict. Our military has developed nanotechnology packages to improve concentration, aggression, team-working, enhance sensory inputs and, significantly, diminish empathy. Pilots, long-distance drivers, coders, performers, actors, sportsmen and women routinely use nanotech, and the image of the nano-snorting Levent trader who can't start the day without inserting a nozzle into his nostril is beyond a cliché now. We routinely use nanoagents to improve concentration, sociability, power of recall, to increase our ability to learn or give us access to secure short-term information. We can buy moods, emotions, aspects of personality quite foreign to us. Young people on a night out can take sociability, eroticism, dis-inhibition. We give it to our schoolchildren at exam time without a thought. To even gain admission to this group I had to inhale a nanoagent which placed a contact number in my short-term memory. What we are engaged on is a massive, unregulated and improvised experiment in reprogramming ourselves. The true end of nanotech is not the transformation of the world, it's the transformation of humanity. We can redefine what it means to be human. No doubt there is some ugly adolescent expression like "neuro-hacking" to describe it, but my point is: this cannot have gone unobserved by those with agendas of political, social and religious evangelism, those for whom hearts and minds is victory. Nanotechnology is the weapon of choice of the Proselytizer. It is the Sword of the Prophet. I have reason to believe that we have reached a point where this kind of attack is not just possible, but likely.'

Devlet Ceber says in his slow, bell-deep voice, 'This is an extraordinary theory Professor Ferentinou; I'm sure I don't need to remind you of the kind of proof such theories demand.'

'I am aware of it, Professor Ceber. I can give no such proof. All I can offer is to guide you through the sequence of events that have led me to this extraordinary conclusion.

'On Monday an early morning tram was attacked on Necatibey Cadessi by a woman suicide bomber; it made the news briefly. Professor Saltuk mentioned it in his introduction to our sessions. The only victim was the woman bomber herself. That is unusual. Police swarm robots arrived at the scene to control, contain and identify victims. They were not the only ones. I have evidence that another group – almost certainly the group who coerced that poor woman to her death – were observing the bomb site with their own surveillance machines.'

'Now, surely you must offer this evidence.' Professor Ceber is a leading legal theorist on the left. Georgios dips his head in respect.

'I plead a journalist's defence,' he says. Ceber nods. 'These machines appeared to have been tasked with identifying, following and keeping surveillance of selected victims from the bombing. One of them is a neighbour of mine, a young man called, Necdet Hasgüler. He's a feckless sort, of little ambition and with a troubled past; he is being looked after by his brother, Ismet, who runs a study group, and is something of an amateur shariat jurist himself, from the ground floor apartment. The last sort of person you would imagine gaining the ability to see djinn.'

Beskardes raises his eyebrows. Murmurs around the horseshoe of delegates. Saltuk fidgets and frets, trying to find an excuse to cut

Georgios short. The insouciant jackdaw is nowhere to be seen.

'Not just djinn, but visions of the Green Saint, Hızır, all manner of creatures from religious mythology. Round my part of Beyoğlu, which is still traditional in outlook, this makes you something of a religious celebrity. This young man's visions could easily be dismissed as traumatic stress; but why go to such efforts to spy on a mere bomb victim? Then Selma Hanım tells me that Necdet Hasgüler is not alone, there is a veritable plague of visionaries: a man who finds his neighbourhood over-run with tiny machines, a woman who consults with the peri and other supernatural creatures as some form of oracle. Now, we all know that remarkable is unremarkable in Istanbul and miracles happen every morning before breakfast, but all these individuals appeared within hours of the bomb attack and, please mark this, all live within the catchment area of the tram line. Perhaps a coincidence, I don't believe so. There is more.' Georgios takes a sip of water. His voice is cracking and dry. 'I did some research. I found physical evidence that allowed me to trace the robots back to a hire facility in Kayişdaği on the Asian side of the city. That is also the location of the Kayişdaği Compression Station on the main Nabucco pipeline under the Bosphorus to Europe. The final piece of the puzzle fell into place last night when young Necdet Hasgüler was abducted from the street outside his own home by unknown assailants.'

A murmur of concern, into which Ceber speaks.

'Professor Ferentinou, you use expressions like "final piece of the puzzle", but what you have presented us with is a series of unsubstantiated, disconnected events. I don't see how you get from these to a theory that the European Union is under threat from nano-terrorism.'

'I am aware of that,' Georgios says. 'My evidence you will have to take on trust. How I explain these events is this. There exists a terror cell in Istanbul developing a nanotechnology weapon. They organized the attack on the tram, it was an experiment. They selected victims to observe for symptoms that their nanoagent was effective.

They see that it is and they are now working to a full-scale attack. They will introduce it into the gas pipeline at Kayişdaği, from which it will be carried into Europe.'

'They'll need replicators for that,' interjects Yusuf Yilmaz, a popular technology journalist on *Cumhuriyet*.

'Yes, I'm certain they will,' Georgios says, 'I'd imagine they could replicate exponentially using the hydrocarbon as feedstock. The word that was given to us was *gas*.'

'Why, if they've been observing Mr Hasgüler, would they now need to abduct him?' Ceber asks. Saltuk is furious now, rolling his pen between his fingers, picking at a piece of flaking varnish on the desk, foot unconsciously kicking kicking kicking; all the tiny aggressions by which stifled rage expresses itself.

'Their surveillance of Mr Hasgüler failed. Their robot was destroyed in an accident; it was from the wreckage that I managed to trace it to Kayişdaği.'

'These are substantial suspicions, Professor Saltuk,' Ceber says. He is persistent in his examination of Georgios' theory but he is fair. 'Why did you not take them to police?'

'My assistant is my neighbours' son. He has the technical facility. But he is only nine years old. I wouldn't want to place him in any danger.' The delegates understand his second, unspoken fear, *or attract any accusations to myself*. 'I believe there's another motive to Mr Hasgüler's abduction. They wanted to be very sure of the nature of his visions; are they simply hallucinations, or do they come from an underlying religious fervour?'

'Expand on this please, Professor Ferentinou,' Ceber asks though the room already knows Georgios' answer.

'Certainly. I believe their goal is the religious conversion of a sizeable portion of the population of eastern and central Europe.'

'Nonsense.' Ogün Saltuk spits out the word, a wad of rage. 'Arrant nonsense. Replicators in the gas, terrorist cells, nanotech jihad; this isn't speculation, this isn't even blue-sky, this is pure science fiction.' The lone writer looks up and utters a clear 'Excuse me!' but Saltuk's bile is high and he talks over the man. 'No no no, this will not do. I want Professor Ferentinou's statement, all the questions and answers, struck from the records of this session.'

'Why?' Ceber asks. 'Firstly, Professor Ferentinou's theory is perfectly valid in terms of the purpose of this session. Secondly, he gives evidence of a crime; the abduction of this Mr Hasgüler. Thirdly, if there is any merit in them, as Professor Ferentinou himself said, it is imperative that police and security forces investigate immediately.'

'You asked for "blue-sky thinking",' Yusuf Yilmaz the journalist says. 'You got it. What's wrong with that? In terms of the Professor's evidence, it makes sense.'

Saltuk's lip-chewing has come a cheek-twitching.

'Evidence? A nine-year-old boy is hardly a credible authority. There is blue-sky thinking and there is palpable fantasy. We require some intellectual rigour here, not an exercise in join-the-dots and seeing a face. No no no, I can't allow this because the Professor has made the cardinal error of deducing too much from inadequate sources.'

There is a cardinal error here, Georgios Ferentinou thinks, *but it is you who have made it, Ogün Saltuk. You have alienated your own experts. And to that first error add a second and fatal error, that you don't know, but your audience knows, and I know, and with which I will now kill you.*

'You say "inadequate sources",' Georgios says. His hands are steady now, his voice is steady now, and clear. 'Should you not rather say, "minimal sources"?'

'What?' Saltuk sees it now. There is nothing he can do about it.

'Cognitive discontinuity, the theory that intelligence, working on minimal information can make leaps of intuition far beyond those achievable by directed thinking; that's the theory, if I remember correctly. A sufficient, rich and diverse ecology of information, with no data outweighing any other, isn't that the theory?'

Ogün Saltuk can't speak. There is a cognitive discontinuity here. He is being shown that he does not understand his own theory.

'What is the title of your book, Professor Saltuk?' Georgios Ferentinou asks. Ten years he has waited for this and at the end it is a pitiful and poor thing to see a man destroyed in a public forum. But Georgios will have it, every syllable of it. No one revenges like the Greeks.

'*Great Leap Forward*,' Saltuk says. To his credit his voice is clear and loud, but his face is pale as sick.

'Yes, "How Ignorance Really is Bliss",' Georgios says.

Saltuk blusters about sessions running over time and hastily calls another coffee break to try and regain a measure of composure but everyone knows what has been done here and that the Kadiköy Group is finished. All around the salon small groups have spontaneously formed, talking nano, dissecting Georgios' Great Leap Forward, debating the neurochemistry of faith. Ogün Saltuk stands apart at the window, isolated, insulated by a coterie of MIT staffers. There is no need for Georgios to be here. He would slip away quietly but Emrah Beskardes catches him at the top of the faux-rococo staircase.

'Thought you'd get clean away?'

'I don't think I have anything more to contribute,' Georgios says.

'I'm glad that when it comes to pure unalloyed aggression, humans still have it over rooks.'

Georgios blushes. 'No no, I shouldn't have done that; I said too much, I let my temper carry me away. I was cruel.'

'Well, it was a pleasure spending overpaid and underworked afternoons in your company, Professor Ferentinou. I have learned something new.' Beskardes shakes Georgios' hand. 'I must read some of your work.'

'It's economics, it's a dismal science. My driver's here. It was a pleasure to meet you, Dr Beskardes. I shall never look at crows the same way.'

'Keep an eye on those crows,' Beskardes calls after him down the gilded stairs. 'They really are bastards.'

*

'The djinn tell me you studied nano engineering,' Necdet says to Big Bastard. Two wordless hours since Green Headscarf and Big Hair left the room. Raised voices, a radio turned on to cover the dispute, slammed doors. Big Bastard edgy and volunteering nothing, not asking, not answering. 'They told me a concierge had emphysema. They told me a woman was pregnant before she even knew it. I'm going to tell you about that one. My brother is a local shaykh, he opens the book, he gives judgements in domestic disputes, things like that. People come to him for advice. A woman who works in the art gallery next to us came to find out if she was pregnant. Out in the street, I saw her karin upside down in the earth and from it I was able to tell her what she wanted to know. How did I know this? It wasn't creatures from the universe of fire and it wasn't God. I just knew something no one else knew. Knowing without knowing, I think there are lots of ways that can happen. Maybe there are chemicals we sense but never register. Maybe it's electrical. I think we get thousands, millions of bits of information every day that we've lost the ability to read or that we filter out because there's just too much stuff to be conscious of. It's knowing without knowing. So I see the way you handle that gun, and that your hands are quite delicate, and that the lettering on your T-shirt is really neat and I know you're the one designed whatever's in here.' Necdet touches forefingers to forehead: horns of Iblis. 'And by the same way, I know that you and Green Headscarf are together – I hope you don't mind me calling her that, I'd rather use my own made-up names than any you'd make up for me. You're both Alevis, it's obvious. And I know in the same way that the reason her sister volunteered to be the bomber on the tram is because she's from that Valley of Saints and Shaykhs you talk about. She was there on the night of the Divrican attack. Green Headscarf was at university. She was with you that night. You won't tell me what happened to those people. What did she see?'

Big Bastard looks up. He's trembling with quiet rage. He has been trembling with it for years, Necdet thinks.

'If God truly were inside you, could you bear to look at it?' Necdet says.

Big Hair and Green Headscarf enter the room again and take up their customary places. Their faces are harried, edgy. Green Headscarf's fists clench and unclench inside her sweater sleeves. Necdet sees Surly Fucker hovering and fidgeting and pacing within earshot in the adjoining room.

'Have you ever looked at a map of our country, Necdet?' Green Headscarf says. 'It's a map of the human mind. We're split by water over two continents, Europe and Anatolia. We are seven per cent Europe, ninety-three per cent Asia. Conscious Thrace, unconscious, pre-conscious, sub-concious Anatolia. And Istanbul – have you ever seen a neuron, Necdet? A brain cell? The marvel is that the synapses don't touch. There is always a gap – there must a gap, otherwise consciousness would not exist. The Bosphorus is that synaptic cleft. Potential can flow across the cleft. It's the cleft that makes con-sciousness possible.'

'I don't understand what you're saying,' Necdet says. 'This is nonsense.' In the other room Surly Fucker stops pacing. Necdet holds his breath. The pacing resumes. *You are fragile. These people are insane.*

Green Headscarf shakes her head in incomprehension.

'It's fitting, it's right. Anatolia has always been the cradle of civilizations. New consciousnesses were born here. The Europeans have always looked down on us, they used to call us the Sick Man of Europe, but I tell you, it's Europe that is the Sick Man. We have wisdoms from thousands of years of civilizations and empires and religions but they never listened to us because they invented the Enlightenment and the Renaissance and capitalism and democracy and technology and those are the monologues of the twenty-first century. Maybe they'll realize that the future is going to be a dialogue. Maybe they'll realize that ideas can come from the Islamic world – new ideas, ideas the world has never seen before, completely revolu-tionary ways of thinking about what it means to be human.'

'They,' Necdet says. 'You're talking about ... whole countries.'

'They're ignorant, they can't imagine anything outside their experiences so we will take them completely by surprise,' Green Headscarf says, now rocking on her knees. Necdet notices that Big Bastard can't look at her. He grips the gun tightly. His face is flushed. This is terrifying and dangerous. They are insane. They have done insane things. They are not amenable to reason. They will carry out their plan. 'It's ignorance to think that, ignorance and arrogance. We are against ignorance. We are for the perfect knowledge of God.'

They have to kill me, Necdet thinks. *They are going to do it just before they go out on their mission. They will kill me. Surly Fucker will do it. He's the only one here can kill. I will be dead. I can't think about that. Oh God oh God will it be quick, what will I see, will it hurt, what is it like not-to-be, to be dead? Oh God oh God. How can I stop them?*

'We've enough data to know that the experiment has been a success,' Big Hair says. Green Headscarf's eyes are closed. She moves her lips in silent utterances. 'Congratulations Mr Hasgüler.'

'All I did was take a different tram to get in to work earlier!' Necdet shouts. 'Who are you to decide to bomb a tram to test your theories about human consciousness? Who is your sister to blow herself up in my face and spray me with nano you designed and you engineered? Who are you to decide that I need to see djinn and green saints and know things no one could or should know, but that's all right, it's God-inside. Who are you to take me off my street in front of my house and bang me into the back of a van and bring me here and hold me prisoner and talk shit? It's all shit, shit shit. Who are you, who are you bastards, who are you to decide to make me your experiment and now the experiment's, well, we all know what happens to the rats and monkeys don't we? Help me!' Necdet bellows in despair. 'Help me! Oh God please help me! Someone!'

Big Bastard lunges forward and strikes Necdet hard in the chest with the butt of the assault rifle, knocking wind and words clean from his lungs. Necdet collapses, limbs curled up like a desiccating spider, gagging for breath.

'Please understand that there is no revenge or personal malice or religious fanaticism in this, Necdet,' Green Headscarf says. 'We are not Kurdish freedom fighters, we are not Islamists. We are God's Engineers. You are confused and afraid now, but, in a very real way, you will achieve a place in the Paradise we will build.'

Necdet rolls away. In his corner, universes of knowing pour through the human-shaped green void of Hızır.

Can watches the Gas Bubble pull away from the yellow marked drop-off zone in front of the school and merge with the afternoon school run's daily ruckus of hootings, veerings, swervings and silent swearings. He waits until it's safely around the corner into Aşariye Cadessi. Inside the gates, tiny children beneath huge backpacks mill around on the concrete schoolyard. Can steps away from the gate into the cover of the wall. Eyes are sharp at Yildiz Special School. The morning shift is gone, the afternoon shift lines up on the coloured ladders painted on the concrete, one child per rung. Can slides further along the wall until he can no longer see anything of the schoolyard. For a moment the street is empty of pedestrians. Can quickly turns and walks away from Yildiz School. He walks quickly, but not so quickly as to look like a child escaping from school. The crossing on Aşariye Cadessi is a danger point; he imagines adults noticing him and his proximity to the school, maybe the heavy hand of a teacher coming back from lunch. Will the traffic ever end? Then the little crossing man is green and he is safely across into the labyrinth of soks and lanes to the south of Cihannuma. The narrow streets are choked with traffic on foot and wheel; vans push pedestrians into doorways and porches, teenagers on mopeds steer between knots of women with headscarves and men in shirt sleeves and ties. Can falls in behind a group of men in business suits, unconsciously matching his stride to theirs. Old men at tables in folded-back çayhane doors with no better way to live their lives than watching the street observe his swagger and nod and smile. Can lifts his shoulders, straightens his back. He unfolds his shades from one of the big pockets of his practical Boy Detective pants and slides them up his nose. He's a man, out in the city. There's purpose in his steps.

At the top of Horoz Stairs Can is stopped by a dazzle of sunlit sea. It blinks, it blinds, it shimmers. Can is thrilled and appalled: this is the furthest he has ever been on his own. The plan had been to take the tram to the Marmaray and shuttle under the Bosphorus to Üsküdar Metro. But he is free in the city and far from home and no boy of Istanbul has ever resisted the sea-call. Can skips lightly down to the glimmering water between antique shops and small cafés, the sidewalk descending in long, low steps, each the width of a house front. The apartment balconies are bright with geraniums in terracotta pots. Wisteria weaves through the wrought-ironwork, dripping early blossoms. A thin cat with a twisted back leg looks up from licking to study Can but he is insufficient novelty to warrant any effort. Smells assail Can now: coffee and mint and mastic, old metal and charcoal and furniture polish. Lemon and diesel. The asthmatic tang of gas, the sour of rotting fruit. The salt of the sea, deep and clear.

Horoz Stairs delivers Can on to Çirağan Cadessi. He knows this place. There is Sinanpaşa Mosque, there is the tram stop in the middle of the street, there, beyond the Dolmabahçe Palace, is Neca-tibey Cadessi where Can sent Rat dodging the truck tyres and the guillotine tramwheels, chasing the white van that lifted Necdet. But that was screen-life. That was life in 2D. It is another sensation to feel the tug of slipstream and the seismic rumble of a tram passing, to see the gulls circling over the minarets of Sinanpaşa, to smell the oily bilge water lapping against the quays. This is not a game. Can crosses the road and strides along the seaward footpath, thumbs hooked into the shoulder straps of his backpack. Everyone, every-thing he sees has purpose. At the little garden at Cezayir he pulls out his map to check the ferry routes. It's doable. It will work. A good detective is flexible, has information at his fingertips, thinks fast.

'Single please,' he says to the man in the ticket booth, half hoping that he will ask him why a nine-year-old boy asks for a single to Üsküdar, why a nine-year-old-boy is asking for a paper ticket, paid for with paper money, rather than using his ceptep, what that thing is he has wrapped around his wrist; what is that, is it a snake? The man slides him his ticket and his change. Can files on to the ferry. Clanking metal, banging ramps as cars and vans drive on, the thrum of engines and the swash of screws, all come to him as whispers and murmurs. Can climbs as high as he can to the topmost deck; only the flags of the nation and the European Union higher than he. The ferry carries him out alone into the Bosphorus. The wind is cool in his face, the first cool he can remember for a long time. Can leans forward over the rail; not Boy Detective now but Master and Commander of the Üsküdar ferry, which has become a landing craft, invasion-bound, preparing to storm the Asian shore. The ferry surges between clashing rocks of moving metal; cutting across the wake of a monster gas carrier. The Cyrillic letters on its side are each the size of a car. Now the ferry nimbly skips under the bows of a mass-transporter, its flying bridge peeping over tier upon tier of stacked containers. Rectangles of colour. A Lego ship. He knows this ship. He has seen this mosaic of containers before, a wall of colour moving past the windows of the expensive private clinic where he was fitted with the ear-inserts. This is the ship that took away all the sounds in the world. He always knew it would come back some day. Can rushes to the side rail and gazes up at the towering cliff of slow-moving metal. Slowly, painfully, he works the plugs out of his ears. He winces as adhesions tear and scabs crack. There is a lot of wax and encrustations and flakes of hardened skin. Then the plugs pop free and the audible world rushes in. It is as if every container piled ten high on the deck of the great ship has sprung open and released the sound trapped inside. Gulls are harsh and shrill and sound like summer mornings. The flags snap and belly above him, a full, satisfying noise. Engines: the diesely metallic beat of the ferry over the deeper, felt-more-than-heard pulse of the bulk carrier. Water, he can hear water. Feet clang on metal staircases, a radio crackles behind him on the bridge, girls chatter down the rail from him, men's voices behind him, in the shade of the awning. Sounds have places; he looks up, not knowing how he knows to do that, to find the source of the drone in the sky; a big plane lowering itself down over the Sea of Marmara. Small sounds, tiny sounds. Treble whisper from earbuds nearby, the wind over the wires that stay the radio mast. Can turns slowly, identifying and locating each sound in turn. He looks at the little, waxy plugs in the palm of his hand. He throws them far out into the wash from the receding bulk carrier.

The ferry sweeps past the Kız Kulesi tower on its tiny island. Can can hear Asia. It sounds like cars and emergency sirens. The ferry throws its engines into reverse with a great roar and swash of water. Now the ramp starts to lower, with the clank of a mechanism new to Can's sound-scape. One by one the vehicles start their engines. How it echoes around the steel box of the car deck. Passengers push past him, he can distinguish every one of their voices as they swarm down the metal stairs. Different. Every voice is different. The world is sound.

Can falters at the top of the concrete ramp. All the sounds that have been separate and distinct now merge into an intimidating wall. Everything is big, loud and close. He doesn't know how to pick information out of it. There's a tightness in his chest. His breath is shallow. He threw away his plugs. Why did he do that? The tightness gets worse. But is it his heart, the Long QT, or is it what they told him about his heart, that everyone has believed all his life? A thing is different from believing a thing. Maybe what everyone believes about his heart is no longer true. He got better. People can get better. Any time he's been to the doctor recently they've attached their machines to his earplugs not his chest. Can sits down on the oily, plastic-strewn rocks beside the ferry terminal and closes his eyes. He focuses his hearing, pushes it inward, down, into his chest. He listens to his body. There, small and light, fleeting at first, then, when he hooks on to its rhythm, the base of all. His heartbeat. It's good and steady and strong. There is no click or flap or wheeze in it. This tightness, this breathlessness, maybe it's everything new and loud and up-at-your-face and exciting. Maybe this is what adventure feels like. Can lets go of his heartbeat and opens his eyes. There is the big ship of hearing, heading up the big bridge, all the sounds in the world still spilling from its containers. This is Asia, another continent, but it is still Istanbul, still his city. Can gets his map out. Üsküdar Marmaray Station is across three big roads. That is easy for the Boy Detective.

The Marmaray Station is a concrete pit driven deep into the rock and shale and silts of Üsküdar. Can rides down through the many levels of tubes and people, ticket gripped in his fist. It was exciting to hear himself ask for a single to Kayişdaği and hear the clerk name the price. The noises here are different, the ticking whirr of the escalator, the slap of a poorly fitted handrail. Distant automated voices calling trains. It's cool down here, the air smells of electricity and concrete and old time. These are deep tunnels. Sounds travel far and strangely through the corridors, words cling to walls, some footsteps ring like pistol shots while others are soft as rain. The arrival of the train is the most thrilling thing Can has ever heard. First there is distant, dinosaur booming in the deep tunnel that becomes a bass rattle. Hot air blows in Can's face. Lights appear in the darkness, then all of a sudden the train is on him, bursting from the tunnel in a rush of banging metal and rattling cars and shrieking brakes. Announcements overhead. Warnings to stay clear of this, beware of that. Can steps on to the metro train. Doors whoosh and slam. The sudden acceleration sends Can reeling into a seat. He was listening to the whine of the motors. A chime, a robot voice telling him the next station.

The train is busy, every seat full, strap hangers in the doorways. Next to Can is a teenager who has been unable to take his eyes off the machine wrapped around Can's left wrist.

'What's that?'

Can ignores him. It's not in his Detective Plan to talk to people on public transport.

'No, come on, I'm curious, what is it? Some kind of tattoo or weird ceptep or jewellery or something?'

He reaches out to touch Can's arm. Quick as a knife Snake lifts his head and stabs it at the young man. He recoils into his neighbour, a middle-aged woman, proper and traditional.

'It's a snake, he's got a snake!'

'It's a toy, it's a toy!' Can shouts, holding his arm up. But the damage is done, the alarm is spread. A man is talking into his ceptep. He could be calling IETT staff. The metro train brakes into the next station and Can is out through the doors as they are still opening. He vanishes into the crowd on the platform, turns his back to the train and slips Snake off his arm. He loops tail into mouth and slings him around his neck, a bling chain, hidden by his plain and anonymous T-shirt. He'll take the next train. A Boy Detective is always resourceful.

'You live here?' Aso asks as Leyla turns the Peugeot into Güneşli Sok beside the Fethi Bey teashop. 'I didn't know there were any of these really old tekkes left.'

'It's cheap,' Leyla says. 'I don't care about the history.'

Cousin Naci unfolds from the back of the car. It's like a late night TV show where a woman in a sparkly catsuit unfolds herself from a perspex box. 'Cool.'

Aso surveys the balconies leaning out over the cobbles, the shuttered gallery beneath the beetle-brow of the roof. 'This really is something. This could be seventeenth Christian century.'

'The plumbing is certainly seventeenth century,' Leyla says. Aso ducks down Güneşli Sok, pulls himself up the wall to peer over. She watches him scrape the toes of the new shoes she made him buy.

'There's an old dervish graveyard in the back,' Aso calls. 'Original Mevlevi grave pillars.' He drops back to the greasy steps. 'It's amazing that an old wooden tekke has survived this long.'

'Especially given the wiring.'

'You're so lucky to live here.'

Practical Cousin Naci has gone to the front of the dervish house. 'You should see this.'

The double doors of the Erkoç Gallery, the old wooden doors of the Adem Dede Mevlevi house carved with the Tree of Life, iron rivets between each branch, have been cross-banded, corner to corner by yellow *Police Incident: Do Not Cross* tape.

'It is one thing after another,' Leyla shouts. 'I've had enough of this.' Dealer after auctioneer after crook, obstacle after obstacle. Beyond every achievement a frustration because it would never do to get too far, to be too successful. That would be impious. Now it's the police. This has a simple solution. Leyla reaches out to rip the tape away.

Naci clears his throat and points to the top right corner. Concealed among the cobwebs and silk egg-purses of true spiders is a police surveillance bot, all legs and eyes.

'Are you looking for Ms Erkoç?' The man who owns the teashop across the square is calling. He's called something like Bülent; Leyla doesn't like either of Adem Dede Square's çayhanes. The guys are pervy, the way they sit and watch, and watch.

'What happened?'

'The police arrived at about ten this morning, went in, spent maybe about an hour in there, took a few things away and then taped the place up. That's twice in two days the cops have been here. I've just got the paint off from their last visit.' Leyla's balcony is still orange polka-dotted. Some of it had spattered into a blouse and pants she had stood out to dry. When she gets paid she'll get a cleaner. That's what Ms Erkoç would do.

'Do you have any idea what they took?'

'No, but you could ask Hafize.' Leyla frowns, puzzled. 'The girl who works there. She's over in the Improving Bookstore, waiting to see what happens.'

Hafize, is it? Leyla's private name for her is Miss Priggy. Leyla has caught many a glance, a sniff of disapproval from her when she trusts her business heels on Adem Dede Square's cobbles or saunters across to Aydin's stall for a gossip magazine in her short house-shorts or puts out the empty wine bottles for the recycle. Husband and a headscarf. They grant an unwarranted sense of moral superiority. Disapproval from a glorified shopgirl, who's five years younger than her as well.

Leyla's never been in the Improving Bookstore. It smells like an elementary school, of cheap paper and phenolic inks, poorly bound and covered in that thin card that is smooth on the outside and teeth-on-edge scratchy on the inside. The windows catch the sun full and in this sun Hafize sits at a little table with tea.

'It was the art crime squad. They were led by an officer called Haydar Akgün. He'd been in before to see Madam Erkoç, I remember him. I didn't like the look of him then. I asked him why he was here and he said that I didn't need to know and he didn't have to tell me but Madam had been charged with obtaining antiquities under the meaning of the 2017 Antiquities Act with a view to selling them illegally to persons outside Turkey. He said this was a very serious charge and that I was to render him all assistance or I would be charged with obstructing a police investigation which is a very serious charge as well. That's the way they talk, policemen, when they want to intimidate you. Of course I asked to see his identification. He got annoyed about that but he showed it to me. He had to. That's the law.

'I saw him taking prints and miniatures and the computers and then the police women ordered me out and sealed the gallery up.'

'Miniatures?'

'Paintings. Persian miniatures. The Isfahan masters, they're the most sought after.'

'Not a miniature Koran? Not the other half of this?' Leyla sets the contract on the tea table.

'Persian, silver cover, eighteenth Christian century. Yes, I've seen the other half of that. I remember it well because it's a sign of disrespect to do that to a holy Koran.'

'Or a sign of great love,' Leyla says.

'Madam Erkoç bought it as part of a job lot from a man on Monday.'

'Topaloğlu.'

'Yes, from the Grand Bazaar. I didn't think much of him, he tried to hoodwink Madam with a poor fake of the English artist Blake. We saw through them at once. I settled up with him, Madam doesn't handle money. I remember wondering where the other half was.'

'It's here,' Leyla says.

'I can't offer to buy it off you,' Hafize says. 'Madam Erkoç makes all the buying decisions and she can't do anything until she's finished with the police. Even then, she won't give you very much. It's pretty but they were mass-marketed for pilgrims.'

'I don't want to sell it,' Leyla says slowly. 'I want to buy the other half. Can you sell it to me?'

'The police have closed the gallery. I'm only here until I'm told what to do next.'

'If we could get into the gallery, could you sell it to me?'

'I don't want to annoy the police.'

You irritating, idle, docile, sanctimonious woman. Well you suit Miss Priggy.

'I need this now. Aso, tell her.'

Hafize prefers studying her manicure to Aso's explication of the irregular financial set-up of Besarani-Ceylan. Leyla is not sure how much she understands of the white heat of the new entre-preneurialism and the asymptotic curve of twenty-first-century nano-engineering development. Leyla cuts Aso off as he starts on the technical specifications of the Besarani-Ceylan transcriber.

'I will give you a thousand euro. Deal?'

Money she understands. Deal.

'A thousand euro?' Aso whispers to Leyla as she leads him, Hafize and rearguard Naci up the narrow wooden staircase off Güneşli Sok.

'We'd have that between us. Kenan has an ATM in his shop anyway.' The stairs open on to the north side of the gallery that overlooks the garden. 'I live in there.' But Aso is more interested in the fountain in the courtyard.

'You've got your own garden. I'd never be out of that. Who's your landlord?'

At the end of the gallery a door leads to a narrow, dusty, cobwebby corridor. A high window in the right wall has been cheaply boarded up.

'That's the Professor in there. On the other side of this wall is the main stair case that goes up to the kid's apartment.'

'How did you discover all this?' Hafize asks. Something you don't know, shopgirl.

'You know the kid has these toy robots that change shape? I caught him watching me with them once. He tried to get away but I followed them. He's got runways and boltholes all over this building. He never did it again.'

'Not that you can see,' Hafize says.

A door on the right opens into a forgotten gallery that runs along the tekke's front. Shreds of hot light stream through the latticed window. Leyla is directly over the main door of the gallery. A spit would hit the cobbles of Adem Dede Square but this is a world away, a hidden place. Where the gallery turns right to follow Vermilion-Maker Lane Leyla stops at a painted-up door.

'Has anyone got a knife?'

Naci unfolds a multitool. Leyla flicks at wedges of paper packed into the doorframe. Dust flies up, sparkling in the grid of sunsquares. A headscarf is not so bad an idea. The last wedge falls to the floor, Leyla inserts the blade into the frame and levers the door ajar. She opens it a crack. A plane of light cuts the air of the old gallery. Leyla squints through the gap.

'It's clear.' She opens the door on to the gallery of the semahane of the Erkoç Gallery. 'This was all one gallery originally and at some point someone thought it was a good idea to split it in half.'

Aso leans on the rail. He takes in the octagonal gallery, the old wooden dervish cells, the brass chandelier, the railed-in dance floor where the smaller treasures have been displayed in glass cases.

'I've seen old hamams converted to carpet shops but this is just beautiful.'

Hafize covers her mouth in horror at the desecration. The walls have been stripped half naked. A few thin volumes remain on the display shelves. The manuscript pages have been scattered like leaves in the Storm of Mother Mary. She stoops down to lift the sacred texts but sits down on the floor, overcome by the scale of the offence.

'Later,' Leyla says gently.

Some of the cases have been hacked with lock-pick nano. From the scant remains Leyla guesses they held Christian crosses. Where the old dede would have stood when dervishes danced in this hall is the case with the miniature Korans. It's untouched. There it is. Oh, there it is.

'Have you got a key?'

Hafize opens the case. Leyla lifts the prize. Back in her left hand, front half in her right. A thought would unite them. She doesn't. She knows that if she did thunder would crack, a djinni appear, or a superhero, or she would bring some terrible nano-doom down on Istanbul, devouring the towers and minarets from the top down. Superstition, but in a place like this superstition is strong.

'Let's go.'

'A thousand euro, madam,' Hafize says.

They scrape it. Hafize counts it forwards and counts it backwards and hands them fifty euro back for blessing. She handwrites a receipt.

'Now can we go?'

They come down the creaking dusty steps on to shadowy Güneşli Sok to find the car blocked in the street by a big red tow-truck parked across the mouth of the lane. The driver hangs his arm out of the window. Abdullah Unul leans against the cab drinking tea. Another man is with him. He's young, tall, hair going Afro, sunken cheeks emphasizing good cheekbones. Stubble, pale blue eyes.

Where did the DNA for those come from? He looks nothing like how Leyla has imagined Mehmet Ali.

'I do rather like birds,' Abdullah Unul says. 'They're busy, active little things. They make do. Have you ever thought, if Istanbul were to have an official bird, what would it be? I bet you'd think stork straight away. Maybe a sparrow. Me, the official bird of Istanbul would have to be the seagull. What do you see dancing around the Ramazan lights, what's following the ships up and down the Bosphorus, what's facing into the wind on the rocks down by the water side. The common or garden gull, that's what. For all those reasons, the seagull for me is Istanbul, but mostly because it practises kleptoparasitism. You may not have heard of that. I'll explain. It's a behaviour when one animal takes prey from another that has the job of catching or killing it. In seagulls it's letting some other bird do all the hard work of catching the fish or a bit of bread and then taking it off them as they're about to eat it. It's the reason they're the success they are. So, I'll have that Koran. Both parts. To be honest, I'd prefer cash, but I imagine there's a market for that gadgetry you have out there in Fenerbahçe.'

Naci steps forward. Abdullah Unul twitches back his jacket to show an ivory handle.

'No, son.'

Leyla rages. It's the rage of helplessness, of having no options but needing to do something. She is so angry and powerless she could do something silly. Launch herself at Abdullah Unul and bite out his throat. Run back up the stairs on a mad chase through the dervish house. Drop both halves of the Koran down the drain grating at her feet. Resorts of desperation. There is no brilliant solution to this one. This one she loses. She hears a door open behind her. She glances around. The spooky guy who thinks he's some sort of dede.

'Shaykh Ismet,' Hafize shouts.

'What's going on here?' Ismet says.

'This is a private matter.'

Leyla sees how Ismet sizes up the men, the truck, the stand-off.

'These people are under the protection of the Adem Dede Tarikat.' Ismet puts himself between Hafize and Leyla.

'This is none of your business son.'

Then the men start to emerge from the door to the old kitchen on to Güneşli Sok. Five, ten, twenty. They form up behind Ismet. They are darkly dressed. Their faces are serious as men's faces should be after study of the Holy Koran.

Abdullah Unul sighs, shakes his head and does the gun reveal again. Ismet clicks his tongue and makes exactly the same gesture. Time hangs, then every other tarikat moves his jacket or pulls up his T-shirt to show the weapon there.

'Okay,' Abdullah Unul says. The tow-truck driver starts his engines. Abdullah Unul pushes Mehmet Ali towards the truck.

'He stays.' Naci's voice is clear and commanding. Abdullah Unul chews his bottom lip, shakes his head, breathes deep through flared nostrils, then goes around to the other side of the truck and gets in. Engines rev. The red tow-truck drives away through the narrow alleys of Eskiköy.

The lawyer is a junior in a first work suit but his shoes are decent. Adnan thinks of commenting that the firm could have sent someone more senior, but he's no dazzling paragon in his Galatasaray shirt and jeans. He blends too well with the street thieves, brawlers, pick-pocketed tourists and travel insurance scammers. The kid can't pick him out until Adnan nods to him.

'Mr Sarioğlu, I am Cengiz Bekdil, from Özis Turan Kezman.' They're a big commercial practice used by Özer that still keeps a small criminal division on the basis that modern business practice is a complex thing. *Don't switch companies yet*, Adnan thinks. *You may be about to have a major career boost.* Bekdil's handshake is as good as his shoes. To the desk sergeant, 'Is there somewhere we can talk in private?'

The sergeant frowns at the disturbance – the Cup Tie burbles at the frustrating edge of audibility on his radio – but lifts up the counter and nods Adnan and Bekdil through to a statement room. The table is covered in empty tea glasses.

'What's the score?' Adnan shoots back to the sergeant as he closes the door.

'One all.'

Adnan winces. Bekdil sits across the table from him, leaning forward. His hands are lively and dancing.

'The situation is this, Mr Sarioğlu. Your wife has been arrested on a charge of smuggling antiquities out of Turkey.'

'What's their evidence?'

'She was allegedly caught transferring a rare historical piece to her gallery in Eskiköy with an intention on selling it out of the country without proper export documentation. The object is currently at the gallery. The police have cordoned off the area. Ms Erkoç claims to have found it quite legitimately through her own research. Against that, and what makes our case slightly more tricky, is that she was arrested as part of a larger operation against organized antiquity smuggling.'

'Ayşe is not a smuggler.'

'Of course, Mr Sarioğlu. However, she did in confidence tell me that many of her pieces – religious artwork, that's her speciality? – have come from irregular sources. Of course, we'll argue that it's entrapment.'

'Yes, good, but what are you going to do right now?'

Bekdil has a trick where he pulls in his bottom lip when concentrating or irritated.

'I'll apply for bail. I'm confident she'll get it, though it may be quite substantial. Are you in a position, Mr Sarioğlu?'

'I'll post the bail.'

'Excellent, excellent.' Bekdil clasps his hands and shakes them in pleasure. He may wear a twenty-year-old's suit but in his heart, in his inner spiritual age, the one you are all your life, he is an Anatolian great-uncle, the kind who gives you money for school uniforms and his old pick-up for your first car. 'Between ourselves, and off the record, I suspect the prosecutors will offer a plea bargain.'

'Ayşe's not pleading guilty to any minor charge. If you get a name as a traitor in her business, no one will ever deal with you again.'

'With respect, that is for my client to decide, Mr Sarioğlu. I'm going to go and see if I can set bail.'

They rise from the table of sugar-silty tea glasses.

'One last thing: this object, what was it?'

Bekdil sucks in his lower lip.

'Have you ever heard of a Mellified Man?'

'What is that?'

'I don't know either, Mr Sarioğlu but, it's worth somewhere in the region of a million euro.'

'Just gone two one,' the sergeant offers as he lifts the counter for Bekdil and Adnan.

'Cimbom?'

'Arsenal.'

Adnan mouths a silent *fuck*. The sergeant turns the radio a fraction so that Adnan, leaning against the desk, can listen to it.

'Volkan's been substituted. Van Rijn went for his bad leg in a sliding tackle on the edge of the box. Should have been a penalty and a red card; we got a yellow and a free kick and they're talking about Volkan being out for six months.'

'Russian referee,' Adnan says. The sergeant's mouth forms a wise O. Behind the wire-toughened glass Bekdil argues with two policemen in well-ironed suits. One is short, nicotine-skinned, balding. He looks too warm. The other is tall, well-groomed in a nanoweave suit that shifts from blacker on black to a dizzying moire mesh of patterns. Silver at his cuffs. He makes Bekdil look cheap. Flash fucker. Bekdil's hands spell *negotiation:* open to plead, palms down to reject, beckoning in to reason, weighing up, scissoring to cut through to clarity. Detective Flash Fucker does all the police talking. Nods all around finally. Bekdil slips into the interview room. Adnan glimpses a hand on a table, silver rings on the fingers, antique silver at the wrist. Ayşe. Then the door closes.

'As I suspected, the bail is substantial,' Bekdil says, returning to the front office. Flash Fucker is looking at Adnan through the glass. What kind of cop affords a suit like that? They should be checking him for corruption, not hard-working gallery owners trying to make a go in Queen Bitch City. 'We can arrange for it to be deposited from our funds . . .'

'How much?'

'Twenty thousand.'

'I said I'll get it.'

'We take cards,' the sergeant says. 'Not Amex, though, and there's a two per cent surcharge on credit cards.' He proffers the reader. Adnan taps in the zeroes and they seem to be the mathematics of this day's jarring incongruities. Zero times zero is zero. Zero times anything is still zero, but divide by zero is infinity. That's the logic of this day. Ayşe arrested. An antiquity smuggling ring. A million euro. A Mellified Man; he can't even begin to imagine what that is. All the while the game burbles away on the desk radio. Adnan watches the money vanish from his account into the Istanbul Police account. The sergeant tears off the print-out receipt with a flourish.

'You can apply for repayments either online or on our twenty-four-hour bail-bond hotline.' He picks up the phone and calls through to the police behind the glass. Flash Fucker opens the interview room door and there she is: Ayşe. She is tired and furious but her eyes are bright. Her hair is mussed, there's a ladder in her tights. The toes of her boots are scuffed, but her face, her make-up is perfect. Her eyes hold that dark light deep in them that Adnan has learned over years to recognize and respect. Her bag is pulled aggressively up high on her shoulder. It is possible to wear a bag aggressively. It is as if he hasn't seen her for years. Then she is out in the front office. Flash Fucker catches Adnan's eye, nods in acknowledgement. *You think you know me, do you? Well, you do. I am your enemy.*

Ayşe picks up the paperwork from the desk sergeant and brushes past Adnan's open arms.

'Not here,' she whispers. 'I wouldn't give those bastards the satisfaction.'

Adnan and Bekdil follow her out on to the hot street. Ayşe angrily flicks out a cigarette, lights it, inhales with tight pleasure. Smoking on the street be damned.

'Well Ms Erkoç, I'll keep you apprised of developments,' Bekdil says. Ayşe waves away his offer of a handshake. 'It's a complicated case so it will take some time for the Public Prosecutors to formulate charges. I'd be surprised if anything happened before the summer, but I'd still like to arrange a meeting early next week to present you with the likely chain of events and your options. There is a very good lawyer specializes in art and antiquities; if I may, I'd like to retain him. He knows his stuff. Mr Sarioğlu.' Bekdil's details jump to Adnan's ceptep in a handshake. 'If you need anything, don't hesitate to call.'

Then he is hurrying away along Imran Öktem Cadessi with rather short steps for a man.

'I'll call the car,' Adnan says. 'Come on, let's go home.'

'I don't want to go home,' Ayşe snaps. 'I want a coffee or something. I stink of police.' She looks around her at the flat grey face of the street, that not even spring sun can inspire. 'Not here.' Her boot heels clop down the cobble of Terzihani Sok. Adnan follows her across the sun-dazzling Atmeydanı, the ancient Roman Hippodrome, dodging tour buses and taxis, Chinese tour groups following high-held umbrellas, keeping enough distance to fully appreciate the magnificence of her anger. No regret, no remorse, never a waver of guilt: how he loves her. She bangs down on to a stool at a çayhane in the wall of the Sultanahmet Mosque. Patrons stare, even in the heart of tourist Istanbul this is traditionally the world of men. 'Two coffees,' she orders and then sits, chain smoking. Adnan knows she'll talk in her own due time.

'Do you know what the final score was?' Adnan asks the waiter as he sets down the tiny cups of coffee.

'It was a draw. Two all. Second leg at the Emirates next week.'

'That's all right,' Adnan says. It makes him feel ridiculously better.
'Not bad, though I'm a Beşiktaş man myself.'

Ayşe throws her coffee down in one.

'They fingerprinted me. That stuff doesn't come off, it's all over
this dress, it's ruined, not that I'll ever be wearing it again. They
took my DNA; they made me open my mouth and stuck a swab in,
like I was a common car thief or something.' She lights another
cigarette, throws her head back, draws in the smoke and flutteringly
exhales it in a wisping blue veil in that way that has always aroused
Adnan with its unconscious movie-star sophistication. 'I had it. It
was in my hands, I opened the sarcophagus and looked in, the first
eyes in two hundred and fifty years to see it. I touched it. I tasted it.
It was sweet, like nothing has ever been sweet before or ever will be
again. I had it in my hands.'

'Bekdil seems all right.'

'Fuck Bekdil. No; Bekdil is all right. He's about twelve years old
but he's good. How much did he tell you?'

'That you'd been lifted as part of a larger operation cracking
antique smuggling.'

'That doesn't make me feel any better. No, did he tell you what
it is, this antiquity I'm accused of trying to sell out of the
country?'

'Something like a "Mellified Man"?'

'Do you know what that is? It's a legend. It's a fairy tale. It's a roc
egg or a djinn lamp or a flying carpet. It's the jewels of Aya Sofya
and the tears of Mary. It's a human body mummified in honey. It
shouldn't exist at all but I found it.' Ayşe lights another cigarette.
'Honey trap was what it was. I don't think that bastard Akgün even
knew it existed, he just gave me enough clues to make it plausible.
And dangled a million euro in front of me.'

'I can't follow this.'

'A client came to a gallery; well dressed, knowledgeable. He had
a provenance of the existence of an eighteenth-century Mellified
Man from Iskenderun and would pay me one million euro if I would

deliver it to him. And I did – Adnan, the things I've seen. I got him his Mellified Man but he was a cop from the antiquities division. Fucker, I should have known; that cheap airport aftershave. He knew that my looking for a Mellified Man would bring out every statue-seller and icon pedlar from here to Bursa. Fucker.'

'A million euro. Ayşe, if it's money . . .'

Ayşe suddenly touches Adnan's face. 'Adnan; it was for me. A purely selfish exercise; to show I can do the deals too. I can make the money. I can play the big game.'

A shadow crosses the table. Adnan squints up at the unexpected drop in temperature. There is a cloud across the sun, a small, laugh-able bubble of vapour but there is another behind it, and another, and behind it a wall of cumulo-nimbus towering behind the dome of Aya Sofya. Adnan's heart kicks; now the enormity of what he has achieved in Turquoise has a solid, physiological form. The proof is written across the sky.

'I was the bait. I was set up from the start. I should have known. I was blinded by it. A Mellified Man – to find a thing like that, one of the last wonders of the world; could you have refused?'

Adnan shakes his head, mouths the word *no*.

'They try and scare you in there. Çandar, the other one; he's just a station plainclothesman, no idea what this is about except he's supposed to play bad cop to Aykut's good cop. Jail, fines, losing the business, bankruptcy; I can't go to jail. It would kill my mother. I did bad enough marrying you, Adnan. Then they try and play Prisoner's Dilemma – please. Just a fine, maybe a suspended jail sentence – that would still finish it. The game is over and there isn't any other game that interests me. If I can't see another Ashkenazi Pentateuch or an Isfahan miniature or a Blake illustration . . . there is no life without Blake. It's as simple as that. I can't go to court; I can't lose the gallery. Fuck fuck fuck fuck fuck!' Ayşe stabs her cigarette out in the ash tray.

'You need a better deal,' Adnan says. 'Not just a plea bargain, but immunity from prosecution.'

'Well, yes darling, but that's only for whistleblowers who bring down state institutions ...' Ayşe stares as Adnan gets up from his chair and begins to pace around the tables of smokers and drinkers. He wanders into the old Hippodrome, looks up at the Egyptian obelisk, wanders back. When Ayşe tries to ask him what has gotten into him Adnan presses his finger to his lips: *ssh don't speak*. It's a plan, pure and simple, perfect and entire; as totally and instantly there in its every detail as Turquoise was when it appeared to him written on the smoked glass of an elevator. Only this is much, much bigger than Turquoise.

Adnan sits down on his wicker stool, hooks up his ceptep.

'Bekdil. Adnan Sarioğlu. Thanks for taking the call. I need to talk to you, urgently. You might want to bring a couple of the partners with you. Well, you either bring them or you'll bring them later. What's it about? Well, we might say, you're a good lawyer, but you're not a dealer.'

The last unit on the right, next to the ElmaÖrap apple packing unit, upstairs from the accountants; that's where they're holding Necdet, the Boy Detective deduces. He's been past three times, the last a saunter among kids heading from the close of afternoon school. The young man with the scrubby moustache in the security booth doesn't worry Can; grown-ups never notice anything and between buzzing trucks in and out his time is spent watching the sports channel or playing with his ceptep. But there are cameras and a quick check on the BotSpotters forum pegs two Samsung FB118 Security drones pinned to the map of Bostancı Dudullu Business Park. Pattern recognition, gait and facial analysis AI were all introduced on that particular model and they come with equipped with RFID tag darts as standard. The consensus among the commentators is that their attention piques after three passes. Can took care to snap his photographs on his first recce, shooting low from the hip, clickety-click of the ceptep. It was a risk, opening up the phone, but as soon as he realized he would need photographs he also realized he had forgotten to add a camera to his Boy Detective Check List. Next case he'll know better.

Kayişdaği is a flat, ugly place, nothing over two storeys high, all wedged tightly and meanly, paint peeling and plaster mould-stained, plastic, wide streets patrolled by wide cars, dust everywhere. Dust on the white Toyota pick-ups, dust on little three-wheeler citicars, dust on the tin dome of the small cheap community mosque, dust on the plastic store signs. All the women wear headscarves. There are a lot of babies and very small children. Some don't look very clean. The sound is flat out here, thin and high-pitched. The sun is very strong and hot. Can has slapped on half a tube of factor thirty.

Can thinks he has chosen the stake-out well. The Kapçek teashop faces on to the side of the business unit where Can suspects Necdet is being held across Bostancı Dudullu Cadessi. The road is wide and busy, two carriageways of constant traffic. Samsung FB118s are smart enough to disregard background vehicular traffic; scanning and identifying every car is within their capabilities but it would leave them little else for janitoring. Can will hide behind walls of moving vehicles. Beneath the teashop awning he can sit and work on his computer and carry out his investigation. No one will dream of asking him what he's doing. *Çayhane* is a recognized way of life.

Can nods to the clientele as he takes a stool at a table by the street.

'Gentlemen,' he says nonchalantly. The men of the Kapçek are less well shaven, their faces thinner, their hands browner, the folds at the corners of their eyes deeper drawn, but they are of a type with Mr Ferentinou and his old Greeks. Can slides his computer out of his backpack and opens it up. The proprietor is at the table. He's younger and skinnier than Bülent and has rather prominent teeth.

'Sir?'

Can looks at him over the top of his Detective shades.

'Ayran please. Over ice.'

Ayran on the Asian side is cheap and very very good. Can takes shots through a straw as he opens up the BitBot application while loading the photographs from the ceptep chip directly into Pano-ramika, which whipstitches them into a fully explorable three-sixty model of Bostancı Dudullu Business Park. He needs to get the Bots over there to check out locations and faces before it's too dark to see. There's the van. It hasn't moved since it arrived here last night. If he zooms he can make out Rat Baby hooked on to the rear fender. It makes Can giggle in glee at his cleverness. BitBot is ready. Can slides in the earphone and taps up the haptic field. A wave of his fingers and Snake comes to life around his neck, disgorges his tail and slithers down Can's arm on to the table.

Old men and proprietor alike stare.

'It's a toy,' Can says. He crosses his hands, spreads his fingers and Snake becomes Bird.

'Why didn't we have toys like that when I was a kid?' says a chubby, smiley man with a grand moustache.

'God keep us so my grandsons never ever get to hear about those,' says the grizzled man with cheeks sunken from missing teeth.

Now Can will really make their eyes pop. A flick of his hands and Bird flitters up from the table, over the traffic constant along Bostancı Dudullu Cadessi, spiralling up like a stork on the heat beating up from the blacktop, high over the solar roofs of the business centre. The first part is the tricky part, bringing in Bird unseen by the Samsung Sisters and reconfiguring it so Rat and Rat Baby rejoin. He makes a high pass, all eight-camera-eyes wide angle. It's a risk, if he enters their patrol perimeters those bastarding robots will see at once this is no ordinary bird. There. Opportunity. Can drops Bird on to the roof of an inbound truck stopped at the security gate. He pulls his fists apart. Bird transforms to Snake and wriggles down the back of the truck to the fender. Another conversion and Snake is Rat, clinging behind the licence plate. The truck swings wide to reverse up to the ElmaÖrap bay, Rat hops off the trailer at the maximum of its articulation, scurries under the wheels to leap, dis-sociate and mingle with the simultaneously leaping and dissociating BitBot swarm of Rat Baby, releasing from the back of the white truck. Rat reforms in mid-air, full and complete, then rolls under the van out of sight of the twitching eye-antennae of the Samsungs. In.

Can feels an audience on his shoulder. He turns round to see that the old men have all moved their chairs round to watch the transforming robot show playing out on his silkscreen.

'Never mind your grandchildren, I want one of those,' the çayhane owner says.

'Is this for television?' says Sunken-Cheeks Missing-Teeth.

'But seriously son, where did you get those things?' There's a sour one, like the nasty old Egyptian in Adem Dede Square. There's always a nasty one. 'What devilment are you up to with them?'

Can's heart flaps and beats like a pigeon trapped in a balcony. His plans never allowed for the fact that other people might be suspicious of his detective work. The detective is always right and straight. His goodness is never questioned. Now that it has been, other realizations clutch at Can's chest. Any one of these men might be bad guys. The bad guys might walk in at five o'clock every day to order ayran fresh from the fridge. Sour One might be sour because he's a policeman. Chubby-Good-Moustache could be a teacher or a social worker or someone from the ministry for children. People with the power to stop his investigation and send him back home. Then Can knows how to work it.

'My brother has been kidnapped.' The men start back. Here's what I'll say when you say, *then call the police*, Can thinks. Oh, it's finger-snapping brilliant. 'He owes money to these men.' The men relax back with an audible *oh*. 'Except he doesn't. Except there's been a mistake. Except I got this tag on him, and found him here, and when I find where he really is, I'll get in the rest of the family and they'll smack them up, the money lenders.'

'Are you making this up?' Sunken-Cheek Missing-Teeth asks.

'No,' says Can with the little upturn at the end that he uses on his parents when he wants to double-bluff them. 'Really.' Now you don't know what to believe, but I am telling the truth. Sort of. Can has another Brilliant Detective Idea. This will really confuse them. 'Have you noticed anything or anyone strange coming or going from the end unit?'

The proprietor shakes his head, in bafflement rather than negation.

'Kids,' Sunken-Cheeks Missing-Teeth says with a dismissive wave of the hand.

'Do your parents know you're out?' Good Moustache says, half-joking. Only Nasty-Man-Egyptian keeps his eye on Can as the others return to their çay and cards. Can flexes his fingers. Peace at last.

Can sends Rat out from under the white van along the foot of the wall to cover behind the garbage. Just like a flesh rat. There he converts to Snake and goes up the wall behind the drain. Easy easy so easy. These people with their clunky big Samsungs are no match for the Boy Detective and his BitBots. This is the plan: take Snake out along the walls, clinging to the roughly painted cinderblock easily with the nanoscale hooks that bind and release from different forms, finding cover in the shadow of window sills and eaves. Windows are the big goal: a good look in through each one. Can snaps his fingers in excitement. This is so good. He is so clever.

Through the first window: an empty room with a broken-down sofa, a desk with some electronic equipment that won't resolve properly on Snake's limited field of resolution.

Through the second window. Snake lifts his camera-jewelled head over the edge of the sill. Three mattresses, some sheets, flat looking foam pillows. Empty water bottles: many. Empty fast-food containers: several. Black plastic refuse sacks: bulging. Magazines, books with dull covers and scrolly writing.

The third window. Desks are pushed against the wall, the floor space is taken up with styrofoam crates and cardboard boxes. Here Can spots his first human. A young man sits at a desk at the side of the room where he can see both door and window. He has curling hair and blue eyes and the kind of almost-beard men grow first when it's time to experiment with facial hair. He might be one of the men who kidnapped Necdet, Can can't remember the faces too clearly. The man's intent on his work on a silkscreen computer. Can fiddles with the focus but can't get a clear shot of the screen. He daren't linger, the man could look up at any moment. But there is an angular object under the desk. The young man shifts in his chair and now Can sees the object for what it is: an assault rifle.

In the Kapçek çayhane Can starts back from the screen. A little gasp puffs out of him. He looks around quickly, guiltily to see if anyone else has seen the gun. The men seem happy with their cards. Quickly Can pulls Snake away from the third window and on to the fourth.

Here is Necdet. He lies on his side on a mattress. Can's angle is acute and he cannot see the face but the man is wearing the same clothes he was when Can saw him bundled into the white van. Can will always remember that. Squatting on her heels, facing Necdet, is a woman. She wears a headscarf but her face is young. She has fashionable glasses, jeans and boots, Her heels come a little off the floor. Her lips are moving, she is clearly talking to Necdet. Audio was never very good on BitBots. It's much harder to get decent sound than an acceptable picture. Can is sure he's never seen this woman before. The man behind her, cross-legged on a mat on the floor, is vaguely familiar. He is one of the kidnap crew. He is a square man, he looks old to Can but he never was very good at age over fourteen. They all look the same. He has dark skin, an eastern complexion, and wears a SuperDry T-shirt going at the collar. He has a big sport of hair at his throat; that's what's wearing away at the T. A big assault rifle lies comfortably across his thighs.

Everyone but Necdet is in a position where they could see peeping Snake as plain as a minaret. Can pulls Snake in to safety under the window sill. He's found him. He's found Necdet. He's seen the people holding him, and something of their plan. They have guns. He always thought they might but the truth knocks him back. What does he do now? One immediate must. The BitBots are low on power.

The çayhane owner is startled to find Can behind him as he washes glasses. Can holds up his power adaptor.

'Can I use some electricity? I'll pay you.' The teashop owner silently plugs in the cord. Can carefully adjusts his seat so his back is to a wall and he can see both street and teashop, a lesson he has already learned from the terrorists. He risks a mid-air shift into Bird and a swoop across Bostancı Dudullu Cadessi. Mr Ferentinou once told him that people find things moving away less interesting than things moving towards them. Bird's arrival makes the card-players look up from their game.

'Needs recharging,' Can says. The hour of charging is endless and agonizing. The light is going. The teashop owner is impatient. The men have drained all interest from their cards and will soon start with their questions again. And he has no idea what is going on over in the house of terror. Planning is good. Think strategy. Greater Istanbul Department of Planning and Building Control will have architect's plans for the business park. As he shuffles through the search menus, Can wonders that the planning office for Istanbul contains Istanbul, flat and drawn on paper. A two-dimensional city. Bostancı Dudullu Business Park. Easy. Can plans his assault. He will take the easy option through the accountants'. He will gain entry by a vent brick, then work his way up through the wall cavity. This is very easy for Snake to do. Along the floorspace: the office suites are generously endowed with air vents. Marrying plan to memory, he locates the one closest to Necdet.

Green lights all across the board. BitBots are go.

The accountants are closing up as Rat skitters behind their feet, along the wall. By the time it hits the vent it has reconfigured into Snake and goes straight through the terracotta slats without a beat. Up up. Can grins in delight and concentration as he maps Snake's camera feed – looming, sudden, wide-angle, bizarrely lit by Snake's limited LED output – on to the architect's plans. This is the best game in the world. Over the top of the cinder-block inner wall and the raftered space of the underfloor stretches before him. Cables: follow them. Ducting. He's there. The vent is a grille of blinding light. Can stops down the cameras and crawls closer, nano-scale by nano-scale. Snake's nose is millimetres from the vent cover. A dark shape fills the visible horizon. Can hisses air over his tongue in concentration as he opens up the cameras into wide-angle. The dark mass recedes into substance and shape. Necdet, lying on his mattress, but his back is to the vent, and worse, beyond his reclining shape, the upright shape of the guard, facing the vent. He could not fail to miss a metre-long robo-snake emerging from the ventilators.

Only patience will see Can's plan succeed.

For an hour Can sits at the monitor, not moving, not making a sound, looking at Necdet's hunched back. The last truck has left the apple-packers. Even the security man has closed down his booth and locked the gates. The Samsung F118s still patrol and lights now burn in the apartment over the accountancy firm. The traffic along Bostancı Dudullu Cadessi carry lights. There's a stupendous sunset unfolding beyond the flat tin roofs of the business centre.

'Is someone coming for you?' the proprietor of the Kapçek çayhane. The nosy men have all drifted away, one by one, unsatisfied by the non-resolution of the story of the Robot-Toy-Boy vs the Money-Lenders of Kayişdaği. Can is alone between the day and the evening shifts.

'I'll not be long,' Can says but he hasn't solved the problem of where to stay the night. He has not even thought of it until now. But stay he must, until the Boy Detective saves the day.

A movement. Necdet has turned over. Now Can carefully, a millimetre at a time, moves Snake's head so that it is directly looking at Necdet's face. He goes close with the cameras. Necdet looks bad. He is unshaved and his hair is greasy. Crusty stuff from bad sleeping gathers around the corners of his mouth and eyes. Necdet's closed eyelids flicker. Open them open them. They flicker again. Open. Necdet opens his eyes. Now, the Boy Detective shows his brilliance.

Can flicks up a new command window, moves his right hand into the haptic field and snaps fingers to thumb, like a duck quacking. Across the boulevard, in the offices above the accountants, Snake starts flashing his LEDs at Necdet's face.

Wake.

I don't want to wake.

Wake!

Leave me alone.

How can that be? Wake! Open your eyes.

I don't want to open my eyes. I'll see how much closer I am to them killing me.

Who am I? Recite!

You are Hızır Khidr al-Khadir Khidar Khwaja Khizar Khizr. You are the Green One.

What am I?

You are the Undying One, Eternal Wanderer, the Righteous Servant of God, Tutor of the Prophets, Lord of the Men of the Unseen, Master of the Assembly of Saints, Lord of the Waters of Life, Initiator of those who walk the Hidden Path.

Open your eyes!

I see the edge of a mattress, a thin grey hard-pile carpet, the junction of two white-painted walls scuffed with trainer-marks, skirting board, sockets, vent . . . What would you have me see, Green Saint?

The vent. Something flashing in the vent. Not flickering, not arcing. Flashing. Rhythmically.

This is real, says Hızır in a voice of springtime.

Necdet blinks twice. The light blinks back, twice. Something in there with a mind, something that recognizes him. Something that knows he's here. Something that followed him? One blink, one flash back. What's behind the lights? Necdet tries to make sense out of the strips of shape behind the vent slats. It looks like a snake head. A snake head with spider eyes, a dozen dot-eyes, blinking light at him. A machine of some kind. A robot snake. He's seen a robot snake before. He was in the garden of the dervish house. It was all new and fresh but threatening at the same time. He was new then. It must have been just after Ismet took him away from Başibüyük to build a new life for him. He had been sitting on the edge of the little fountain, skinning up, when a movement on the edge of the roof had drawn his eye. Snake! He dropped the half-rolled skin, breathless in fear. At first he had thought it was a flashback or a flashout or some hideous flash-in, all his sins manifesting themselves. Then he saw that it was a complicated machine, hanging over the edge of the sloping cloister roof, watching him. And another time, when he discovered the tiny triangle of the old dervish graveyard behind the kitchen cloister, a movement in the grass, and that same snake-robot had darted away from his feet, coiled up a cylindrical tombstone topped with a conical Mevlevi headdress and, to his astonishment, turned into dust that coalesced into a bird. The bird spread it wings and flew away. He had always thought it some kind of parable.

The kid's robot. The kid's found him. How? Doesn't matter. The kid's found him. Someone knows he's here. He has to get a message out, but he's locked in a room with an armed guard who is going to kill mercifully, painlessly, without prejudice and in the name of God when the operation is finished with a toy robot stuck up the air vent flashing lights at him and a deaf kid at the other end of the line.

The deaf kid can lip-read.

Once for yes, twice for no, Necdet mouths slowly and clearly. There is a long pause, then the spider-eyes flash once.

Don't flash unless I ask you, Necdet says. Big Bastard is as much a prisoner in this room as Necdet and plays mental games with the walls, the lights, patterns in the carpets, knots in the skirting, anything to break the boredom.

Flash.

Listen carefully. At the end, I will ask you if you understand. Call the police. These people are terrorists.

Necdet feels the repeated 'r's move his jaw against the mattress.

His head will have tilted, just a fraction but Big Bastard will have noticed that.

'Hey, Necdet, you awake?'

'I am now.'

'You need water or the pot or something?'

'Does it matter?'

Necdet never takes his gaze from the half seen shape in the vent. He says nothing for several minutes, listening for the soft noise of Big Bastard making himself comfortable and inattentive again. The kid doesn't move, doesn't flash.

Call the police, Necdet mouths. *They have some insane plan. Nano-technology; they won't tell me. Call the police. Be careful. Go now. Be quick. They are going to kill me. Do you understand?*

A blink of light. Necdet closes his eyes. The next time he looks he cannot see anything behind the slats of the air vent. He had forgotten the most famous attribute of the Green Saint. Hızır: help from beyond comprehension.

Hasan the barber wraps the wad of kitchen roll around the tip of the screwdriver, douses it in lighter fuel and ignites it. Quick as knife he wafts the flame close to Adnan's ears, left, then right, and repeat twice before he douses the brand in the flowerpot of sand on the counter. A wash of heat too quick for pain, the smell of burning hair. This is the heart of barbering, the intimate violence, the placing of yourself in the seat of a man who can bring so many blades close to your eyes, ears, nostrils, jugular. A splash and gasp of kolonya and the ritual is done. The door bell clangs; there is the courier, on time to the second, with the flat boxes under his arms.

'Mr Sarioğlu?'

The other three Ultralords of the Universe, perched along the bench like old men at a winter tram-stop, point at the freshly groomed man in the chair. Adnan swirls off the sheet, opens the top box and shakes out the virtuous white new shirt.

'I'm just going to change here, all right, Hasan?' The barber bows a fraction and flips over the *Closed* sign. Adnan peels off his Galatasaray top. The new shirt falls around him like a blessing. The tailors know his skin better than anyone except Ayşe.

'I've got the same for you, Kemal. I wasn't sure of the size so I just guessed and went up one.' He kicks the flat boxes over at Kemal. Adnan Sarioğlu's rules for life. Off-the-peg is a false economy when a bespoke Istanbul tailor will keep your statistics on file, cut and assemble a suit in an hour and deliver it across the city by courier. 'With respect, gentlemen, he's the only one needs to be there.' Kemal gingerly lifts the jacket out of the folded tissue.

'When I was a kid, I saw this old American silent comedy film. It was pretty funny so it can't have been Charlie Chaplin. There was this scene where the funny man was standing in front of the barn, with an open door right at the top.' He fastens up his cufflinks and kicks off his shoes. 'The joke is that the barn wall blows down, right on top but he's positioned so that the open door goes right over him. That's good timing and that, gentlemen, is pretty much what I intend to do with Özer.' He steps into his slacks, adjusts the waistband. New shoes on. 'Özer is coming down. We all know that. But what if, instead of the Levent Tower coming down around our ears and hoping we walk away with our asses, we arrange a controlled demolition? Kemal, get that fucking suit on; without you we do not have a hope.' Adnan pulls on the shoes; left, right. They're pretty good for cheap slip-ons. 'Kemal has the details: names, accounts, transactions, codes, times, everything. I have the deal.'

'Immunity,' Kadir says. His team shirt and baseball cap sit uneasily on him, he looks like a British prince at a music festival.

'Correct.'

'We deliberately destroy Özer?' Oğuz asks.

'It's going to fall anyway. How much does it owe?'

'Somewhere not far off two point seven billion euro,' Kemal says. He stands in the middle of the tiny, one-chair Alemdar barbershop in his Cimbom top with his pants off. 'When did you find out about the Cygnus X error account?'

'I told Adnan,' Kadir says.

Adnan raises a finger. 'Kadir, shut the fuck up. He told me the day before the deal went down, straight after the meeting with Larijani. We thought you were a threat to Turquoise.' He meets and holds Kemal's eyes. Straight is the only way to play this now.

'A threat? A threat? Fuck you, who cleared the money, who ran the back office, who snorted Larijani's coded nano – you want to try that some time, that's a whole basket of fun. What were you going to do? Go on, what were you going to do?'

'We were planning to cut you out of the deal.'

'Cut me out? Me? Out? The fuck . . . And how were you going to do that exactly, knowing what I know? Hm?'

'Kemal, put the suit on.' Oğuz is about to open his mouth with some stupidity. Adnan stabs a finger at him. 'You say nothing. Only I talk here. Put the suit on, Kemal.'

'What is this, like some gangster movie where they all fall out after the heist? What were you going to do, you fuckers? A bit of a kicking? A car going into the Bosphorus with a body in the trunk?'

'Put the fucking suit on, Kemal.'

'A hit? No . . .' Kemal's mouth chews air; implications fall on him, sharp as glass. 'You fuckers. You fuckers!'

'No,' Adnan very clearly and slowly. 'It was a tailored nanotech package. I was to swap it for your usual dose. It would have scrambled your memory; you wouldn't have known what was yours and what was the nano's.'

Kemal remembers, he remembers every little detail. 'That cough . . .'

'Is why you're talking to me here today.'

'You bitches!' Kemal screams. 'You sneaking, scheming, faithless little bitches.'

'Now put the suit on. We have to go.'

'Why the fuck should I ever work with you?'

'Because we need each other, one last time. Just do this one thing and we need never see each other again, but you need to put on the suit, Kemal.'

Kemal is defeated but he is an Ultralord, he is a paşa; he tosses his head back in a final gesture of contempt. 'Clever of you to pull this little one out of your ass after the wifey gets in trouble.'

Two moves, and Adnan has Kemal by the scruff of his Galatasaray shirt; breath to breath.

'You do not ever, ever talk about Ayşe,' Adnan hisses and then Kadir and Oğuz are in to separate them. Adnan slowly exhales, straighten the lapels of his jacket, matches the sleeves.

'We go to meet Bekdil and whoever else he's persuaded to come along to the Anadolu Hotel. We tell him about Turquoise. We tell him about Cygnus X. We tell him Mehmet Meral's personal intervention in the Cygnus X accounts. You give him the codes, he sees the accounts, he sees the errors, he sees the off-balance-sheet losses, he sees the authorizations from the top floor. We tell him that Özer is rotten from the head, that the company has no assets, that it's manipulated its share price, that it has lost billions and that it is effectively bankrupt. For this we want immunity for Turquoise. Yes and I want any charges against Ayşe Erkoç dropped as part of the bargain. Bekdil goes to the Financial Regulatory Office. We tell it all over again to them. We tell it as many times as we need to until we get our immunity documents in our hands, our cash in our pockets and the regulators take Özer apart like an Eminönü Rolex.' Adnan shakes the new shirt out of its shallow box and holds it out to Kemal. 'Put the suit on or don't put the suit on, but wear something. You see, we do this one thing, you and me, and we get everything.'

Kemal snatches the shirt, turns away. He shudders as he takes off his football shirt. For an instant Adnan thinks he might cry and that would be the worst thing. Then he pulls the pure cotton over his turning-flabby torso, buttons it up, fixes the cuffs. There is work to be done. *But I saved your life and I saved your ass and you hate that*, Adnan thinks. *It kills you that you will forever be in my debt for that.*

He tightens his tie, adjusts his cufflinks to perfect symmetry. This is the true Deal Day suit.

In the Improving Bookstore Can once found a wonder: eleven huge leather-bound volumes, cheek to cheek on seldom-visited shelves, gold-edged pages thick with dust. The names on their spines were *The Encyclopaedia of Istanbul*. They went as far as G, but they were illustrated, so in their pages you could not just read about the histories of horse-carriages and steam ferries but you could see them, all drawn out, four to a page, and also Hezarfen Ahmet Çelebi who flew from the Galata Tower to Üsküdar on wooden wings, and the siege engines of Mehmet the Conqueror and harsh Ottoman tortures that made Can feel light-headed and strangely excited. His parents refused to buy them for him at any discount from the bookstore owner, but Can remembers vividly that the last wolf in Istanbul was shot in 1943 in the old graveyard at Eyup, and the drawing; a slobber-jawed, mad-eyed monster leaping on to the blazing rifles of the wolf-finders, who all have good moustaches.

Can wonders how sure Mr Koçu the writer was about 1943. He's heard something with big claws and teeth and slobber snuffling and scratching around the end of the concrete pipe. He hugs Monkey closer to him. The machines give off warmth even in resting. Once the sun is down, concrete loses heat rapidly. He shivers and drapes his rainproof around him.

The extraction had been successful. That's what they called it in games when they had to lift out the Star Troopers. The extraction. Like a tooth, or plugs from his ears. Funny now that he can hear any-thing and anyone, that Necdet had to talk to him silently, in lip-reading. It was dark by the time he worked back under the floor and down the interior wall and wormed out the ventilation brick. The Sam-sungs were silhouettes against the high yellow floodlights but outside the lighted areas the dark was deep. It had been easy to disengage Rat Baby and reinstall him on the back of the white van. They were terrorists. They had a plan. They might move before the police came.

Terrorists. The word made him feel funny; not scared, not excited, like both of those but deeper in his belly, right in the core of him, something hot and dark and strange, something Can and at the same time not-Can. Terrorists are old men with beards in robes and young men moving their hands like rappers. Terrorists don't wear good jeans and boots and SuperDry. But at the same time he saw the guns and the boxes of serious stuff. Can can't work that out. Terrorists are not supposed to be people at all.

He'd coiled Snake around his arm, unplugged the charger and rolled up the computer. 'Thank you,' he called to the teashop man. 'I'm going home now. Home.' The teashop owner didn't charge him for the electricity. Can bought a plastic bag of sensible food from the store at the gas station and wandered along the dusty, street-lit roadside. *Call the police*, Necdet had said. *These people are terrorists. They have some insane plan.*

Call the police. Go home.

Promise me you won't have any more to do with this, Mr Ferentinou had said. *Terrorist plots don't get solved by old men and boys; they're solved by police, the security forces, with guns. You must promise me this or you can never come here again.*

He broke his promise. Mr Ferentinou would never speak to him again. He can't go home. Call the police then. But would they believe him? They must believe him. It's the truth. But it's full dark now and he hasn't seen another soul since the gas station on this business park arterial and the traffic never stops and the noise is just noise and louder now, closer and more isolating in the night. Can didn't know what to do. Then he saw the construction site behind the security fence, the warnings and the diggers with metal shutters over their cabs to keep out thieves and boys, but most of all the concrete water pipes. No construction site fence can defeat a nine-year-old. The pipes were still warm with the heat of the day, desirable and discreet yet unoccupied by anyone else. No ashes or food packaging or coils of dried human excrement. If the terrorists moved, he could monitor them in privacy. No one would disturb him here. Can snuggled in and opened his backpack.

Now he's eaten all his food and he's getting cold and the concrete is hard and the curvature of the pipe won't let him sit up fully and he can only lie in one direction and the last wolf in all Istanbul is out there or something worse than a wolf, like a tramp or a drunk or a Terrorist and he's paralysed by the enormity of what he has to do.

Call the police!

Shaking with dread, Can switches on the ceptep and hooks it up. Now he's visible to the communications world.

'Police please.'

'Putting you through now.'

'Hello, hello, is that the police in Kayişdaği?'

'This is Kadiköy police station. How can I help you?'

'A friend of mine, he's from Eskiköy, that's over on the European side, he's been kidnapped and they're holding him in the Business Park off Bostancı Dudullu Cadessi.'

A pause. A sigh.

'What's your name son?'

'Can. Can Durukan.'

'And how old are you?'

'I'm nine. He's being held by terrorists, I've seen them, they've got guns.'

'Terrorists, is it?'

'Yes, terrorists, they've got some plan, they're going to make an attack. You'll need to get the army in, this is too big for just the police.'

'Is it now?'

'Yes, they've got assault rifles and bombs and everything.'

'I'll tell you what's not too big for the police and that's sending round a patrol car to give you a good hiding for wasting police time and misuse of a emergency line. It's a serious offence, misuse of an emergency line, and in case you'd forgotten, sonny, we get an automatic fix on your location, so we can go round right away and deal with nine-year-olds who think it's clever to waste police time.'

'Then come round and I'll show you it's all true,' Can shouts but the police officer has disconnected. 'Something terrible is going to happen!' The ceptep stays resolutely silent. Wrong wrong wrong. He did that wrong wrong wrong. He should have said he was a missing person. Mom and Dad will have reported it to the local police. They would have a crew car round to him like a shot. But they would just bundle him into the back and send him home. That's the reason he can't call Osman and Şekure, or even Mr Ferentinou. Home first, questions later. By the time he persuaded anyone – if he persuaded anyone – it might all be too late. The upstairs office might be empty. The van might be filled up with those crates and boxes and driving out through the gates. Necdet – what were they going to do with Necdet? Can hasn't thought of that. No, someone has to stay here. Someone has to keep watch. Someone has to find a way to warn people, beat the Terrorists and save Necdet. And that has to be Can Durukan. It's up to him.

Can hugs Monkey to him. Its heat is niggardly and he doesn't know when he can recharge him next. He's spent into his toe-of-shoe emergency money already: gas station food is so expensive, one hundred euro goes nowhere. It's cold and he is a long way from home and he doesn't know how much longer he can go on making it up as he goes along. How he wishes that wolf would go away.

Gold on black, stars above and the drifting constellations of ships and ferries against jewelled Asia. Across the Golden Horn, the neon of Eminönü and the floodlit pinnacles of the great mosques, crowned by wheeling flocks of seagulls. The taxi pulls off into the blur of lights along Rıhtım Cadessi, Georgios Ferentinou waits on the pavement, evening pedestrians pushing past him, enchanted by the night.

Georgios has never been to this restaurant. Georgios can't remember the last time he was anywhere more grand than Bülent's teashop. His has become the type of life that does not admit restaurants. He regrets that. He used to love going out. But the maps of Istanbul have changed and all his search bots throw up are the four-and-a-half-star pointlessness of customer reviews so he asked Bülent where he would go with his wife if they were to have a wonderful night. Bülent hasn't been to this restaurant either but it's by the water and has a Bosphorus side terrace and the staff in uniform to open taxi doors and take coats and it purrs with glamour. When that night of wonder comes, when the expense ends and there's room for wants over needs; that's where they'll go: the Lale.

'Sir?' The cloakroom boy has stepped out of the golden glow on to the street.

'I have a table reserved. Eight o'clock. Ferentinou.'

The maître d' comes over and touches his ceptep. 'Professor Ferentinou, welcome. You're the first to arrive. Would you like a drink at the bar or shall I take you to your table now, sir?'

A moment of panic. Georgios had booked the Lale and then been vertiginous with fear. Would the clientèle be young and fashionable? Would it be too loud for conversation? Would people stare at his clothes? What narratives would they invent for the old man and the old woman at the Bosphorus side table? Would he know the social conventions? Would the maître d' snark?

'I think I'd like to go to the table now.'

'It's ready for you, sir. Please follow me.'

The maître d' leads Georgios through the restaurant and he is a waddling bulb of a man and he is the oldest person in the room and his clothes are odd and ugly and look uncomfortable on him and the people at the tables are young and glamorous and well dressed and good looking and impossibly articulate and vastly more wealthy but there's a spring in his step and a lift to his chin and a brightness to his eye and a firmness to his intent because he defeated Ogün Saltuk in his own think-tank, in front of Turkey's fashionable minds, defeated him with his own weapons, wrested from his hands those weapons he had stolen from Georgios all those years ago. He defeated his ancient enemy and that makes him as young and strong and smart as anyone in Lale.

The table is beside the water, a railing between him and the Bosphorus. The water smells deep, as it does when the Storm of the Red Plums or autumn's Storm of the Passing Cranes carry its scent up the hill to Eskiköy. Georgios is encircled in light. The candle lantern on his table. The glittering arc of the bridge. A cruise ship a glowing mosaic, moving slowly down the channel from the Black Sea. Aircraft, a helicopter, the navigation beacons of kitesails south in the Marmara. The water catches the lights and shatters them in ripples and glances. Looking down at the cat-tongue ripples, Georgios sees tar-stained polystyrene and an empty bleach bottle. But at every moment some fascinating movement of light seduces his attention. He feels beyond time and age.

'Sir, your guest.'

Georgios stumbles to his feet. He's sky-struck, night-mazed. He's not ready for Ariana. But here she is, stepped out of forty years. He can't look at her. He daren't look at her. Georgios fumbles a bow, then comes out from the safety of the table to kiss her on both cheeks, in the European fashion. She smells of lavender and salt sea and sky.

'Thank you, thank you for coming.'

The maître d' scoops the chair deftly in behind Ariana. He catches Georgios' eye in a glance that says, *I understand, sir, we will make it special, sir.* Now Georgios dares look at her. His last image of Ariana was of her walking off the ferry at Haydarpaşa in another century. He has carried that icon for forty-seven years. He looks and he can no longer remember that face. This is Ariana Sinanidis. Face thinner and lined by idealism become determination. Hair massive and dark and curling, hair he could bury his hands in, now made more dramatic by two streaks of grey framing her face. He had thought her eyes wouldn't change, couldn't change, but they are larger and the light in them more luminous. She carries herself with ease and grace. She is the mother of gods. The skin of her hands bears the minute lozenge-pattern of age, her nails are French-polished. Georgios sees no rings, nor the old imprint of one on the third finger of the left hand.

'This is a wonderful place,' Ariana Sinanidis says in English. 'Forgive me, my Turkish has slipped a bit.' The shawl slides from her shoulders, baring them. A flow of warm air eddies in over the black water. It carries scents of rose and diesel fumes.

'Of course.' Georgios switches languages effortlessly. 'I'm sure you're finding Istanbul much changed.'

'In some ways, I hardly recognize it. In other ways, not so much. The old apartments and old houses are still there. There are still some of the same shops. Some of the names and frontages have changed but they are still selling cigarettes and newspapers. There's still a Lotto cart at Kazancı Mesjid. The fountain at Çukurlu Çeşme Sok still drips. Things look smaller and closer together.'

The sommelier enters the natural gap in the conversation. Drinks are ordered: Georgios water, Ariana a Scotch whisky, a man's drink. She asks the sommelier for a particular brand. The sommelier doesn't have it but suggests a similar distillery. It's acceptable.

'If I may be so bold, what brings you back to the Queen of Cities?' Georgios is fascinated by her fine fingers around the heavy glass. He wonders how he seems to her; does anything remain of the lean, shy, inadvertent revolutionary, or is he just a scarcely recognizable bulb of tired flesh?

'Business. My family still owns a number of properties in Beyoğlu and I'm trying to tie them together into a trust fund.'

'Do you have children?'

A flicker of a shadow. 'No. Mine wasn't that kind of life. But I have grand-nieces and -nephews I'm very fond of and I think they should have something. We're not getting any younger. But I have hopes for them. Did you?'

'No, no. Nothing like that. An academic, bachelor life for me. I live alone. I moved down to Eskiköy about ten years ago when I lost my position at the university – there are almost no Greeks left in Beyoğlu now, and those there are are old and tired like me. I've an apartment in an old dervish house; it's rather lovely in its way. It suits me. I don't need much excitement. There's a neighbour's lad,

I'm very fond of him, he's like a grandson. An only child. He has a health problem. I worry about him, but you can't be too careful, people accuse first and ask questions later these days. Everyone is guilty until proved innocent. But you've been very successful.'

Ariana takes the compliment without self-effacement or affectation.

'I think what you mean is that I manage compromise. Success would be reducing the number of dead children. I'm sorry, that's crass, and arch. I'm doing less fieldwork these days; it's mostly seminars and lectures. What you can't say when you're up there on the podium is that NGOs are the world's worst to work with. They all have their own specialisms, they all have their own agendas, they all hate each other. Give me governments or warlords any time. At least you know where you are with them. Small groups are the natural social organizational level of humans and the hardest to work with. Politics doesn't understand groups.'

The menus arrive. The dishes are sophisticated and sumptuous and illustrate how meagre and monastic Georgios' life has been; if not ever at the level of eating out of a tin with a spoon, content with sparseness and monotony. This is dizzying, he wants everything, he can't choose. Choose he must, choose he does and after the order has been taken Ariana talks more about her work in international peacemaking, It has taken her around the world to different countries all with the same core problem, males killing each other. Ariana's achievements are immense, but Georgios gains the impression that she is no longer certain it was a life well-spent. There can never be an end to violence as long as there are young males.

'I'm afraid I was never very good at caring about other people,' Georgios says. Over the first course there is no talk at all. It would be a dishonour to the chef.

'And on all your travels, did you ever come back to Istanbul?' Georgios asks as the plates are lifted.

'No. Never. Not until I had to. I've been away from Istanbul much longer than I ever lived here. Athens is my home.'

'You are remembered here.'

Ariana scoops up her scarf and pulls it around her.

'I'm not sure I want to be. It makes me feel like a ghost, one that's not dead.'

'Did you go to the old house?' Ariana shakes her head. 'It's long gone, it's been a backpackers' hostel for about twenty years.'

'Good,' she says.

The main courses arrive; lamb for Georgios, fish for Ariana. She orders rakı with the barbounia, which is correct. Georgios has always thought fish too simple, too unrefined for the best restaurants. A thing dead on a plate. His lamb is glorious, full, mouth-rewarding. On what thin fare has he been wasting himself? He wants it to go on forever but the pleasure of food is its finitude so he eats around the lamb, leaving the flesh to the last. The main course is finished, the evening is slipping past like lighted ships and he has not said what he must.

'Did you keep in contact any of the old group?'

The shadow again crosses Ariana Sinanidis' face.

'I didn't dare. I knew they had agents in Athens.'

'That was wise. Do you know what happened to them?'

'I know that Arif Hikmet died five years ago.'

'He refused to take their deal.'

'Inform on others.'

'Yes. And they needed to make an example. When the government changed he was let out but he never got the post at the newspaper back. He went into politics: he formed a minor party on the left that was eventually rolled into the People's Party of Toil and eventually the Turkish Workers Party.'

'Devlet Sezer?'

'Devlet Sezer died ten years back. Cancer. Smoked himself to death. He couldn't get published so he wrote an anonymous column in *Hürriyet* about the hidden history of the city and old Istanbul characters. He became a minor celebrity.'

'Recep Gül?'

'He went to Germany and became an Islamist. Well, as Islamist as anyone gets in Turkey. Guest-worker discrimination was his issue. He worked through the mosque network. He was killed in an arson attack on a hostel in Dresden, the former East Germany. They were very bigoted against Turks in the former East.'

'And Merve Tüzün?'

'She got three months for agitation and when she came out she couldn't get a teaching job. She became a poet. She writes under the name of Tansu. She's well regarded, she has quite a lot in print.'

'Tansu. I think I've heard that name. She always used to read at those sessions in the Karakuş Café. It was dreadful, adolescent stuff.'

'Seemingly she's improved.'

Ariana sits forward now.

'Arif Kezman, what about him?' As she says each name, Georgios sees them in the crowd at the Karakuş Café, slowed by time and remembering, faces impossibly young, hair impossibly full and long, clothes just impossible; slowing with the act of recall until they freeze, each one, mouths open, fists in the air, feet off the ground, arms around each other, jacket flaps flying; or on the picket line at Taksim Square, mouths contorted in a yell, a chant, hands slapping away the muzzles of army rifles; or blinking, posing in the sun, arms around each other like brothers, champagne flutes in hand, against the blue and white of Meryem Tasi's pool. The Revolutionaries of 1980.

'Arif you won't believe. He's a TV presenter.'

'No!' exclaims Ariana Sinanidis, captivated now.

'Oh yes. A huge star. He's old now and pretty much retired. He used to host a show called *Brother Mehmet* where they would put soldiers on national service together with their families. It was incredibly popular.'

'The army?' Ariana shakes her head. The lights of Istanbul are caught in her hair. 'Arif?'

'They still haul him out every year for the New Year show. Made up to the eyeballs, he is. He can hardly move from botox.'

Ariana laughs. She tosses her head back, shows her fine teeth, wrinkles her eyes. It's a young woman's laugh. Then she covers her mouth and kills the laugh as she remembers those lives wrecked on the hard rock of 1980.

'Ariana,' Georgios Ferentinou says, 'there is something you must know, something that has gone unsaid for forty-seven years.'

They came for the Kurds and they came for the Armenians. They came for the Jews. Then they came for the Greeks.

Tobacco smoke, year upon year, had permeated the glossy paint of the room in Üsküdar so deeply that the walls smelled of diseased lung. It was not a smoky, burning smell; it was vile and metallic but clearly human and unclean. It stank of phlegm.

'Do you know Ariana Sinanidis?' the lead inquisitor asked.

'Yes,' Georgios Ferentinou said very simply. 'Yes, I do.'

The third intelligence man, the one who was not making notes, took photographs from a large manilla envelope and laid them out one at a time on the desk. Georgios and Ariana in the front line at Taksim. Georgios and Ariana with a loud-hailer. Georgios and Ariana handing out leaflets. Georgios and Ariana running down Istiklal Cadessi. Georgios and Ariana huddling in a doorway, glancing up at unseasonal rain.

'You are, ah, involved with Miss Sinanidis?' the inquisitor asked.

'I am,' Georgios said. 'We are a couple. I am her ...' he hesitated over the word, ' ... lover.' He saw ballpoint-pen man write carefully, *fucking her?* and circle the question mark twice.

'You're an economist,' the inquisitor said casually, squinting at a sheet in his folder. 'That's a good subject, a useful subject. You can get a good job with a qualification in economics. The big banks give top jobs to economists. Turkey needs economists. The government can use economists.'

'I want to stay in research.'

'Oh, do you now?'

Photograph man opened another envelope. Only one picture this time, a big, grainy blow-up of people standing around a truck at a border post.

'Is your family settling in well in Greece?' the inquisitor said.

'I believe so.'

'Do they not have universities in Athens? Schools of economics or whatever they are?'

'I prefer to stay in Istanbul.'

'For academic reasons?'

'For academic reasons.'

'Not personal reasons. Romantic reasons. Reasons to do with Ariana Sinanidis.'

'I said it was for academic reasons,' Georgios snapped. Ballpoint man tutted loudly.

'That's good,' Interrogator said. 'It's good to have that focus and dedication. Many an academic career starts brightly – even brilliantly, then sex comes along, and it's all scattered to the winds. It would be a shame if that were to happen to you.'

'Are you threatening me?'

'I'm advising you, as your own adviser at the university would. She is very good looking, isn't she?' Interrogator slipped a close-up of Ariana Sinanidis out of Georgios' folder and turned it to each intelligence man in turn. Photograph-man took it and studied it closely. 'In a classical way. A Greek nose. A real looker. We've all been young men, ruled by our cocks, we've all had that blindness, done stupid things, made poor decisions. She's a known trouble-maker and *agente provocateuse*. You've just been easily led – and I don't blame you son; young men, like I said, are ruled by their cocks but they're also ruled by their hearts, and it's a romantic game, politics, protest, revolution. Young men should be idealistic, they should be revolutionaries. Enjoy it before you become old, pragmatic men like us. You have a great future in front of you, lad. You won't be an office grunt like we are. Don't throw it away for a moment of summer madness.'

Georgios looked at his hands resting lightly and symmetrically on his thighs. He looked at the photographs of his small, romantic rebellion. He looked at his family at the check-point, moments before the truck was searched and half their valuables were confiscated. He breathed in the dying-lung odour of the interrogation room.

'Meryem Nasi,' he said.

'Good lad,' the interrogator said.

The security forces raided the Yeniköy house that night. The neighbours had been warned and took themselves discreetly elsewhere. The riot troops smashed in the front door with a small battering ram. Others went over the wall and across the terrace, past the pool, kicking over the drinks trolleys and upsetting the patio seats. They stormed across the white carpets and past the grand piano and the sculptures and the paintings. They found Meryem Nasi in her kitchen with an open bottle of wine in one hand and a telephone in the other. She went properly and politely, without screaming or violence, though she did shout 'get Ossian' to her friend Elif Mater visiting from Madrid. 'He's my lawyer.'

She turned up three days later in a dumpster at the new Metro station at Yesilyurt. Formal identification could only be made through dental records.

'I gave Meryem Nasi's name to the police,' Georgios says. Ship lights shift behind him. 'They killed her. They had me in a room, all day. They lifted me from the university and took me to a room in Üsküdar and I told them everything. I couldn't stop. When you're somewhere like that, when you realize they have you and can do anything they want with you, you tell them anything they ask. They asked about you. They seemed to think that you were high up in the protest movement. I told them Meryem Nasi was the main organizer of the protests, that she was running a left-wing cell, that she knew everyone. They arrested her. I didn't think they would kill her. That was when I had to get you out of Istanbul. I gave them her name. You know that, everyone knows that, everyone's known that for forty-seven years. Georgios Ferentinou betrayed Meryem Nasi to the security police who killed her. Forty-seven years a Judas, I've learned to live with that. But what no one knows, what I've never told anyone, is that I gave them Meryem Nasi's name to keep you safe.'

Ariana says, 'I know.'

Georgios doesn't hear her, or if he does, he doesn't register what she has said, he is about to work out more of his long expiation, then he trips over those two words.

'What?' Sometimes you remember that that view from your window, that chink of vista, is of another continent. Sometimes the seasonal winds remind you that that stripe of water that runs through the heart of your city is the unbounded sea. Sometimes you discover that those palisades of clouds along the horizon are mountains.

'I know. I've known for years. Oh, I never had proof, no one ever spoke, everyone who was involved in 1980 knew what talking could do. In those first few weeks in Athens, it was mad then, I was mad then, and I did blame you for Meryem's death. I hated you, I hated what you'd done. I hated that I'd loved you and you had betrayed that. I think what I hated was what had happened to Turkey, to Istanbul, to the world I had known; and knowing I could never go back.'

'Did you?'

'What?'

'Love me?'

'Georgios, we were twenty-one years old, we were wild, we were dazzled, it was a long hot summer, we knew nothing. We were kids. Thinking that a few placards and leaflets and some poetry in a café would blow the generals away like chaff. We were not serious people. The police, the army, the generals, they were serious people. We had no chance. That was when I realized what you must have done. And then I felt guilty, for so many years, that I had lived because Meryem had died, and that you'd been forced to make that choice.'

Georgios' heart is hammering. His hands shake, yet the the world seems suspended around him, lights hanging like mosque lanterns, wheels upon wheels of light. The foundations on which his life has stood for forty-seven years are swept away. What has been, what could have been, are churned up together. The life he led, the life he imagined and then put away, folded neat as an unused wedding suit; those years, those years.

'A word would have been enough. A letter, an email, even a call. Just a word. I thought the reason you never came back was because of me.'

'No, oh no, not you, never you,' Ariana says. She reaches across the table to clasp Georgios' hands in hers.

'Do you think . . .'

'Don't think. Don't ask. That will kill you. We have the lives we have and that's all we can know. We have those lives because of what you had to do. We were young and thought we were invincible and and we threw ourselves into the gears of history and it ground us up. But don't ever regret. For a few moments we were the most brilliant stars in the sky.'

Ariana Sinanidis suddenly shivers.

'Oh, a chill breeze there.'

'Thank God,' Georgios says. 'Çarkdönümü Fırtanası.'

'The Storm of the Turning Windmills,' Ariana says and pulls her scarf around her bare shoulders.

Friday

9

This morning Adem Dede Square is blessed. The air is clear and cool and smells fresh as a loaf or a morning newspaper. Every sound is crystalline, distinct; the Istanbul drone opens up into layers and lines and levels. The rumble of traffic, the conversation of radios. Footsteps on staircases. A voice shouting for someone to get a move on. A car engine suddenly bursts into life then settles into a tick-over. The hiss of the gas burners in the rival çayhanes, the moil of boiling kettles. Aydin turning the crisp pages of the morning daily at his stand. The drip of water into the fountain's scalloped basin. The old dervish house clicks and creaks as its timbers expand in the sun. Birds; sparrows shrieking and dipping low through the alleys and soks. High over all a blackbird flings his song over the rooftops toward the Golden Horn.

Father Ioannis looks up; the storks still glide over the ragged quadrilateral of sky above Adem Dede Square, sliding down to their ancient nesting grounds among the grave pillars of ancient Eyup. The Christ of the Immanent. The sacrament of silence is the sacrament of hearing.

'God save all here,' he greets the Greeks of Eskiköy around their little table. 'That is a much more seasonable day.' He sits heavily down on his low stool. Lefteres does not return his greeting. He sits hunched on his stool, shoulders up, head down, a sick vulture of a man. His face is yellow, his eyes bulging. His left hand covers a laminated A4 sheet. The edge of the sheet is worked with a pretty floral design and there is a hole from a thumb-tack at the top. 'What's with our friend?'

'They made him take it down,' Bülent calls from the kitchen, pouring Father Ioannis his tea.

'Who, what?' the priest asks.

'Those tarikat boys,' Constantin says. 'From over there.' He nods across the square to the shadowed mouth of Güneşli Sok.

'The Hasgüler kid?' Father Ioannis stirs his tea. The sugar crystals whirl briefly before dissolving. 'The so-called Shaykh Ismet?'

'The so-called Shaykh Ismet has a lot of friends,' Bülent says. 'They faced down some hood trying to muscle his way into the square.'

'It was insulting, irreligious and inappropriate.' Lefteres speaks now. 'It was disrespectful of women. Disrespectful of women! Those Wahhabis! In future all matters of community policing must be referred to the tarikat of Adem Dede. The tarikat of Adem Dede? Car mechanics and house painters and ignorant little gecekondu gobshites who never got a day's education past medrese. Street judges? Street law? When you were born on this street, when you live in this street, when you've worked there for fifty years, when you've seen and remember all the changes that have happened to this street and city, when you know the name on every door in every house, when you sit and take tea on this street every morning in life; then, *then, maybe* you can presume to talk to me about street law. They're not from here, they don't understand how it works. It's not kadıs and community courts and street shariat. It's knowing someone here, having a word there. This is still a shame society. Shame works. Not "street law." Street law? I am the fucking street law, your pardon, Father.'

But everyone at the low brass table knows that Lefteres' power is broken. He has been challenged and beaten. The time of the lampoon is over. This is the age of divine law.

'They have guns now,' Bülent says darkly. He pulls up an empty stool. 'A lot's happened since yesterday morning, Father. The police have closed down the Art Gallery.'

'Ms Erkoç's?'

'They arrested her. Seems she was knee deep in smuggling. They raided it yesterday morning just after you left, took away boxloads of stuff, sealed the place up. Then, just as suddenly, they unsealed it and brought it all back and it seems she's in the clear.'

'How does that happen?' Father Ioannis asks.

'Gas trader husband,' Constantin interjects. 'Works for Özer. There's more to this story.'

Bülent leans low over the table to draw in his audience.

'Then the girl who lives in apartment two, you know, the one sometimes wears the short shorts, she has this run-in with some gangster, just there down Güneşli Sok. That Ismet and his mosque mates turn out, there's a showdown and we find out they've armed themselves.'

'God and his mother have mercy on us,' Father Ioannis says and every Greek at the table crosses himself.

'It's on the back of that they take the lampoon down.'

'I'm not drinking in this teashop again,' Lefteres declares. 'This is not a safe place for Greeks.'

'Tell him about the kid,' Constantin says quickly but Lefteres has spoken everyone's fear.

'Necdet Hasgüler isn't the only one who's gone missing,' Bülent says. 'The boy who lives in apartment five.'

'The deaf one?' Father Ioannis asks.

'He's not deaf,' Bülent says and Lefteres, Constantin and even Father Ioannis chorus, *he's got a heart condition*. 'It seems he went off to afternoon school same as usual. Except,' (and here Bülent leans forward to draw the old Greeks into conspiracy) 'he never made it back. His mother goes to pick him up, she waits, she waits some more, she waits a long time. Finally she goes into the school. Sure doesn't it turn up that the boy never made it in at all? He's gone. Disappeared. His ceptep's off, there's no way of tracking him. Şekure Hanım is distraught, what with his condition and everything. Remember: any sudden loud noise, and the electrical patterns in his heart go berserk. An engine backfiring, builders dropping stuff into a dumpster; those could kill him. Of course they call the police. That's the third time this week they've been round here.'

'There go the property prices,' Constantin grumbles.

'Now, the police are playing it down, being discreet, just in case the lad hasn't wandered off or met with an accident, God between him and evil.'

'God and his Mother.' Father Ioannis kisses his cross.

'If anything's happened to the kid, those Islamists will blame us,' Lefteres says.

'It turns out there's someone may know where the Durukan kid is,' Bülent says. 'Our very own Professor Ferentinou. Do you remember all that stuff we were talking about? Robots and gas terrorism and people who see djinn and that tram bombing back on Monday. Georgios thinks it's all connected, and he let the kid in on his theories. Filled his head with all kinds of nonsense. And now the boy's decided to go and play detective.'

'How old is the boy?' Father Ioannis asks.

'Nine.'

'Well, the police will have it in hand now, thanks be to God,' the priest says.

Bülent grimaces.

'It's not quite so simple. You see, this is breaking news. On the ticker. Georgios only found out this morning that Can was gone – you know how close he is to the boy.'

'Too close,' Lefteres growls.

'I'm confused here,' Father Ioannis says. 'Georgios always makes it his business to know everything that goes on here. He always says that it's like his map of the universe. How could he not have seen police arriving?'

'He wasn't here, was he?' Bülent says. The Father frowns, puzzled.

'Ariana,' Constantin whispers. Father Ioannis' wild grey eyebrows raise.

'He's over with Şekure Hanım now,' Bülent says. 'They're going to go and find him. The father's talking to the cops.'

'What do they think they can do?' Father Ioannis opines. 'These things are best left to the police.'

'If you had a child, you'd go,' Bülent says. 'Whatever the police tell you.'

Father Ioannis touches his brow. 'Thank God and his Mother, the kid's all right.'

'I didn't say he was all right,' Bülent says. 'I said he had an idea where he is.'

'Where is he?'

'Over on the Asian half. In the same place as the people who lifted Necdet Hasgüler. He said something about a terror plot?'

Lefteres looks up, startled from his impotent old-man anger.

'What now?'

A man is striding across Adem Dede Square. He's young, short, hair prematurely receding, a heart-shaped face and a small moustache, all of which make him look older than his years and lend him a comic air, as if he is aware that the world is his audience. No one knows who he is but it's clear from his stride that he knows what he wants. He wants the Greeks of Adem Dede Square.

'Does anyone here know Necdet Hasgüler?'

Bülent gets up from his seat slowly.

'Who wants to know?'

'My name is Mustafa Bağli. I work with Necdet. At the Levent Business Rescue Centre. He didn't turn up at work yesterday, and again today. I'm worried something bad may have happened to him.'

The four men at the table trade glances.

'Something bad did happen,' Bülent says carefully. 'On Wednesday night he was abducted.'

This Mustafa's eyes widen. 'Was it the police?'

'Why do you ask?' Bülent says.

'Because I saw the police take away one of the other ones.' Excitement blurs his words.

'The other ones?' Lefteres asks.

'The other ones who'd been caught by the tram bombing. The Peri Lady of Ereğli. Necdet sees djinn, she sees peri and fairies and wee folk. We went to see her and the police raided the place. Took her away. I think Necdet may be in great danger.'

'Necdet is in very great danger,' Lefteres says. His mood has brightened, like the Storm of Mother Mary clearing the bruise-dark skies of autumn. He has a purpose again. 'It wasn't police lifted Necdet.' He jerks his head at a disturbance across the square where a little silvery gas-powered three-wheeler trundles from its garage on to cobbled Vermilion-Maker Lane. 'There's the man you want. Quick, catch him. Tell him what you told me. Before they get away!'

Mustafa salutes his thanks to the teashop men, sprints across the square, shouting and waving at the slow-moving citicar, low on its suspension, unaccustomed to Georgios Ferentinou's weight. He runs up beside it, raps the glass. The car stops. The customers of the Adem Dede çayhane watch the discussion through the open window. Mustafa clambers in. The car sags lower as it resumes its journey down steep and cobbly Vermilion-Maker Lane.

'So, let me see if I've got this right: a mum, a retired professor and someone from a business rescue centre are taking on terrorists,' Father Ioannis says. 'I only hope the police stop them before they do any serious harm to themselves. What is a business rescue centre anyway?'

'Never mind that,' Constantin rasps. 'I want to know what went on at his meeting with Ariana Sinanidis.'

Father Ioannis fingers knots in his prayer rope, slipping them through, one by one. Blessings by their nature are fleeting. Only God is eternal, and Istanbul.

They're coming.

Necdet wakes. Grey dawn light fills the upper room. He is alone but from his position on the mattress he can see feet in the next room. He counts four pairs of shoes moving in and out of the room, up and down the stairs. Voices: Green Headscarf; orders from the tone of her voice. He can't make out any words but they all seem to agree on something.

Now. Prepare yourself.

Big Bastard enters the room and in one movement grabs Necdet by the collar of his T-shirt and hauls him to his feet. But Necdet has obeyed the voice of Hızır. He is awake and aware. He is focused.

Clench your fists. Thumbs out.

Big Bastard whips cable tie around Necdet's wrists and pulls the zip plastic tight, pinning Necdet's arms behind his back. Big Bastard hooks into Necdet's left arm, Big Hair the right. Necdet digs in his heels, goes limp at the knees, struggles and twists as they wrestle him out of the back room to the stairs.

'Where are you taking me? Oh God no! Don't kill me, don't kill me!'

Surly Fucker clatters down the stairs behind the three struggling men. Necdet feels a ring of cold metal pressed under the base of his skull.

'Not a whisper or I will blow your head right off your neck.'

The white van has been backed up to the front of the building so that the open doors will screen the abduction from any early Kayişdaği traffic but the lift is so fast, so smooth that Necdet is in the back, the doors closed and the van driving out the gates without even a single truck-gardener's delivery pick-up noticing.

Green Headscarf and Big Hair drive. Necdet is seated on the floor between Surly Fucker and Big Bastard. With his hands bound behind his back, Necdet's balance is thrown. He can count the turns by the number of times he veers left into Big Bastard's legs, right into Surly Fucker's. His back is pressed against a pile of equipment, the styrofoam cases, plastic tidy boxes and cartons he saw in the upstairs room.

'Where are you taking me?'

'To glory, Necdet.'

You will not be killed. They need a potential hostage.

It's dark in the back of the van, the overhead bulb burned out. Needles of laser-light beam through holes in the bodywork, cracks in the floor. Planes of illumination stream into the van body around the door but, above the top lock, does Necdet see a flicker of green?

Now relax your hands.

Necdet pushes himself back against the equipment to mask any movement. His fists are aching, the blood throbbing in his fingers. He lets go, he folds in his thumbs. The binding relaxes, there's a gap. Necdet pulls. It hurts, it cuts but he can feel the plastic start to slip over the balls of his thumbs.

This is the mission. This is the day. They're going to do it. Where are the police, why didn't the kid get the police? Maybe the kid did. Maybe they're keeping a low profile, waiting until they're out in the open, in position before they make their move. Maybe they want to see if there's a second, back-up group in case the first is captured. Whichever way, he's in the middle of a holy war. *Hızır*, you've never failed me yet; help from beyond comprehension, help me now.

The van bounces to a jarring stop. The light as the doors bang open is painful. Necdet tests his ties. They will give. They will tear his hands to shreds but they will give and he will be free. To do it now would be a leap into blind white light. He wouldn't make it more than three metres. Hızır will tell him. His God-sense will know the best time. Big Bastard is almost gentle as he helps Necdet down from the van.

They're parked outside a basket-ball-court sized industrial station, a rectangle of fat yellow pipes and bright blue valves and big metal wheels wrapped around a mass of white machinery, all housed under a corrugated aluminium roof. At one end of the installation stand three vertical cylinders, each the height of three people. Piped in and piped out, they look like monstrous village water pumps. The site is defended by a chain-link fence with a razor wire overhang to deter climbing boys and is tucked incongruously away behind a small rundown shopping complex, overlooked by a new-build housing project. Wire, pumps, gate are all generously tagged with Özer Pipelines' logo.

The gate is dealt with so quickly the trespassers almost seem to walk through it. A pass with a doorcode cracker, a squirt of lock-burn nano and they are in. Big Hair reverses the van as Big Bastard hustles Necdet out of sight from the housing units. Surly Fucker closes the gate. The assault of God's Engineers on Kayişdaği Compression Station has begun.

Cold hurts, Can realizes. Cold makes his fingers feel like they will snap. Cold turns his feet to steel hooves. Cold locks every bone and muscle. Cold is in every cell of his body. Can is shivering and he can't stop. He can't move. He has to move. The alert has sounded. Rat Baby is moving.

The cold came in the night. It swept in from the east over Kayişdaği and came into the pipe with him and woke him up. It would not let him sleep again. For hours Can has sat in his pipe, coat pulled around him, eking out the warmth of the BitBots. He had always thought it would be thrilling to stay up all night, like the day they took his hearing away and Turkey joined the EU and he sat up late late to watch the silent fireworks and the painted man fall from the front of the Adem Dede teahouse. Staying up all night is hard and boring and endless and cold cold cold. No one is ever cold in adventures. In adventures, no one ever tells you that cold is much more dangerous than jackals or city dogs or the last wolf in Istanbul. A Boy Detective can freeze and only be found when the construction crews' crane lifts the concrete pipe.

That concrete is so cold it burns. But the alert has sounded, the alert has sounded. Can forces limbs into motion, painfully unfolds fingers, shuffles lifeless stone feet forward. Is this what it is like to be old, like Mr Ferentinou? It's a dreadful thing. He emerges from the pipe into the light. The sun is still under the horizon, the air is grey and pitilessly cold. Can blows into his fingers. Work work work. He opens the computer. Slow slow slow to boot up. Can cries in frustration as his fingers trip, numb and stupid, over the keys, blunder through the haptic field. He is almost weeping by the time he manages to open the command application. He overlays the map. Necdet is close. The van is on the highway. Here is the construction site, there is the road: Can hobbles out of the jumble of pipes to watch the white van speed past in the early commute. North-east. Kayişdaği Compression Station, just as he thought. He reconfigures the BitBots. They're low on power. He'll need a charge point soon, or failing that, somewhere he can buy a couple of gas canisters for the catalytic charger.

Better now. Out on the highway he can at least soak up a little sun. On the highway he has a direction and a purpose. The heat is slow to penetrate the core of cold inside him but the sun gains in strength every minute. He tries to take his mind off the pain and the hunger by imagining how it would be if people were like flowers and could live from the sun. You would never be cold. You would never be hungry either. Plants are never hungry. The nights would be terrible. People would dread the night even more than they do now. They would fill it with much worse things than ghost wolves of Istanbul. Cold demons, ice horrors; that might be terrifying enough.

This is a long road without any shops and the traffic is heavy and constant. He wonders what they think of a boy with a pack and a bird on his shoulder, striding along the dusty verge in the early light. Do they even notice? Osman hardly notices anything when he heads to work in the morning. There is a tea and news stand at the corner where Bostancı Dudullu Cadessi crosses Kayişdaği Cadessi. Can doesn't like tea but he buys a glass. The tulip-shaped glass is like a drop of molten gold in his fingers. He can hardly stand the pain but he sips and feels warmth shine through him. A second glass and the cold is gone from everything but the tips of his fingers, toes and nose and the sun is up and hard and bright. With the last of his folding money he buys three gas canisters for the emergency charger. He squats around the back of the stall on the kerb and checks the laptop while Bird recharges from the catalyser. The van has stopped moving. It's right on top of Kayişdaği Compression Station. Can tries to click his fingers in delight, winces with the pain and awkwardness. But the Boy Detective is back.

It's a long trot up Kayişdaği Cadessi but by the end of it Can has everything planned. It is a very good plan. He is so clever. The compression station is tucked away in the middle of a built-up area. The map shows him that there aren't any useful çayhanes where he can sit all day and survey the gas plant. There is an arcade of shops at the end of the alley and a gas station with a 24/7 and a little traveller's chapel across the road. Boys are always hanging around gas stations and 24/7s and he can sit in the entrance to the mescid and no one will know he is there. Then he will send Bird over to scan the area. If they haven't brought the Samsung nightwatchman robots, he will use Bird. If they have, it will be Rat or Snake. Either way, he will shoot footage, lots of footage. When he called the police last night they didn't believe what they heard. Maybe they will believe what they see. Oh, it is a brilliant plan. He's even starting to feel warm.

Şekure Durukan goes down on her knees before the concrete pipe and picks up the applecore, the empty water bottle, the gözleme wrapper. She lifts them up in her two hands as if praying. Then she begins to wail; deeply, inconsolably, the shrieking of a woman at the funeral of her mother. Pipeline workers look up from the morning tea, distressed.

'This is where the call came from,' the police sergeant says.

'And you didn't act on it?' Georgios Ferentinou asks.

'If we acted on every call we got from a nine-year-old kid, we wouldn't do anything else,' the sergeant says.

'You didn't think it odd that a nine-year-old was calling from a construction site after dark?'

'We didn't check the location until the Beyoğlu police told us a child was missing, probably in Kayişdaği.'

As soon as the car had turned out of Vermilion-Maker Lane Şekure Durukan switched to autodrive and called Beyoğlu police. *Theory about the missing boy. Kayişdaği. Trying to be a detective. Finding some man who was supposedly kidnapped from Eskiköy.*

*Kayişdaği, in Kadiköy. Has some notion there's a terror plot. Yeah kids.
Going over there now.*

Then she turned on Georgios Ferentinou.

'You put him up to this.'

'I told him expressly not to go off on his own. I forbade it
absolutely. I told him that he was not to get involved, that this was
dangerous and a matter for the police.'

'Forbade him absolutely, did you? Do you know anything about
nine-year-old boys? Forbade it absolutely. What city are you living
in? And all this disappearance, mystery, conspiracy stuff, did you tell
me? Did you think to tell me? It's only my son after all. Did you ever
think that maybe his mother should know about all these theories
and conspiracies you were cooking up down in your apartment.
Who said he could go to your apartment anyway? My God, he
was in your apartment. He's nine years old! Oh my God. How
often did he go? Did he ever take out his earplugs? Did he? Did
you not know that could kill him, or did you just not care?
Sneaking around behind my back. The lies, oh the lies, the bare-
faced lies, after all we did for him. You told him it was dangerous.
You might as well have thrown petrol on a fire. How long has he
been coming down to see you?'

'About a year and a half. Ever since he got those ...'

'Those things, God I wish I'd never set eyes on the bloody things.
As soon as he gets back home, well that's the last he's seen of those
things, I'm telling you.'

'Mrs Durukan, your son is a highly intelligent, highly creative,
highly energetic boy who's been forced into an unnatural ...'

'Unnatural? Of course it's unnatural. Do you think we want this
for him? Do you think we want to keep him cooped up in the house,
afraid in case a random noise stops his heart beating? It's all for him,
you know. We could have been somewhere bigger, better by now.
But I don't begrudge it. Don't you ever think that about my Can.
I love him. Mr Ferentinou. I love him.'

'Guys,' Mustafa interrupts from the back seat, 'I don't know if you've noticed, but I can see your ceptep and the Beyoğlu police have been calling for about three minutes.'

That call had taken them to this construction site off Bostancı Dudullu Cadessi and an applecore, an empty water bottle and wrapper from a sandwich.

Why did I not defend myself? Georgios Ferentinou asks himself. *Because you are right, Mrs Durukan. I have done wrong. Everything you have accused me of is true. I could have told you from the moment I trapped the BitBot under my tea glass and the boy came knocking on my door; I didn't. Because I didn't want to share it with you. I wanted him for myself. I wanted a son. I wanted a tiny family of my own. You wouldn't have let me have that, and now you never will.*

Şekure Durukan cries unashamedly at the discarded trash and Georgios knows it is a thing he will never and can never do.

Mustafa has been asking around the area. Georgios thinks him a strange cove; worldly-wise with a fool's knowledge but wide-eyed to the wonders of the world. He cares about Necdet very much. Georgios finds it touching.

'A couple of people say they remember a kid with a bird on his shoulder?'

Şekure Durukan composes herself, dries her face with a moist wipe.

'That would be one of the forms his toy robots take. Bird, he calls it.'

'Bird, hm, very original. It seems this bird-kid was heading up the road, north-east.'

'Kayişdaği,' Georgios says.

The sergeant has been taking a call on his police ceptep. He looks up at the word.

'Kayişdaği?'

'Kayişdaği Gas Compression Station.'

'The station got another call from your son. He's at Kayişdaği shopping precinct. We're the nearest car. Come on.'

Şekure Durukan follows the police cruiser as if she is driving the

Istanbul Otodrom. She pulls in at the five moribund shops that call themselves Kayişdaği Shopping Precinct. She runs into the street, waving her arms, signing frantically.

Georgios and Mustafa cross the road to the gas station.

'Can! Are you there? Can!'

'The boy's functionally deaf, Mr Bağli.'

But he's not. Can never has been deaf. *Did he ever take out his earplugs?* Mrs Durukan had said in her torrent of fearful accusations. He's a boy on a great adventure. Of course he will have taken them out.

'Can!' Georgios calls. His voice is not made for shouting, it cracks and wavers. 'Can!'

Mustafa stops, shakes his head, as if troubled by an itch. Then Georgios hears it too, an all-pervasive, insect hum, like a billion filigree wings.

'Whoa!' Mustafa exclaims. Georgios follows his eyes up. The air above the gas station warps and moils, shimmering like heat haze, then in the flick of an eye coalesces into a dust storm of swarmbots.

At oh eight thirty-three on April 16th 2027 black vans of the Financial Regulatory Authority arrive in the Levent Plaza as the Kebab Prophet is opening up his stand. Men and women in suits and yellow hi-viz tabards with *Maliye Bakanlığı* and the symbol of the Turkish Ministry of Finance between their shoulders spring from the backs of the vans and push their way, politely but authoritatively, through the throng of early-starters blearing in to the day's work. They march into the headquarters of Özer Gas and Commodities, brush past security with a wave of an authorization and head for the elevators, reading maps of the building off their eyewriters. At every level, in every division, they fan out through the open plan offices, author-izations held high. Most here this early are cleaners; the few workers early to their pods stand up, crane to see the snaking lines of black and yellow. Some phone out only to be cut off in mid-call. The ceptep network has shut down.

Simultaneous with the attack of the black vans, Artificial Intelligences of the Financial Regulatory Authority assault Özer's information structure. All outgoing electronic communication is shut down; email, messaging, conferencing, online accounting, ebanking, automated trading links. Screen by screen, the brilliant leaves of the Money Tree go dark. Reinforced by quantum mainframes in Ankara, the AIs effortlessly crack the passwords to Özer's communication network and try to shut down all external and internal telecoms. Here they first encounter resistance; a picket of trip-wire AIs summon antibody-ware that attempts to reprogramme the attackers' operating code. Billions of copies are corrupted and erased. The AI war lasts thirty seconds before the Maliye Bakanlığı breaks the defence. That's long enough for Özer suicide-AIs to put out a general Mayday to all managerial levels.

Oh eight fifty. The Özer Tower is isolated, cut off from the financial world, a solitary spike of glass and steel, a pulled tooth. The Financial Regulatory Authority agents move through the building, sealing filing cabinets and isolating servers. Özer is being closed down. Now the paralysis is broken and the few Özer managers in the building remember the official end-game strategy of dead and shred. In glassed-in cubicles and corner offices, senior staff take EMP memory-killers to drives and cepteps, crush flash memories beneath heels or pour vials of nano through computer ventilation slits. Özer's forty floors hum with the now-shrill, now-labouring shriek of shredders, like a rainforest being felled at once. Dead and shred. There's a business legend that shredded paper is outsourced to be sorted and reassembled by African children. Up and down the Özer Tower windows open their permitted crack and shed a ticker-tape storm of shredded documents, twisting and tangling on the wind. Paper shreds snow down on the workers in the Plaza, baffled at the police lines now barricading the entrance to the building. A man with his jacket tries to run the cordon; the police lift him off his feet and throw him down hard on the marble steps.

Oh nine hundred. Four men in suits carrying briefcases walk down

Istiklal Cadessi and enter the Muhtar Branch of the Anadolu Bank. Staff are still preparing their work spaces as the men make their way to the enquiries desk. The woman on the desk calls the manager, who takes the men one at a time through the security door to an office at the back of the bank. She takes their iris scans and two signatures, one on an authorization, one on an indemnity and in return gives each one a plastic wallet containing fifty hundred-thousand-euro bearer bonds. There is another signature here, on a receipt. Then she solemnly shakes hands. The men came together, they leave separately, each steering his own way across Istanbul.

Oh nine twenty. Senior management arrive at the same time as the press. Flittercams are first on the scene, swooping over the Levent Plaza, spiralling up around the tower in the hope of a shot of an FRA agent hauling a manager away from a shredder or a computer, diving down for an action cut of the massive titanium Ö of the Özer logo in Levent Plaza, the umlauts kept hovering over it by a clever trick of magnetism, before themselves hovering and darting to steal snapshots of the faces and match them to the image database of Özer executives. By the time the satellite vans with the journalists arrive the FRA agents have begun porting out servers and boxes of documents on trolleys. Already the leadlines for the lunchtime bulletins are written. Özer collapses in Turkey's biggest corporate fraud. Bankruptcy of the Century. Over for Özer. Police escort a steady stream of junior managers and early-shifters from the building. The workers ranked outside cheer them raggedly. The cleaners receive special applause. They punch their fists in the air. The line for the Kebab Prophet's stall reaches across the Plaza and down the boulevard. He calculates the sales and calls his nephew and niece to run out to the cash and carry. The news reporters have begun to interview the workers. Özer, bankrupt? No, they knew nothing. There was no sign. How has this happened? Özer was a great little company. What will they do now? When are the police going to let them in, they have family photographs in the desk drawer. Where are Süleyman Pamir and Etyan Ercan and Mehmet Meral?

In the Bebek apartment, in the Kanlıca yalı, in the Mercedes pulled over at the service station on the E80 expressway, Süleyman Pamir and Etyan Ercan and Mehmet Meral each take a vial from a plastic case. They snap off the seal. Each hesitates a moment before inserting the nozzle into the preferred nostril, but only a moment. It's not death. The greyware designer promised that. But it is not-being, of a kind. Each inhales and then settles back into his chair or sofa or car seat with a shuddering sigh and images and sounds and smells, the memories of lives they never lived, experiences they never knew, fountain up through their forebrains and they forget who they were.

Oh nine forty-five. Maliye Bakanlığı completes its control of Özer Gas and Commodities. Extra- and intra-nets are shut down, codes and passwords are in the hands of FRA investigators, online banking, trading, ecommerce, supply and logistics are closed down. Artificial Intelligences are stood down and deactivated one by one as FRA audit AIs follow the scent of money; moving out from the Levent tower to subsidiaries, clients and service providers. Automated legal systems generate injunctions against Özbek Consulting, Özer's auditors, SarayTRC Bank and the Nabucco Pipeline Corporation. Across Anatolia compression stations fall silent as the pumps stop. The Money Tree hangs black and dead in the middle of the trading pit. Line managers gather their sections group by group across the Plaza and shout instructions to go home, come back tomorrow for further information and to empty desks and collect personal effects. Özer Gas and Commodities has ceased trading. The last of the paper snow spirals down to Levent Plaza. The Kebab Prophet has never seen such takings.

Oh nine fifty. Adnan Sarioğlu walks down Istiklal Cadessi, down through the filling streets, weaving between the electric drays and the clusters of women and the little white vans delivering fish to the market of Balık Sok. His step is bold and light. He feels as if his next footfall could carry him off the world completely. He is dizzy with the vertigo of daring. He did it. He has four million

in convertible bearer bonds in his briefcase and a signed immunity
from the Financial Regulatory Authority's chief prosecutor in the
left inside pocket of his jacket. In his right, a matching document
from Haydar Akgün of the Art and Antiquities Division. He
destroyed Özer in the corporate fall of the century. His feet can
take him anywhere. For the first time in long memory there is
nowhere he has to be, nothing he has to do. The tourist tram
clanges past to the terminus at Tünel; a crawling, grating, gloriously
impractical fancy. He can just see the top of Galata Tower over
the high nineteenth-century frontages, and now the first glimpse
of the Golden Horn and it is the deepest, bluest thing he has
ever seen. Boats skip and chug across the water and it seems new
and fresh, like when he came off the bus from Kaş, the beach-
boy afraid of the water. Adnan's heart leaps; on Yüksek Kaldırım
Cadessi he breaks into a trot. He feels a million kilometres tall,
capable of covering all the seven heavens in a single stride. There
is the Galata Bridge, lined with fishermen, trams cruising the
centre strip and on the far side of it the domes and minarets of
Sultanahmet. He's running now, dodging the traffic, which slams
to an auto-brake halt, horns blaring, sending waves of disruption
up and down the busy boulevards, cutting in front of trams
swinging up from Müeyettzade, on to the bridge, running past
the fishermen with plastic bottles of secret bait and tool boxes of
hooks and lures and buckets of tiny Golden Horn fish.

Meet me on the bridge, he had said. Over the open water. And there
she is, in the middle of the wide pavement away from the rods
and casts of the fishermen; frowning slightly but elegant, strong,
magnificent, her hair a pyramid of black curls; looking the wrong
way but then she sees him and he waves his arms like a mad penguin,
a penguin in a suit and now he's not a flightless bird, he's a plane
coming in to land, like the big white Airbus turning over the water
on the approach to Istanbul; he holds his arms back like wings and
runs crazy now so that the pedestrians step back and call out, watch
out for the mad man in the suit. Ayşe smiles, grins, tosses her head

back and shakes her black curling hair and there they meet, over the water, in the middle of the Galata Bridge.

Necdet first sees the bird as God's Engineers unpack the truck. It swoops down from a high balcony on an apartment block that stands hard against the compression station's perimeter wire. The peculiarity of its flight draws his attention. It is ugly and mechanical, badly timed and uncanny, like a badly animated pterodactyl he once saw in a movie. The proportions are wrong, the wings are too long, no bird's ever had a tail like that. The head. The head ... It turns six eyes on Necdet as it glides past, then up over the roof of the pumping station.

The engineers, laying the equipment from the back of the truck in precision rows, do not see the bird. Now that it is all in order and its proper place Necdet notices that there are four of everything. Four cardboard cartons, four plastic crates, four styrene impact cages.

The cardboard cartons contain devices Necdet cannot identify, a hybrid of domestic cleaning spray and boxing glove. One each, worn over the hand. Weapons of some kind. They take large cartridges as ammunition, six to a magazine. One magazine each. Big Hair and Big Bastard both try theirs for fit and heft. They practise aiming. They seem pleased, slapping the devices into the palms of their hand. Good. Good.

The bird swoops again, from the shops to the new housing unit. Again it looks at him. Necdet knows what it is now. *Help me*, he mouths.

From the plastic crates the team take what appear to Necdet to be necklaces. They fasten them around each other's throats with much care and great devotion. There are tears in Green Headscarf's eyes as Big Hair clicks the fastening around her neck. They are very tight necklaces. Choking tight. Each has a jewel in the centre. Necdet remembers where he saw this jewel before. It shone from the throat of the woman on the tram. She reached up and touched it and blew her head off. She was Green Headscarf's sister. From what Green

Headscarf said, Necdet thinks that she must have had a terminal disease of some kind. These people don't have terminal diseases and the death necklace was not a suicide device. Suicide was incidental. They are devices for explosively delivering nanoagents. God's Engineers will not be taken. Necdet tugs again at the cable ties. Lubricated by fear sweat, the balls of his thumbs slip a little further through the loop. Big Bastard casts an eye over at Necdet. He stands meekly, back to a concrete roof pillar.

A third time the alien bird robot takes flight. It's low, very low, dangerously low; pull up, fly right boy. It skims the razor barricade, moments later Necdet hears a click on the roof.

Now the styrene shells. Big Hair attends to these. He cuts binding tape and unwinds bubble wrap. Nestling inside each is a brushed aluminium cylinder the length of Necdet's forearm. These are the nano warheads. Four of them. Four warheads. Four pumps.

Necdet hears movement on the roof, like the slither of a scaled creature. He doesn't worry now that Big Bastard or Surly Fucker will hear. This is divine hearing, Hızır manifesting himself in the audible world. The snake robot is up there.

On the bench by the door of the little mosque-chapel where old men sit when the weather is warm, Can bounces up and down with excitement as the pictures come in from Bird. He has it, oh he has it. That is clearly a pumping station, just as Mr Ferentinou suggested. There is the white van inside the wire. It will be tricky to get Rat Baby back from there. Afterwards, maybe. After what? He hasn't thought of afters.

Next picture. There is the woman in the green headscarf and the big man in the SuperDry T-shirt. Guns! Look, guns! That surely is enough to get the police to pay attention to him. The next sequence of shots shows boxes and crates laid out on the ground and people squatting beside them. More guns. There is Necdet, beside a pillar with his hands behind him. There is Necdet closer, looking straight at Bird. He knows.

There's no time to talk. Can unfolds his ceptep and sends the picture directly to the stored contact for the Kayişdaği police. Now you'll believe a nine-year-old boy!

Next, help Necdet. Can crosses his sun-warmed thumbs in the haptic field, flaps his fingers. Bird glides down to land on the pump-house roof and, as its claws touch metal, Can bursts and reforms it into Snake. He has enough visuals to build a map and work out Necdet's position underneath the roof. He sends Snake snaky-snaking one scale at a time down the pillar next to Necdet.

Look at me look at me look at me.

The eye contact is fleeting but the twitch of the head, the flare of the nostrils say, *I've seen you.* Can sends Snake around the back of the pillar, blindside to the terrorists. Now comes the hard stuff; lip-reading Necdet from the side on. What is he saying? Gg ard. Ig hard.

'Big bastard,' Necdet giggles. 'Big bastard!' A gas station attendant pulling on his rubber boots after prayer in the corrugated iron mescid stares at the crazed boy. Big Bastard. That can only be SuperDry. He is big. Can thinks he looks kind, and a little lost.

Get above Big Bastard.

This is hard. He has to move slowly and carefully so as not to be seen, keeping Necdet in camera, upside down, where Snake's traction is least strong. His tongue sticks out in concentration. He's forgotten ever being cold to the bone. He's forgotten that there is anyone around him or even where he is by the time he inches Snake into position above SuperDry's head. It's going to be a drop isn't it? It's going to be an Evil Shock Snake Drop. The thing he always wanted to do to the woman in Apartment 2, to make her scream. Evil Snake Attack! He catches Necdet's eye, focuses on his lips and Necdet looks away.

Wait.

Don't look at the snake. But how long can the kid hold it there, upside down under the roof. *Don't wiggle, don't let them see you almost have one hand free.* Though his fingers feel like they are in a vice, as if his fingertips will explode in showers of blood at any moment.

Big Hair has opened his computer and jacked it in to a panel on the pump-house controls. He taps keys. He reads outputs from his eyewriter. He seems pleased. Another sequence of keystrokes. Four oval panels, chevronned warning black-and-yellow, slide open on the pump housings. Big Hair smiles. Green Headscarf helps him load the canisters, one per pump. They fit very neatly into the spaces. Necdet wonders what Özer usually inserts into those chambers. It keeps his mind from the pain as he saws his thumbs back and forth, back and forth against the rasp of the plastic cable tie. The panel doors close again.

Necdet looks up, startled. The noise was so gentle and pervasive it had receded into the unheard background, like traffic thunder, but now that it has stopped, its absence is deafening. The hum of the pumps has stopped.

'The pumps are down!' Big Hair shouts.

'What?' Surly Fucker says.

'The pumps are down. Listen, nothing's working.'

'Get them back up again,' Green Headscarf says.

'It could be a scheduled diagnostic, in which case I can over-ride it.' Big Hair hits keys. 'No. It's a central command from pipeline control. Let's see if I can work around this. No. It's network wide. Özer's entire system has been shut down.' Even Big Bastard is on his feet. Necdet glances up. Good boy. Snake tracks him across the underside of the roof, writhing behind pipes and conduits.

'Is that possible?'

'I'm looking at it. It's like Özer has disappeared.'

'Get me a fucking spanner, there must be a way of doing this by hand!' Surly Bastard barges in between Big Hair and Green Headscarf. Then Necdet hears a new noise, a small noise growing bigger and this is not Hızır hearing, for Green Headscarf and Big Hair and Surly Bastard and Big Bastard all look up: a buzzing like a billion insect wings.

'Swarmbots!' Surly Bastard shouts and thrusts his hand into the glove-weapon.

'Now!' Necdet shouts. Snake drops from concealment on to Big Bastard's head. He screams, reels back, trips, falls on his back, pawing and shrieking at the oldest fear of all: a snake from above. Necdet tears his hands free. In two steps he reaches the sprawling Big Bastard, scoops up his assault rifle with bloody hands and drives the butt hard into his belly. Big Bastard projectile vomits.

'Forgive me brother.'

Necdet smashes him on the side of his head and runs. A hurricane of swarmbots barrels towards him down the alley. He sees the God's Engineers swing their boxing-glove weapons and tighten their fists. Swarmbots fall from the air like black snow. Swing, aim, fire in silence. Squadron by squadron, the air is swept clean of flying robots. Swarmbot carcasses rain on his shoulders and scalp. Necdet runs for the open street. Two white robotic rats, one large, one very small, race before him. Then, in a thunder of rotors, the helicopters arrive.

A voice is calling Can's name. A voice can't call Can's name. That's not allowed. That is game over. That is come away, come home. A second voice. He recognizes Mr Ferentinou. Not now, Mr Ferentinou. He has a mission to accomplish, a case to solve. Now he sees his mother coming past the shops, looking all around her as if he might be hidden in the gutter like a rat or perched on the roof like a bird, signing his name with her hands. He could always ignore the signing. Now he sees Mr Ferentinou on this side of the street coming, and another man he does not recognize with him. They're coming towards the gas station. There is the Gas Bubble. Beside it is a police car. Not now not now not now. Can slips from the bench and moves inside the small red-painted porch of the little tin mescid. He pretends not to hear his name. Then the metal chapel vibrates to a new sound. The air itself thrums. Necdet peeps out from his hiding place. The sky over Kayişdaği curdles and breaks into swarmbots, dark as smoke. Can gasps. He would have missed the action on his feed from Snake had he not heard Necdet shout, 'Now!'

He reacts without thought, smashing his fist down through the haptic field. He sees SuperDry's face white with fear; then Superdry, Necdet, Compression Station tumble over each other in wheeling images.

'Evil Snake Attack!' Can shouts in glee. 'Evil Snake Attack!' He's running blind. Get out. Get them out. Mission accomplished, Boy Detective. *Size of a rat!* Can commands. *BitBots to me!* He hopes Rat Baby gets the command and disengages from the white van.

The swarmbots whirl into a vortex, tower high over Kayişdaği and plunge into the alley that leads to the pumping station. Then they start to drop from the sky. Can gapes. Whole sub-swarms fall like hail. His screen stutters and blanks. Can squeaks in fear. Insect robots rattle from the corrugated iron roof of the mescid.

'EMP guns!' Can breathes. This is the greatest action movie the world has ever seen. Rat and Rat Baby come running harum-scarum down the alleys, staggering, reeling, tumbling as each new pulse shot sweeps another wing of swarmbots from the sky. 'Get here get here get here!' Can hisses. One targeted shot could kill them both. Necdet. Here comes Necdet. He's covered in blood and carrying a big big assault rifle.

With a huge noise that beats the cavity of Can's chest like a drum, two helicopters come in low and fast over the little minaret of the mescid. They turn over the apartment blocks behind the ratty shops. One holds position over the compression station, the other slides across the street to hover above the 24/7. Everyone is on the street. No one moves. The roar of its engines drives the air from Can's lungs and the thoughts from his head. It is the most exciting thing he has ever seen. Rat and Baby Rat race across the street scattering dead swarmbots like desiccated flies. At the mescid door they leap and in mid-air explode into their component units, then come together again as a soft hive of BitBots. At the same instant the armoured cars turn into Namik Kemal Cadessi.

*

The figure stumbling from the alley is bloody and wild and carries a gun.

'Necdet?' Mustafa calls. The figure looks up, confused. 'Necdet!' Mustafa runs to him. Dead robots crunch under his feet. The beating of the helicopters fills the entire world. Necdet throws away the gun as if it is the leg of a dead man. Mustafa hugs Necdet to him like a brother.

'Come on, come with me, you're all right. It's me. Mustafa. Mustafa from the Rescue Centre. Come on, there are police here, they'll look after you.' The police sergeant is already hurrying to assist. Then everyone freezes as the big six-wheeled armoured cars pound into Namik Kemal Cadessi and seal off the street in both directions. Front ends unfold like insect mandibles into shields and ramps. Figures in orange suits and orange breather masks pour on to the street. On the backs of their suits and the brows of their enclosed helmets is a rosette of black inward-pointing arrows on a yellow background. The figures are armed. They move to cover the street. Loudspeakers blare even over the helicopter thrash.

'This is the security service, attention attention. This is a nano-hazard alert, this is a nanohazard alert. Leave the area immediately, leave the area immediately. Do not take anything with you. Move back beyond the APCs.'

But Georgios Ferentinou sees the scuttling BitBots.

'Can!' His voice vanishes into the wall of noise. 'Can!' He walks towards the little red-painted mescid beside the 24/7. The loud-speaker repeats the order. Can appears in the door of the mescid. He is frightened and very very small. 'Can!'

A figure emerges from the alley, a thin man with big frizzy hair. He waves an assault rifle, charges towards Georgios and the filling station.

'Sir! Get down! Sir!'

The shots are deafening. The thin man's back explodes. He goes straight down in the black snow of swarmbots, limbs splayed like a crushed spider. In the door of the mescid Can Durukan freezes. His chest spasms. His eyes bulge. He raises a finger and drops to the ground.

'Help help!' Georgios Ferentinou ducks and scuttles towards the mescid.

'Sir! On the ground!'

'Get an ambulance!' Georgios shouts. The din is appalling. Can is limp and pale. He doesn't seem to be breathing. 'Oh God oh God. Can Can Can Can Can.' He doesn't know what to do, he doesn't know what to do. 'Help me.' No one can hear you, Georgios Ferentinou.

The soldiers in the orange nanohazard combat suits move from cover to close on the alley. A man comes running from the compression station. He is unarmed but his face is wild with anger, like a fighting dog. He charges at the soldiers, lifts his hands to his throat. A single shot drops him dead.

'Come on, come on, Can, you'll be all right.' Georgios tries to lift the boy but he is old and fat and the child is heavy and floppy and awkward and he can't get a grip. He hauls Can under one arm and drags him out of the mescid on to the street in squatting shuffle. 'Don't shoot! Don't shoot!' He pulls a handkerchief from his pocket and waves it. Now a woman walks from the compression station. She wears glasses and a green headscarf. Her hands are held up. The soldiers hold their aim. She walks confidently and boldly, with purpose, without fear. One of the soldiers moves his fingers over the back of his heavy gauntlet.

Georgios Ferentinou drags Can towards the line of army vehicles. The woman walks up to the soldiers. She smiles and raises her hands to the necklace at her throat. She looks startled. The soldier taps his gauntlet. Then the other soldiers seize her, wrestle her to the ground, tear off the necklace and cuff her.

'Help me!' Georgios Ferentinou shouts. He is at the end of his strength. Orange-armoured troopers break from cover. Two take Can, one helps Georgios back behind the lines.

'He needs an ambulance. It's his heart!' Georgios shouts. He can just hear approaching sirens over the helicopter din.

'We'll look after him,' says the soldier who helped Georgios. The soldier raises his hands, releases seals and takes off his nanohazard helmet. It takes Georgios a moment to recognize the face for he last saw it in circumstances so different that the incongruity beggars understanding. It is Major Oktay Eğilmez and Georgios last saw him on the deck of the Kadiköy ferry.

'It's as well somebody paid attention to you, Professor Ferentinou.'

'The boy ...'

'We'll look after him. Medic.' A soldier in orange, his helmet off, looks up from cleaning Necdet's bloody hands. 'When you've finished, please check over Professor Ferentinou. Our tip off was accurate, it was gas. We just never thought it would be nano-technology delivered through the supply system.'

'Who are they?'

'We've no idea. They're not on any of our watch lists. We're making their equipment safe now. They're a technologically sophis-ticated crew, and that alarms us. We have one prisoner, that's all we need.'

The ambulance has arrived. Blue lights pulse. Georgios watches the paramedics roll Can on to a gurney and load him into the back of the vehicle.

'I need to go with him'

'As soon as we've checked you out, we'll get the police to run you down.' Major Eğilmez removes a glove. 'I'll be glad to be out of this thing, I'm telling you. Thank you, Professor Ferentinou.' He offers his hand. Georgios, still dazed, soldiers and vehicles and helicopters and casualties whirling around him, accepts it. 'Well done.'

Major Eğilmez bows briefly to Georgios and goes to talk with Şekure Durukan. Soldiers help her into the back of the ambulance and close it up. Sirens wail briefly, the ambulance moves off. Soldiers zip the bodies into bags. The police unwrap incident tape and corral refugees. Radio crackle. People mill. Mustafa sits on the kerb with Necdet, one arm around him, the other holding his hand like an old, true friend. Georgios stands alone. The helicopters lift from their stations in beautiful synchrony, bow to each other and peel off across Kayişdaği.

A ceptep is calling.

Leyla Gültaşli pulls the pillow over her head. It has a cool side. For the first time in weeks, the pillow has a cool side.

The ceptep is still calling.

Let her enjoy a few more moments of being a goddess.

By the time Ceylan-Besarani's scattered staff made it by their diverse means to Bakirköy the word had spread and most of the building was in the apartment with fruit punch and beer for the drinkers and sweetmeats. Leyla could hear the music from the street as she swung the Peugeot into its parking space. Party poppers and streamers and a gauntlet of silly string greeted her entrance. The din was of police-summoning levels, had there been anyone left within earshot to complain to them. Uncle Cengiz pumped her hand and pumped her hand and bellowed congratulations she could not hear. Aunt Betül hugged her. Sub-Aunt Kevser hugged her. Cousin Naci, her self-appointed bodyguard, cleared the crowd in the living room to allow Leyla on to the balcony to receive the thanks of Great-Aunt Sezen. The old woman kissed her on each cheek. Then family friends and freeloaders all fell silent as Leyla presented the matriarch with both halves of the Koran. The old woman took them, spoke the Bismillah and put the sundered pieces together.

'Never let them be disunited again,' she said. There were tears on her face. Leyla found she was bawling. Cousin Naci was grinning and crying at the same time. Then someone put on the old *arabesk* music, the good kind, the country kind that gets everyone dancing and the girls were up in a line, tops pulled up to bare bellies, nodding and laughing to each other and moving it moving it moving it to the beat, then the boys were up in a line with their arms up and though Uncle Cengiz was like a lump of masonry Cousin Naci was a great mover, light on his feet as big guys so often are. All that taekwondo.

They beckoned Aso, he shook his head – no no no nanotechnologists don't dance – but again they beckoned come on come on come on get up and this time he did and watched their feet to get the steps. He was a dreadful dancer but Leyla saw his heart in it, and a light in his eyes. Then the girls replied with an old Ibrahim Tatlıses remix and Aso cried that he knew this one, he grew up to this one, his mother sang this one around the house and he stood in front of the line of aunts and sub-aunts and cousins and danced and Leyla thought *That's for me, isn't it?* In the midst of the mad dance Leyla noticed her ceptep was calling and she slipped out into the comparative quiet of Great-Aunt Sezen's balcony. Demre calling. Her mother was proud of her, her father was proud of her, her sisters were all proud of her, all that money hadn't been wasted. She got teary all over again.

Then Yaşar finally arrived with Zeliha who had made-up and dressed up and turned from office grump into some mad glam vampire and again the party poppers and the silly string and the confetti flew. The uncles and the aunts and the neighbours stayed in the living room dancing around to *arabesk* but the young ones put the sing station on in the main bedroom and Zeliha took the mike and became a smoky-voiced, tortured torch-singer. *Where's my contract?* Leyla shouted at her but Zeliha was deep in her diva. Two hours later she was still singing. There was no one left in the bedroom but she needed no audience other than herself.

Aso whirled Leyla home through the hour of parties. Taxis and Mercs. Short dresses, coloured shoes. Sharp young men with precision stubble. The hip and the beautiful spinning from club to bar to club. *All Istanbul is celebrating*, Leyla thought. *And Istanbul is mourning, and Istanbul is dreading and Istanbul is hoping. Istanbul is everything*. It was four a.m. when the Peugeot hummed into Adem Dede Square. The air was cool. The silence was immense. Aso could feel the djinn, packed like running fish, waiting, watching, neither good nor evil.

'You know, I've never asked, but where do you live?' Leyla said.

'I've got an apartment out in Bostancı,' Aso said. Home, family, significant others. Leyla has never thought of Aso having a life outside nanotech.

'How's Yaşar?'

'He's staying at the house.'

'What about Zeliha?'

'Oh, she's staying on the folding bed in Aunt Betül's room. Yaşar's been poking her for months.'

'I didn't know that.'

Aso hesitated to close the car door.

'Oh, yes, I meant to say.'

'Yes?'

'I think we might, you know, keep you on full time.'

A ceptep is calling. Calling and calling and calling. Leyla pulls the pillow around her ears but it won't shut out the sound. Answer me answer me. She flings the pillow across the room.

'Yes!'

'Leyla, it's Yaşar. Özer Gas and Commodities has gone bankrupt.'

The page is calf vellum, four hundred and fifty-three centimetres by two hundred and twelve, twenty-two millimetre binding margin, verso. The body text is from the Pentateuch, the Book of Ruth, Chapter 4, verses 14–22, a genealogy of King David. The text was written in a fine Ashkenazi hand some time between the late twelve hundreds and the early thirteen hundreds in central France or southern Germany.

The Pentateuch text is set out in a central panel framed by three decorative pillars forming two arches. The space within the pillars is filled with vine decoration, a sinusoidal plant stem sprouting small fan-shaped leaves. The stem on the right column is more richly textured, with a central spine and banding. The head and tail of each stem unfolds into a fantastical beast, matched serpent heads meeting under the Pentateuch text at the bottom, more fabulous creatures altogether at the head. On the left a winged dog-creature crosses a trefoil-ended tongue with that of a winged chimaera of goat and giraffe. The outlines of the beasts, the snakes, the vines and flowers, the pillars and arches and fine detail, are all written in micrography. They are built from lines of minute text, so fine it strains the naked eye. The text is *masorah*, commentary and traditional wisdom customarily written in the margin of the page. The artist here has playfully turned it into decoration. Worlds within worlds.

Ayşe Erkoç looks long at the micrographic panel before hanging it on the wall. It is her favourite piece in the collection, the one from which she would never be parted. She would face fire and weapons for the Ashkenazi micrographic panel. She remembers buying it at an auction with the last of the money from her father's will. Before the Ashkenazi panel she had only eyes for illustration. After it she walked for months in a world made from words, spelled from letters, a world transcribed from the mind of God on to the receptive surface of the earth.

Ayşe and Hafize have distributed the boxes across the semahane according to the wall space their contents occupied. Ayşe sets the Ashkenazi Pentateuch in its place. Behind it in the box is the Constantinople Golden Canon Table, an early illuminated concordance. The glass is cracked. The Directorate of Antiquities and Museums has no respect for old and beautiful things. Ayşe lifts it, looks long at the beautiful medallion busts of the four evangelists. They are worked in gold. She puts it back in the box.

Adnan is underneath desks hooking up power and wireless.

'I'm good at doing books too,' he says. His good jacket is hung over the back of a chair to keep it smart. The briefcase of bearer bonds is laid flat on the seat. 'Or maybe you need someone to drive a bit of a bargain? All reasonable offers considered. I've suddenly made myself unemployed.'

'You've got four million euro. You don't need a job.'

'I've got four million I need to get rid of quickly, painlessly and easily, before Maliye Bakanlığı and the FRA start sending audit AIs to take a little look at the spending patterns of ex-Özer traders.

Who's made off with the tea fund, awarded themselves a little golden send-off, passed off twenty million euro of cheap Iranian gas as best Baku. Had you thought of expanding the gallery, maybe move it out of this place somewhere a little less like a morgue?'

Ayşe turns on him.

'It's finished here,' she snaps. 'The damage is done. I always said it's reputation first, reputation last, reputation always. I just didn't think that reputation would be mine.' She goes to the cluster of fine old early Republic era desks at the centre of the dance floor. 'I'm sorry. That was uncalled for. No, love, Gallery Erkoç is over. I'm going to sell on the stock.'

Hafize looks up from arranging a wall of miniatures no larger than her thumb.

'You found the Mellified Man,' Adnan says. 'That has to count for something. It's a fucking legend. It's like the Sword of the Prophet or the Holy Grail.'

'I got half of Istanbul's antiquarians arrested. I got my old friend Burak Özekmekçib charged and he may lose his licence and Ahmet and Mehmet looking at six years and a multi-million euro fine, and I walk clean away, without stain or taint to my character. How is that going to look to them? What are they going to think? We can never talk about this. Whenever the name of Ayşe Erkoç is mentioned, it'll be the name of a traitor. But ... but ...' Ayşe squats on her heel so that she can look Adnan, sprawling on his back, strangely vulnerable like an infant in a cradle, in the eyes. 'But, despite all that, I tasted the Mellified Man.'

'How did he taste?'

Ayşe loves in Adnan that he knows when to be serious.

'Sweet. The sweetest thing. Nothing will ever taste the same after it. I think I understand Barçin Yayla. Nothing in the world could ever look as bright as the secret name of God. There would be colours no one had ever seen before. That's why he could contemplate burning his eyes out with acid. It would be an act of supplication to God. I don't believe in God, that option isn't open to me.'

THE DERVISH HOUSE

'We could get out of Istanbul,' Adnan says. 'Just go, start somewhere new. Back to Kaş, I could set up a couple of businesses, maybe
an outdoor pursuits centre, mountain bike, hike, kayak, scuba. By
the time I've paid enough bribes to keep the whole thing quiet,
I might get some change from four million.'

'Darling; sun, sea, me. No. I don't do outdoors. I do beautiful
things, lovely things, rare and precious things. Istanbul is me. I evaporate if I go beyond Bursa.'

Adnan sits up, points TV-presenter pistol-fingers at Ayşe.

'By the way, that yalı: could we put that on hold for a year or two?
The first thing they'll start looking for are property sales.'

Ayşe sits down on the foot-polished wooden floor of the semahane
beside Adnan, bodies touching naturally, intimately.

'Darling, you can put the yalı on hold permanently. It was you
wanted it. I never liked it.'

'What was wrong with it?'

'Oh for God's sake, man! It's the wrong fucking side of the
Bosphorus!'

They laugh. It's forced and desperate but it holds a kernel of all
laughter; it recognizes the ridiculousness of human existence. It
celebrates it. They lie side by side, laughing the best laugh they can.

'Madam?' Ayşe squints up at Hafize against the chandelier
lanterns. She holds out an envelope. 'When the police had you,
I sold an object to customer. A neighbour. Leyla Gültaşli? You'd
recognize her if you saw her. She lives in apartment 2.'

'What did you sell?'

'The half Koran. The miniature that man Topaloğlu sold you on
Monday, just before.'

'His name is never mentioned in this building again. The half
Koran? Well done finding a buyer for that.'

'I didn't sell it. She was looking for it specifically. She gave me a
thousand euro.'

Ayşe sits up.

'That's a hell of a lot more than it's worth.'

'It was worth much more to her. Madam, Adnan Bey, I overheard what you were saying about setting up a business, needing to get rid of a large amount of money quickly. I have a suggestion.'

10

It's 1783, the Islamic year 1197, and Mahtab, the wife of Kurosh Tehranian, a civil servant in Tabriz, is drawn by a shine of silver in a bookseller's in the city's old bazaar. A miniature Koran, silver cased, a crystal magnifier in the cover, very beautiful. The perfect Koran for a traveller or a trader, a soldier or a pilgrim. It's for this last that Mahtab buys it. After years of saving and economizing on his civil service pay, Kurosh Tehranian is finally going on the Hac in fulfilment of a lifetime's yearning and obligation.

It's 1827/1243. Salman Tehranian, a member of a diplomatic mission of the Qajay Dynasty of Tehran, travels to Constantinople to negotiate Ottoman support in the Russo-Persian war of 1826. At Konya he falls sick. The mission continues to Constantinople while he remains under the care of the hospital of the Tomb of the Mevlana. He dies three months later. He wills his most treasured possession, a silver-cased miniature Koran, to Yusuf Horozcu, who nursed him with love and dedication. The mission to the Sublime Porte of the Ottoman Empire fails.

It's 1858/1275. Listed among the dowry goods of the marriage of Fikriye Gören to Atıf Ceylan, a furniture maker of Hacıevhattin is a miniature Koran, described as 'of Persian make, silver filigreed, with crystal lens.' To obtain permission to marry their daughter, Atıf Ceylan had to prove his merit as a cabinet maker and build a wonder. He made a trunk of fabulous beauty, a chest of treasures, worked with floral patterns of the greatest intricacy, but it was unlucky. At the age of sixty-three Nilufer Gören tripped, struck her head against a corner of the chest and died. The family took the chest outside and burned it.

It's 1916/1335. Abdulkadir Hasgüler's many plans and favours and small bribes to minor officials finally fail and he is armed and uniformed and sent down to the ferry that will take him to the train to Çanakkale and across the Dardanelles to Gallipoli. At the quay his mother gives him a keepsake to return him safe to Istanbul: the family miniature Koran, cut in half. *It will always seek to be one*, she says as the ferry belches smoke into the evening sky. By its power Abdulkadir survives the shot and shell and hell of Gallipoli and returns safe to Istanbul to found a mighty, sprawling, brawling family.

It's 2027/1448. At a desk in the semahane of the Adem Dede dervish house, Adnan Sarioğlu and Ayşe Erkoç buy both halves of the Gültaşli Koran for two million euro. In so doing they become the owners of Ceylan-Besarani nanotech, with Yaşar Ceylan and Aso Besarani as executive and technical directors. They shake hands over the table. Leyla Gültaşli and Hafize Gülek witness the contract.

'Right then,' says Adnan Sarioğlu. 'You're highly talented boys but you know fuck about making deals. The deal is, I make the deals. You do the science, I'll do the money. I will be working out of this building. You will continue to work out at the Nano Bazaar. I am not having any place that calls itself Nano Bazaar on my business card, and I'm not running the risk of coming out at six o'clock and finding the Audi up on blocks. I will be out to see you but not often. You may be glad of that, I don't care. I want to spend as little time as possible around geeks, techno-hippies, nano-fairies and idiots who wear goggles. The administrative headquarters of Turquoise Nanotech – we've decided that's the name, by the way, you can retain Ceylan-Besarani, or Besarani-Ceylan or whatever the hell you want to work it, for the transcriber when you get it – will be here.'

'This is the registered company office,' Ayşe says. 'Everything will be managed out of here. We'll honour existing contracts for six months, after that, contracts are renegotiated and everything is dependent on results.'

'Excuse me.' Leyla Gültaşli raises her hand. 'I still don't have a contract.'

'When you're operations manager you can write your own.'

'Operations? I was marketing . . .'

'Adnan and I are the face of the company,' Ayşe says curtly. 'Leyla, operations. Yaşar and Aso, technical directors. Zeliha will continue to manage the Fenerbahçe end. Hafize, PA to me and Adnan, maternity permitting. Turquoise Nanotech is a commercial company. We're here to make money. If we happen to change the world while we're doing that, that's a bonus.'

Five days is a long time in business, Adnan thinks. On Monday he only expected to pull off a gas scam, put a deposit down on a mansion and watch Galatasaray beat Arsenal. It's Friday and he's destroyed a major corporation, bought a nano company and missed Galatasaray play Arsenal to a draw. He could never have imagined the fall of Özer, how fast, how far. But Kemal knew, Kemal had known from the moment the first error showed up in the Cygnus X account. The same multiplying force of the financial instruments that allows the extraction of unimaginable profit also generates unlimited loss. Now the vultures pull at the corpse of Özer but he got out. He got out intact, he got out with the money. The Ultralords of the Universe always get out from the exploding base. Empires crumble but the money never rests. The money whirls around the world, never ceasing because if the money ever stops, everything stops. It's Friday and Adnan killed a great little company.

'We've work to do, right away. We've an advantage in that the collapse of Özer will knock out the Idiz team but even as we sit here they're talking to money people. Our advantage won't last. We have to get to market first. So everything goes into prototyping the Ceylan-Besarani transcriber.'

'Besarani-Ceylan transcriber,' Aso Besarani says.

Little letters, Ayşe Erkoç thinks. Words written from smaller words written from words too tiny to read. In this room, at this desk the policeman Akgün had wondered whether the power of micrography grew the smaller it became. The Hurufis believed the final name of God was written into every atom. The world is written. Reality is transcribed, endlessly copied from moment to moment. The secrets of the universe may be inscribed on to the human heart.

'Tomorrow we start.'

Yaşar raises a hand.

'I need to know I won't be bothered by Abdullah Unul.'

'Abdullah Unul is a small-time hustler and coercer of cornershops. If it's big-time crooks you're after, just take a trip down to Levent Plaza. They're all out there looking for new jobs. I can deal with Abdullah Unul. Now, ladies, gentlemen.'

On cue Hafize fetches the tray with the glasses and the bottle of champagne. There is pomegranate spritzer for her. It's good for pregnant women. She tackles the champagne cork as if it is a loaded shotgun but it pops, and there is foam, and five glasses.

'Ladies and gentlemen, Turquoise.'

The first toast is drunk.

'Ladies and gentlemen, profit.'

As the second goes down Ayşe takes the Koran and twists it in two parts. The back she slides across the desk to Adnan. The front she puts in her bag. People who collect miniature Korans buy them for the stories they attract.

'Profit,' says Ayşe Erkoç.

Adnan leans across the desk to his new working partners.

'Gentlemen, would either of you, by any chance, be football fans?'

The woman police officer is tall and very striking in her neatly belted uniform and gun but still Georgios is not aware of her until she speaks a second time.

'Hm?'

'We can get a car to take you home. It's not a problem.'

'Oh no, no no no, I'll wait.'

'The doctors have said they won't let anyone other than immediate family in today.'

'That's all right. I'm more than happy to wait. You see, I have something of his.' Georgios lifts the heavy-duty supermarket bag-for-life on his lap.

'Can I get you a coffee or something?'

'No, no, I'm fine, thank you.'

Georgios sits on the centre of the three plastic chairs outside the door of the private cardio ward. He sits very upright, ankles and knees together, hands clasped around the bag in his lap. Institutional sitting. The hospital corridor is painted the same diseased-lung yellow as the interrogation room in Üsküdar. The smell is leaking back through the years. Or perhaps it is not memory; a hospital could very well smell the same as a secret police cell: body fluids, fear, hope, terror. Death. He's read all the notices on the wall three times. The health warnings are either irrelevant or would have killed him by now.

The policewoman touches her ceptep to the vending machine, waits, touches it again, bangs it. Bangs it again.

'I've something to give him, you see,' Georgios says, hoping that the policewoman will ask what he has in the bag. 'I'm returning something to him.'

The machine grudgingly disgorges half a cup of tarry coffee. Georgios peeps into the carrier bag. The interior swarms with insect motion. The BitBots, broken down into their individual component microbots, hiving like wasps, a ceaseless boil of blind robot energy. Mindless automata in their individuality, intelligent in society. Intelligence as an emergent property, a property that cannot be predicted from the behaviour of the individual components. He would assemble them but he doesn't have the control unit. Later he'll take the bag over to the free charge point to power up.

He found them swarming like silver wasps in the gutter at Kayi-şdaği Compression Station, a pool of liquid light, after the ambulance drove away. A dog was sniffing at them, leaping back when the threatened BitBots reared up in their preprogrammed defensive reaction. The çayhane owner had a plastic shopper – the one Georgios now carries – and was trying to work out a way of scooping them in. Beyond the police cordon the news men jockey for pictures.

'Those aren't yours!' Georgios cried. 'They belong to the boy. They're his pets.'

'Pets?' the çayhane owner said. *Toy*, Georgios had meant.

'I'm going to the hospital. I'll give them to him.'

Together they corralled every last BitBot in the bag-for-life. Then the Terrorist Incident police who had corralled everyone away from the compression station noticed people they had not yet processed and came over to take details and ask questions. They took Georgios into the back of the mobile control room van.

'So were they trying to launch a nanoagent attack through the gas supply?' Georgios asked the questioning officer.

'Who, sir?'

'The terrorists. Were they trying to introduce a nanoreplicator into the distribution system?'

'I can neither confirm nor deny that, sir.' The policeman frowned. 'I can say that this has been a major incident. Can I see some identification, sir?'

Georgios fumbled out his Kadiköy identity tag. The officer ran it through his scanner.

'This is an MIT security clearance, sir.'

'Yes, officer, I was doing some work for them recently, a security service think-tank. We were investigating the possibility of a terror attack using a nanotechnology agent. There was a boy, a nine-year-old, he has a cardiac condition, a very serious cardiac condition. He was taken to hospital; do you know if he's all right?'

'You're the one rescued the boy.'

'Yes, I am.'

'Are you family?'

'I'm a neighbour. A friend of the family. He's like a son to me. A grandson.'

'I can arrange to have a car take you down there.'

'That would be very good. Thank you.'

'There are some officers at the hospital. I'll let them know you're coming. I'll need contact details; we will have to question you in some detail.'

'I understand, officer. If I can help in any way, officer.'

'Is that your bag, sir?'

'Yes, just some of my old stuff. I carry far too much around with me.'

Old men, plastic shoppers, street mutterers and pigeon feeders.

'Was it a nano attack?' Georgios asks quickly.

The policeman gave no answer but as Georgios was helped down the steps to the waiting cruiser the officer said, 'Professor,' and when Georgios looked, he nodded curtly.

He clutched the bag of BitBots to his chest all the way to Kozyatağı Central Hospital.

A woman in green scrubs comes banging out of the cardiac ward.

'Doctor.' She stops with an audible sigh of exasperation. 'Is he all right?'

'Are you family?'

'I'm his grandfather.'

'We've stabilized the heartbeat. He was anoxic for several minutes. We've run a scan and we haven't detected any neurological damage. Now that doesn't mean there isn't any but he has youth on his side. Kids are robust things.'

'Thank you, Doctor.'

'You still can't go in. Immediate family only. Grandpa.'

Stabilized. Anoxic. The terrible euphemisms of doctors. Georgios remembers the terrible looseness of the boy's body, everything flopping, impossibly heavy, lifeless, no movement no breath no life. No life. The dreadful panic. Not knowing what to do. Not knowing what he should do. *Can Can Can Can Can*, he had shouted.

The television in the nursing station, burbling away to itself, is showing footage from the gun battle on the afternoon news. The street looks very wide. The camera jerks wildly. He hadn't noticed there was so much smoke. That must be him, that round, ridiculous little man, trying to run in a crouch with Can tucked under his arm, waving his white handkerchief. Men in bright orange nanohazard suits lope towards him, waving their arms: *get down get down*. Why do they always order people to get down?

'Officer.' The policewoman comes. She smells very fresh, of the iron and a musky bodyspray. She's married. Georgios envies her husband. 'The woman, the one they captured before she could blow herself up, do you know what's happened to her?'

'I would imagine she's being questioned.'

'I mean, she's all right?'

'Of course, sir.'

'Good, good. I'd be very interested to hear what she has to say, but I suppose that'll have to wait for the trial, if we even hear about it then. It'll be one of those trials where the public aren't admitted, I suppose.'

'Probably, sir.'

The news anchors have serious faces. In the space of two hours he watches himself seven times, dragging the boy, waving the handkerchief, dragging the boy, waving the handkerchief. New footage is added as it comes out of edit. There is the big fellow in the SuperDry T-shirt, running across the street firing. He goes down. Did he fire the shot that took Can down? Georgios had never seen anyone collapse before. They went straight down, so fast, so hard.

'Necdet!'

The policewoman is there in an instant.

'Sir, quiet please. It's a hospital.'

'The young man, the hostage, Necdet. What happened to him?'

'He's being treated in another centre. Sir, you probably should go home. Nothing's going to happen here. I can get you a car, you can call back tomorrow.'

No, I need to hear Can speak. I need to hear him tell me I'm innocent, that I've done nothing wrong. I need him to forgive my sins and absolve me. He saw how Şekure and Osman looked at him as they were taken out from the cardiac room for a brief press piece. They blame him absolutely. They will never forgive him. He has abused their son as completely as if he were a paedophile. *I only helped him go where his own curiosity led him*. You can't lock up a nine-year-old boy in a prison of silence. You can't take away half his world and expect him not to want to explore the absence, not to push his intelligence and faculties into the forbidden. If he had had a son, Georgios might think different. *If I had a son whom a single noise could kill*. They won't let him see Can again. He knows it. Georgios is terribly, terribly afraid that they will take him away. They'll get compensation and they'll move out of the dervish house and then he will be utterly alone.

It is a terrible thing to be caught up in current affairs.

'I'm going off shift in about ten minutes, if you want me to take you back to Eskiköy,' the policewoman says.

'Officer. I might.'

'Well, I'll just visit the ladies room first.' The corridor is empty, backs turned, attention away from the fat old man in the dark suit. Georgios tips the contents of the carrier bag on to the floor.

'Go to him,' he whispers. As he suspected, the BitBots are bonded to Can's smell. The puddle of gnat-sized robots seethes and shifts: waves, spikes, strange geometrical patterns, then with breathtaking alacrity snaps into a thread and winds slowly under the ward door. Georgios watches until the rag-end vanishes.

This is what his world has come down to. Year upon year, decade upon decade, Georgios pulled the borders of his life in around himself, drawing the circle tighter: Istanbul University. The economics community. The Greek community. Eskiköy. Three old Greeks and a teashop owner. The dervish house apartment, its white walls full of cities he is afraid to visit. A plastic chair in a hospital, an empty carrier bag on his lap.

He has lost everything.

The policewoman is bathroom fresh and vigorous.

'Are you coming then?'

'Yes, yes, can I just make a quick call first?'

'Go ahead.'

463

Georgios shuffles to the ceptep-safe area. He has done enough without his phone call interfering with the machines firing modulated patterns of charge across Can's heart. The phone rings. It will be tight. He may have mistimed it. Hope, old man. Allow yourself to hope. The phone rings. Is answered.

'Ariana. Don't catch the plane. Not today. Don't catch the plane. Don't go.'

The last light catches the upper gallery of the dervish house. From buses and trams the workers are coming home, criss-crossing Adem Dede Square on their various paths to apartment blocks and konaks of Old Eskiköy. If they are more leisurely than lately, if they bustle less and stop and talk on the steps and in the soks more, it's because at last, at last, at last the heatwave has broken. The cool has come. This is an evening to enjoy in the proper Istanbul fashion. Some stop to buy a paper from Aydin, some fruit or bread from Kenan, or coffee from Bülent or his eternal rival Aykut across the square. The shutters roll down on the Improving Bookstore. Early evening unfolds over Adem Dede Square like a flock of birds taking to the air and all Leyla Gültaşli can think about is keying Adnan Sarioğlu's Audi.

'She's run an art gallery!' Leyla says to Aso. 'What does she know about marketing? I set the deal up, I did everything, and what do I end up with? Operations. I should be out there with with Adnan, getting the meetings, talking to the distributors, doing the deals.'

She settles for kicking the Audi's tyres. It is a beautiful car. It would be vicious and if she's feeling anything it's underappreciated not vicious and anyway Bülent at the teashop across the square is watching.

'That's capitalism,' Aso says. His face is turned to the sky, he stands very still, feeling the air against his face. He looks like a saint.

'You're pretty damn cool about it.'

'I have a million reasons to be.'

'Two million reasons.'

'Tell me. Of course they'll want to pay themselves large directors' salaries and sink as much money as they can into capital assets, but they're still getting it cheap.'

'Are you happy with it?'

'We get to develop the Besarani-Ceylan transcriber. We get to fire the starting gun of the next industrial revolution. We get to change the world in our own lifetimes. Downside, the name sucks. We'll talk about that. The licensing percentages are a little low. Then again, it's the law of large numbers. Very very large numbers.'

'And I'm going to have to find somewhere new to stay, I mean, no way can I keep on living here, it is just too damn close to the shop . . .'

'Leyla,' Aso says, 'shut up. Just shut up. Enough business, enough career, enough money, enough deals. It's a beautiful evening.'

It is, she realizes. It has crept over her as it has crept up the sky, minute by minute, a huge purple streaked golden twilight. The air smells new. The light is heartbreaking; all the more luminous because in a few moments it will be lost. Bülent has switched on the little fairy-lights around his shop front; Kenan's shop glows from within. Lights come on in the apartments around Adem Dede Square. Leyla's never loved the square, never loved the dervish house, never loved Eskiköy. This is a place without horizons, without panoramas or sweeping vistas. Wherever you look, you only see another building. The houses feel to her like they are pressed up against her window, full of eyes and mouths and loud lives. It doesn't welcome the young, it's too full of history and old memories. She understands why the rest of the girls left as soon as they could. There are many women here but it's not their world, it's old and male and secretive. She's never loved it and never will and now she has decided to move out she can't wait to be gone but this evening she almost could.

'You know, I might go back home.' Leyla sees Aso suddenly freeze. *Why, what, who, me?* She adds quickly 'Just for a visit, just to make sure everyone's all right and everything's where I left it and the tomatoes are still growing. Just touch back home for a day or two, that's all.'

He froze. He looked shocked when she said she might go home, as if he would never see her again. As if he might miss her. That's incredible. But the lesson of Demre, the secret of her chaotic, messy, ever-expanding family, is that love is always under your nose. You love what you see every day.

'Aso,' Leyla says suddenly, 'let's go for dinner. I don't know where, just somewhere away from here where we don't have to talk business and I can kick off these heels.'

'What, you mean, somewhere like a date?'

'No, somewhere to go and eat. Yes, like a date. Somewhere lovely, somewhere you can see from, somewhere with a view, somewhere you can get wine and good table linen and people who'll be polite to you because you're wearing a suit. Somewhere we can be a little bit glamorous. Aso, what do you think?'

For a moment he doesn't speak. Leyla fears she's blown it, run away at the mouth, overtalked her pitch. Maybe she always was a shit marketeer and achieved what she did by sheer self-confidence. Which is running out through the soles of her business heels like water.

'Yes,' Aso says, 'yes, I'd like that very very much.'

You are the Boy Detective and you are lying in a big bed that goes up and down and changes shape with a thought. There is a mask on your face and a tube in your arm and machines watching over you like people praying. You feel the hair-tip tickle of a haptic field. That's how the machines are watching you. That steady blue line the beat of your heart. That grainy, pulsing ghost is your heart. It keeps going and going and going, without rest. You are amazed at that. Beneath the screens are numbers and smaller displays but you can't read them without turning your head and the nurse has told you not to do that because you might pull out a tube, dislodge the thing sitting on your chest.

You're wearing just a pair of pants. That's odd and creepy. Strangers must have undressed you while you were in the black, in the no-time, the place that is deeper and darker than any sleep. You remember a noise, a sudden, big noise and something like fireworks going off in your chest, except that each burst was bright red pain through your heart and up your chest into your head, burst after burst after burst until the red all joined up. There was nothing but red. Then you woke up in this bed in just a pair of pants. You think you may have been dead for a while.

The doctor is good. The doctor you like. She's gruff and no nonsense and always looks impatient as if she has ten thousand more important things to do than talk to you but you think you can trust her. She will answer your questions if you can catch her in flight and tells the truth.

When she heard about the earplugs her face became more and more serious. 'That's medieval,' she said. 'That's not a cure.' There's a new way of treating Long QT syndrome. Like the earplugs, it takes noise – in this case the noise of electrical patterns across the heart going crazy – and turns it upside down and feeds it back on itself so that the great roars and shouts drown themselves out and all that remains is the small, constant voice of the heart. It's much more complex than that but it's what this nano-plastic spider sitting on his chest is doing and what the smaller, smarter one will do when they put it into his chest and it wraps its spindly legs around his heart. It will be the new tech that's not quite machine and not quite living. Protein computing, she calls it, though Can suspects that the doctor doesn't understand it either. But she has a plan.

'We'll give you a couple more days to recover and make sure there's no underlying trauma or damage and get you fit. Then we'll go in and fit the spider.'

'I'll be able to hear.'

'You always could hear.'

When you dream, and you dream often and brilliantly from all the drugs they drip into you through that tube, you don't dream of the gunshot that stopped your heart or the police swarmbots falling out of the sky like snow, or even Necdet seen through the mouse-hole in the office above the accountants'. You dream of the container ship, sailing away up the Bosphorus to the Black sea, and all the doors of the containers bursting open and all the sounds in the world pouring out.

Şekure and Osman only leave the room to eat or go to the toilet or talk to the newspapers. They're drowsy now, dozing off in their chairs. A magazine falls from Şekure's hand and flops to the floor. You watch them. You've been watching them a lot. It's easy to fool them that you're asleep. Not so the nurse. Nurses are canny. Nurses know everything.

Şekure and Osman had been out talking to the news when she came into the room. You didn't need anything, she came in because she knew you would be awake.

'Is that your grandfather outside?'

You had to think a moment.

'Yes.'

'He says he has something for you.'

'What?'

'It's in a bag.'

'Can he come in?'

'Not today. Immediate family only.'

'But he's my grandfather.'

The nurse smiled.

Then you did sleep, but not for very long because you were woken by the feeling of something moving against you, something long and very smooth and very soft but with a cat-tongue prickle at the same time. It moved along your upper arm, under your armpit, which almost made you laugh from ticklishness, down your side to slide over your hip on to your belly. Something presses against your navel. You carefully carefully lifted the sheet that is all that covers you and there, beyond the plastic scar of the heart-spider, Snake raised his jewelled head.

You are the Boy Detective and you have just solved your first and greatest case. Nothing will ever be quite as exciting and important. That's all right. This case almost killed you. But that's all right too, because the hospital will make it better than it ever was. And here is Snake, your faithful sidekick with Monkey and Rat and Bird, curled on your stomach. It's almost dark now. The nurse tells you that Mr Ferentinou has gone home. You hope he's all right. Şekure and Osman are asleep, leaning against each other like birds in a cage. Even the machines are quiet and in that quiet you push down, push down like you did at the shore at Üsküdar when you had the attack. You push down and listen to your heart. Bu-duh. Bu-duh. Bu-duh. It is good. It is very good.

'Yah!' Adnan Sarioğlu roars as he knocks out the autodrive, floors the gas and launches the howling Audi into the drive-time traffic streaming sedate and orderly Asia-wards over the Bosphorus Bridge. The cars scurry, the cars scamper. *Coming through.*

Ayşe puts her hand on the wheel.

'Don't go back to Ferhatpaşa. I can't abide that apartment. Sell it, get rid of it. I don't need a yalı, I don't need a Bosphorus view and mooring for my speedboat; I just need to be back in Europe again. We can afford somewhere decent; run the money through my family, or through the gallery. Just, not Ferhatpaşa, not tonight. Let's get a hotel; somewhere good. Somewhere we can look like a couple of millionaires. By the water.'

'Hell yes. Hell yes. I think I know somewhere.' Adnan taps into the drive AI. 'When I was in Özer ...' Adnan pauses. 'It's odd saying that. It's like missing a tooth. When I was in Özer with the boys, we used to call ourselves the Ultralords of the Universe, you know, after that kids' TV series, Draksor, Ultror, Terrak, Hydror: Ultralorrrrds ... That's the kind of thing you did in Özer. There was another cartoon I used to love, I think it was a remake of an old American thing from way back. There were these two kids, a boy and girl, and they each had half of a magic ring. Usual thing, they fight crime, they battle demons, all that, but when they got in trouble, they could join the two halves of the ring together, shout *Shazzan!* and this big fat djinni in harem pants would appear and kick animated ass. Of course, you realised pretty quick that the show was only interesting if the bad guy had stolen one of the rings or the djinni was trapped somewhere and the kids had to rely on their own ingenuity.'

Adnan takes out his half of the Gültaşli Koran and holds it in his hand. Ayşe matches it with hers.

'Shazzan!' Adnan shouts. Ayşe completes the book.

'Shazzan!'

Then Adnan flicks on the autodrive and reclines his seat and goes straight back, grinning like a millionaire, and Ayşe laughs and shakes out her hair and reclines her seat and rolls on to her side to face him and the Audi arcs high over the Bosphorus through the unceasing traffic and ever-flowing river of lights.

There are many quiets in the garden. Necdet Hasgüler sits on the rim of the fountain catching different quiets like butterflies. There is the quiet of insulation; how the soft, organic woodwork of the dervish house reduces the growl of the city to a murmur. Stone and concrete reflect, wood absorbs. There is the quiet of small things; the trickle of water from the fountain, the soft pad of the lizard that lives in the fountain's base, the bird that stoops down to perch on the gallery eaves, examines him with one eye, then the other, then flies away again. There is the quiet of being; the dark wooden pillars of the cloister, the blue and white tiles, the marble of the ablutions fountain, the smells of water and old sun-bleached wood and earth and greenery. There is the quiet of absence: no people, no voices, no words, no needings or questions. There is the quiet of presence: no one in the tiny garden but Necdet and the Green Saint.

'Hello friend,' Necdet whispers. Hızır nods from his seat on the stone bench where the roses grow. The army doctor who had patched up his hands and examined him after the rescue at Kayişdaği told him a story about the Mevlana, the great saint whose order built this tekke. The Mevlana had a friend, Şams of Tabriz, a spiritual friend, the other half of his soul, one spirit in two bodies. Together they explored the depth of God in ceaseless conversation. The dervishes grew jealous of the one-in-twoness and quietly killed Şams of Tabriz. When the Mevlana was unable to find his friend, the only possible conclusion was that they had merged and Şams was now part of him.

Why should I seek?
I am the same as he.
His essence speaks through me.
I have been looking for myself.

Necdet knows how long Hızır will be with him.

'And the others?'

'We'll monitor them of course, but there's no reason to hold them. They're not sick. Like you they have passed through a delusional phase into a stable configuration. It seems to grant them extra faculties that we don't have the concepts, much less the language, to explain. More conscious? Differently conscious?'

'How long will it last, Doctor?'

That when the doctor had told Necdet the story of Şams of Tabriz. As God wills. These things turn. As his brother brought him to safety, helped him, cared for him, now he will help Ismet. The brotherhood is strong but men are stupid when they band together. The street shariat is strong and it can be a great good, but their work could easily spin apart through rivalry or dogmatism. If Ismet calls him a shaykh, then a true shaykh he will be. Shaykh Necdet. The whirl is in everything

You have made me real, Friend.

The perfume of verdure in the little garden is suddenly heady, dizzying. Tomorrow Necdet will go back to Başibüyük, to his family, to his sister and try to put right his old wrongs. Tonight, the evening azan has broken out from the loudspeakers of the Tulip Mosque. The dervish house accepts the sound, the invocation of the call to prayer swirls in the enclosed air of the tekke garden, swells and ebbs. He might go and pray.

This is the azan calling ikindi from the minarets of the three thousand mosques of Istanbul. This is a stork spiralling up on the thermals high above the corporate towers and Levent and Maslak. This is an atom of carbon bonded to four hydrogen atoms; star-forged, hurtling through the gas pipeline beneath the Bosphorus towards Europe. This is a Mellified Man, sleeping on a bed of honey until the trumpet of Israfil wakes him. This is three men dead and cold in an army morgue. This is the Little Virgin of St Pantaleimon's spreading her protecting veil over the twenty million souls of Europe's greatest city. This is lovers in a rented room washed by the sound of the sea. This is the Storm of the Turning Windmills, singing in the lines of the skysails, licking the water of the Bosphorus to restless cat-tongues. This is the secret name of God, written across Istanbul in letters too great and yet too small to be comprehended. This is the stir of djinn and rememberings, which are not as different as humans think, in the twilight of Adem Dede Square, outside the old dervish house. This is the turn, this is the whirl, this is the dance that is woven into every particle of the universe. This is the laughter of Hızır the Green Saint. This is Istanbul, Queen of Cities, and she will endure as long as human hearts beat upon the earth.